BOOKS BY TIM MCBAIN & L.T. VARGUS

Casting Shadows Everywhere
The Awake in the Dark series
The Scattered and the Dead series
The Clowns
The Violet Darger series
The Victor Loshak series

NIGHT ON FIRE

NIGHT
ON
FIRE

a Violet Darger novel

LT VARGUS & TIM MCBAIN

NIGHT ON
FIRE

PROLOGUE

The groom had just peeled back the bride's veil when the smell of smoke hit.

Wait. Was that right?

In the ensuing panic, Jason couldn't remember the exact sequence of events anymore. Flashes of the day came to him out of order — a useless jumble of memories that pulsed through his head as he tried to escape the burning building.

In his mind, he could see the church as it had been before — rows of silent people. Sitting. Fidgeting. Fingers picking at their clothes and faces. Waiting for the ceremony to start.

Sunlight streamed through the windows up along the vaulted ceiling and glittered on the shiny wooden backs of the seating and the rails that divided the main altar from the nave. The glow shot through the stained glass and splotched sections of the wall in royal blue and red, elongated rectangles of color that stretched along with the angle of the sun.

The minister stood next to the lectern, an older man sporting thick glasses, smiling, fingers laced around a bible that he clutched to his chest. A little smile blossomed and ebbed on his lips, never fully leaving.

Above all, Jason remembered the anticipation building to something palpable. All of those waiting people. All of that anxious energy. It multiplied like bacteria, created a warmth in the air that made the room stuffy, made it hard to breathe.

In another flash, he remembered kissing Fran on the cheek in the little prep area in the chamber off the main floor of the

1

church that she called "backstage." Remembered worrying, for just a second, that he might have messed up her makeup or something. Everything about all of this seemed so delicate, so precious, made him feel so out of place. Part of him worried that he was going to blunder in and trample something, that he'd go to touch something and watch it fold up like moth wings, ruined.

Even the kiss itself had caught him off guard. He didn't show affection that way often — considered himself the strong, silent type — but in that moment he'd lost himself, forgotten himself. Fran was his niece, almost like a daughter to him, and now she was all grown up, getting married.

He could still remember her laughing as a toddler — head tipped back, eyelids squinted to slits, little ringlets of hair bobbing along with the quaking round belly — laughing harder than he'd ever seen any child laugh. And he still associated that image with the woman she'd become — her sense of humor still as core to her being at 26 as it had inexplicably been at two. She taught improv now and periodically toured with a local group doing sketch comedy, made laughter for a living, albeit toward the starving artist end of the economic spectrum. Still, she'd always favored pursuits of passion to those financial, just like him.

The emotions that came along with her wedding surprised him, gripped him like a fist clenching in the center of his chest, overwhelmed him. His skin had tingled from the moment he'd arrived at the church, throbbed with pins and needles.

He'd never had kids of his own. Never would, according to the doctors. Maybe that meant more to him than he'd realized until today. And maybe that diagnosis from Dr. Miller played a bigger role in the divorce than he'd let himself consider — the straw that broke the marriage's back.

Only sitting in the packed pews did any of this occur to him, in the quiet of the church, in the stillness of being alone while surrounded by people. He saw his life from a different perspective in this place — a fresh angle — saw the way his mind usually distorted aspects of the truth like those warped boxes of red and blue light that stretched out along the wall.

Funny how it all worked, life. You kept so busy that you only got the faintest glimpses of what you really wanted, who you really were — fleeting little glances at the truth that only came to you in the quiet moments if you looked for them out of the side of your eye.

And the big truth here seemed plain enough. Fran was as close as he'd get to fatherhood, and now she was a girl no longer. Her new life started today. They were all here to witness it become official, this ceremony cementing it to the satisfaction of both God and government.

Dennis, the guy she was marrying, seemed like an all right guy. Tall and long-faced with bad posture. Worked at a big marketing company. Something to do with computers, Jason thought. Kind enough, though. Agreeable. Gentle.

Except...

Maybe Dennis was a bit of a puss, if Jason was being totally honest. Scared of snakes and spiders. Unable to fix anything around the house. Hell, he had seen the kid's face pucker into a contorted mess of wrinkles whilst sipping something as watered down as Coors Light, for Christ's sake. Bitter beer face on more than one occasion.

Not much of a man by Jason's old school definition, maybe,

but he treated Fran well. That was something. So much had changed, Jason knew. Maybe the world was different now. Maybe the way we treated each other was all that really mattered, the only real way to judge someone's character.

His mind fast-forwarded to the main event. He sat in the pews among all the people as the ceremony got underway, shocked to find tears forming in his eyes as Fran walked down the aisle. Tears. He couldn't remember the last time he'd cried. Had forgotten, somehow, that it was something that happened to you rather than something you did, the involuntary nature of the act striking him as strange, almost cruel.

He tried to fight it, the crying. Tried to squelch the emotions. Tried to will his eyes dry. Like he could wrestle his feelings, pin them to the ground and make them submit. Cast them out with some brute force of will power.

But the nostalgia only tugged harder at him as things proceeded. It submerged him, pulled him out into the deep. An angry ocean of emotions lurching in his skull. Chaotic and overwhelming.

And his consciousness drew up into that storm in his head until he couldn't make out the words that the minister said. Instead, he experienced them as a drone streaming along with the image of Fran's veil lifting, her green eyes looking deeply into the groom's, like watching a foreign film with the subtitles turned off.

The smoke smell hit then, a blackened stench like that of charring meat on a barbecue with a foul chemical note intertwined. Jason felt his nose wrinkle.

He blinked a few times as his mind processed it. With an effort, he managed to break his gaze from Fran and Dennis, swivel his head to scan for the source of the bad smell.

Someone yelled then.

"Fire!"

And then everything moved very quickly.

A stampede of human bodies swarmed for the door. All shuffling feet and swinging elbows. Seeming to move as one frightened creature rather than individuals.

Screams and moans shattered the silence of the ceremony. Strange throaty sounds rising up — the screech of frightened animals.

Jason could hear his breath in his head. Too loud. Wrong.

The same room that had harbored that reverent quiet one second, convulsed with panic the next.

Twirling black smoke filled the space all at once. Clouded everything, its opaqueness rapidly thickening. It billowed from the little chamber off to the side of the main sanctuary and began to eclipse the sun streaming in those windows above, casting a darkness over everything.

Jason pressed forward into the mass of human bodies clogging the space between him and the exit, eyes looking past all of them to the double doors ahead.

The main chamber of the church tapered to a small foyer — an architectural funnel overflowing with humanity. The stampede had moved from the pews to this narrow doorway all at once, and all the torsos piled against each other. But their forward progress ended there.

No daylight peeked from around the edges of the door. Nothing.

The mob could only shift and jockey for position and thrash into each other.

The wall of bodies closed around Jason. Cinched him so tightly that he moved along with the whims of the crowd. They lifted him off his feet, swept him up in the swell of mankind pressing on the front door that wouldn't seem to open.

He could picture an impossible image in the frenzy: the mob somehow lifting itself up like a tidal wave in the ocean, lurching up and up before folding itself forward with great momentum, crashing into the door, rolling back out to sea.

And as shoulders and elbows dug into his ribcage, a set of words opened in his head. Interrupted the present. Held him strangely still as though catatonic. Whittled all the panicked sounds down to quiet.

We're going to die here.

We are all going to die in here.

The sounds of the mob returned, brought him back. The wood floor groaning beneath all those moving feet. And the whimpers. Panicked expressions. A wordless cacophony erupting all around him.

But no. It wasn't wordless after all. He could make out one word rising above all the din. A raspy voice, full-throated and deep.

"Locked."

Locked. It took a second to make sense of it. The doors were locked. They were trapped inside.

Again, he swiveled his head.

The black smoke undulated behind them. A strange wall of murk that twirled and tumbled about itself like liquid.

Still, it was the only way out. Had to be.

He pulled the collar of his shirt up over his mouth and knifed his way back through the mob, moving toward the smoke, moving into it.

He got low as the black surrounded him, one hand holding his collar over his lips, the other patting along the ground to try to feel his way along.

The windows were too high. He remembered that, even if he couldn't see it now — all of the stained glass congregated far up toward the vaulted ceiling, out of reach.

But there had to be other doors. Another way.

He felt along. Fingers scrabbling over the textured carpet, knuckles butting into the leg of a pew now and again.

The heat gripped him as he reached the last row of pews and moved into the open. It was right on top of him and so intense it seemed to flush sweat out of every pore right away, made his vision blur and flicker along the edges. His mouth and throat felt raw, but he didn't let himself dwell on it.

He squinted. Tried to see anything at all in the murk. But the black smoke rolled endlessly up. A thick wall of it undulating everywhere like some creature that belonged at the bottom of the sea.

Light erupted to his right. A curtain went up all at once. Flame climbed it and devoured it. Sent raining sheets of melted fabric down, sizzling and flickering and half-liquefied. He jumped back, just missing the fallout.

But the curtain told him where he was. It meant he was near the little side chamber, the little backstage area where he'd kissed Fran.

God. Fran. Was she OK?

He pushed the thought away. He had to focus on finding a way out.

He stepped around the flaming curtain, moving faster now.

He couldn't remember, but he thought there'd been a door in that little prep chamber. Thought. Hoped.

His fingers found the wall. Traced along it. Patting it. Frisking it.

He could hear the fire just next to him, though he couldn't see it. Hissing. Spitting. Mocking him. Threatening.

The screams back toward the door intensified — the sounds of fear turning to those of pain — and Jason stiffened. Froze. Listened. He suspected the fire had reached the mob now. Inevitable.

Focus. Keep looking.

If he could find a door, he could yell for the others. Try to lead them by sound to the way out. Save them.

His fingers traced and retraced the seam before the realization hit. A doorway.

He jerked his hands for where the knob should be.

Nothing.

Panic.

Bile in his throat, on the back of his tongue.

His hands flailed where the door handle should be. Fingers brushing the smooth steel of the door.

The empty space seemed impossible. Something from a nightmare.

Too hot. Hard to think now. Sweat cascaded down his spine. An endless flow.

He focused. Slowed down. Worked his hands in wider arcs.

The protrusion bashed into the back of his knuckles. Found it.

He twisted the knob. Pulled the door open.

A rectangle of light sliced into the smoke. Tendrils rushed

into the opening, twisting like tentacles into the open air.

He stumbled through the threshold into the light, into the cool. Down two concrete steps. Collapsed on hands and knees in the grass.

Very faint now. Head spinning.

Breathe.

Breathe and then yell for the others.

The wind hurt scraping into him, cold and fresh as it was. Ached in his throat and on his tongue as it sucked past into his lungs.

But the cool surrounded him. Enveloped him. Beat back the heat at last.

Safe. He was safe.

He breathed. In and out. The spinning in his head slowing, leaving him.

Need to yell for Fran. For Dennis. For everyone.

He pushed himself off the ground. Trying to sit up.

But no. Something was wrong.

The heat surged in him again. Flushed his face. Too hot.

His breathing went ragged. Uneven. Not working right.

He coughed. Choked.

And his face clenched. Pulled taut. Felt like all the veins there constricted into piano strings.

He swiped a hand at his forehead, and a wad of melted flesh sloughed away at his touch.

CHAPTER 1

A blast of warm air tugged at Darger's hair as she passed from the plane into the skybridge and proceeded with the rest of the passengers into Terminal 3 of Los Angeles International Airport. The flight from Virginia to California had been delayed due to lightning at Dulles but was otherwise uneventful. No turbulence, no screaming children, no overly-talkative seatmates.

The air felt different here, that was for sure. Warm, dry, and scented with pine and salt. Back in Virginia, they were at the tail end of a moist, muggy summer. She couldn't remember the last time it hadn't rained for at least part of the day. During the most recent downpour, the basement below Darger's apartment had flooded, and her landlord had to have a handyman come install new gutters.

She passed a bank of windows near the gate showing off a picturesque row of palm trees. As a kid, palm trees had always looked like some sort of weird Dr. Seuss animal to her, with an impossibly long neck and a shaggy green mane that obscured the face.

Crossing through a food court area, Darger got a whiff of freshly ground coffee beans coming from Starbucks. Her mouth watered, and she considered that a healthy shot of espresso would go a long way in warding off any looming jetlag. Then she saw the line stretching halfway across the food court and decided against it. She was already running late as a result of her delayed flight, and she had a ride waiting. She needed to collect her luggage and get a move on.

She glided down two escalators to the baggage claim area and wriggled through the crowd to Carousel 2. The horde shifted and swayed, a sea of people. Together their voices combined to form one collective murmur. Here and there a raucous laugh or shriek of a child stood out for a half-second before being swallowed up again by the babble.

There were other sounds, too. Suitcases clattering to the ground and wheels bump-bump-bumping over the seams of the tiled floor. Shoe heels squeaked. Somewhere to her left, someone slurped at the dregs of a drink through a straw, a hollow gurgling noise as they tried to suck up the last few drops.

At least three different languages were being spoken in her direct vicinity: English, Spanish, and Korean.

Someone coughed. Another person called out, "Callie! Callie, come back here." Darger watched the woman turn and mutter to her husband. "Please go get Callie before she starts climbing on that thing."

A slight bulge in Darger's jacket pocket kept causing her to shift her right elbow. A fresh set of FBI credentials to replace the ones she'd tossed over the bridge in Detroit. Had they always been this bulky, or had she grown that accustomed to not having them on her person? She'd only been on hiatus for a couple of months, but somehow it felt like years had passed. There'd been surprisingly few hoops to jump through to return to her duties with the BAU. Whoever Loshak knew higher up the chain, they must have been a Big Fucking Deal.

Fifteen minutes passed. The mass of people in the baggage claim area grew slightly more agitated. A game of telephone started up and passed through the crowd, and Darger heard her flight number.

"Were you all on Delta 1128?"

Darger and several people clustered around her nodded their heads.

"So I guess the thing they use to get the luggage from the plane to here — the train, or whatever — I guess it broke down, so they had to switch all the luggage over to another one. They're almost finished, but it'll be another fifteen minutes or so."

The throng groaned and sighed with annoyance at the holdup.

Darger reached for her phone and glanced at the clock. From what she knew about L.A. traffic, they were probably already going to be late for the meeting. Shit.

She opened her contacts and dialed, but there was no answer on the other end. She texted instead.

Still at the Baggage Claim. Some sort of delay. Fifteen minutes, they said.

She should have just rented a car like she usually did, then this could have been avoided. She'd still be late to the meeting, of course, but at least she wouldn't have made someone else late, too.

Instead of putting her phone away, she kept it out and used the dead time to flip through her case notes.

Loshak had called only a few days after she'd gotten her shiny new badge and ID via FedEx.

"Got something for you, if you're ready to roll. There's a mutual acquaintance of ours working out of the L.A. field office that specifically requested our expertise."

"Los Angeles? That's where we're headed?"

"Tinseltown, indeed, but I don't know if I'll be able to join you. I've got a speaking engagement and then a conference that'll run through the 10th. You know how I love to work the criminology con circuit, hang out in a crowded conference room that smells like boiled ham, so I can shake the hands of sweaty people from all over the country."

Darger had been looking forward to working with Loshak again, so it was a little disappointing to hear she'd be flying solo for the time being. She managed to stifle that feeling and put her game face on.

"Tell me about the case."

"Serial arsonist," Loshak said. "Guy torched a church last week in the middle of a wedding ceremony."

"Jesus."

"Yeah. Twenty-six dead. At least seven of them were kids."

Darger closed her eyes and sighed.

"Nearly all the survivors had to be treated for severe burns. Some had damaged lungs. A real mess. Crazy thing is, the majority of the dead weren't even burned. Untouched by the fire. They died due to smoke inhalation."

"You said serial arsonist. He's done this before?"

She heard papers shifting in the background, Loshak paging through the file.

"There was a single casualty at a previous scene, an older woman, retired junior high principal, last name Galitis. Died when her house went up in flames at three in the morning. A few months before that, back in May, there was a small structure fire on some abandoned property. Anyway, they found evidence of the same incendiary device, for lack of a better term, at all three scenes — a two-liter bottle of gasoline of all things. Crude. Simple. Not much of a device at all, I guess, but…"

She swiped past photographs of the crime scenes on her phone now. Charred bodies. Destroyed buildings. Evidence markers. Crime scene tape.

Darger was jotting a reminder to look into the dead retiree's background when she noticed a distinct shift in the crowd noise. It was like someone had suddenly turned up the volume on the steady murmur.

At first she assumed the baggage from her flight had finally started circulating, but she hadn't heard the obnoxious buzzer sound that usually announced that the carousel was about to start up.

Something was definitely going on, though. She heard shouts echoing across the large chamber of concrete and tile. She wondered if a fight had broken out. It wouldn't surprise her. People were typically fairly on edge while traveling. With the added delay of their flight and then the snafu with the baggage, she could imagine someone with a short fuse snapping.

She skirted around a family decked out in matching Hawaiian shirts, trying to see what all the commotion was about.

There was a young woman breezing through the baggage claim area. Her platinum blonde hair was pulled into a messy ponytail, and she wore dark sunglasses despite being indoors. She clutched a phone in a hand with long pink stiletto nails.

She was flanked by two men and another woman, who appeared to be with her. But another group swarmed around

14

her like flies and seemed to be trying to get her attention.

"Cici!" one man yelled, then threw himself onto his knees so he could snap a photo of her with a camera sporting a giant telephoto lens.

That was when Darger realized they all had cameras, all of the people buzzing around the woman. A few of them were just using I-phones, but one of them had a full-size TV camera propped on his shoulder.

A celebrity being followed by the paparazzi, Darger thought. How very L.A.

The name "Cici" didn't ring any bells for Darger, and the woman hadn't looked familiar. A pop star from one of those singing shows, maybe. Darger could never keep track of that kind of thing.

She went back to her notes, thinking over what she and Loshak had discussed when he'd given her the case.

"I can't say I'll be sad to miss out on this one," he'd said.

"Why's that?"

"Arson is always ugly. It's one of the worst ways to go, and it makes for some of the grisliest cases to work. From my point of view, anyhow. And dealing with the arsonists themselves — the psychology of it — can get a little bleak. I don't know. They don't inspire a lot of faith in humanity, I guess you could say."

"Any thoughts about this case in particular?"

"I didn't dig too deeply in the file, but... a wedding? Seems awfully personal."

"You think the killer knew the bride or groom? That they were targeting someone specifically?"

"Could be. Could be the bride, the groom, someone in the wedding party. A family member. Or just one of the guests. Or it could be that this particular wedding was chosen at random. But I think the fact that it was a wedding says something, regardless. This person is very angry."

"Well, let's take a step back. The three motives for setting fires are money, revenge, and fun. I'm assuming we can rule money out," Darger said. "Unless the same person happens to own both properties. Or stands to benefit from all the life insurance policies, if there were any. Though I also assume that's the first place the police looked."

"Bingo. So far they've found zero connection between the victims or the targeted properties. That doesn't rule it out completely. There could always be some bizarre tangled web that leads to someone profiting off the various fires, but I'd say it's a doubtful prospect."

"So that leaves revenge and fun," Darger said. "And if you haven't been able to tie together the victims or properties…"

"Then it rules out revenge as motive, at least tacitly."

"So he's setting them for fun."

She used the male pronoun theoretically, even though nearly all convicted arsonists were male.

Just because most of them are, she thought to herself, doesn't mean they all are.

It was a mistake she'd made once and had vowed to never make again.

"That's what my gut says."

"Great," she said, her tone dry.

"Yeah."

She knew Loshak was thinking the same thing she was. That the "for fun" type of arsonist was the hardest to catch, because they often chose their targets at random and behaved rather erratically in general. Impulsive types, largely.

She tacked on a few notes to the end of her profile — things she wanted to be sure to hit hard during her presentation — and then a sound like a basketball shot clock sounded. The baggage carousel was finally moving, and she could see suitcases and duffel bags already sliding down the chute at the far end.

For once, luck seemed to be on her side. Her suitcase was one of the first onto the conveyor belt. She recognized it at a distance because of the twist of bright orange yarn tied to the handle. A trick her mother had taught her long ago.

She edged her way around to one corner of the giant oval-shaped machine, trying to head off her bag. She extended her arm, grabbing for the handle of her suitcase. It was just within her grasp, but someone elbowed in front of her and beat her to it.

"Let me get that for you."

It was a masculine voice, and Darger was instantly annoyed. She knew that was irrational. He was surely just trying to be gentlemanly. But if she needed help, she'd ask for it. She didn't need someone barging into her personal space, as if she were some kind of damsel in distress, incapable of lifting a damn suitcase.

The man's fingers snatched the suitcase upward, hoisting it easily from the conveyor belt and setting it on the floor beside him and just slightly out of her reach.

He smiled down at her benevolently, and now she was really ready to give it to him. She was already late, and now some dickhead wanted to play games with her luggage. Was he trying to be cute, holding her bag hostage like that?

17

Darger opened her mouth to speak, and at the same time the man lifted a hand to remove his sunglasses. She stopped, recognizing him.

The man was Casey Luck.

"How was your flight?" he asked, still grinning.

Her irritation fled instantly.

"I didn't recognize you. You're... tan. And you've got stubble."

"Plus, I shaved off the mustache."

"Aww," Darger said, pretending to mourn the loss.

"Yeah right. I know you hated it."

"I told you it was nothing personal. I hate all mustaches equally."

"Yes, I remember it well. Very even-handed of you. Fair and balanced and all that. Let's go."

They threaded their way through the throngs of humanity to the parking area outside, where Luck's Lexus was parked in a restricted area. Darger feigned a heart attack, grabbing her chest.

"Parked in a No Parking zone? Agent Luck, what's gotten into you? You lose the 'stache, grow a little stubble, and suddenly you're Mr. Rulebreaker?"

Luck chuckled as they climbed into the car.

There were other things that were different about him, too. He looked a little thinner, and instead of a suit and tie, he was wearing a sports jacket and khakis.

"I don't know if I've ever seen you not wearing a tie."

He gave her a wry look.

"Violet, you've seen me wearing nothing."

Snorting, Darger said, "Fair enough. You're just looking

18

awfully casual, is all. Relaxed, even. It's very… un-Luck."

He made a face like that had hurt his feelings.

"I can be relaxed," he insisted. "Besides, everything's a little more casual out here."

Darger raised an eyebrow. "Even the FBI?"

"Even the FBI."

CHAPTER 2

The chorus of "Hang On Sloopy" by The McCoys filtered out of the speakers as soon as Luck turned the key in the ignition. He steered them into traffic and soon they left the airport behind them, heading for downtown.

Something about the radio playing oldies felt fitting with all the palm trees and mid-century architecture passing by outside Darger's window. Part of her always thought of that era of history when she thought of L.A.

Her eyes wandered over to the man driving the car. Despite their seemingly friendly greeting, she sensed some unease with Luck. It was his posture, she thought. He was holding his chin just a touch too high. And his back was a little too straight and upright. What did they call that? Ramrod straight. Like even the "new casual model" of Casey Luck couldn't quite relax around her.

She supposed she felt a little of the same uncertainty. Partly because of their history. She doubted things would ever be truly informal between them after a failed romance.

With what happened in Detroit, though, when they'd last seen one another, it was hard to know where things lay between them, even as associates in a professional sense. They'd spoken, of course. Once to go over some of the more pertinent details of the current case and again to double-check her flight arrangements so he could pick her up at the airport. So at least she'd had advance warning that they'd be working together again.

She still felt some resentment that he hadn't spoken up for her after that last case, if she was honest with herself. That maybe he hadn't even believed her that his boss had been working with the mob. And maybe he had some remaining bitterness of his own. Things had gotten messy in Detroit. And Darger wasn't sure how much of that might have led to his current position being in a field office halfway across the country.

There was something else nagging at her, too. After her falling out with Prescott, when Darger had decided that the private sector wasn't working out, it had been a natural decision to go back to the Bureau.

But now that she was here, she couldn't help but wonder if she'd made the right choice.

She let the back of her skull fall against the seat, cradled by the headrest.

Why couldn't she just be sure of things for once? Why was she always doubting her own choices? Maybe that was life. Maybe it only ever seemed like other people knew exactly what they were doing. What they were meant for. Where and who they were supposed to be.

She studied Luck from the corner of her eye. To most people, it would seem like he'd hit the jackpot with this assignment. She remembered one guy in her training group at the Academy. His dream placement had been in Honolulu. He'd been sent to Kansas City instead. She could still see the stunned look on his face when he opened his letter and the way he kept muttering, "Wow... Missouri? Wow."

"So, how's paradise?" Darger finally asked.

"Paradise?"

She swept her hand around, gesturing at the scenic landscape outside.

"Come on, you live in La-La Land. How's it been treating you?"

"I mean the weather is fantastic. Almost unbelievable."

"Are you suggesting you don't miss the seemingly endless winter of the Midwest? The gray, sunless days?"

He shook his head, smirking. "Not even a little."

Darger wondered how Luck's daughter was adjusting to their new home.

"What about Jill?"

"Oh, she loves it out here. We've been to Disneyland five times already. Can't really beat that."

"Yeah, probably not."

They lapsed into silence for a few moments, but something about his original answer about living in Los Angeles was bugging her.

"So the weather is fantastic, but…"

His eyebrows peeked up above the rims of his sunglasses. "Huh?"

"It just sounded like you were going to add that there was something not so fantastic."

"Well, I felt a little guilty at first. We'd just gotten settled in Michigan, and then we had to start all over again."

Darger held her tongue on that. It was part of being in the FBI, the Bureau made that very clear during agent training at the Academy. Agents were told they should be prepared to pick up and move assignments every three to five years.

It wasn't helpful to point this out, though, so she kept her lips sealed.

"Claudia and Ray followed us out here. Jill's grandparents. And at first I thought it was a blessing but…"

Darger waited for him to continue. He shrugged and let out a sigh.

"I don't know. I got kinda used to it being just me and Jill in Michigan. They'd come up for holidays and Jill's birthday and stuff… and I shouldn't complain. They've been great. They're saving me a fortune not having to find daycare, and they love Jill to pieces, but…"

He trailed off again, and this time Darger urged him on.

"But, but, but. What?"

"They're just always around, you know? On the weekends, when maybe I'd like to take Jill to the beach, spend some time with her after working all week, I feel obligated to ask them to come along. Or they invite themselves. And I can't really say no. They do so much for us. And it seems like a small thing to offer."

"Boundaries, my friend," Darger said, shaking her head. "Look, they spend all week with Jill, right?"

"Right."

"Then you're absolutely entitled to some time hanging out with just her, apart from them. She's your daughter."

"But they do—"

"So much. I heard you. But they're not doing you a favor, watching Jill. You realize that, right? They're doing it because it's what they want. It's a reward for them. They didn't move out here for the nanny job. They moved out here to be close to their granddaughter. And they are. Stop feeling guilty."

Luck frowned, and she worried she'd offended him. Maybe she'd overstepped the bounds of their current relationship, offering unsolicited advice like that. It really wasn't her place.

But then Luck blinked a few times and the corners of his mouth turned upward. He turned his face toward her.

"When did you get so insightful?"

Darger scoffed and watched the skyscrapers downtown seem to grow taller through the windshield as they got closer.

"Oh, it's easy to have all the answers when it's someone else's life. You just kind of point your finger and say wrong a lot."

CHAPTER 3

From the outside, the LAPD headquarters looked like a giant mirrored cube nestled in a triangle of concrete. Luck parked down the street in a paid lot. From there they walked back to the shimmering LAPD building, passing restaurants, bars, and storefronts.

A car horn blared. Smells wafted from a food truck set up nearby. Thin, tan, blonde people shuffled everywhere, something a little plastic about many of them.

Darger followed Luck through a set of automatic sliding glass doors. The interior was just as modern as the outside. Everything was brushed steel, sparkling glass, polished concrete. Luck showed his badge to a uniformed officer at a desk, and then they took an elevator upstairs.

As she'd suspected, the meeting was already underway when she and Luck finally pushed through the conference room doors. The rows of chairs were packed with uniforms, detectives, and other law enforcement personnel.

She recognized both the room and the man behind the podium from the press conferences she'd watched related to the case. Newly appointed, Chief Macklin mostly looked the part. His neat crew cut was standard police issue. The beard, less so.

Behind him, an American flag hung limp next to a backdrop emblazoned with the LAPD logo. From the out of context snippet of the speech Darger was hearing, it sounded like Macklin was talking about new leads.

Luck nodded to a man in a gray suit standing near the podium, and, in turn, the man waved them up to the front. As they approached, gray suit leaned over and whispered something to Chief Macklin.

Darger's stomach suddenly felt like a lump of raw dough being kneaded by a dozen fists. She didn't know if it was because she'd missed the beginning of the meeting or if it was the time she'd taken away from the FBI, but she felt even more edgy than usual.

It seemed to take forever to reach the front of the room. She breathed in and out slowly, trying to settle her nerves.

When they reached the podium, Chief Macklin gestured that Darger should take his place in front of the microphone.

"And now I'll turn things over to our profiler, on loan from our friends at the FBI. I'll let her introduce herself and present her findings."

This was it. There was a laptop connected to a projector on a small cart next to the podium. Darger connected a thumb drive with some informational slides relating to her profile and stared out at the crowd of faces.

"Good afternoon," she said into the mic. "I'm Violet Darger from the FBI."

She cringed internally. The Chief had already told them she was from the FBI. Now it probably sounded like she was bragging. That or maybe like she was just an idiot.

And even though her notes were right there in front of her, her mind went blank.

If she'd had just five minutes to get her bearings in the room before she'd had to present her profile, a few seconds to breathe. But she'd literally walked in and been ushered on stage, and now everyone was staring. Expecting her to have all the answers.

She remembered then what someone had once told her about public speaking.

You are here to present your profile... to move the information from Point A — your brain — to Point B — the brains of your audience. Focus on how to do that best, and you'll forget about everything else.

The kindly voice of Ted Fowles echoed in her mind, and Darger knew then that she'd be fine. It was a simple task, after all. One she'd done dozens of times now. She had this.

She swallowed the rest of her doubts and glanced down at her notes, but she barely needed them. She remembered it all now.

"Let's start with the basics: Most arsonists are young, white males," she said, bringing up a chart with more detailed demographics. "In fact, about one-third of them are under the age of fifteen. In this case, however — given the severity of the crimes and the apparent escalation — it's more likely that we're looking for someone older. More experienced, if you will. The geographic spread of the crime scenes, at least, suggests the perpetrator has access to a vehicle or is somehow otherwise able to get all the way from the west side of L.A. to San Bernardino County. These circumstances, combined with the data-driven probabilities, would suggest that we're looking for someone between the ages of 17 and 26 — possibly a little older, but the odds go down as the age goes up."

Her eyes wandered over to Luck, who stood off to her right, and he gave her an approving bob of the head.

"We generally divide arsonists into categories based on

three main motives." She ticked the first two off on her fingers. "The most common are fires started for profit — usually an insurance scam. Second-most common are fires started for revenge — an angry ex-husband setting his former spouse's home on fire, for example. In these cases, the perpetrator may or may not intend for the fire to cause bodily harm."

A click of the mouse revealed a graph of arson crimes in the US grouped by motive.

"Given the fact that we have yet to find a connection between the properties or the victims, we can probably rule out the motives of profit and revenge. That leaves us with the last group: fires started for fun. In these cases the arsonist doesn't have a motive other than loving to see the destructive power of fire in action. This type of arsonist is a true pyromaniac, one who achieves sexual pleasure from starting fires, one obsessed with all fire-related things. Matches, lighters, fire alarms, fire trucks. He sets fires because he loves it, plain and simple."

Darger let her eyes settle on the group of men and women in front of her.

"If we are indeed searching for a pyromaniac, it makes our job that much harder. This is the hardest type of arsonist to catch. He can set fires anytime, anywhere. His crimes are seemingly committed at random. Erratic. Spontaneous. We can't predict where or when he'll strike next, because even he likely does not know."

The next slide she brought up showed a list of common attributes and characteristics for pyromaniacs as children.

"Our pyromaniac would have had an unstable childhood — one or both parents absent, and there was almost certainly abuse and/or neglect by whoever was tasked with caring for him," she said. "Pyromania has also been linked to low serotonin levels and childhood hyperactivity disorders. There's often an incorrect assumption that pyromaniacs have a low IQ, but most studies have found them to have an overall average or above-average intelligence."

Darger proceeded to the next slide.

"But no matter how smart he is, the instability in his childhood will almost certainly carry over into adulthood in terms of his ability to form and maintain relationships. He's probably not married. He may even still live with or somehow rely on a parent or childhood guardian for support. If he is in a long term relationship, his homelife is probably rocky. Substance abuse, domestic disturbances, infidelity. Any and all of these would fit a pyromaniac."

Darger poured herself a glass of water from the pitcher next to the podium and took a sip before she went on.

"Above all, his behavior is marked by impulsiveness. Emotional events and stressors trigger his outbursts. Life problems set him off. It becomes cause and effect. When he gets angry or upset, the emotions create a tension that can only be relieved by setting a fire. He feels an actual physical sense of gratification and even sexual arousal when setting a fire or viewing the damage caused by one. He finds escape from his pain only in torching something."

Darger thought she saw at least a handful of the audience grimace at that thought.

"I imagine at least some of you are familiar with the John Orr case. For anyone that isn't, he was a fire captain and arson investigator for the Glendale Fire Department, and between the years of 1984 and 1991, it is believed that he set as many as two thousand fires. These were fires he'd set and then investigated himself. He was arrested in 1991 and convicted of four counts of murder, but it took years before anyone got suspicious enough to start piecing it all together."

A click of a button brought up a photograph of the convicted arsonist and murderer.

"Orr presents as a classic pyromaniac, and he fits many of the profile characteristics to a T: a childhood fascination with fire, firefighters, and law enforcement. He actually wanted to be a police officer but failed the entrance exam. One pertinent detail is that at the time of the most devastating fire — the hardware store fire that claimed the lives of his four victims — John Orr was 35 years old."

Crossing her arms, Darger continued.

"You'll remember I gave an age range of 17-26. Most experts that have studied the John Orr crimes believe he'd almost certainly been setting fires long before the 1984 fire. So one reason I wanted to bring this up is to remind you that the age range is a suggestion based on the probabilities. It's not gospel, not absolute. Don't let the guidelines in the profile lead to tunnel vision."

She turned and glanced at the larger-than-life photograph of Orr projected on the wall.

"The other reason I bring John Orr up is to highlight the split in his image of himself. Not only did he start the fires and then show up on the scene to put them out and then investigate. He also wrote about them. One of the main pieces of evidence against him was a novel he'd written and submitted to literary agents and publishers. Those who knew Orr and read the book said it was quite clear to them that he'd cast himself as both the hero arson investigator and also the arsonist himself — the name of the villain, Aaron Stiles, was an anagram for 'I set L.A. arson.' So there's a strange dichotomy there, that he can see himself simultaneously as the hero and the villain. That in some ways, he wants to be both. It speaks to the fact that our arsonist, like many other serial offenders — be they rapists or killers — lead a double life."

Gripping both sides of the podium now, Darger shook her head.

"Some of the people he worked with still refuse to discuss or acknowledge the case. I don't think they're able to come to terms with the fact that someone they knew and worked with could have done this right under their noses."

Darger hesitated there a moment, let the silence linger in the room, not sure exactly how to broach this next piece of business.

"Chief Macklin has asked me to suggest a course of action for the investigation moving forward."

Darger resisted an urge to fidget. It was always uncomfortable to be the Fed who swooped in and told the local cops how to do their jobs. The fact that the Chief had specifically asked for her opinion on the topic didn't necessarily make it any easier.

Her next slide had a list of angles for the task force to work.

"Chances are, the investigations into the fires to this point primarily focused on motives involving either money or revenge. You probably looked at building owners, landlords, tenants, former tenants, employees, etc. At the time, that's what made the most sense. But knowing what we know now, it would be wise to revisit those earlier files and expand the investigation. Re-interview witnesses. Rewatch any available surveillance tape. Canvas the neighborhoods. We need to cast a wider net. If we can find a vehicle that was spotted somewhere near several crime scenes in the days leading up to the fires, or someone found lurking around during the investigation or rubbernecking at more than one fire, then we might just find our guy."

It occurred to Darger that the group in this room felt different than most she'd spoken to. Bigger, for one, but there was something else. Something about the quiet, the rigidity of the postures, the proliferation of crew cuts among the uniformed officers staring up at her. She'd heard the LAPD skewed a little more military than most urban police forces, both in operational tactics as well as the culture. Maybe there was something to that.

She took another sip of her water and went on.

"The fire itself only makes these types of investigations more difficult. It destroys evidence of all kinds. Often leaves us little to work with. Without the two-liter bottles found at each of these scenes, we wouldn't even know we had a serial offender on our hands. To that end, I'd like to point out that there's a good chance he's set other fires we don't know about. Dozens. Maybe hundreds, depending on how old he is and how prolific he's been. I'd suggest another team start contacting the various jurisdictions in the surrounding areas to get a list of fires where gasoline was used as an accelerant. Also find out if they've ever found two-liter bottles or perhaps PET plastic residue at a fire scene. In many cases, the fire inspector might not have even classified the fire as arson, so be careful about whose toes you're stepping on. We're not looking to lay blame, we only want as much information as we can gather. If we uncover more fires our guy is responsible for, we might be able to spot a pattern."

She'd reached the last slide and the end of her notes, but she wasn't quite done.

"Does anyone have any questions?"

An older detective in a tweed blazer raised his hand.

"I have a question about the, uh, the plastic soda bottle filled with gasoline."

"Yes?"

"The arson expert says this crude way of starting a fire — splashing gasoline and leaving the empty bottle off to the side — is odd seeing as there are incendiary devices that would be much harder to detect. Which would make it harder to definitively say it's arson. Wouldn't the fact that our guy is using such an obvious method to start the fires be a sign that he's, well... not a genius?"

"It's possible," Darger said. "It's also possible that we're dealing with a young or otherwise inexperienced perpetrator. That he's simply ignorant about what kind of clues he's been leaving behind. Or it could be the opposite. He might know exactly what he's doing, and it's meant as a taunt. These types of criminals are often cocky, aggressive, territorial types. He probably doesn't believe we can catch him, even if he intentionally leaves breadcrumbs to mark his trail. It might be that what he truly craves is credit and attention. As soon as he started leaving a signature, the headlines started rolling in."

That led to the first real murmur in the crowd. The detective who asked the question thanked Darger and jotted something on a legal pad in his lap.

Finding no more raised hands in the crowd, Darger turned things back over to Chief Macklin.

She rejoined Luck off to the side of the room, and he gave her a thumbs up.

"OK. You heard the lady. Cast a wider net. We'll have a team start digging into the surveillance. There's no surveillance set up at the church, but check out the traffic cams for all routes leading into the area. Same for the intersections around the residential fire and the abandoned lot. Another team will go back over any reports of fires for the past… five years?"

He looked to Darger for that last bit, and she nodded her approval.

"Detectives Stoltz and Martin, I want you on the street, head up a major operation canvassing for eyewitnesses. Anyone who might have seen something or someone out of the ordinary. We'll see that you get all the manpower you need to do the job. And I assume our brothers and sisters in San Bernardino will be doing the same," the Chief said.

A woman sitting in the front row said, "Yes, sir."

The baseball cap she wore was embroidered with the San Bernardino Sheriff's Department logo.

The Chief picked up his stack of papers and neatened the stack with a tap of his hand.

"Then I think we're finished here for the time being. This meeting is adjourned."

Immediately a swell in the collective murmur. Bodies rising from the chairs, crowding for the door. Wordlessly, Darger and Luck decided to wait out the scrum.

With the various members of law enforcement streaming past them, Luck took out his phone. Glanced at the screen.

"Shit. Missed a call from Jill."

A loud burst of laughter erupted from one corner of the room where a circle of uniformed officers were chatting.

"If you don't mind, I'm gonna go find somewhere quiet to call her back. You still want to get that bite to eat?"

"Sure," Darger said. "I'll meet you at the car."

She watched him join the mass of people filing out through the double doors.

"Hey, Agent Darger?"

She stopped and swiveled to face him. The man was several inches taller than her, with brown hair and what she considered the classic cop mustache. The badge on his uniform said "MURPHY."

"Yeah?"

"Rodney Murphy," he said, shaking her hand while simultaneously gesturing at the man to his left. "And this is Miguel Camacho."

Camacho's biceps bulged and strained against the fabric of his uniform as he reached for her hand.

"Nice to meet you."

"Got a question for you," Murphy said. "We're supposed to be looking at old fires, trying to find a pattern, right? But I thought you said the pyros don't really follow a pattern, that's why they're so hard to catch."

Darger nodded then pointed to Camacho.

"You two are partners, right?"

"Yeah."

"How long?"

"Four years going on eternity," Murphy joked.

Camacho rolled his eyes.

"Do you know what he ate for breakfast this morning?"

"No," Murphy said, shoulders twitching.

"If you had to guess?"

Without hesitation, Murphy said, "Egg white omelet with spinach and a protein shake."

Darger's gaze flicked over to Camacho.

"Is he right?"

"Yeah, but that's what I eat every morning."

"And that's my point," Darger said with a smile. "Pyromaniacs are still human, and humans are creatures of habit. I guarantee there's a pattern to the fires he sets, it's just not as clear as a fire set for the purpose of money or revenge."

Crossing her arms, Darger sighed.

"You still make a fair point in that it's a long shot. A lot of times, investigators only find the pattern afterward. We might never find one at all. But that doesn't mean it's not there."

CHAPTER 4

Most of the crowd had dispersed by the time Darger reached the hallway outside of the conference room, and she ended up in an elevator by herself. Just as the brushed metal doors began to whoosh shut, a very pregnant woman came bustling out of the ladies' room across the hall.

"Hold the door," she called out.

Darger hit the "DOOR OPEN" button, and the doors slid aside. The woman took a few waddling steps toward the waiting elevator before a file folder slipped from her hand, spilling its contents over the floor.

"Oh, balls!"

The woman gave Darger an exasperated look.

"Thanks, anyway, but it looks like I'll be taking the next one," she said, attempting to retrieve her belongings.

The fullness of her belly prevented her from bending over, so she had to settle for an awkward squat, and Darger was worried she'd tip over like a capsizing ship.

Darger abandoned her post at the elevator door and hurried over to help.

"Let me get those for you," she said, scooping the loose papers and handing them to the woman.

"This is so embarrassing. Here I wanted to make a good impression, and then I go and pull a classic Georgina."

"A good impression?" Darger repeated.

"Well yeah. It's not every day we get a real Quantico profiler consulting on a case. I mean, maybe the L.A. guys do, but we don't."

That was when Darger recognized the woman and her baseball cap.

"Captain Georgina Beck. I run the station out in Yucaipa under the San Bernardino Sheriff's Department."

"Violet Darger."

"I really enjoyed your profile, by the way," she said, waving a hand between them. "I know that's not what it's for, of course. I just mean it was enlightening and all."

Darger nodded, only remembering to mutter a thanks after a second.

"I had some questions for you, if you don't mind."

"Not at all."

"It's just that, to this point we've spent most of our investigation working the revenge angle. Trying to find someone tied to the wedding party or one of the guests, you know? I guess after listening to your presentation, I'm worried I just wasted a whole lot of time sniffing down the wrong trail."

"I wouldn't call it wasted time. You worked with the information you had at the time. Besides that, the profile is only a guide. We never get everything right. So it makes perfect sense to exhaust all the obvious leads and suspects first."

By now they had re-assembled Beck's scattered file, so Darger went and pressed the button for the elevator.

"Well, I guess I'm glad to hear that," Beck said while they waited, but Darger thought she still looked bothered. It was probably hard to deal with something as devastating as the church fire in a small jurisdiction, especially the kids. Darger looked down at Beck's swollen belly.

"I know what you're thinking. 'She's either about 11

months pregnant, or she swallowed a watermelon whole this morning for breakfast.'"

Darger laughed.

The elevator announced its arrival with an electronic ping. Darger gestured that Beck should board first and followed her inside.

"I'd been thinking of driving out to see the scene of the wedding fire. Maybe talk to the owner of the venue, if possible. All with your permission, of course."

"Fine with me," Beck said. "In fact, I'd love to show you around. Give me your info, and we can decide when and where to meet up."

They swapped phone numbers and email addresses and then went their separate ways outside of the building.

The sun made Darger squint as she moved onto the sidewalk. She slid on her sunglasses, regained her bearings, and headed back toward the lot where she and Luck had parked.

The weather was delightful, as she'd been warned it would be. Maybe a little bright for her taste. She smelled the smoky char of a grill as she got down the block, probably from one of the restaurants nearby, and it made her stomach rumble.

Luck waited for Darger in the parking lot, standing near his car. As she got closer, she could see that he was chatting with a couple of uniformed officers.

Luck waved her over and introduced them.

"Agent Darger, meet a couple of guys from the task force — Damon Bishop and T.J. Klootey."

Bishop was a tall black man with his head shaved clean. His partner was shorter and frecklier but solidly built. Klootey's reddish hair sported the classic crew cut, though it was grown out and looking a bit fluffy on top. They shook hands and exchanged the usual pleasantries.

"So this might be a stupid question," Klootey said, "But you usually work cases that involve serial killers, right?"

"I consult on a variety of cases, but yes. Serial murders make up a significant portion of my caseload."

"Is that what this guy is, then? A serial killer?"

It was anything but a stupid question and had been at the back of Darger's mind since she first began studying the files.

"I'm not sure yet. I think that will depend on how his crimes continue to progress. I've been wondering if the fire that killed the retiree, Mrs. Galitis, might have been a fluke. He may have expected the house to be empty for some reason. After that, it's possible that the idea of his fire claiming an actual victim intrigued him enough to try it again, with purpose this time."

"Hence the wedding fire," Klootey said.

Darger nodded.

"I mentioned John Orr during the meeting, and I think there are ideas in his novel that give some insight to both his lack of remorse and the fact that he did, to some degree, relish the idea of taking lives," she explained. "At one point, after the villain in the book sets a fire very similar to the one that claimed the lives of John Orr's real-life victims, he reasons that it wasn't his fault that people died. That they were obviously too stupid to get out. Zero remorse."

Luck shook his head at that.

"Man, there was a two-year-old kid that died in that church fire. How do you not feel any remorse over that?"

"I honestly don't know," Darger answered. "Later on in the

book, the villain attempts to murder a teenage girl. Whether or not Orr ever intentionally killed anyone, I think we can say that he at least fantasized about it. Maybe he even liked to think of himself as a cold-blooded killer. There's an appealing power there, no matter how backward and sick it sounds."

Throughout Darger's response, Klootey had remained attentive. His partner, however, couldn't seem to stop glancing over his shoulder. Darger couldn't figure out if he was rude, up to something, or just kind of a twitchy dude.

She refocused on the question Klootey had asked.

"So to answer your question in earnest, I need more time. If he targets another highly populated area — like he did with the church — then yes. I'd call him a serial killer."

Bishop went rigid, like a rabbit spotting a fox across the field, and Darger knew then that he was definitely up to something. She gave a casual glance across the parking lot and saw one of the cops she'd spoken to inside the conference room climbing into a yellow Ford Mustang. Camacho of the daily spinach and egg white omelet breakfast.

His partner, Murphy, jogged over just as the engine rumbled to life. He rapped his knuckles against the window, and Camacho rolled it down.

Bishop was bouncing on his feet now, sneaking peeks over at the car every so often but trying not to be obvious about it.

Murphy rested a hand on the top of the car and leaned down to say something to his friend in the driver's seat. After a few moments, he knocked his fist against the roof and stepped back.

"Teej! Teej, it's happening," Bishop whispered, his voice on the edge of hysteria.

Finally Camacho put the car in gear and rolled out of the parking space. Almost immediately, there was a loud pop.

Everyone flinched at the sound, and at first Darger thought it was a gunshot. Murphy wheeled around, grabbing for his gun, a terrified look on his face.

The Mustang came to a halt and Camacho lunged out of the car.

"What happened?" he asked Murphy. "What was it? Did I pop a tire?"

Bishop and Klootey were both buckled over at the waist now. Klootey's laugh came out a high-pitched cackle while Bishop's was more of a silent wheeze.

Camacho climbed out and scrambled around the Mustang, searching for the source of the explosion, and Murphy followed as his partner ran circles around the vehicle.

Klootey reached over and punched his partner in the arm.

Swiveling to face her, Luck asked, "Do you have any idea what's going on?"

"Nope."

Klootey peered over at them and managed to choke out, "Inner tube… zip-tied… exhaust pipe."

And then he was losing it again.

Camacho was bent over the rear end of his car now struggling with something.

A few seconds later, he was storming toward them with a blown-out inner tube in one hand. He shook it in the air.

"I told you knuckleheads, the car is off limits! You better hope this didn't do any damage. I just upgraded the exhaust system, and you two jag-offs think it's funny to go messing with it. Not fucking cool."

The two jag-offs were still laughing too hard to speak. Klootey had actually fallen to his hands and knees now.

"Yeah, laugh it up, Klootey!"

Camacho threw the shredded scraps of rubber at Klootey, which landed with a smack against one shoulder.

"Hey man, it was Bishop's idea," he said, aiming a finger at his partner.

As Camacho stomped his way back over to his car, Klootey got himself together enough to stand again.

They watched Camacho peel out of the parking lot, and Darger caught a glimpse of the vanity license plate that read: MACH0M4N.

Murphy strutted over, shaking his head.

"You guys better watch your backs now. You know how he is about that car."

Klootey chuckled.

"Dude is delusional. The car is a ten-year-old piece of shit, and he wants to act like it's a '65 Shelby."

"Yeah, well, he's still pissed about the time you Twinkied it."

"Twinkied?" Darger asked.

"Yeah, it's where you take a Twinkie and you shove it up under the door handle," Klootey explained.

"Now hold on," Bishop interrupted. "You don't shove anything anywhere. See, you got to do it gentle-like, so as to preserve the integrity of the Twinkie. When the person goes to get in their car, they reach up and get a handful of cream filling."

"These two are the pranksters of our division, in case you hadn't noticed," Murphy said, turning to face Darger and Luck.

"Always trying to one-up each other."

"I think what you mean is that T.J. is always trying to one-up me, because I'm the best," Bishop bragged.

Murphy scoffed.

"My point is, watch yourself around these two. They'll tie your shoelaces together when you're not looking."

"Duly noted," Darger said, glancing down at her boots for good measure.

Luck tapped her on the arm.

"You still up for dinner?"

She nodded and followed him over to the car.

When they pulled onto the street, the three guys from the LAPD were still frantically windmilling their limbs in the general direction of where Camacho's car had been parked, reliving their prank.

CHAPTER 5

They drove back toward the ocean, the sun drooping low in the clear blue sky. Luck parked near the Santa Monica Pier, and they ordered dinner at a Caribbean chicken joint. They were close enough to the Pacific that Darger could gaze down the street at it while they waited for their food. It was a gray-blue stripe along the horizon, a little blurred through the veil of smog.

When their number got called, they grabbed their Styrofoam containers and walked down the street to a park with a full view of the beach. Judging from the quiet as they tore into the food, Luck was just as hungry as Darger. A few bites in, however, the edge of the hunger died back, and a conversation finally started up.

"You've teamed up with the LAPD before?" she asked.

"Twice since I've been here. A mass-shooting and a string of burglaries that crossed into Nevada. That's how I know Klootey and Bishop."

Darger swallowed a mouthful of fried plantains.

"I have to be honest, those guys are not quite what I imagined when I think of the LAPD. I guess it's hard not to have some preconceived notions, especially after stuff like Rodney King and the Christopher Dorner shootings."

Luck shook his head.

"I'll tell you what," he said. "I don't envy them. Can't imagine being a street cop or even a detective in a jurisdiction like L.A. There's the danger, of course, but even the guys not on

45

the street… it's gotta wear on you. A city this big, you must see the absolute worst in humanity. Day after day. Unrelenting."

"I guess that means you don't regret switching sides, then?"

"Not even a little bit."

"Spoken like a true traitor," she said with a teasing smile.

He stared out at the beach, so she followed his gaze. The sun was sinking in the sky, coloring it gold.

"So what do you think of paradise?"

"It's beautiful. I'll give you that," Darger said, but she couldn't help but think of when traffic came to a standstill on the highway for over twenty minutes. "Too many people, though."

Even now she could hear the non-stop whoosh and rumble of cars behind her. Horns, the waft of diesel exhaust, squealing brakes. In front of her, down on the beach, people walked dogs, tossed Frisbees, stretched out on towels. The masses of humanity spanning all directions.

Luck laughed as he tossed a chicken bone that had been expertly cleaned of all traces of meat back into his tray.

"Right. I forgot you were such a misanthrope."

"I am not a misanthrope."

"You're not?" he asked, wiping his hands on a napkin.

"Just because I think most people are idiots doesn't mean I hate them."

He laughed again and shook his head.

The sun was just touching the edge of the sea now, a giant molten coin melting into the horizon. The ocean looked like hammered bronze.

They deposited the remnants of their meal in a nearby waste bin and strolled back to Luck's car. It was getting darker now, the nature of the crowd seeming to morph around them — couples holding hands, a pair of teenagers apparently practicing mouth-to-mouth resuscitation, their lips locked together in either desperation or passion.

Just before they reached the car, the lights snapped on along the pier, and a Ferris wheel lit up in the distance.

Luck unlocked the car with his fob, and Darger climbed in.

He turned the key in the ignition and then asked, "You think anyone's actually read John Orr's book?"

"I have."

"Yeah?" he said, in a tone that indicated he wanted her assessment of it.

"Sucks."

Luck chuckled.

They drove back through the city, which seemed to Darger to change dramatically block by block. First it was skyscrapers, then it was the endless rows of small, boxy houses flanked by palm trees. A few blocks later, she could admire the lights of the houses up in the hills. The traffic waxed and waned all the while, catching them for a bit here and there at various clogged intersections and then coming clear for a few blocks.

The weather. The sunset. The views. It really would be paradise if it weren't for all the damn people.

Luck dropped Darger off at the hotel, where he insisted on getting out to pull her luggage from the trunk. Mr. Chivalry or Mr. Rulebreaker? Dude needed to make up his mind.

"Thanks for dinner," Darger said.

"No problem. I'm glad you're here."

He passed the suitcase to her, his fingers brushing over the tops of hers as she took the handle. The lightness of the touch sent a little trail of goose bumps up her arm.

She glanced at his face, trying to see if the contact had been on purpose, but he was already heading back to the front of the car.

"I'll be in touch tomorrow," he said without looking back. "Back to the grind, you know."

"Yep. See you tomorrow."

Darger rolled through the front doors of the hotel with her suitcase trailing behind her. What the hell had Luck meant when he said that? He's glad she's here? Like… in a professional sense? Or was there more to it? And if there was, was it a platonic more or a romantic more?

"Can I see your ID, please?"

Darger glanced up at the clerk behind the front desk. "What?"

"Your ID? I just have to check it against your credit card."

"Oh," Darger said, digging her driver's license out of her wallet. "Right."

The thing with Luck had apparently rattled her enough to render this simple task difficult.

And what about the hand-graze? She glanced down at the place where Luck's fingers had brushed against hers. Had that been an accident?

The hotel clerk handed her a room key along with her license and credit card.

"Enjoy your stay," she said with a picture-perfect Los Angeles smile.

Darger smiled back.

"I will."

As she rode the elevator up to her room, she wondered

what she even thought of Luck's potential advances. She hadn't made a habit of making the same mistake twice. But he seemed different, didn't he? Maybe different in a good way.

Enough of that, she thought, forcing her mind to switch over to thinking about the case.

Arson. Loshak was right. This would be a tough one — tough to crack and tough to deal with.

She thought again about what Officer Klootey had asked — whether or not this guy was a serial killer.

She wondered again if the first victim, the retired middle school principal, had been an accident. They had one prior fire that matched the M.O., but there had been no victims. If he'd set other fires before that — which the profile strongly suggested — they'd very likely been victimless as well. Possibly in isolated or rural locations, like the abandoned property.

Some experts had speculated that John Orr may have set tens of thousands of fires in the wooded areas around Los Angeles throughout his life. After his arrest, the number of wildfires county-wide had dropped by 90%. Setting fires was an utter obsession for this kind of person, something he thought about all the time, every waking hour.

If the retiree was their unsub's first victim, though, was that by design or by mistake? And had he liked how he'd felt when he realized someone died in his fire?

Her gut said yes. Her gut said he'd gotten a taste for murder with the fire that killed the retiree, and then targeted somewhere isolated — somewhere well outside the city — but packed with people to really up the brutality.

Whatever the reason, it was a clear escalation, and it meant things were only going to get worse from here.

CHAPTER 6

The next morning, Darger woke up. Showered. Her phone buzzed as she finished getting dressed. It was Avis. The Toyota Camry she'd requested drop-off service for was waiting downstairs.

When she got down to the little circular driveway in front of the hotel, however, there was no Toyota Camry. Instead, there stood a man in an Avis polo shirt and a Dodge Caravan.

"Miss Darger?"

"Yeah."

"You ordered the rental car for drop off?"

"Yes."

"Great!"

"Where is it?"

"Pardon?"

"The car."

Bewildered look.

"Well, this is it. Right here."

He gestured at the van.

"That's not a car. That's a van."

He chuckled.

"Yes. My apologies, but we were out of — what was it you'd originally booked?"

"A Camry."

"Yes, we were out of Camrys. Actually, we were out of all our base-price model cars. Very busy week."

Darger just stared at the van. Normally, she wouldn't care,

but she was going to catch hell from Luck about driving a minivan. She had a feeling that little group of uniformed officers pranking each other would laugh like hyenas if and when they saw it, too.

"We have luxury SUVs available for a small upcharge, if you'd prefer…"

"No, it's fine," she said.

She was tempted to ask why she'd been able to book a Camry online at all if they were out of Camrys, but it wasn't this guy's fault the company he worked for had a shitty website. No need to give him grief for something he had no control over.

"You'll be charged the same price as the Camry, just so you know. No upcharge for the van."

"There's an upcharge for vans?" Darger said, not able to conceal her disbelief.

He chuckled again.

"The extra seating."

"Right. Well, that'll come in handy if I give an entire family a ride at some point during my business trip."

"Exactly!"

Darger signed the clipboard the man passed her, accepted the keys, and climbed in. She took a moment to adjust the seat and mirrors before getting a move on. A few blocks away, she grabbed a breakfast sandwich from McDonald's and got on the highway heading east.

This drive lacked the scenic qualities of the areas she'd passed with Luck. It was an endless urban sprawl as far as the eye could see: billboards and strip malls and electric substations. The main patches of uninhabited land seemed to belong to golf courses, cemeteries, and landfills.

The weather was nice, at least. Sunny and clear, with just a light haze of clouds hanging above the horizon.

She turned the radio on and flipped around until she found an oldies station. She caught the tail end of "Twist and Shout" and then "I Got A Woman" by Ray Charles. Darger tapped out the drum beat against the steering wheel with her fingers.

Her mind didn't linger on the music for long. It snapped back to the case, to the pool of information she'd absorbed about arsonists through the years.

Many serial killers cut their teeth with arson. It was part of the Macdonald triad, which was a set of three childhood behaviors thought to predict sociopathic impulses later in life — the other two being bedwetting and torturing animals.

David Berkowitz, who would go on to serial killing infamy as the Son of Sam, started fantasizing about killing and setting fires as a seven-year-old. What started as an obsession with fire and explosions turned to something darker when he imagined lighting his babysitter on fire. As an adult, he shot couples sitting in cars in New York, killing six and wounding seven.

Arthur Shawcross had exhibited a long history of setting fires before he went on to kill 14 victims in upstate New York. His army psychiatrist noted that Shawcross derived "sexual enjoyment" from starting fires years before the murders.

Dennis Rader AKA BTK, wrote about what he wanted to be his grand finale — his "opus." Using propane canisters, he'd set a house on fire with a victim — a young girl — tied up inside, hanging upside down. He'd gone so far as selecting a victim and had done extensive sketches that mapped her neighborhood and a partial rendering of her house. Thankfully, he was arrested before he could carry the crime out.

The list went on and on. It wasn't so hard to see the connection between arson and serial murder, Darger thought. They often followed a similar pattern. A build-up of stress almost always triggered the violent acts. These were inadequate personality types. Socially inept at best. Antisocial at worst. Many came from traumatic and abusive families. They felt humiliated and powerless. So the stress built and they had no coping mechanisms. No network of family or friends to turn to for support. They needed an outlet.

Fantasies became the way they escaped.

Any fantasies of normal achievement or accomplishment eventually warped, pushed farther and farther into the extreme, corrupted until only the darkest dreams remained. In their minds, violence became the only power they could wield, the only way they could reassure themselves of their worth, of their agency in the world.

And eventually they tried to make the fantasies real, imagined escape from their problems only in choosing a victim. Finally, they acted, poured all of their humiliation, rage, and pain into the violence, into the fire, into the taking of lives.

Any logic in it was horrifically perverted, of course, but Darger could follow it nevertheless.

In the case of children or young adults, she could see how starting fires would be the baby step for some sociopaths. There was the forbidden danger — what child isn't instructed to not play with matches? And then the fact that fire was so destructive as to be awe-inspiring. Who hadn't sat around a fireplace or campfire and gazed into the flames? There was great power at the end of a lighter, a primal power that could not be tamed.

Darger often told herself when she worked these cases that the killer was only a man, and usually it was true. But in this case, they sought a man wielding fire, an elemental power that cared not whether it consumed the wood and metal of a building or the flesh and blood of a person.

They could stand against a man, she was certain of that. But could they stand against fire?

CHAPTER 7

As she traveled further east, the scenery gradually shifted. The buildings spread out, and she spotted mountains in the distance on either side of the road. She crossed the Santa Ana River, which didn't look much like a river where Darger came from. More hills jutted from the earth straight ahead. She was getting close to her destination.

The highway snaked through a small canyon with green, rocky mountain tops that looked more like Ireland than California to Darger. Except for the palm trees. They were kind of a dead giveaway.

Things were decidedly less metropolitan in Yucaipa. The foothills formed natural barriers to the suburban encroachment, leaving wide open spaces of low, scrubby vegetation. She could see now that snow dusted the peaks of the tallest mountains in the background.

The GPS on her phone told her to take the next exit off the highway, and then she followed the instructions Beck had given from there.

Take a right at the used car lot with the giant inflatable alien. Two blocks down you'll hit Marigold Street. Left on Marigold, fourth house on the left. If you reach the Yucaipa Motel, you've gone too far.

Darger parked on the street beside a knobby-looking mulberry tree and climbed out onto the sidewalk. The fenced-in yard was littered with toys. A molded plastic jungle gym with a small slide. A child-sized picnic table painted bright orange.

A purple bicycle with training wheels and silver streamers in the handles. And one of the little cars powered by pushing your feet over the ground, which Darger always thought of as the kiddie version of a Flintstones car.

The gate out front creaked when Darger let herself through then slammed shut with a clang. She climbed the single step up to the front door and knocked.

Clumps of red and white lilies were blooming on either side of the doorstep, and Darger caught a faint but pleasant whiff. She leaned over to smell them properly while she waited but got too close and ended up with a streak of yellow pollen smeared on her cheek. She wiped it away. No one had come to the door yet, so she knocked again.

Another thirty seconds passed, and she started to wonder if she was in the wrong place. Her eyes darted over to the neighboring houses. Down the street, she spotted the vintage-looking neon sign for the Yucaipa Motel. So she hadn't gone too far.

She double-checked the text from Beck, comparing the address given to the brass numbers next to the door. 324 Marigold. Definitely the right address.

Darger's thumbs tapped out a message, letting Beck know she was outside, but before she could hit Send, the door swung open.

A tall man with dark hair stood before her, clutching a small boy of maybe three or four years old. The boy was squirming and appeared to be covered with a layer of something wet and sticky.

"Violet?"

"That's me."

"Georgina'll be out in a moment. I'm Mike."

Darger stepped inside and put out her hand. Mike stopped her.

"You'd regret that. Wallace here just upended a bottle of maple syrup over his head. I'm afraid I've been contaminated."

Not relishing the thought of a syrupy handshake, Darger retracted her hand.

Beck appeared in the hallway beyond, shaking her head.

"Sorry about that. I have absolutely no leeway when it comes to my bladder these days. When nature calls, it's kind of a matter of life and death," she said. Without missing a beat, she eyeballed her husband and son and added, "What's he gotten into?"

"Syrup again," Mike answered and whisked the boy away, presumably to be hosed down in the bathtub.

Beck rolled her eyes in a way that suggested to Darger that disasters of the maple syrup variety were not unprecedented in her household. She veered toward the kitchen and motioned that Darger should follow.

An electric kettle gurgled and belched steam. Beck lifted it and dumped the piping hot contents into a waiting travel mug.

"You want anything? Coffee? Tea?" Beck offered as she unwrapped a peppermint tea bag.

"No, but thanks."

"I'm stuck with herbal tea until I pop this little fella out." Beck plunked the tea bag into the mug and drummed her fingers against her full belly. "Anyway, I talked to Howard Thorne — the owner — last night, and he's gonna meet us up there at the church."

A minty aroma filled the air, reminding Darger of having a

sore throat as a kid and drinking peppermint tea with honey.

As Beck finished securing the lid of her travel mug, a little girl of about six hurdled into the room. She was clutching a robotic dog toy.

"Mr. Bow-wow needs new batteries."

"Jeez Louise. Again? I just put new ones in last week."

The girl shrugged.

Beck waddled further into the kitchen and slid open a drawer. The pack of batteries she pulled out only had one left. She plucked it from the bubble of plastic, then dug around in the drawer. She closed the drawer, opened the one above it, and rifled some more.

"Well, shoot, honey. We're out of batteries."

"So I can't play with him now?"

"You'll have to wait. Sorry, nugget. I can stop and get some later today, though."

The girl's cheeks sucked inward.

"Shit."

"Morgan!"

Morgan's eyes bulged like a bullfrog's, and she gasped.

"Oops. I meant to say 'fuck.'"

Beck's mouth dropped open, and Morgan clapped a hand over her lips.

"Morgan Marie!"

"I mean fudge! I meant to say fudge!"

Darger had to bite down on her cheek. Something about little kids swearing always made her laugh. She could see that Beck was stuck between scolding her daughter's foul language and trying not to laugh herself.

"Where in the world did you get language like that?"

"Uncle Clay says it all the time," Morgan said.

Beck snorted.

"Yeah. Well, that's a good point."

Beck's husband passed by the kitchen area carrying a folded bath towel and a bottle of baby shampoo.

"Mike, did you hear what your daughter just said?"

He backed up and poked his head into the room.

"Well, it must be bad if she's my daughter, all of a sudden."

"She said the S-word and then followed that up with an F-bomb."

Mike's eyebrows crept up his forehead.

"Double whammy."

"Yeah. What do we do with her?"

"If she wants to talk like a sailor, I say we make her walk the plank."

Morgan put her hands on her hips.

"That's pirates. Not sailors. And we don't have a plank."

"Oh," Mike said before continuing on to the bathroom. "I guess you're off the hook, then."

Beck crossed her arms over her chest.

"Lucky duck. My parents would have washed my mouth out with soap for that kind of language."

The girl's brow furrowed.

"Soap? In your mouth? But why?"

"I guess they figured soap was the only way to clean out all the dirty words."

Morgan giggled.

"That makes no sense."

"I suppose it doesn't. But no more talk like that. OK, kiddo?"

"OK."

Morgan galloped out of the kitchen, leaving Beck to sigh with resignation.

"Just let me grab my stuff, and I'll be ready to roll," she said and marched over to a row of coat hooks near the door. She pulled down a black tote bag and thrust a hand inside.

"Hmm…" she muttered, frowning. "Keys, keys, keys…"

Beck's head swiveled one way and then the other, eyes searching various surfaces for the missing keys. She tried the tote bag again, then patted the pockets of her pants.

"In my pocket," she chuckled. "Of course."

The keys jangled as she pulled them free.

Beck opened the front door and shouted back into the house, "We're going now."

Three different voices called out in response all at once.

"See you later, hon."

"Bye, mommy!"

"Love you mom, and don't forget the batteries for Mr. Bow-wow!"

"Batteries. Yes. Gotcha."

Darger followed her outside and across the yard to the driveway.

"I'd say things aren't usually this chaotic around here, but that would be a lie," Beck said as she unlocked a gray Nissan Altima. "Hope you don't mind the unofficial vehicle. It's technically my day off."

Darger had noticed Beck wasn't in uniform when they were still inside but hadn't considered the implications.

"You should have said something. We didn't have to do this today."

"Oh shush! I don't mind one bit."

At the end of the driveway, Beck paused, glanced both ways, and backed onto the street, heading east. The San Bernardino mountains loomed on the horizon.

"What can you tell me about Howard Thorne?" Darger asked.

"Now, I grew up quite a bit further north of here. Up near Santa Barbara. But Mike was born and raised in Yucaipa. So he knows the Thorne family going all the way back. Howie Thorne's got a few years on him, but he'd heard stories growing up. Howie was apparently a bit of a wild child in his youth. The kind that puts M-80s in mailboxes and TPs his high school principal's front yard," Beck said. "Not what I'd call a full-on delinquent, but certainly no goody-goody. I guess he calmed down sometime in his twenties. Found some religion or other. Buddhism, I think. Anyway, the church itself was one of the first churches in the area, but the Presbyterians ended up building a new deal closer to the city and sold the old structure. The Thorne family's owned the place since... shoot... at least 50 years, I'd guess. Howie's the one that decided to fix the church up, use it as a venue — primarily weddings, you know. They've got a whole homestead out there. They host a garden festival in the spring, and there's a cider pressing and a pumpkin carving contest in the fall. It's a real town institution. Cider and donuts at Thorne's."

Darger nodded, taking it all in.

"You don't think... I mean the blowing up mailboxes thing, that wouldn't be considered the kind of thing you'd expect from your profile, would it?"

"It depends. If it stopped at fireworks, I'd say probably not.

If there was more to it… if he was starting nuisance fires, as well? Then I'd wonder."

"Well, I never heard any mention of fire-starting."

"Did you talk to him after the fire?"

"Sure did," Beck said.

"How did he seem to you?"

"Devastated. Rendered absolutely speechless. Honestly, I'm not sure how much help he'll be even now. He doesn't seem to be handling it so well."

Beck shook her head before she went on.

"Of course, fire out here means something different than it does in the rest of the country. The wildfires are such a threat, I guess, it takes on almost a religious meaning. Everyone is conscious of it all the time. Constant vigilance. We get calls any time a cigarette is pitched out a window on any of the rural highways. Drivers here will actually pull over and try to locate it and extinguish the butt themselves. If the winds are blowing right, one cigarette could take out thousands of acres of forest, homes, businesses. And of course, there's the loss of life. The threat is just so big here. Everyone feels a responsibility to try to stop the fires before they start, do whatever they can to protect each other."

Darger remembered hearing that somewhere before — that the people living out here would pull over at the sight of a flicked cigarette. It was hard to wrap her head around, though hearing Beck lay it out helped the concept get home.

"Shoot, I'm sorry," Beck said. "I didn't mean to carry on like that. I'm sure you know… you know… all of this."

"Don't apologize. You know plenty more than me about the way of things around here."

"I'm— I mean, I understand. I guess I felt out of my element at the task force meeting. I'm just there because one of the fires happened in my little neck of the woods. All of you have so much more experience than me when it comes to anything like this. Look around. Kids putting M-80's in mailboxes is about the most excitement we get out here. A DUI or two every weekend. Possession of narcotics now and again. Petty theft. But violent crime? It's nothing like what the LAPD deals with, what you deal with."

Darger nodded.

"One of my colleagues here in L.A. used to be a cop in rural Ohio. He said pretty much the same thing."

"My hats off to 'em, because I couldn't do it, myself. Wouldn't last a day. Even with this case, I feel out of my depth. This is big city stuff, and I can't stop worrying that I'm going to mess things up somehow."

"How would you mess things up?"

"Hell, you saw me dump that pile of papers outside the elevator yesterday. I'm a klutz on a good day, but the pregnancy just makes things worse."

"Well, if we get to a place in the investigation where you have to balance an egg on the end of a spoon while walking along a balance beam, we could be screwed."

Beck shook her head and smiled at Darger's sarcasm.

"Funny."

"Forget this case," Darger said, turning in her seat to face Beck more squarely. "On a normal day, when you're running things out here, would you say you're a good cop?"

"Yeah."

"Then that's all that matters. The stakes are high in a case like this, sure. But at the end of the day, what ends up solving the big cases isn't much different than what ends up solving the small cases. You do your job. You follow the evidence. So long as you work hard, there's nothing to mess up."

CHAPTER 8

The road wove through the canyons and sometimes up into the hills. Darger watched the blended scenery pass along the roadside — a mix of small subdivisions, open country, and farmland. Most of the fields were planted with neat rows of gnarled old trees.

"This is Oak Glen. Old apple orchard country, if you couldn't tell," Beck explained.

Darger's stomach dropped as they rounded a sharp bend. To the right, the canyon wall rose vertically at almost ninety degrees. And to the left, a sheer drop onto a canopy of pines. She shut her eyes until the landscape on either side leveled out again.

When she opened them, she spotted a wooden sign ahead with hand-painted letters that read, "Thorne's Farm and Apple Orchard." The church lay along the perimeter of the orchard's grounds, Darger knew. It would certainly make a scenic location for a wedding.

Beck slowed the car and took a right onto a dirt lane. It was narrow, with trees and undergrowth crowding both sides. They bumped over potholes and ruts, and then the trees opened up on a large swath of flat land at the base of one of the foothills.

An old white farmhouse stood on the west end of the property, surrounded by a few outbuildings, and then Darger saw it.

The blackened husk of the church stood taller than the other buildings. Flames had chewed through one side of the building, a ragged hole eaten through roof and walls to lay the innards of the structure bare. On the opposite side, the white paint remained intact. Something eerie about that juxtaposition, Darger thought.

Beck parked in a gravel lot that bordered one end of an orchard. The hunched apple trees reminded Darger of stooped crones.

She climbed out of the car and had a brief bout of dizziness. She turned to face Beck over the top of the car, squinting against the sunlight.

"What's the altitude up here?"

"Close to five-thousand feet. You feelin' it?"

Darger nodded.

"Just a little. Kinda makes me feel like a wuss, though. I'm from Colorado, originally, and people back home would give me hell for getting woozy at a measly five-thousand feet."

Beck chuckled.

"Well, your secret's safe with me," she said and glanced around. "Doesn't look like Howie's here yet. Normally I'd say we could start poking around on our own, but considering my current condition —" she gestured at her belly "— and your need to adjust to the altitude, I say we rest our rears right here in the car while we wait, let your stomach settle and whatnot."

Darger settled back into her seat with a sigh.

"Sounds good to me."

She closed her eyes, letting the sensations of the place wash over her. Birds twittering in the trees. A cool breeze stirring the hair at her temples. The sun warming the side of her face.

It was a lovely spot. Peaceful.

After the novelty of tweeting birds and perfect weather

wore off, Darger remembered the videos on her phone.

Aside from the video taken by the fire crew, there were dozens of cell phone videos taken by the wedding guests, plus some footage from a professional videographer hired for the event. It was a rare opportunity for the investigators to stand in the shoes of an actual eye witness. To see what they saw. To hear what they heard.

Darger scrolled through the video files on her phone. They were arranged in chronological order, and she played one of the earliest clips first.

The camera zig-zagged through the crowd of people milling about. Judging from the height of the point-of-view, Darger thought it was probably a kid manning the camera.

Turning toward the church, Darger was able to match up the location of the video with the expanse of lawn out front. It was empty now, but in the video there were two long tables set up with white table cloths. Mason jars clustered near chalkboard signs labeled with the various offerings: beer, wine, peach tea, ice water. White paper lanterns hung from the branches of a live oak tree.

A white-haired woman in a paisley dress and a broad-brimmed straw hat reached out to the camera.

"Joshua! Oh come here, and let me look at you."

She leaned closer, smiling. Pink lipstick leeched into the wrinkled spaces around her lips.

"Just look at what a handsome little gentleman you've grown into."

"Uh... thanks Aunt Dorothy."

The camera took off again, zooming through the kaleidoscope of pastels and florals and chinos. Behind the people, Darger got a good look at what the church had looked like before the fire. It was the type of old church found in many rural areas, beautiful in its simplicity. Comparing it to the wreckage she saw in its place now, it almost didn't look like the same building.

The video paused to focus on a grasshopper. The voices in the background merged into a collective murmur. Darger skipped forward a few minutes and pressed play again.

"—would please proceed inside the church. The ceremony will be starting soon," someone was saying, but the speaker was blocked by the crowd of adult bodies.

They began to file inside, through the front entrance. They were chuckling, joking with one another. Greeting old friends and relatives. A little girl in a pink lace dress ran past, chasing a boy in khakis. Everyone was smiling and in good spirits. Completely ignorant of the tragedy about to unfold.

The boy and the camera proceeded inside along with the rest of the guests. Beck gesturing at the screen with her index finger.

"You see how the crowd bottlenecks right here, as they're passing from the little entryway into the main area?"

Darger nodded.

"The same thing happened once the fire broke out. Everyone ran back the way they'd come in." Beck shook her head. "A hundred-or-so people trying to shove through that one narrow passageway, all at the same time. Even if the doors had been operable, it would have been disastrous."

The low chugging sound of an engine caught Darger's ear. A moment later, an old red-and-white VW bus pulled into the lot, surrounded by a cloud of dust, but in otherwise pristine shape.

Beck's eyes went to the rearview mirror and then over to Darger.

"This is him."

CHAPTER 9

Darger tucked her phone in her pocket, eyes on the VW bus. It pulled in a few yards away from where she and Beck sat, and a man climbed out. He was older, probably in his late 40s judging by the streaks of white and gray in his goatee and mustache. He wore thick horn spikes in his ears, sported two full sleeves of tattoos, and a pair of beat-up Birkenstocks clad his feet. He had a definite old surfer, hippie vibe.

"Mr. Thorne?" Darger asked, extending her hand.

The man nodded, a somewhat vacant look in his eye. Was he high? It wouldn't have been the first time someone had hot-boxed in a Volkswagen. And she didn't particularly care one way or the other, she just hoped he was still lucid enough to answer her questions.

They shook.

"I'm Violet Darger," she said.

He nodded again.

To fill the uncomfortable silence, she added, "I assume you know Captain Beck?"

Another wordless nod, and finally, he spoke.

"Good morning, ma'am."

"Thanks for coming out, Howard," Beck said.

He seemed disturbed and began shaking his head.

"Good morning?" He swiped a hand over his face. "Jesus. What am I even saying? It's not a good morning. I haven't had a good morning since the fire."

He stared over Darger's shoulder at the ruined building,

eyes moist with tears.

Darger and Beck exchange a look.

"Well, we appreciate that you agreed to talk with us," Darger reiterated.

"The only reason I'm here is…" He sighed. "Hell, I don't know why I'm here."

An awkward few seconds passed, with no one saying much, and then Beck cleared her throat.

"Shall we?"

She gestured that they should head over to the church.

Three sets of feet crunched through the gravel, followed by the relative silence of swishing grass.

There was still tape cordoning off an area extending about twenty feet around the building, but that hadn't stopped people from piling up mementos nearby. Flowers and wreaths and teddy bears clustered around the massive trunk of the live oak tree that stood near the entrance of the church.

Darger spotted a cross with the name of one of the victims. Beside that, a bunch of shriveling carnations and stuffed animals. The wind kicked up, disturbing a piece of poster board with a poem titled "Little Angels" written on it in permanent marker.

She followed Beck beyond the tape line but turned back when she realized Thorne was hanging back.

"Are you coming?"

"I don't… I'm not… they said no one's supposed to go inside the taped perimeter."

Darger's eyes slid over to Beck, who raised an eyebrow. She took a step toward Mr. Thorne.

"And I thank you for respecting that boundary, Howard,

but this crime scene is under my jurisdiction. You can come on inside if I give the OK. So come on in, alright?"

He stepped forward, though Darger could tell by the look on his face that he was still hesitant. His hand shook as he pulled the tape aside to duck under it.

They moved closer to the building where more yellow tape was stretched across the main entrance. Signs cautioning against entering had been posted by the fire marshal.

"We'll have to keep to the outside and look in through the openings where we can," Beck said. "I talked to the fire marshal about going inside, but he's worried about the structural integrity of the remaining roof area."

Darger could smell the char now that they were close up to the place, like the remnants of a bonfire. Broken glass littered the ground beneath gaping windows — they were too high to serve as escape routes, but the blast from the fire hoses had toppled them all the same.

They stepped around the glass and peered inside. It was even more obvious why they couldn't go into the building from this vantage point. Aside from the roof above caving in, part of the floor was gone, and the floor that was intact was littered with debris.

Darger slid her phone out and played the wedding video, comparing the interior then and now.

It had been a beautiful space. High windows let in streams of late afternoon sun, dust motes glistening like fairy dust. Blue and red stained glass added streaks of color to the bars of sunlight.

Darger sped the video up, watching in double-time as the guests paraded through the space and took their places in the rows of pews. Beyond that, an arch covered in roses and maidenhair fern served as the backdrop for the ceremony.

Glancing back into the ruined church, Darger saw the remnants of the celebration. Scorched pews. Shriveled flowers. A shattered chandelier. Chiffon hanging in charred and tattered rags.

Darger glanced over at Thorne, who held his hand over his mouth. At first she thought he was trying to block the smell, but then she noticed the rapid blinking of the eyes and the way his Adam's apple bobbed up and down every few seconds when he swallowed. He was trying not to cry.

The wind kicked up, wafting a bunch of ash into the air. A mini cyclone of spent cinders. A singed strand of fabric swayed to and fro.

Darger scooted closer to the gaping doorway. Soot smeared the edge above the opening where the flames had licked at the lintel. She poked her head inside at the small entryway where twenty-six people had lost their lives.

"These were the doors that were locked on the day of the fire?" Darger asked.

"Not locked," Thorne said, his voice pitching high. "We had a break-in the weekend before the wedding. Some local kids forced the door and had a little pow-wow in the sanctuary. Smashed a few beer bottles and broke a window. Standard juvie stuff. We thought we got off easy, at the time. They could have done a lot more damage."

Mr. Thorne paused, staring blankly into the ruined church.

"Anyway, they busted the latching mechanism on the door when they broke in. I needed to repair the handle, but I was waiting on a replacement spindle…"

His voice trailed off. Darger finished for him.

"But until then, the door was essentially locked shut with no way of unlocking it."

The man's shoulders sank.

"Not without tools. No. We'd told them to leave it open, but…"

Darger skipped ahead in the video again. The ceremony was just hitting the exchange of vows when a murmur went through the crowd.

"Do you smell smoke?" one of the voices said.

Heads whipped around, searching for the source of the smell. One man seated close to the altar suddenly pushed up from his seat and pointed at the flickering flame now visible along one wall.

"It's on fire!" he shouted.

Instantly panic broke out. The crowd instinctively stampeded toward the front entrance, the same way they'd come in. But the space was too narrow, the door sealed shut. The medical examiner's report said that several of the victims had injuries consistent with being trampled. After being knocked to the ground by the surging mass of people, they would have been helpless against the deadly smoke. Even once the rear exit had been discovered and some of the survivors pried the front door open from the outside, for many of those still inside, it was too late.

Almost immediately, the entire front half of the church was filled with thick smoke. The black curtain of ash acted like a deadly curtain that concealed any means of escape.

The visual footage on the camera became useless as the person holding it scrambled to find a way out. It was all a blur.

Shaky shots that gave Darger motion sickness. But the audio was clear. Screams of terror. Coughing, choking gasps. The roar and sizzle of the flames.

Darger closed the video and opened a different file, this one taken from the safety of outside the church. The person filming walked around the front corner of the building, focusing on the flames shooting from the windows. It was an absolute inferno. The fire crackled and whooshed like wind.

From this angle, it looked like the flames engulfed the structure so completely that it was no longer possible to believe that there was wood underneath. In this moment, the building was made of fire itself. Inside, there was a periodic tinkling like breaking glass.

The camera swung around to show the people huddled in the lawn, coughing and chugging water. A woman with singed hair clutched a crying child, rocking him back and forth. Another group clustered around a man with a severe burn on his arm, arguing about whether or not ice would help the wound.

"Anthony!" a woman's voice called out.

She came into view then, a smear of ash marking her face. She ran up to a man wiping his neck with a handkerchief and clawed at his arm.

"Do you have Anthony? Tell me you have my baby."

The man shook his head, and the woman turned back to face the church.

"Anthony's still in there! He's still inside!"

She stumbled toward the door, but the man with the handkerchief snagged her arm and held her tight. She struggled against him, wailing the name over and over again and staring at the blaze.

Behind them, a huge beam of wood dropped from the ceiling just beyond the door, sending up a cloud of sparks.

"Oh Jesus," someone murmured, and it was a moment before Darger realized it wasn't on the video.

She swiveled to the right and found Mr. Thorne at her left shoulder, his eyes wide and glued to the screen of her phone.

A commotion erupted in the video now as the people outside the burning church realized that not everyone made it out.

"We have to do something!"

Mr. Thorne listed, his knees buckling. Beck and Darger reached out at the same moment to catch him, just barely managing to keep him from going down.

"Do what?" another voice responded. "The whole thing's engulfed! We have to wait for the fire department."

"Turn it off," Thorne begged. "Please. I can't… I can't listen to that anymore."

Darger silenced her phone and returned it to her pocket.

They led Mr. Thorne over to the live oak tree and lowered him to the ground.

"This shouldn't have happened," he said, eyes watering. "I still don't understand how this could happen. This was such a happy place. I grew up here. My kids grew up here. I've had nothing but fond memories. Nothing but good things to associate with it. And now this."

A tear loosened its grip on his eyelashes and slid down his cheek.

"The church had been abandoned for most of my childhood. Used for storage, equipment for the orchards. My playhouse on rainy days. I was the one who fixed it up, turned it into a venue. I tried to make something for the community here. A shared space. A place for people to come together and celebrate some of the biggest moments of their lives, and then… something like this happens and it all comes crashing down."

He studied the church for some time before turning his face away and closing his eyes.

"I keep seeing the families, the mothers and fathers of the children who died, on the TV saying all this stuff… that those responsible for the deaths need to be held accountable. And if I'd only repaired that door sooner, those kids might still be alive. Does that make it partially my fault? Am I responsible? That's what the reporters on my front lawn want to know. That's the question they ask me when I go out to get the mail in the morning." Thorne wiped his cheek with the back of his knuckles. "How do I answer that?"

Darger knew he was feeling guilty, wondering if he was to blame for this tragedy unfolding on his property.

"I don't think anyone blames you. Not really," Darger said. "It's just that most people don't know what to do with the grief. It overwhelms them and comes out as anger, and the anger makes them feel like something should be done. That someone should be punished. And someone does deserve to be punished here, but it isn't you. Someone set this fire on purpose. That's the responsible party."

Thorne bowed his head, his body shaking with sobs. Darger placed a hand on his shoulder.

"I will find him."

CHAPTER 10

"Well, you called that one," Darger said.

Beck raised an eyebrow. "Hm?"

"The first thing you said when we got here was that you didn't think he was handling this all very well."

She glanced back at where they'd left Mr. Thorne to gather himself while they continued their circuit of the place.

Beck followed her gaze and nodded.

"I feel for the guy," she said. "It seems like such a small thing. An inoperable door. But you add fire into the mix and suddenly something as small as being able to open a door could be the difference between life and death for some of those folks. In any case, legally speaking, even with the inoperable door, the venue was up to code as far as the proper number of exits and so forth."

They passed the doors in question again, and Darger couldn't help but stare into the gaping opening. What might have happened had those doors been unlocked that day? How many of the victims might have survived?

Darger thrust her hands in her pockets and turned to Beck.

"Any chance our arsonist could have been the one that broke in? He might have been checking the place out as a possible site for a fire and just made it look like kids. Maybe even sabotaged the door handle on purpose."

Beck shook her head.

"We got the kids on camera, and they all had alibis for the time of the fire, so we've crossed them off the list of suspects for the arson."

Darger hadn't recalled seeing any security footage from the church in the evidence she'd received.

"There's security cam footage from the day of the fire?" she said, not able to keep the eagerness from her voice.

"No. The kids filmed themselves breaking in, believe it or not."

"You're kidding."

"I wish I was," Beck said. "And I'll be the first to admit that I wasn't a perfect angel as a youngster. We might have gotten up to some mischief here and there, sure, but we weren't dumb enough to incriminate ourselves by documenting it."

Darger's chuckle was interrupted by a sharp intake of breath.

They'd reached the back end of the church, the top of which was a skeleton of blackened wood and splintered beams. The utter destruction was startling.

Darger played a new video, this one from after the fire department arrived. Firemen in reflective suits shouted to one another through the thick haze of smoke and steam. They re-arranged hoses, changing positions, trying to gain control over the fire. On one side of the lawn, paramedics administered oxygen and first aid to some of the survivors.

Behind them, the flames flickered and danced. A column of black smoke rose like a mushroom cloud into the sky.

Over the low roar of the fire, Darger suddenly heard something whistle and pop, and then what sounded like several small explosions.

"What is that?" Darger asked.

"Fireworks. They were going to do a little show once it got

dark. Can't do much out here, on account of the forest fire risk. The weak stuff — what the state of California calls the 'safe and sane' fireworks — are all you can purchase, and even then they're only legal to buy from June 28 to July 6. I guess all the restrictions make what little we can do extra special."

The video footage jumped to a new angle, this one giving a clear shot through the entrance of the church. The entire inside glowed like a furnace, everything colored in shades of yellow and orange. The wind kicked up and the flames danced higher, roared louder. Smoke roiled and fluttered.

Darger skipped through the rest of the footage from the afternoon and into the evening. Red and blue lights twirled against the sides of the church in the fading light of day. The fire crews still bustled about, talking into radios and issuing orders, but there was less urgency in their movements. By now, they knew the church was a lost cause.

As the video zoomed out to give a fuller picture of the church, something shifted near the peak of the steeple. An almost imperceptible shudder. There was a muffled shout and one of the firemen ran forward, waving his hands at the two men running the hoses at the front of the church. They stepped back just as the roof caved in. The front facade crumbled and fell, landing where the men had been standing only a few seconds before.

More pieces of the roof collapsed in on itself, falling to pieces. Cinders and sparks flew into the air, looking like a thousand fireflies released from the blaze.

The screen went black as the video ended. She opened the last file, footage from the day after the fire.

In the gray light of dawn, men from the local fire

department hauled and shifted debris away from the main door of the church. They cleared a path inside, then set to work reinforcing key structural points so that the investigative work could continue without fear of the remainder of the roof collapsing. A pair of hydraulic struts supported the main doorway while wood rakers were used to shore up other parts of the structure.

Outside the church, debris was raked into little piles — scorched bits of wood siding and shriveled wedding flowers instead of the traditional dead leaves of autumn.

Darger skipped past most of the raking and hammering and drilling, and then the fire investigation team and coroner were given the all clear.

They found the first bodies just inside the main interior doorway — what looked like a couple huddled together, though it was hard to be certain in this blackened state. A camera flashed to document it, and then bright yellow body bags were brought in and wrapped around the figures, one then the other. The lengthy operation of logging and processing the dead had just begun.

Darger fast-forwarded a little more. Body after body found, photographed, bagged, and carted off — the camera flash flickering in fast motion as she watched the sped-up video.

Something caught her eye, a change, a lull in the rhythm of the flashes. She rewound a little bit. Watched.

Men helped clear away a cracked pew to reveal a body below — a body smaller than all of the others, tiny legs bright white and stark against the smears of dark soot.

This was the first of the children they'd find.

The assistant coroner snapping the photos raised his

camera just like he had with all the previous bodies, but his arms shook. After a second, he lowered the camera and cupped a hand at his brow, stepping off to the side to gather himself.

CHAPTER 11

Darger attempted to question Thorne again once he'd pulled himself together — simple questions like whether or not he'd noticed anyone or anything suspicious in the days or weeks leading up to the fire.

"If you're asking me whether I had any inkling that this would happen, then the answer is no. Hell, if you'd told me ahead of time that this was going to happen, I wouldn't have believed you. It's too awful to comprehend. Even now, standing here in front of the wreckage, I can't quite wrap my head around it."

Howard Thorne seemed to her a man broken, and she didn't think she'd get anything further out of him. She thanked him for his time, and then she and Beck watched his slouched form drift back toward his Volkswagen. He moved like a much older man, and Darger wondered how many years the stress of this had taken off his life already.

Glancing at her watch, Darger winced when she saw how quickly the morning hours had already melted away.

"I've got to head back soon," Darger said. "I'm supposed to meet up with Agent Luck this afternoon."

Beck nodded.

"Let's get a move on, then. I don't suppose you'd mind if I run a quick errand on the way. If I don't bring home batteries, I'll never hear the end of it."

Darger smiled, remembered Beck's daughter and her robotic dog toy.

"Not at all."

((

They parted ways in Beck's driveway, Darger heading toward the street and Beck to the house.

Just as Darger was climbing into her rented minivan, Beck paused on the stoop and called out to her.

"Agent Darger?"

"Yeah?"

"I really appreciate you taking the trouble to drive all the way out here."

Shaking her head, Darger said, "It wasn't any trouble."

"No, it's just... sometimes when you're running a small outpost like this, you tend to get overshadowed by the big city happenings. Some folks might think our problems aren't as big as what goes on in L.A. But this fire... there were a lot of people in this town affected by it. Most of us knew at least one of the victims, if not more. And it means a lot for you to come out here. To get to know the place a little. It's important, I think."

Darger nodded.

"It is. Thank you for showing me around," she said, giving Beck a final wave. "I'll be in touch."

The scene shifted in reverse as Darger drove back into the city, the green hills reminiscent of a backdrop from The Lord of the Rings transitioning to an endless sprawl of strip malls, apartment buildings, and small mid-century homes.

Their killer was here somewhere. Hiding in a crowd of some 13 million people. The idea of finding him was daunting when she thought of it that way. But her whole job was to narrow the suspect pool.

The fire at the church, that was the key. It had been a spectacle, for one. But because of its isolated location, she was certain it hadn't been a random choice by the arsonist. He knew the place. Maybe not the church specifically, but the town. There had to be a connection there.

Her mind instantly jumped to Howard Thorne, remembering what Beck had said about the wild days of his youth. That part might fit the profile, but the rest didn't. He was too old, for one. Then there was his display of grief, which had seemed genuine enough to her.

Lastly and most damning was the fact that he ran Thorne Farms, which by all accounts was an institution in the community. No, their killer was someone who felt like an outsider, she was sure of that. Even if he played the part of a normal person sometimes, it wasn't who he really was.

Still, she felt it was best to exhaust every avenue, so Beck would be looking into Thorne's background, just in case.

The steady hum of the car's tires on the road lulled Darger into sort of a daze, and her thoughts wandered to the captain and her family.

Beck had to be around the same age as Darger, and yet she was able to balance a husband, kids, and her career. Darger couldn't even seem to juggle a single relationship with her job. Seeing Beck manage a full life like that made Darger feel like she was some kind of failure as an adult. Like she wasn't a real grown-up but some kind of overgrown adolescent. Still figuring things out. Doomed to spend the rest of her life figuring it out, maybe.

The Los Angeles skyline came into view as she crested a small rise, the details of the skyscrapers blurred through layers of smog.

Darger sighed, willing the somber and self-pitying thoughts from her consciousness.

She wasn't a psycho who got his kicks lighting up a church full of people, at least. That was something.

CHAPTER 12

The automatic doors whisked aside with a whoosh. A janitor mopped the floor near the entryway, filling the space with the scent of lemon cleaner.

Darger crossed the lobby and took an elevator to the fourth floor. The steel doors opened on a long corridor with windows on one side and a series of rooms on the other. She wasn't sure which one was right, but she heard voices coming from an open door further down the hall.

Boots thudding against the tile floor, she made her way down the passageway. The voices grew louder, enough that she could make out what they were saying now.

"The guy is just completely fucked up, right? Dressed in an undershirt and boxer shorts, no pants. Blows a 0.2 on the Breathalyzer. He can barely stand, let alone drive, so I don't know how he hadn't already wrapped the 4-wheeler around a telephone pole," the voice said. "He's a big guy, too. Probably 250, wouldn't you say, Teej?"

"At least," a second voice responded.

"Maneuvering this beefcake into the back of the patrol car is no easy feat," the first voice said. "He's flip-flopping around like a marionette, not exactly fighting us, but not helping either. Swaying, you know. Letting gravity have its way with his dangling limbs. Teej is swearing. I'm breaking a sweat."

Darger reached the open door and peered inside. Officers Klootey and Bishop were leaned back in swivel chairs. Luck sat on the edge of a desk nearby. A pair of over-the-ear headphones rested around Bishop's neck.

"But we finally get him inside, and I lean across to buckle him in, and that's when the gates of his bladder open as if by divine intervention, gallons of fluid spilling forth like the great flood the prophesies spoke of," Bishop continued.

"He peed on you?" Luck asked, and Bishop nodded.

"We are talking an extraordinary amount of piss," Klootey said, spinning the wire of a pair of earbuds like a lasso.

Bishop shuddered.

"Thank Christ I keep an extra uni in my locker."

Darger rested one shoulder against the door frame.

"Are you boys swapping watersports stories again?" Darger asked.

Luck turned his stubbled face toward her and frowned, apparently not approving of her joke.

Klootey hissed out a laugh.

"Hey, wasn't Albert Fish into the old golden shower?"

Nodding, Darger said, "Oh yeah. And it was common at the time for widows to post classified ads looking for marriage prospects. Fish used to write obscene letters to them, and apparently he often went into great detail about his urophilia. He mentioned it in one of his famous confession letters, as well. And that wasn't even the grossest thing he was into."

Klootey stopped spinning his wire lasso.

"Yeah? Like what?"

Darger gestured to the styrofoam containers nearby.

"Did you guys just eat?"

"Yeah."

"Then you don't want to hear it. Trust me." She turned to Luck. "So you got some interviews lined up for us?"

Luck rose to his feet.

"I actually came up here to ask if these guys might have any ideas," he said, smoothing his tie, though she noticed he still wasn't wearing a jacket. "What do you think? Any witnesses that might warrant a second pass?"

Stroking his chin, Bishop appeared to give it some thought.

"Hey, T.J. What was the lady's name... the one that lives next door to the Galitis fire? The one that called 911 that night."

"Something with a P, wasn't it?" Klootey squinted. "Peyton?"

Bishop shook his head.

"Not Peyton, but that's close. Palin? Pay... Payne!"

"Payne, yeah. That's it."

Bishop spun in his seat to face the two agents.

"Mrs. Payne. She's the one you should talk to."

"Yeah?" Luck said.

Bishop nodded.

"She seemed like the type that kept an eye on things around the neighborhood, you know?"

Luck raised his eyebrows at Darger, which she took as him asking her opinion.

"I'm game," she said with a shrug.

"You said it's the house next to the retiree fire?"

"Teej, look up the old lady's address for our man Luck."

Klootey drummed his fingers against his keyboard and leaned closer to the screen.

"8045 Aspen Avenue."

Luck jotted this down then glanced up at Darger.

"Ready to roll?"

"Always."

CHAPTER 13

"This is it," Luck said, turning his Lexus onto Aspen Street.

A neat row of single-story Cape Cods, Spanish bungalows, and Ranch style houses in pale yellow and sky blue and various shades of beige lined the street. The rectangle of front lawn afforded to each home was modest but well-kept. Aside from the modern cars parked on the street, the neighborhood probably looked pretty much the same as it had when it was built in the 1960s.

The car slowed, coming to a halt in front of the burned-out shell of the former Galitis home. It stood out like a rotten tooth in an otherwise picture-perfect smile.

Darger undid her seatbelt and climbed out, unable to tear her eyes from the fire-ravaged house. The roof was gone entirely. The front of the home was a ruin of blackened wood and charred siding. Many of the windows had been broken out by the flames or the fire crews and covered with plywood, but one window on the west side of the house remained, its glass opaque with soot. Where the vinyl siding on most of the house had melted away in the blaze, a scrap here was left untouched. Enough that Darger could see the house had been dove gray, with white shutters.

The fire hadn't touched only the house, either. A pair of banana trees stood sentry on either side of the front door, the topmost leaves singed by the inferno. The planting of hostas along the foundation of the house had probably once been lush and green, but now the foliage was shriveled and brown.

Darger squinted, trying to imagine what the front of the Galitis house had looked like before the fire had destroyed the facade. Her eyes roamed to the house next door. The neighboring homes had been saved, luckily. The house on the right was similar in appearance to the Galitis house, the same general size and shape, with white shutters, but robin's egg blue siding instead of gray. And where the lawn of the Galitis house was bordered by boxwoods, the front yard of the house next door was lined with chain-link fence.

Luck followed her gaze.

"Should we head in?"

She realized then that the blue house was their intended destination. The home of the woman who had called 911 the night of the fire.

"After you," she said and followed him across the sidewalk to 8045 Aspen Street.

The hinges of the metal gate let out an ear-piercing shriek as Luck pushed it aside. Several signs were attached to the gate via loops of wire. The largest was a black and white sign that said NO PARKING. Beside that was a smaller sign with a list of other prohibited activities: NO SOLICITING, NO RELIGIOUS PAMPHLETS, NO FUNDRAISING, NO SURVEYS. A third sign featured a simple silhouette of a skateboard crossed out with a large red "X."

Instead of grass, Mrs. Payne's lawn was paved in white gravel. The collective crunch of their feet hitting the stones must have been loud enough for the homeowner to hear them, because before they'd made it halfway to the front door, it swung open.

"Good afternoon," Luck started. "We're—"

"Blind or illiterate, clearly."

A small, pear-shaped woman stood with the screen door as a barrier between them.

Luck paused, eyes swinging over to Darger then back to the woman.

"Sorry?"

The woman crooked a finger back the way they'd come.

"You saw the sign?"

Luck glanced over his shoulder.

"Uh. Yes, ma'am."

She crossed her arms.

"So if your eyes work, I have to assume you can't read. Sign says this is private property. You know what that means?"

"Yes, but—"

"It means I'm not interested in whatever it is you're selling, and that goes for religion as well as encyclopedias, or whatever it is you people go around hawking these days. Probably Obamacare plans or some such nonsense."

Luck's mouth hung open, at a loss for words. Darger bit her lip, trying to keep herself from laughing.

The woman turned on her.

"And what are you smirking about?"

Darger cleared her throat, putting a final stop to the inappropriate chuckle that was still trying to worm its way out.

"Ma'am, I'm Agent Darger with the FBI. This is my colleague, Agent Luck. We were wondering if we could ask you a few questions."

The woman pursed her lips, trying to keep her tough facade in place, but Darger could see the sudden flicker of curiosity in her eyes.

"FBI? Well why didn't you say so?"

When they didn't immediately approach the door, the woman waved an exasperated hand.

"Are you just going to loiter there on my stoop, or are you coming inside?"

Luck reached the door first. Grasping the handle, he opened it wide and gestured that Darger should enter ahead of him.

They walked into a living room that looked like it belonged in a time capsule. The oranges and browns in the carpet and walls suggested the 1970's, while the strange dark green upholstery of the furniture evoked a decade or more earlier still — perhaps the 40's or 50's. Darger ran her fingers over the back of the couch and found the fabric slightly more coarse than canvas.

"All I can say is, it's about time someone downtown started to take me seriously."

She motioned for them to sit with a flail of the arm.

"Sorry?" Luck said as they sat.

The couch was beyond firm. It felt like sitting on a stone slab with a layer of tent canvas draped over it.

"I've called — I don't know how many times — and no one ever does diddly-squat about the hippie trash across the way." She waved a hand toward a large picture window with a view of the street. "You know they just let their trash cart set out there all day, and I have to look at it. Every Thursday, just setting there. Everyone else pulls their cart in after the truck comes, but not them. Oh no. And I've spoken to them a number of times about it, but come trash day, there it sets."

She sniffed. The pink from her lipstick had seeped into the

hairline folds at the corners of her lips.

"I'm certain they're growing marijuana and god knows what else over there. I can smell it on them. Reefer."

"You know that marijuana is legal in the state of California, ma'am."

"It's not legal to sell it, not without a permit. I've complained to the city, but they don't do a thing. You said you're Feds?"

She eyed them almost suspiciously.

The Adam's apple at the center of Luck's throat bobbed up and down as he swallowed.

"Ahh, that's right, ma'am."

"So that'd mean you're way above the local, uh, law enforcement. Right?"

"I don't know what you mean."

"You've got more clout. More sway. More authority than the dumb-dumbs down at city hall."

"I don't know about that," Luck said, shooting Darger a desperate look.

She shrugged at him. He was the local, not her.

"We don't really have jurisdiction in city affairs, ma'am."

She made a raspberry sound with her mouth.

"Then what good are you?"

Darger wondered how they'd gotten on the topic of trash carts and pot when they'd come to talk about the fire and realized they hadn't even asked about the fire yet. In fact, they hadn't asked any questions at all. The woman had just gone off, dominating the conversation as if she were filibustering on the Senate floor. If Darger didn't say something, they might never get back on track.

She broke in before the woman could build up another head of steam.

"Mrs. Payne, is it?" Darger said. "We're actually here to talk about the fire."

"The fire?"

"That's right."

The woman blinked a few times, looking unimpressed.

"Well, if neither the LAPD nor the federal government are going to take any interest in an illegal drug ring operating right under their noses, then I don't know what I can do about it. After all, I'm only one concerned citizen."

Darger worried the conversation was about to go off the rails again, so she redirected quickly with an easy question.

"How long have you lived here?"

It was a trick she'd learned when she was a victim advocate. The easiest way to get someone talking was to ask them a question where the answer was a number, because numbers were simple. Finite. With kids, she always opened by asking how old they were. With teenagers, it was what grade they were in. And with adults, how long they'd been at their current job. Or how long they'd been married. How many kids they had.

When the answer was a number, it was a simple fact, the opposite of something open-ended. That made a certain type of person comfortable.

"Twenty-two years," Mrs. Payne said.

Darger permitted herself a small smile. It always worked. But her satisfaction didn't last long.

"And I don't like to speak ill of the dead," the woman added, "but every one of those years has been outright misery since that woman and her spawn moved in next door. I don't know why everyone's making such a fuss about the fire, to be frank. Judy Galitis was an airhead. I told the fire investigators when they were here, the idiot probably left the stove on and burned herself up."

"There's overwhelming evidence that this fire was set intentionally, ma'am."

Mrs. Payne sighed.

"That's what they told me. And I'll repeat what I said to them: if someone intentionally set that house on fire, then you can be sure it was Judy Galitis herself. She and that daughter of hers have been running insurance scams for years."

Darger was already getting the feeling that Mrs. Payne had an axe to grind with the late Judy Galitis, but if the Galitis family was acquainted with insurance fraud, it was something worth noting.

"What kind of scams?"

"Oh, I suppose you know that poor Judy was disabled? They say that's why she didn't make it out of the house. Couldn't get to her wheelchair," Mrs. Payne said. "Well, it serves her right, doesn't it? After all the years of faking her illness, she finally got her comeuppance."

Darger couldn't help but notice the twinkle of glee in Mrs. Payne's eye. She stifled her own disgust.

"What makes you think Ms. Galitis was faking her illness?"

"Please! One day she's in the wheelchair, the next day she's up and about, puttering around her garden. Painting her mailbox. Having company over," Mrs. Payne said, leaning against the tufted back of her armchair. "Oh yes. Frequent visitors. Men, usually. A different one every evening, if you catch my meaning. They were boinking over there, sure as you're alive. And this reverse harem of hers always used my parking space."

Darger glanced out the window. She'd noticed as they walked down the sidewalk that there were no driveways in the neighborhood. Everyone parked on the street.

Luck must have been thinking the same thing, because he said, "You mean they parked on the street in front of your house?"

The wrinkled mouth tightened, flexing all the little pink lines.

"Yes, on the street in front of my house," she said, clearly annoyed at the clarification. "They certainly don't park on the sidewalk, now do they? Something would actually be done about that, I suppose."

"I don't think there are generally assigned parking spaces when it's street parking, ma'am."

She huffed.

"Well in my day, it was common courtesy not to park in front of another person's house, as they just might need to park there themselves. They have the whole rest of the street to park on."

"Of course," Luck said, and Darger sensed he was trying his best to sound genuinely sympathetic. "I imagine it's very inconvenient for you to have to park your car elsewhere and walk."

The woman rolled her eyes then, as if talking to Luck were some great chore.

"I don't have a car. You think I drive in this cesspool of a city? With all the illegals driving around with no license and no insurance? My friend Louise Snelling got into an accident with one of those types. Smashed up her Buick and left her high and dry! No, thank you. I don't need any of that."

Darger cleared her throat.

"Mrs. Payne, what we'd really be interested in hearing is whether you remember seeing anything out of the ordinary in the days leading up to the fire."

The woman crossed her arms over her chest.

"I've got the phony cripple next door who sets herself on fire. The deadbeats across the street in their tie-dye shirts slinging hashish. And then there's the delinquent kids on skateboards and hover-things, loitering on my sidewalk as soon as school's out. And you want to know if I've seen anything out of the ordinary? I'm surrounded by freaks and free-loaders. Everything I see is out of the ordinary, but I don't suppose you're going to do diddly-squat about any of it."

"Our focus right now is really on the arson investigation, ma'am," Luck said. "Besides that, the FBI really doesn't have jurisdiction here."

"Typical."

With a wordless glance, Darger and Luck concluded that they'd gotten all they would from Mrs. Payne. They thanked her for her time and showed themselves to the door.

Luck waited until the door was closed behind them to mutter, "If not for your profile and the other fires, I'd think she was the one that torched the Galitis house. Talk about sour grapes."

Darger considered this.

"She would be a great bet if we were dealing with a revenge arsonist. But unless we can tie her to the church fire, it doesn't fit."

"Yeah, I know," Luck agreed.

When Darger turned left outside the gate in Mrs. Payne's yard, Luck stopped and hooked a thumb over his shoulder.

"Where are you going? Car's over here."

"We came all the way out here," Darger said, not pausing to answer. "Figured I might as well take a peek at the alleyway where the fire started."

Luck caught up with her at the end of the block. They looped around the corner house and entered the narrow passage that ran behind the homes. It was wide enough for two garbage bins to stand side-by-side, but not much more. And indeed, it appeared that the main function of the alley was for the residents to store their garbage and recycling bins.

Spinning slowly in a circle, Darger studied the houses surrounding them.

"He picked a pretty good spot to start the fire," Darger said. "Almost none of the houses have windows that face this way."

She pointed at one of the few windows in sight. It was small and appeared to be frosted glass.

"Probably a bathroom window. Not much chance someone's going to spot you from there unless they get lucky."

"You think he's familiar with the area?"

Darger nodded.

"The church fire scene felt the same. I mean it's practically nestled in the mountains. Perfectly isolated. He didn't come across that spot randomly. He chose it."

"So he'd been there before."

"I think so. The problem is, Thorne Farms sees a lot of visitors. He could have been there for a wedding or for one of the other hundred events they have. You know their website says ten thousand people stop by the cider mill every fall?"

"And in a city like this, there could be tens of thousands of people that know this neighborhood, too. Utility workers, delivery drivers, all the nearby residents whose commute takes them through."

"I told you," Darger said, shaking her head. "Too many people."

CHAPTER 14

The door was open, but Luck rapped his knuckles against the wall as they entered the room where Klootey and Bishop were still combing through surveillance footage. The two LAPD officers were right where they'd left them, hunkered down in front of computer screens.

Klootey lifted his feet and spun around in his chair theatrically at the sound of Luck's knock. He fixed them with a big, toothy grin.

"How'd it go?"

Luck sighed.

"She had a laundry list of complaints about her neighbors, but absolutely nothing helpful in terms of the investigation."

Klootey nodded along with Luck, giggling all the while.

"We call her Miss Pain-in-the-ass."

"Clever," Luck said. "And accurate."

Darger narrowed her eyes.

"Wait. You know her? From before the fire?"

"Everyone knows Miss Pain-in-the-ass. She racks up, oh, about a dozen calls a month, at least," Bishop said, glancing over at his partner who nodded in agreement.

Luck's back straightened, and he crossed his arms.

"So you idiots sent us out there as one of your stupid pranks?"

Their raucous laughter was answer enough. The two of them sounded like a pair of hyenas.

"What the hell is wrong with you?" Luck asked. "This is a

serial arson case. You can't be screwing around like that."

"We couldn't resist." Klootey shook his head, still snickering. "It was too good, man. She's such a piece of work. I bet she gave you an assload about Judy Galitis faking her illness and all that?"

Darger and Luck nodded in unison.

"Yeah so, the deal with that is Judy Galitis had Relapsing-Remitting Multiple Sclerosis. Meaning she had good days, and she had bad days. Sometimes her symptoms would disappear altogether. Suddenly she could walk again. Do most of the stuff she did before she got sick. And then — WHAM!" He slammed his fist into the flattened palm of his other hand. "The MS would knock her on her ass, and she'd be out of commission for days, weeks, even months. Right back in the wheelchair and all."

"You verified this?" Darger asked.

"We got it from the daughter and confirmed it with the specialist she saw over at UCLA. It all checks out. Galitis wasn't faking shit."

Darger couldn't help but feel a sense of vindication that bitter old Mrs. Payne had been dead wrong about everything.

Bishop leaned back in his chair, hands behind his head.

"According to Galitis' daughter, the feud goes way back."

"Seemed pretty one-sided for a feud," Darger said.

"You wanna talk one-sided? Listen to this. Judy Galitis was big into gardening, right? Had this one particular flower that was her favorite. She grew all kinds, even bred some of her own hybrids. Anyway, I don't remember the name of it, but the daughter said it was some kind of vining plant. Liked to climb up stuff. A couple of 'em twined their way over to Mrs. Payne's side of the fence, and I guess you saw her lawn, if you can call it that."

Darger envisioned the sterile space in her mind.

"Chain-link fence and gravel."

"Yeah. Real cozy, right? So she spots some of these vines on her turf, and she hops over into Judy Galitis' yard and rips 'em out of the ground, all the way down to the roots."

"All of them?"

Bishop nodded.

"Called them 'invasive.' The daughter also told us that when she was in high school, Mrs. Payne used to call the cops on her for playing music while she was studying. We're talking like Beethoven or some classical shit, and Payne would call up and complain about the 'loud partying' going on next door. I mean, she's just too fuckin' much, man."

"Any idea what started the vendetta?" Luck asked.

The other two men shook their heads.

"Daughter said it was that way from the day they moved in. She just had it out for 'em, man. I mean, I don't even think it was personal, really. She harasses pretty much everyone on the block."

Bishop stroked his chin. "As my mama would say, 'That woman would yank out a stop sign to argue with the hole.'"

Luck blew out a breath, frowning.

"What the hell makes someone turn out that way?"

"Lack of sex would be my guess," Klootey offered, then laughed heartily at his own joke.

"Anyway, you Feebs need a taste of dealing with the civilian wildlife every now and then," Bishop said. "It's good for you. Keeps you honest."

With a disapproving scoff, Luck said, "You guys are a pair of assholes."

That got another chuckle out of Klootey, but Bishop attempted to look contrite.

"Hey man, just 'cause she's a Nagasaurus Rex doesn't mean she couldn't have had some good information," he said, then started to laugh again. "Lord knows, she's nosy enough."

Luck raised his hands in disbelief and looked to Darger for support, but all of Bishop's talking had given her an idea.

"What about the daughter?" she said.

Luck frowned.

"Of the deceased?"

"Yeah."

"What about her?"

"Well, I'll bet she spent a lot of time at her mom's place. Checking in on her. Helping out."

A glance at Bishop indicated her guess was correct. She turned back to Luck.

"Maybe she remembers something. Something she saw or something her mom told her about," Darger said. "Let's go talk to her."

CHAPTER 15

Caroline Galitis' apartment was on the second floor of a yellow stucco building in Rancho Park. Darger followed Luck up the exterior stairs, trailing her fingers along the wrought-iron railing.

They knocked on the door of number 27, and a dark-haired girl answered the door. She was 26, a lab tech and grad student at UCLA, according to Bishop. She looked younger than that to Darger, but then everyone under thirty had a tendency to look more and more like kids the older she got. In this case, it was the girl's eyes. They were big and blue with impossibly long lashes that lent an innocent appearance to her face.

Caroline invited them in and offered to make tea. Luck declined, but Darger accepted. She'd found that many people were more comfortable during interviews if they had something to do with their hands.

The studio apartment was small and appeared to be new digs for Caroline — aside from the mix of IKEA and secondhand furniture, there were stacks of moving boxes taking up most of the living area.

In the small kitchen, Caroline filled a kettle with water from the sink. Darger saw her glance at the card they'd given her when she first answered the door.

"You said you're from the FBI?" she asked, setting the kettle on the stovetop.

"That's right."

"This isn't a good thing, is it?" Caroline blinked. "I mean, if

106

the police investigation was going well, they wouldn't need to call in the FBI, would they?"

"It's not necessarily good or bad. It's just… complicated. Sometimes when an investigation grows to encompass several jurisdictions, the FBI is brought in to help facilitate things. Especially with a serial offender. I assume the police asked whether you'd ever been up to Thorne Farms?"

Caroline nodded slowly.

"I couldn't believe it, when they told me they thought it was the same person that had set fire to my mom's house." She covered her mouth. "Why would someone do something like that? My mother never hurt anybody. And all those people at that wedding. There were little kids there. Why?"

Darger could have explained that it was about power. That they were dealing with a very insecure man trying to prove his superiority to the world and to himself. But she didn't think it would mean much to a girl mourning the loss of her mother.

Instead, she said, "That's what we're here to find out. And we were hoping we could ask you a few questions about your mom."

The girl nodded, and Darger went on.

"Can you remember anything unusual in the week or so before she died? Maybe she mentioned noticing someone in the neighborhood that didn't belong?"

Caroline was rifling in one of the cabinets and stopped abruptly. Her wide eyes were even wider.

"It's so weird that you say that."

"Why?" Luck asked. "What happened?"

"Mom had been having trouble sleeping, which isn't out of the ordinary when she's having a flare-up. But she'd been complaining that a noisy car was waking her up in the middle of the night. Honestly, I thought it was tinnitus. It's pretty common with MS. And the noises she was describing seemed right for it." Pulling a box of green tea from a shelf, Caroline shook her head. "But then I stayed over one night, and I heard it, too."

Darger was about to ask exactly what it was that she'd heard, but the girl suddenly gasped.

"Oh god," she said, stifling a sob. "That was only two nights before the fire."

Caroline wrapped her arms around herself and leaned against the counter.

"If the fire had been that night, I could have done something. I could have gotten her out of the house."

The girl's voice was barely a whisper, but Darger heard the pain in it nonetheless. The sharp edges in her told her to push on, that the girl had something. But the softer side, the part that used to be a counselor told her to give the girl a moment.

She saw that Luck was poised on the edge of his bar stool, ready to fire off the question — What did you hear? — but she gave an almost imperceptible shake of her head.

Caroline sniffled and wiped her nose with the back of her hand.

"That's what's so frustrating about all of this. A thousand What-Ifs pop into my head on a daily basis. It's almost constant. What if the smoke detector in the kitchen had been hardwired, like it was supposed to be? If she'd had that extra two minutes it took for the hallway outside her bedroom to fill with smoke, that could have been the difference. Or what if she'd been having a good day that day? If she hadn't needed the wheelchair, maybe she would have made it out."

Darger said, "You're bargaining."

Caroline lifted her head.

"What?"

"There was a psychiatrist named Elisabeth Kübler-Ross. Back in the 1960s, she worked with the terminally ill and came up with a framework for the grieving process. It starts with denial. I'd guess the first thing you thought when you heard your mother was dead was, 'This can't be true.'"

The girl nodded emphatically, her eyelashes glittering with tears.

"I thought it was a nightmare. I kept waiting to wake up."

"The second stage is anger. Once it becomes clear that all of this is real, we want to know why. Why this had to happen. Why someone would do this. And because there aren't any satisfying answers to those questions, we get angry. We rage against the unfairness. The randomness. Sometimes you'll probably end up feeling angry at everyone and everything. People and situations that have nothing to do with your mother's death."

A choked laugh burst out of Caroline's throat.

"OK. Yeah. I totally blew up at work the other day. I'd just cleaned the microwave in the break room, only to come back the next day and find it absolutely caked with someone's leftover spaghetti. I screamed at a whole room full of my coworkers, and then I burst into tears. I've been so embarrassed about it, but you're saying it's... I don't know... normal?"

"It is normal. And even though you can go back and forth and even skip around between the various stages, you seem to be right on schedule when it comes to the third stage."

"Bargaining?"

Darger bobbed her head.

"Now you start thinking of all the ways the fire could have been prevented. All the scenarios in which you might have been able to save your mom. It's your mind's way of trying to prevent this terrible tragedy retroactively. But you can't undo what's already happened."

Tears brimmed again in Caroline's eyes. She smeared her sleeve across her face.

"I know. It's just… it's like my mind won't let go of it."

Reaching out, Darger patted the girl's arm.

"That's OK. It's part of the process."

The kettle whistled, and Caroline set about making the tea.

"Are there more?" she asked as she poured boiling water into a small green teapot.

"More?"

"More stages?"

"Ah," Darger said. "Yes. Two more. After bargaining comes depression."

Caroline managed a wry smile.

"Oh, great."

"I know, right? Like, why couldn't they make one of the stages Nonstop Ecstasy and Bottomless Margaritas?"

That got a snort of laughter out of Caroline.

"Not gonna lie. It blows. It's the worst stage, by far. You'll have days where it hits you hard. Unfortunately, that's just part of the shitty rollercoaster." Darger accepted the steaming cup Caroline handed her. "The important thing is not to let yourself get pulled in too deep. You're going to be sad. That's a given. But you need to reach out to people when it all starts to feel like too much. Friends. Family. A therapist or support group. Heck, you can call me if you need to."

"Seriously?"

"Sure. Why not?" Darger said. "I mean it. You're going to hit a point where you'll want to talk about it, but a lot of times, people don't. They isolate themselves because they feel like no one can possibly understand. Or they don't want to burden someone else with their pain. But you need to do it. Don't wall yourself off from the world, OK?"

Caroline sipped her tea and gave a small nod.

"Good. Eventually, you'll reach the final stage, which is acceptance. Sometimes people mistakenly think that means they'll be OK with what happened. That they get to move on and leave the grief behind. But I think it's more like you come to terms with moving forward with the grief. Because I don't think it ever really goes away. Not with a loss like this."

Sliding open one of the kitchen drawers, Caroline removed a silver picture frame. She set the photo on the counter and angled it so Darger could see. Turquoise water shimmered like glass against white cliffs. In the foreground, Judy Galitis and her daughter hovered in mid-air, the photograph taken mid-jump. They wore matching sarongs and gap-toothed grins.

"You have the same smile," Darger said.

Caroline's fingers brushed the edge of the frame.

"This was just before she was diagnosed. We were in Corfu. We did a whole tour of the Greek islands. We kept saying we'd go back, but..." Caroline shook her head. "There was always a reason or an excuse not to do it."

Luck, who had been quiet for some time, said, "Isn't that life?"

Darger's head swiveled around to survey him.

"Makes you want to jump up and do all the stuff you've always said you wanted to do."

Caroline's brow furrowed, but she nodded in agreement.

"It does. It really does."

Darger was both impressed and surprised at Luck's comment. And she was confident that they could move on in the interview, now that a path had been paved through Caroline's grief.

"Caroline," Darger said, and the girl blinked at her with her frank blue gaze. "You mentioned something before, about your mother hearing a noise at night?"

"Right! Gosh, I almost forgot about that. I thought it was just tinnitus, because—" Caroline stopped herself. "No wait, I already said all that."

"You said you heard it, too?" Darger prompted.

"Yes," Caroline nodded. "The Tuesday night before she died. I went over and made dinner. Linguini with clam sauce. It was one of her favorites. But anyway, I slept in my old room that night. It faces the street. And sure enough, in the middle of the night, I'm awakened by this... this weird noise, just like mom said. I got up and looked out the window, and saw a car idling across the street."

Luck sat forward in his seat. "You saw the car?"

"Only for a minute, then it drove off."

"Could you tell the make and model?"

"Sorry, I don't really know cars. It was an SUV. It looked black, but it was dark, so... I guess it could have been any dark color, really."

Luck was busily entering notes into his phone while she

talked.

"Do you remember what time it was?" Darger asked.

"Almost four AM."

"And the noise," Luck said, "what did it sound like?"

She closed her eyes and frowned, looking every bit like a fifth-grader focusing on multiplying eleven by twelve.

"It was this high-pitched squeak or chirp." She shrugged. "I don't know how else to describe it."

"Could you make the noise for us?" Darger asked.

Caroline blushed.

"I don't really know if I can…"

"Come on," Darger encouraged. "Was it more like — squeak-squawk-squeak-squawk! — or — scrEEeeEEee?"

She made the most high-pitched, chirpy sounds she could. She wasn't going for accuracy. She was merely making an ass of herself so that Caroline would feel more comfortable.

It worked. The big blue eyes crinkled at the edges as Caroline fought off laughter.

"No, no," she said. "It was more like — chirpy-chirpy-chirpy-chirpy-chirpy-chirpy-chirpy!"

"You got that?" Darger asked Luck.

He nodded, replaying the recording of Caroline's chirping from his phone.

Creases formed along Caroline's forehead.

"Was that actually helpful?"

"It might be," Darger said.

When she'd finished her tea, Darger thanked Caroline for answering their questions, and then she and Luck excused themselves.

Back in Luck's Lexus, Darger fastened her seatbelt. She

studied him as he turned the key in the ignition and put the car in gear.

"You did good in there," she said. "That stuff about doing the things you want to do before it's too late. That was good."

"It's the truth, isn't it?"

"Yeah." She slid on a pair of sunglasses and adjusted her sun visor against the late afternoon glare. "I just remember you getting a little squeamish around the grieving family members before."

He shrugged.

"I may have learned a thing or two here and there. From you, mostly."

"Hmm. Well, if you learned it from me, then I guess I should be giving myself the praise." She made a show of patting herself on the back. "Good one, Violet."

Luck rolled his eyes.

CHAPTER 16

Bishop's head snapped up.

"What kind of car noise?"

Sliding his phone from his pocket, Luck played the recording he'd made of Caroline Galitis.

Bishop snapped his fingers and pointed at the two agents.

"Bad serpentine belt!"

"Seriously? You can tell that from the noise she made?" Darger asked.

"Yep. I'm just that good," he said, wheeling over to his computer.

He tapped at the keyboard, opening and closing a series of videos from the surveillance they'd been sifting through.

"Here we go." Bishop unlooped the headphones from around his neck and held them out. "Check it out."

Darger stepped forward and donned the headphones.

With a tap of the spacebar, Bishop played the video. It was distorted with a fisheye effect, and after a moment Darger realized it must be one of those doorbell cameras. The video segment was taken at night, with everything rendered in shades of gray. Seconds ticked by and nothing happened. The road was deserted. And then she heard it. A faint chirping sound. It almost sounded like crickets, but the noise gradually got louder. Light flared on the right side of the screen. Headlights. The high-pitched squeal swelled to a peak as a dark SUV rolled across the screen.

"Where is this from?"

"A little secondhand shop, maybe two blocks down from the Galitis house," Bishop said. "This is the night before the fire."

"How do we know it isn't just someone that lives in the neighborhood?" Klootey asked.

Darger aimed a finger at the time stamp on the screen.

"This says 11 PM. Caroline heard the same thing a few days before at 4 AM."

"So?" Luck asked.

"So, someone in the neighborhood would more likely be on a schedule. If it was the same car at the same times, then I'd consider it's maybe someone on the night shift, coming home. But to be rolling through at 4 AM and then 11 PM? On week nights? And Caroline said the car idled at the curb for a while before taking off. That doesn't sound like a local. I think it could be him," Darger said, then turned to face Bishop. "What do you have the night of the fire?"

"I don't remember seeing this car on there, but I've been churning through the footage pretty quick. The only reason I remember it at all is that this jag-off—" he pointed at Klootey "—cranked the volume on the computer all the way up when I went to take a leak. Almost blew my eardrums out when that squeaking piece of shit rolled by."

Bishop scrolled through the video files, the thumbnails shifting up and then down on the screen.

"Huh. Looks like we don't have footage from this camera that night."

"Well that's convenient," Klootey muttered.

Bishop shrugged, "It's a DIY set-up. The shop owner warned me that his wireless feed goes down every few days or so. He has to reset it or it doesn't record. Sometimes he forgets."

"Have you checked him out at all?" Luck asked. "It does seem a little too convenient, is all. He could be worth looking into."

"Especially if he owns an SUV with a bad…" Darger eyed Bishop. "What kind of belt was it?"

"Serpentine belt," Bishop said. "I had a Chevy Malibu a few years back. Noisy as hell. Camacho's the one that told me to get the belt fixed."

"Let's check out the feed you've got from other cameras, see if we can't spot this noisy bastard on the night of the fire," Darger suggested. "It'll go faster if four of us search."

Bishop waggled an elbow at the other computers in the room.

"Take your pick."

Darger and Luck each chose a computer and began sifting through the "night of" footage. Darger spent the next hour staring at video from various traffic cameras surrounding the Galitis scene. The good news was she could narrow her search down to the half-hour during which the fire was set. The bad news was they'd pulled feed from a dozen different traffic cams, and there was no telling which one might have the footage she was looking for.

After an hour and a half in front of the screen, her eyes stung, and she needed to pee. She'd just rolled her chair back away from the desk when Luck held up his hand.

"I think I've got something."

Darger joined the two cops in their huddle around Luck's monitor.

117

He rolled the video clip. It was grainy black and white security feed from the parking lot of an apartment building down the street from Judy Galitis' residence. Twenty-two minutes before the fire was called in to 911, the same dark SUV went cruising past.

At least it looked like the same vehicle. Without sound to confirm the squeaking belt noise, it was hard to be definitive.

"No audio on this feed?" Darger asked.

Luck frowned.

"Afraid not."

Darger crossed her arms. Still, it was something.

Luck squinted at the screen.

"You know, my in-laws had a car a lot like this. A Toyota 4-Runner. I'm not saying it's the same make and model or anything, but it's the same size, same general style, so probably from around the same time period. Maybe we can narrow it down to dark, mid-size SUVs from, I don't know, 2007 through 2012?"

"Good thinking, Luck," Klootey said. "There's only about 8 million vehicles registered in L.A. county. And roughly half of all vehicles sold are SUVs. So with your additional criteria, it should only be another few million to go through. Can't imagine it'd take more than a decade or two."

"Hey, dickhead, at least I'm trying to come up with something useful instead of sending people out on snipe hunts for a laugh."

"Whoa, whoa, whoa. Correct me if I'm wrong, but you ended up getting something from the daughter, did you not?" Klootey said.

"Yeah, so?"

"Guys," Darger said.

They ignored her.

"So the way I see it, I steered you on the proper path with my keen eye for detail and preternatural sense for working the evidence at hand. Just had a feeling about ol' Mrs. Pain-in-the-ass, the Klootey tingle they call it, like a spidey-sense type of deal, and thankfully for all of us, I trusted my gut."

"You're kidding me if you think—"

"Hey, dumbfucks!" Bishop interrupted.

When he had the attention of Luck and Klootey, he motioned toward Darger's computer, where she'd brought up a list of 2009 mid-size SUVs with photographs.

"There's no fucking way you're going to be able to ID the car with this. The video's grainy as shit," Klootey argued.

"But Luck is right," Darger said. "We can narrow it down."

She tapped Luck's screen with her fingernail.

"Look. It's got those rail things on the roof."

"Roof racks," Bishop said.

"Yeah. So, check out this list." She scrolled through the photos of the mid-size SUVs on her screen. "Only some come with roof racks. And some have them laid out crosswise."

"Roof racks can be added aftermarket," Klootey said. "This is nothing."

"Nah." Bishop shook his head. "It's not nothing. Come on, Teej. We've been at this for hours, and this is the first scrap of anything we've found. It makes sense to tease out whatever we can from it."

They spent the next twenty minutes shaving their list down, which at times turned into a heated debate, mostly between Luck and Klootey.

"What about the GMC Envoy?" Luck asked. "It's got the right roof rack style."

Klootey scoffed.

"No fucking way. The profile is all wrong. Look at how chunky that thing is. No finesse. The SUV in the video is way sleeker." He leaned back in his swivel chair, feet up on the desk in front of him. "Besides that, the grill on the GMC isn't right."

"You can't even see the grill in the video," Luck argued.

"Yeah, you can." Klootey leaned forward and poked his finger into the monitor. "Right there."

"That's glare from the other car's headlights. And would you mind not smearing your sausage fingers all over my screen, please?"

"Glare, my ass," Klootey said with an antagonizing smirk.

After all the bickering, they'd narrowed the possibilities to six models. Not ideal, but it was a starting point. Given the poor quality of the video footage, Darger thought it was better than they could have hoped for.

Once they were finished with the main thrust of their task here, it seemed all the energy fled the room. Time had flown past, somehow transporting them from the afternoon directly into the night, and all Darger wanted to do was get back to her room to sleep. She had a feeling the same must be true for the others as they packed up to head out in near silence.

And suddenly, with the sway of exhaustion creeping in, the new lead didn't seem so promising. Like Klootey had said, they'd only succeeded in narrowing the list to millions of vehicles in the surrounding counties, maybe the high hundreds of thousands if they were lucky.

"You OK?" Luck said, shaking her out of the spiraling

thoughts. She realized that Bishop and Klootey were gone now. The room felt very empty.

"Yeah, I'm fine. Just tired."

"Well, let's get out of here."

CHAPTER 17

The man stoops in the shadowed place between the parked cars, the place where the streetlights cannot touch. He pours gasoline from a red plastic can into an empty two-liter bottle of Sierra Mist.

Licks his lips. Nervous. Excited. Alive.

The fuel trickles into the bottle with a sound a lot like pissing. Loud.

He swivels his head to see if anyone hears. Sees the glow staring back from all the suburban windows, TVs flickering inside most, but not a soul stirring. Good.

He turns back to the dark place where the gas sloshes.

Gasoline is not his favorite accelerant, but it's what he has handy most of the time. We all make little sacrifices when it comes to our passions in this life.

Besides. This one won't be like the church. Nothing quite so grand as all that. This one is just a little warning. A little entertainment. Nothing too serious.

What do they call it? Firing a shot across the bow. That's all.

He walks a block and a half. Rounds a corner. Slows as he moves close to the sports car he means to light up.

Images of the flames to come flicker in his skull. Bright pictures. Orange smears that engulf all things around them.

But no. No. Not this one. Small, he reminds himself. And yet…

Couldn't it spread? Become something serious? Of course it could. But that part isn't up to him. It's up to the wind, up to chance, up to whatever gods watch over this place.

In the end it is always up to the fire. Always.

Something nags him. Makes him hesitate a moment. Something he needs to remember. It hits him: He'd stowed the gas can near the driver's side tire of his SUV. Needs to remember to grab that. Alas, the Sierra Mist bottle won't be coming back from this journey.

Now he shuffles forward, the hair on his arms standing up as he moves back into the light. He considers standing. Walking upright like a normal man. But better to stay low, some animal part of him thinks. No feints to normalcy or nonchalance here. Stay in the shadows, strike, and get out. Quick and savage. Like a wolf leaping straight for the goddamn jugular.

He kneels before the Mustang. Hesitates there a moment. And he gazes upon the house of the owner, or at least the one he thinks is the owner's. Holds his breath as he does it.

Blue light brightens and darkens on the wall. But no figure appears there in the window. No threatening silhouette. No vigilant watcher to find him out.

When it comes to these dark deeds, these dark matters of the heart, the shadows will mostly conceal you, he thinks. If you're smart enough to let them.

His heart hammers now in his chest. The level of excitement tingling in every follicle on his head, in the meat of his palms, in the tips of his toes, and all points in between.

Why did it feel so good to deceive them? To get away with it?

OK. No more waiting.

He takes a big breath and twists the cap off the plastic

bottle.

He has to chew his lip to hold back from giggling a little as the first spritz of gas flings out of the bottle.

☾

He still remembers how it all started for him. That first brush with fire, the first taste of the power it wielded without mercy.

He was 13, and it was just about a month after his dad's heart attack. Like any true working-class hero, his father had worked himself to death. A lumberjack who died on the job, draped in sweaty flannel. Massive coronary. Dead before he hit the ground.

The funeral was hard. Pain like he'd never imagined. Loneliness he couldn't shake. Surrounded by all those people and lonelier than ever. Then, somehow, even after the acute hurt of the wound had started its long, slow fade, things just kept getting worse.

Homelife got so dreary. Mom crying all the time. Drinking until she passed out. Putting all of her anxiety and guilt on him when she was awake.

With dad out of the picture, their income dropped to zero. The power company pulled the plug on them within weeks. He ate generic brand cereal, a Cocoa Puffs knockoff, with water instead of milk for every meal.

And the few friends he had at school all seemed to be away for that stretch of summer. Off at camps or on family trips.

So he started going out on his bike at all hours. Long rides by himself. Alone. He fled the city, took the twisting roads up into the hills where there were more trees than faces, tried to get as far away from everyone as he could.

It was there, on a canyon road near Griffith Observatory just after dawn, that he found it.

He came upon a Porsche smashed into a California sycamore. The front end wrapped around the thick trunk entirely, as though attempting to bear hug it, metal contorted into impossible angles that made him think about all those phony psychics bending spoons. But the little sports car wasn't just mangled, it'd become a fireball at the end. A blackened shell that wept its plastic contents into dark puddles that hardened on the ground around the accident as well as on the car's floor.

Based on the gashes in the mud, they'd taken quite a tumble before landing here, veering nearly sideways, grazing one tree and stripping a good hunk of bark away so a gouged chunk of white flesh lay exposed like a bite mark, before finally reaching that final collision point and bursting into flames. The news reports later estimated their speed to have been in the 120 mph range.

The driver had been thrown from the vehicle on the impact with the first tree — in some way spared from the worst of it. No seatbelt. His body launched through the windshield — catapulted — and then smashed under the car. The skinny little legs sticking out from under the twisted steel. Probably a quick end. Merciful to a certain degree.

The woman in the passenger seat didn't fare so well.

Her nose was just about smashed flat, a detail strangely discernible even after she'd burned to black char. Most of her teeth lay on the floor below, congealed in the plastic goo that seeped down from the dash as the fire consumed it.

But the claw marks in one unburnt remnant of upholstery told the real story. She was trapped. Conscious. Terrified. Confused.

And the fire took her.

He was looking at the aftermath of what must have been a stunning special effects sequence. Horrifying and disturbing, and in its own way, awe-inspiring. Except this wasn't movie magic. It was real.

Everything about the scene was a spectacle, yes, but those torn places in the seat and the curved little scratches near the door handle, those were what took his breath away. Jesus. It reminded him of something that might happen to a rodent or possum or something. Some creature too dumb to avoid traffic or whatever. A groundhog. Not a real live human being.

After that, he thought about fire all the time. And he learned a word for its effects. Sublime. An awe-inspiring aesthetic experience that is rooted in an elevated quality — in this case, rooted not in the beautiful but in the terrifying. Like experiencing a storm at sea, a tornado, an act of brutal violence like a punch that knocks out teeth, or an explosion. Any of these experiences can overwhelm the senses, make one shudder, fill one with wonder so intense it becomes nauseating. To him, that was what distinguished a beautiful experience from a sublime one.

Bring on your shock, your horror, your total astonishment. Bring on the sublime.

But fire? Fire trumps all the rest.

Fire is destruction in its purest form. Naked energy. Raw power. It devours solid objects. Erases everything it touches. Crisps skin. Melts faces. Brings all to ash.

Night on Fire

He set his first fire out in the hills three weeks after he came upon the little accident. It didn't do much, and he didn't see what little it did. He'd splashed some lighter fluid everywhere and lit it. When he heard the whoosh and saw the bright flash, he panicked. Rode his bike away at top speed. Going back the next day revealed just a little patch where the grass had turned brown. Nothing more.

But he was determined. And he was willing to learn.

CHAPTER 18

Officer Miguel Camacho woke on his couch in the dark, gasping for breath. Confused. Groggy. A little frightened.

What the hell?

Screaming. Screaming had awakened him. Hadn't it?

He listened. Nothing now. A dream, maybe.

The TV flashed blue light at him, a flicker that brightened and darkened on the walls around him, shifted the tones of the shadows every which way.

He took a breath. Rubbed his eyes. A little of the alarm drained away as he pieced together what was happening.

Beer commercials on TV provided the first clue as they gave way to the local news. That put the time somewhere between 11 pm and midnight or so.

He must have fallen asleep watching Thursday Night Football again. Sheesh. Why were the games on Thursday always so damn boring? Low scoring. Poor execution in all three phases of the game. NyQuil Football, he liked to call it. Tasted terrible and knocked him the hell out.

The screaming picked up again and snapped his mind away from the NFL. The shrill sound snaked a little chill down the length of his spine, a sensation that reminded him of a dog's hackles going up.

He sat forward on the couch. Listened.

Yes. The screaming. That's what had shaken him awake in the first place, he remembered now with certainty. Incessant screaming.

But not the screaming of a human, thankfully. It was that damn Pomeranian over at Gus Miller's place, Cheeto. Thing went apeshit every time a squirrel came within a few hundred yards of their property. One of those mean little dogs that probably leaped to bite the nose of any idiot foolish enough to try to lean down and pet it. He'd heard Klootey refer to this type of dog as a Scrotum Shredder once. Thinking about that made Camacho chuckle under his breath.

He stood then, gathered dishes from the coffee table, and took them out to the kitchen and rinsed them in the sink. The shocking cold as he first turned on the water made him think about how much that sleep-warmth had already settled over his body as he dozed in front of the TV.

He didn't think he could shake the tiredness, and he didn't feel like fighting it. Better to get things cleaned up and head to bed. Another Thursday night wasted on the No Fun League.

Flipping off the water seemed to turn the volume of the rest of the world back up.

Cheeto was still screeching away out there. Livid. The barks came faster now. More urgent.

And then the dog's cries hit a higher note and cut out all at once.

Again Camacho's skin crawled.

Shit. That didn't sound good.

No. Worse than that, he told himself.

Wrong. It sounded wrong.

He stood still. Listening. No further sounds came.

Staying so light on his feet so as to remain soundless, he crept back out to the living room, moved to the front window, standing so he just peeked through the slitted space over the top of the curtains.

He peered out into the places where the streetlights gouged openings into the darkness. The shapes out there took a moment to make sense to his eyes, the contours at first seeming to craft some abstract painting of light and darkness before the shapes of the parked cars on the street came into focus.

He held his breath. Waited a few seconds. Watched that street portrait for any sign of movement.

Nothing stirred out there that he could see. Maybe the sound wasn't wrong after all. Just the normal routine. The squirrel went home and the dog laid back down. Or maybe Gus Miller did the unthinkable and let his goddamn dog inside for once so it'd stop screaming at the whole neighborhood willy-nilly. Anything was possible, Camacho figured, even if the likelihood of Gus Miller lifting a finger for the good of others seemed quite a stretch.

But then something did move.

A flitting of the shadows along the cars. Something low to the ground. Too big to be an animal, he thought, but it moved like one.

He squinted. Looked for it. Now he couldn't see anything but the cars.

Shit.

His heart hammered in his chest, squeezing harder and faster with every breath. He thought of his gun, locked up in his bedroom. Then he considered the notion that his sleepy mind was playing tricks on him, his imagination already half-sauced with dreams, but no. No.

He'd seen something out there. He was certain of that.

He stared into the blackest gap between the streetlights,

where he'd last seen movement. Fixed his eyes there with such intensity that he started to see those squiggly lines and pink blotches he sometimes saw in the dark.

Again something moved. Not an animal. A man.

He squinted harder. Pushed his nose right up to the glass. Chewed his lip as an outlet for the anticipation, teeth gnawing right up to the edge of pain and holding steady there.

His chest ached to take a breath. Not yet. Not yet. Something was happening here. Something.

Wasn't it?

Bright light burst from the nothingness, and Camacho flinched, sucking in a breath at last in shock.

A writhing wall of orange whooshed up from the blackness all at once.

CHAPTER 19

Luck and Darger arrived on the scene outside of Miguel Camacho's home within two minutes of each other. Darger hadn't quite made it to her hotel parking lot when she got the call. She figured Luck hadn't made it home, either.

The fire itself had done no real damage, apart from frying some grass and leaving a dark splotch on the street that looked wet.

Still, Camacho was rattled, chest heaving, eyes darting everywhere. She imagined seeing a blaze whoosh to life outside one's place of residence had that effect on people, especially after one of the detectives spotted the Sierra Mist bottle that even now reeked of gasoline lying in the grass near the Mustang. That close of a call would shake anyone up.

Luck bent over a table set up by the crime scene techs, studying the bottle where it sat in its plastic baggie shroud.

"Might get lucky and get something off it," he said. "Prints or DNA."

At his words, a new realization dawned on her. Darger sighed.

"No."

"What's that?"

"We won't find anything on the bottle."

"How do you know that?"

"Because he left it on purpose," she said. "Intentional or not in the earlier fires, this is his calling card now. He dumped it because he wanted us to know this was his work."

132

His gaze went from her and back to the evidence baggie.

"Christ," was all he could say.

Another moment passed before he spoke again.

"Ready to talk to Camacho?"

"Let's do it," she said.

Luck pulled the officer aside from all the twirling lights out front and had him sit on the couch in the living room. Darger closed the curtains to block out all the commotion the best they could.

She thought he looked calmer inside, but it was hard to be sure. She figured it best to launch right into it. Maybe he'd heard the screech of the serpentine belt.

"Did you hear anything suspicious before the fire?"

"Yeah, actually. Neighbor's dog was screamin' his damn head off just before. He's a noisy fucker as a rule, but this was next level barking."

"What about other sounds?" she asked.

She had to be careful here. Couldn't lead him. The last thing she wanted was to put the idea of a noisy car in his head.

"I mean… like what?" He shook his head. "Jesus! It's weird as hell to be on this side of the table. I'm supposed to be the one taking witness statements. Not giving them."

"You're doing fine."

He chuckled.

"Don't feel like it. I feel like my memories are all jumbled up."

"That's the adrenaline. Sometimes it helps to go through things step by step, so let's do that," Darger suggested.

After a nod from Camacho, she went on.

"You're on the couch, watching football. You notice your

neighbor's dog barking. Then what?"

"I was clearing some of the crap from the coffee table. Rinsing dishes in the sink when—"

Camacho's face tensed.

"What is it?"

"Cheeto stopped barking."

"Cheeto? That's your neighbor's dog?"

Nodding, Camacho rubbed his knuckles along the side of his face.

"Jesus, I hope nothing bad happened to the little guy. He's an annoying little shit, but, I mean… dogs are innocent creatures, man."

"What happened next?"

"I went back out to the living room. To look out the window."

"What did you see?"

"Nothing at first. Just blackness. And then something moved."

Darger waited. She could tell by the way Camacho's eyes moved up to stare at a blank space on the kitchen wall that he was in full-on memory mode, and she didn't want to interrupt that.

"The way it moved, at first I thought it was an animal. But it was too big. I waited. And then I saw it again. It was a man."

"Could you see what he was doing?"

"It was a split second. Just his silhouette moving past a light in the distance. If I would have blinked, I would have missed it."

"And then?"

"And then I was practically blinded by the light of the fire.

It was so bright and it went up so fast. Just whoosh! And then flames. I thought my car was toast for sure."

"Did you hear him at all? His footsteps as he ran away? A car door slamming?"

Camacho's brow furrowed so deep it was almost comical.

"Nuh-uh. No." He swiveled his gaze to meet Darger's. "And that's kind of weird, isn't it? To hear nothing? No car door? No engine? That means he got away on foot."

"So he parked somewhere else," Luck suggested.

Darger was still staring at Camacho. She knew what he was thinking.

"Or he didn't drive here at all," Darger said.

"Because he lives close by," Camacho finished.

Luck screwed up his face. "Seems like a bit of a leap."

"Not if you pair it with what we got earlier," she said, then turned back to Camacho. "You know the sound a car makes when it has a bad serpentine belt?"

Camacho nodded. "Yeah. It's like a constant high-pitched cricket noise. Almost as annoying as that little mutt Cheeto."

"Have you heard that around here recently? Someone driving by your house at night, maybe?"

"No," Camacho answered, frowning. "Why?"

"We think our guy might drive an SUV with a bad serpentine belt. Both Caroline Galitis and her mother heard it driving by the house in the nights leading up to the fire," she explained. "And it's like I said before, these guys are creatures of habit. If he scoped out the Galitis house before he started that fire, he would have done the same here. Except you haven't heard a bad serpentine belt."

"Because he walked here," Camacho slammed a fist on the

table triumphantly. Then his look soured. "Jesus, though… does that mean this guy's been watching me and shit? That's creepy as hell."

CHAPTER 20

The SUV creeps through downtown Los Angeles, another dark shape blurring past like all the rest. Unnoticed. Anonymous. For now.

Maybe someday the whole world will know his name. Maybe. That is the goal out here in Hollywood, right? To see your name in lights. To plaster yourself on billboards, posters, the cover of magazines. He smiles a little at the thought.

He can still see the fire flickering on the ground just shy of the Mustang every time he closes his eyes. Nothing too dramatic tonight — it didn't so much as blister the paint on the car — but the excitement still throbs when he remembers, the flames putting him right back under their spell.

After the church, it's probably better to lay low anyway. Take it easy. Just a little pick me up, one little jolt. Like the jump scare fake-out in the horror movie to reset the tension before the next big reveal. That's what tonight was.

Yeah. A jump scare. He likes that. He likes that a lot.

With the window all the way down, the air rushes in, blasts its cool against his cheeks, ruffles his hair. Makes him feel alive. In motion. Unstoppable. Restless. Important.

Driving through the city always feels this way. Like it's foreshadowing something big.

He works long hours — real work, not some showbiz puffery — and when he's done, he's too wired to relax, too amped to shut his head off. So he drives. Swoops down and around random streets. Shoots through alleys. Spirals and zigs

137

and zags every which way. Only ever able to see as far ahead as the headlights show, which is fine by him. Better to live life that half a block at a time, forget the rest of the world.

Be here now. All the way here.

He circles the city like there's a drain at the center, the whirlpool spinning, slowly pulling until it swallows him, until it swallows everyone. He can almost see it when he closes his eyes — the grate at the center of Los Angeles, the hole that eventually sucks down all of the scum and flushes it out into the sea.

Or maybe some nights he circles it like a vulture. Sniffing around for freshly dead meat, which the city offers up daily. Shot. Stabbed. Crushed in cars. Drunk and drowned and washing up on the beach. Or best yet — burned to a blackened husk. Well done, you could say.

So bring out your dead. Offer up your humble sacrifices. Because the god of Los Angeles? He's no merciful deity. He is out for fucking blood.

Again, he smiles at these thoughts, at how deeply people misunderstand the city he was born and raised in.

This city does not care about you. It does not care what happens to you. It's chasing its own dream, serving only its own desires. Looking out for number one. It will gladly grind its heel into your skull to get that one step higher toward the top of the heap. And still the masses flock here to get trampled. Fresh meat for the grinder every year, every month, every day.

Here it feels like the concrete never ends. You could drive forever and never reach the end of the city, never find the edge. Zooming past skyscrapers, zipping beneath underpasses, coiling around corner after corner, the periodic tree jutting up from the cement for decorative purposes.

He weaves a circuitous path through the city. No particular place to go. Just time to burn. Intersections to hurtle through.

Red light. Yellow light. Green light.

He lights a cigarette, cups his hands around the lighter's flame to shield it from the wind sucking into the window. Loves everything about this little ritual. The feel of the fresh cigarette filter clenched in his lips, the tangy smell of the unlit tobacco, the little snick of the lighter wheel, the fire's bright glow flickering just under his chin.

He breathes smoke, hears a little click in his throat as he inhales, hesitates with the swirling gray cloud in his chest, and then he lets it come spilling out, his nostrils turned to two chimneys for this moment.

People mill along the sidewalks here, clusters of humanity huddling outside of gas stations and liquor stores, partially lit in oranges and yellows by the streetlights and store signs. He watches them as he rushes past. Sees faces and forgets them just as quickly. Three seconds of their lives witnessed, noted, and erased forever.

He loves Los Angeles at night. The bustling dark sprawl. Endless and pointless. Positively brimming with emptiness. Movie stars and murder. The biggest stars in the world flock to the same few restaurants here, living the dream, and a few blocks from them? A bunch of toothless nobodies whose last remaining dream comes spiraling down the glass tube of a crack pipe.

The dream and the nightmare unfolding on the same street, sometimes on the same block. Welcome to fucking Hollywood.

As if on cue, a bum stumbles out of an alley, picking at his last couple teeth with his fingernails, all scrawny with that big swollen belly one gets from malnourishment. He brings a paper bag housing what looks to be a pint bottle to his lips, tips his head back and freezes there, pouring cheap liquor down his gullet. A brutal image, startling, but after the customary three seconds, he's past it. Moving on. Never looking back.

Good thing I don't give a fuck about anybody but me, he reassures himself, chuckling a little between hits on his cigarette. It'd suck to have worry about such things for real. To actually care. Of course, I know empathy is important. That's why I have so much of it for myself.

Thinking of it that way makes it seem funny, the city as a whole. Absurd. Ludicrous.

L.A. is all well and good during the day, he thinks, but the city is a different animal at night. Something that can't be tamed. Something wicked that glitters with bad intent when all those lights flick on — all fluorescent glow and flitting shadows.

Through his windshield, he sees it all. Watches it all. The pimps and prostitutes. The thugs. The junkies. The drunks. The rapists and pushers and pedophiles. They all come creeping out at night.

And the killers who walk among them. So many killers.

This is the place where the Manson family roamed, where the Night Stalker stalked, where Robert Kennedy took a bullet to the skull just like his brother did, where OJ Simpson just about sliced his ex-wife's head off, allegedly. Black Dahlia. The Menendez brothers. The Wonderland murders. The list of famous L.A. murders goes on and on.

The way he sees it, Los Angeles is a monument to this kind

of savagery. A city perhaps best captured in the footage of the Rodney King beating, in the videos of the riots that ensued.

A city that burns.

Periodically, the hills catch on fire. The Santa Ana winds carry the blaze far and wide until driving down the highway into the city looks like driving through the gates of Hell — walls of flame stretching vertically up the slopes, consuming everything on both sides of the asphalt. Sad little highway signs that seem suspended in the middle of all of that fire, hovering in the little gap above the blacktop. A furious orange glow surrounds everything, all the world's hatred focused here, made real, spontaneously combusting, burning out and trying to take the rest of the world with it.

Destruction.

He drives out in the hills with the wind in his hair now. A few miles south of here, the Manson family butchered Sharon Tate one summer night. Scrawled their piggy messages on the walls like the blood of the dead was finger paint. Off to the east, the Night Stalker carved a bloody path from Sun Valley to Whittier to Diamond Bar, peeled the screens off of windows to crawl into suburban homes and wipe out families as they slept. Ravaging the suburbs, robbing and raping and killing, etching his name into pop culture immortality just like all the movie stars.

It fits, he thinks. All the violence feels right.

The basest appetites rule this place. Lust. Greed. Wrath. It's a place that offers up worship of a kind. Worship for a god who demands a blood sacrifice, a god who wants his pound of flesh, a god who will make you a star if you come sit on the casting couch with him for a little while.

He sees the ones who've been used up by the Hollywood machine, too. The has-beens and the never-wases crawling all over this place, the ones still competing for the love of strangers, the ones who'd drink a bottle of Drano to book a Geico commercial, wearing their sad stories in the lines in their faces, waiting for something that's never coming.

The dream. The spectacle. The audience's stamp of approval that validates it once and for all: you are special. You do matter. You really are here.

He watches it all through panes of glass. One side, the tinsel, he sees come through the TV screen, but the real shit he sees through the windshield, through the driver's side window, through the portals sliced in the sides of the buildings that expose the insides. When he drives down through it, he sees the real thing.

He sucks on his cigarette butt, feels the smoke twirl inside him again.

You can see so much if you really watch, he thinks, if you pay attention to people. You see secrets in the way a woman angles herself away from her lover. See the unasked question in her chewed lip. See the reservations in the way her arms stay folded tight to her chest, as though clutching one's torso might keep them safe. Not in this place.

If you focus your eyes, you can look right through people. Stare holes clean through to the meat of them, to the innards, all the way through.

At a stop light he massages the back of his neck. Feels how long the day has been in the way those muscles ache. Long hours. Days that bleed into each other.

Sometimes he thinks the fires are a way to divide the days.

The big blazes he sets mark an ending of a chapter so a new one can begin. Burn out the old way of things, the old way of thinking, bring this little piece of time to ash, and start over. The phoenix can only rise from the ashes, right? So burn the fucker down, another piece of the endless city, another piece of the endless night.

Change. Transformation. A chemical reaction set in motion by his lighter's flame.

The city wants a spectacle? This he can provide. Over and over like endless sequels. This franchise is going strong. The future is bright. White hot, you could say.

See your city on fire. See your city dead. A breathtaking display. Step right up, folks. This one's not to be missed.

Here the violence seems to be for excitement. For entertainment. The fires serve as just another dramatic set piece in the place that cranks them out endlessly. Action. Thrills. Something exciting, something visceral every ten minutes or you'll lose the audience. Them's the rules.

Now the scenery outside changes. The glitz of Hollywood replaced by the industrial look of the rougher outlying neighborhoods.

Driving through Compton and Watts at night gets the heart pumping. Danger. Chaos. Confusion. Sets the adrenaline coursing in the blood.

Everyone knows the history. Bloods and Crips. The Mexican Mafia. The 18th Street Gang. MS-13 with their charming motto: rape, control, kill. It's been estimated that in total there are over 120,000 gang members in L.A. alone.

The gang violence isn't what it was years ago, when gangs ruled certain neighborhoods mostly unchecked, contested blocks of the city essentially turned to war zones. But the gang presence remains even so, the threat still palpable when he hurtles through the turbulent neighborhoods. A doomed feeling circulating in the air. Something desperate, a danger he can feel like a vibration, a violence he sometimes thinks he can smell, some bodily musk hanging over them in a cloud.

In the summer, especially, you can hear the restlessness bubble over every few blocks in the rough places. Music blaring. People yelling. Fighting. Worse. The sound and fury of this place coming unblocked, coming unglued, ready to get hands-on with the next motherfucker who makes eye contact, itching to lose control.

Every summer night, the pedestrians pour out onto the streets and linger there. Wandering souls. Purposeless and plentiful. So many people living right on top of each other. What better for them to do than bash each other's brains in? To fight over the scraps.

And still, there is something funny about all of it, too, he thinks. Funny in a morbid way. Tragedy and comedy go hand-in-hand, don't they?

Funny like a razor in an apple on Halloween.

After Robert Kennedy took that bullet behind his ear at point-blank range, fragments of skull shot all through his brain. Still conscious, he lay on the floor of a hotel kitchen, dying. He asked if everyone was OK and was told yes. "Everything is going to be OK," he turned and said to no one in particular. He got quiet after that. When they brought his wife to him, he made eye contact with her and seemed to recognize her, but he still said nothing.

As the EMTs loaded him onto a stretcher, he finally spoke

again. He said, "Don't lift me." Those were his final words.

See? Funny.

But it fits once again. The morbid story suits this place, and it suits him. He loves the thrill. Loves the violence. Lives for it. Finds it disturbing and hilarious all at once.

Driving down through L.A. with that threat of harm all around, he feels alive. Alert. All the way awake. He can breathe it in the smog, taste it on his tongue, hear it in the voices raised in the ghetto each and every night.

You don't find that trapped behind a desk in some bullshit suburb, bored to fucking death.

So he drives on. Presses deeper into the night.

And he pictures the hills on fire. The flames turning everything red and bright. Soon. Soon it becomes real again.

It's a spectacle the people crave, and a spectacle he will give them.

CHAPTER 21

Darger didn't sleep well that night. Too many thoughts raced through her mind as she replayed the interview with Camacho again and again.

It was just before dawn when her phone rang the next morning, a thin line of amber light already brightening the eastern horizon.

Seeing Luck's name on the screen, Darger skipped past the formality of a standard greeting.

"What do you have?"

Not missing a beat, Luck said, "Chief Macklin had his people go back through the list of potentially disgruntled or otherwise unstable former police and fire employees."

Darger bounced her foot up and down with impatience. This was not news. It was the plan they'd come up with last night, after talking with Camacho.

"Yes. And?" she said, struggling to keep her tone cordial. She needed some damn coffee.

"We found a guy. Ivan Sablatsky. 26 years old. Lives about a third of a mile from Camacho. Maybe a two or three-minute jog if you know the shortcuts through the alleyways and whatnot."

"And I bet he does."

"Yep," Luck said.

"What's his history?"

"He was a short-lived member of the Los Angeles Fire Department. Station 12. He actually passed the initial psych

146

test, made it to the probationary period and then washed out when he failed a random drug test."

"Drug of choice?"

"Cocaine. He claimed it was a one-time thing, but the department has a zero-tolerance policy, so that was it."

"And what does he do now? Does he have a job?"

"Yeah, but it's a weekend-only gig. He drives a forklift at the Anheuser Busch plant."

"And what about a dark SUV?"

"He's got a 2014 Mercury Mariner. A little newer than we were thinking, but it's the right body type and has the roof racks that run parallel to the length of the car. Only the thing is, it's sort of a silvery-blue color."

"How dark?"

"I mean, I wouldn't call it dark at all. But it's hard to say what it might look like at night, under street lights or on crappy CCTV camera footage."

"What about his family life?"

"Divorced. And get this: the house he lives in is actually owned by his sister. We don't think she lives there, though. It's listed in the county registry as a rental property."

Darger nodded to herself. It wasn't perfectly consistent with the part of her profile that said he may still live with a parent or guardian, but it was close. One step away.

"Do we have any background on his childhood?"

"Not yet. I made it clear that any inquiries into his background should be done very discreetly to avoid spooking him," Luck said. "Oh, but we did get one other thing. He's got a DUI on his record. Happened about a month after he was dismissed from the fire department."

"Everything else seems to fit," Darger said. "The problem is it's all circumstantial at the moment. I can't imagine LAPD managed to get a search warrant on any of this."

"Nope. We're stuck in limbo until we get something solid on him."

"So what's the plan? Surveillance?"

"For now, yes. Three shifts, two cars per shift."

Darger ground her back teeth together. She knew watching and waiting was their best shot, but it was slow and tedious. She'd rather they bust down this Sablatsky guy's door and toss his place. He probably had a whole treasure trove of pyro gear in his garage. But there were always those pesky things called Due Process and Probable Cause.

"If we can catch him in the act of starting a fire, that'd be pretty rock solid," she said. "Where should we meet up? My rental is probably a little more inconspicuous than your Lexus. I can pick you up."

Luck cleared his throat.

"Well, there's a bit of a snafu with that. I tried to sign us up for a few shifts, but Chief Macklin more or less told me he'd prefer that we tag along with the locals versus manning our own vehicle."

"What?"

"I think he's worried the FBI will try to horn in on his collar."

Darger made a disgusted noise. One thing she hadn't missed while she was away from the FBI was all the interdepartmental dick-measuring.

"Anyway, I'm about to head out with a team for the morning rotation. I put you down as a third wheel with Klootey and Bishop for this afternoon, three o'clock to eleven. But we can swap if you want."

"Nah, that's fine with me," she said, figuring Luck would have more time to spend with his kid if he kept to normal hours. "Call me if anything goes down."

"Will do."

CHAPTER 22

Sunglasses shield his eyes as he walks into the diner and takes his typical seat in a booth in the back corner. He doesn't remove the knockoff Ray-Bans, even though the interior of the building is well shaded. Better to keep covered up.

This diner always smells like wood shavings, a pungent stench that seems to change along with seasons. In winter, the odor strikes him as being just like sawdust, dry and a little sharp. It shifts in the summer, though, to something earthy and damp, dank like that red mulch people spread around the plants outside of dentist offices and the like.

When the waitress comes around, he doesn't even need to speak.

"Your usual, I presume?" she says, smiling.

He nods. Watches her.

Betsy. He is always conscious of her body when she's near. Preoccupied with her physicality. He wonders sometimes if she can sense that in her subconscious mind, if she can feel it like a disturbance in the atmosphere, something aggressive or dangerous or alien in her presence. Something wild. Something… something wicked this way comes.

She jots a little flourish on her pad, pen flicking in her fingers, and then her eyes come back to his.

"Any big plans for today or just the S.O.C. — same old crap?"

"Same old for me. What about you?"

"Working. Sleeping, waking, and working again. You know

how it is, I'm sure."

He nods again.

"Can I ask you something?" he says, almost surprised to hear the words coming out of his mouth.

"Sure, hon. Ask away." Again she smiles when she says it, lips all sheening with lip gloss. Moist.

"What's the deal with grits?"

Her eyelids flutter. He's surprised her.

"What's the… deal with them?"

"Yeah, I mean, I see them up on the sign every time I walk in here. Bowl o' grits. $1.99. But I've never had 'em. Don't really understand 'em. Like… what do you put on them?"

She laughs a little, nodding now.

"Butter. That's how I like them. Some people go the sweet route — add syrup or brown sugar or whatever, sometimes honey, but I prefer the savory presentation. Add a little salt, some butter, or maybe some bacon or cheese."

"And you have 'em with breakfast or what? Kind of like oatmeal?"

"Well, they're sort of like if you made oatmeal out of corn, but I like grits better with dinner. Shrimp and grits. Chicken and grits. Stuff like that."

"Damn. I'll have to try them."

Again, she laughs, and her tongue flicks out to touch her teeth.

Flashes in his imagination fight for control of the movie screen in his skull.

Part of him sees the two of them together. Naked flesh mashing together. Body parts entwining. Lips enfolding. Hips working.

Another part sees gasoline spritzed over her face. Glugging out of a two-liter Mountain Dew bottle and gushing over her dome. Drenching her hair. The chemical vapors visible as shimmers in the air all around. Her eyes blinking, open so wide, eyelashes all wet. She whimpers a little. Shivers. Bound at the wrists. And the flame of his lighter presses closer, closer, closer.

"You don't want to change your order, do you hon?"

Her question shatters his fantasy. Draws him back to the present. Confuses him.

"What?"

She gestures at the pad of tickets in her hand.

"I'm asking if you want me to change your order. Bring ya some grits instead of the usual?"

Their prior conversation comes back to him, feels far away after the intrusion of fantasy images.

"Oh. No. No, maybe next time."

"Well, all right. I'll be right back with that coffee and pie, Jim." He can hear the wetness on her lips now. Little smacks. Subtle but there.

Jim. That's how she knows him. It isn't his real name. Just the nondescript placeholder he uses whenever he's off work. Out in the metropolis. Among the people. It provides a way to be anonymous as he explores the city. Pokes around it like it's a hornet's nest. A way to keep the life he lives out here separate from his other life.

Jim. An alter ego in a lot of ways.

Jim could do anything, be anything, totally free to pursue whatever impulses bubbled up from his subconscious. Totally unblocked.

Jim. A character. A piece of work. An unlikely protagonist to our tale.

Jim. A lone wolf. A man who does as he pleases, who pursues his desires no matter how dark they might get.

Because we all have primal urges, dark impulses that come spewing out of the places in ourselves where our eyes can never go, the parts of our brain leftover from those initial stages of evolution, the wild animal trapped in there, held back.

Sexual desires.

A lust for violence.

A variety of bodily appetites, concerns, and preferences.

A way of seeing the physical world, looking right through the niceties, the social framework, the agreed-upon lie that defines daily life in modern civilization. Sizing this place up in a dead-eyed way, seeing what's really there, what's real.

The lizard brain. That's what some people call it. The limbic system. An emotional part of the brain so ancient it cannot process language, and ironically enough the place where the human animal makes its decisions. He heard some egghead go on about it in some YouTube video, a fancy lad with an accent he could never quite place.

But be it from a fancy source or not, the concept makes sense enough to him. Trust isn't based in words. It isn't rooted in reason. It isn't even a choice. You trust someone or you don't. It's a feeling. Inevitable. Untouchable. Something happening to you, not something you control.

Betsy swoops back with the aforementioned pie and coffee. Smiling as always. Inviting.

He tries to look down her shirt when she sets the mug and plate in front of him. No joy. The green fabric of her sweater crawls a little too tall up her chest. Blocks out his eyeball's advances.

Still, he can see the shape of her, and that's something. That's plenty.

When he gazes at her, he gazes on all of femininity. Stands in awe of it. Wants only to worship it. To sacrifice himself to it in some violent ritual.

If she notices his leering, she shows no signs of it. Smiling as ever. Lips so wet she could dab them three times with a paper towel and they'd still be moist as hell.

Here in this diner, Jim is a known entity. A regular. A familiar face. He didn't plan it this way. He typically prefers anonymity, wants to interact with the people while remaining disentangled. Unknown and unknowable.

But he sensed the opposite happening here with Betsy, and he let it happen. Liked it in a weird way.

Perhaps it was Jim who liked it, Jim who let it happen.

Jim. The wild card. Unpredictable. The mysterious stranger looking out through his eyes.

And he wonders of Betsy for the first time: Does she always make sure to wait on him for the tips? Or could it be something else? Something more?

He sips the coffee. Considers adding a little plastic cup of creamer and decides against it. It's good today. Not at all acrid like it sometimes gets, none of that burned note that lingers on his tongue. Must be freshly brewed. Not having cooked down into black sludge on the goddamn burner for four hours does wonders for its flavor.

He severs the pointy tip of his slice of apple pie with the side of his fork, spears it, and shovels it into his maw. Delicious as always. Some burst of spice in there he can never quite identify. Something exotic, maybe. Nutmeg or some fucking thing his family could never afford.

Betsy catches his eye from behind the counter. Her smile faltering for the first time that he can remember.

He follows her gaze to the TV mounted in the corner above the counter, and what does he see?

Fire. His fire.

The flames lick out from the doors and windows of the blackening church. Melting. Consuming. Chewing it up.

Firemen in the foreground of the shot spray jets of water in every orifice of the structure, but the endless streams seem powerless against the destructive orange engulfing this place. Producing a little steam here and there but reducing the shriveling destruction of the church not at all. The news producers must love this footage as much as he does, as often as they keep playing it.

"Ain't that awful?" Betsy says to no one. He can hear the fear in her voice, the somber melody, the tiniest tremble to her words.

"Hell of a fire," Jim says, shaking his head. He can't help but smile a little.

She looks at him, then. Really looks. That scared expression still adorns her face, corners of the mouth turned down, a sag around the eyes that seems to carry much worry.

And for a second, he thinks maybe she sees him. Looks through the artifice to see him for real. Fears him. Knows the awe-inspiring power that he wields. And maybe that excites her. Compels her. Confounds her. Arouses her.

"It's just so visceral," she says. "So horrific. Dying that way."

She shudders as she says it, and he can see how stimulated she is, body wavering just like the shimmer of those gasoline fumes in his imagination.

And Jim wants something. Jim wants something bad.

He wolfs down the rest of the pie in three bites. Chews. Swallows. Washes it down with the scalding black brew.

And Jim stands. Approaches the woman behind the counter.

Their eyes lock, some invisible beam snapping his pupils to hers as though by way of electromagnetic force.

He doesn't think. Doesn't blink. Doesn't hesitate.

He lets the words, Jim's words, come pouring out of his mouth.

"I come down here all the time. I started thinking about that, you know? And I didn't know why that was. Ain't like the food is so great. No offense. But I see you when I'm down here, and I like seeing you. Really like it. So I guess that must be it."

He hesitates a moment there. Lowers his sunglasses to the tip of his nose so they can make real eye contact before he blurts out the climax of his speech — a move he thinks the cocky hero might have pulled in a 1980's action movie, back when movies still kicked ass.

"Bottom line, what I'm trying to spit out is this: You wanna get a cup of coffee with me one of these days? I can take you someplace a little nicer than this."

He shrugs one shoulder as he speaks, exuding nonchalance, and he sounds strong. Sounds confident. Sounds just like a man who knows what he wants and is well accustomed to getting it, sounds just like the Jim they all know and love around these parts.

But her smile falters harder than before, even the moisture on her lips suddenly seeming to die back to a faint dampness. That inviting lushness wilting all at once. Her head starts shaking a "no" before she speaks the rejection.

"I'm sorry, honey. I don't date customers. Official company policy, you could say. Had a couple bad experiences."

Her eyelids crinkle up as she talks, her makeup cracking a little. She looks much older now.

Jim blinks hard once. Slides the sunglasses back up to the bridge of his nose. Then he nods. Thumps the counter lightly with the heel of his hand.

"Oh. Right on."

He doesn't sound deflated. Doesn't sound particularly invested. Doesn't sound vulnerable at all.

The waves of lava inside lurch up the walls of his skull, ache only to burst forth in a molten tidal wave, to melt, to burn, to destroy.

To incinerate.

To kill everything he touches.

He somehow remains upright, though he can't feel his legs as he walks back to his table and leaves his usual tip.

CHAPTER 23

The SUV rips out of the diner's parking lot and scuttles up a hill. His foot jams the accelerator. The vehicle turning savage at his touch, a hateful machine, growling like some psycho dog frothing at the fucking mouth.

He still sees her, Betsy, appearing there in his mind's eye, stupid makeup cracking like old stucco around her eyes, and he still wants her just as bad as ever.

Jim wants and cannot have. Not supposed to work that way, is it?

He grips the wheel tighter. Feels the skin at his knuckles pulled taut. Feels the vibration of the churning engine in the meat of his hands.

Rage. Pain. A fire inside.

In moments like these, he thinks pain and anger are the same thing coming out in different ways. Pain is bleeding internally, all the wet red gushing and sloshing around inside that bag of skin. Wounds no one can see. Wounds that cannot heal. Like dry rot in a wall.

Anger takes the same feelings and turns them outward, fuels the aggressive part of him that wants to get hands-fucking-on with whoever made him feel this way.

Shank. Bludgeon. Kill.

Attack. Attack. Attack.

Cover the whole world in gasoline, acetone, ethanol.

Set the fucking night on fire.

He catches his reflection in the rearview. Peels away the

sunglasses. Looks himself in the bloodshot eyes.

The world does not care about you. It would never accept you as you are. So fuck it. Let it burn.

Now he slows, drifts to a stop at a red light, and the hair on his forearms stands up tall. Overwhelming to suddenly go still after all that rushing forward. The car's growl trims back to a muted purr. Sounds good now that he got that damn belt fixed.

Feels empty to stop pressing onward. Hollow. All things turning weightless. Like nothing that happened back in that diner was real. Like his wounds themselves aren't real. Just more figments in his head to keep him company.

Imaginary friends, right? Just hangin' out with Jim.

Wait. He clenches his jaw as the question occurs to him: Is Jim his only friend? Maybe. Maybe so.

No. Fuck that.

Fire. Fire is the only friend he will ever need.

He licks his lips. Turns from the windshield to face the screen out the driver's side window instead, like changing the channel.

The sun rises from the east, a blushing red rising from the ocean at the horizon. Fitting, he thinks.

Seeing red. Inside and out.

And looking out the window at the sky gone scarlet, he knows now. He knows just what to do.

The light turns green.

Go.

CHAPTER 24

The sunlight reflecting off of the LAPD building changed the strange glass cube from silver to gold that afternoon. Darger met up with Officers Klootey and Bishop in the parking lot behind headquarters and followed them to a parking garage where they climbed into Bishop's personal vehicle — a spotless Honda CRV, red, with the new car smell still intact.

"Gonna be a long shift. We should grab some grub," Klootey said.

"I have to stop for gas anyway. We can load up then."

"Nah, man. I'm talking about real food. There's an In-N-Out on the way," Klootey said, then turned in his seat to face her. "You like burgers, Agent Darger?"

"Who doesn't?"

"That settles it. To the In-N-Out, my good sir."

Bishop winced.

"In-N-Out is so sloppy."

"That's what's good about it."

"Yeah, but this is a new car. Tanya will have my ass if I mess up our new ride."

"Jeeee-sus," Klootey said, rolling his eyes. "I'd call you pussy-whipped right now, but I wouldn't want to offend the lady."

"Oh, that's nice. Real nice, man."

"I'm fucking serious, Bishop. You've gone limp-dick on me. You come out for Friday night brewskies and leave after one beer?"

Darger started to feel a bit uncomfortable with the tone of the conversation. She would have wondered if they'd forgotten she was in the backseat had Klootey not just mentioned her.

"I told you we were meeting her parents for brunch in the morning."

"Brunch! Fuck me, dude. This is exactly what I'm talking about. Ever since you got engaged, it's like…" Klootey's face darkened.

Darger got the sense of a married couple bickering, when it started out good-natured and suddenly turned bitter. She held her breath, bracing herself for an awkward shift in mood.

"It's like what?"

Klootey blinked, as if sweeping away whatever he'd been about to say next. Then he grinned and socked Bishop in the arm rapidly, reminding Darger of one of those punching nun toys.

"I'm just saying, I miss the Bishop that used to kick ass instead of kissing ass."

The car jerked to the left as Bishop raised his elbow to try to defend himself from Klootey's punches.

"Knock it off, dickhead! I'm trying to drive."

Despite the fact that Klootey relented, Bishop scowled over at his partner.

"I'll get you your goddamn In-N-Out, but if I hear one more word about me being whipped, I'm gonna pull this car over and show you what a whipping is."

A demonic smile spread over Klootey's mouth.

"Whatever you say, man. But I don't know how you're gonna manage to whip anyone's ass when your balls are locked securely in your girlfriend's purse. Hey, maybe you can ask her to let you get 'em out — like before this supposed whipping, I mean — but I doubt she'll let you. From what I can see, your girlfriend runs a pretty tight ship."

Shaking his head, Bishop signaled for a right turn.

"She's my fiancée. And you're an asshole."

Klootey only cackled in response.

At the gas station, Bishop got out to pump gas, and Darger accompanied Klootey inside to procure beverages and snacks. There was nothing worse than a stakeout without ample food and drink.

Mountain Dew was Klootey's beverage of choice. He stocked up on half a dozen 1-liter bottles of the stuff, though she presumed he would split them with his partner. Darger stuck with water. As tempting as something caffeinated was, she had to consider her bladder. The guys could guzzle their Mountain Dew all afternoon long, and when nature called, all they had to do was find a secluded corner in which to relieve themselves. Darger wasn't so lucky.

But she'd done enough stakeouts now to know her limitations. As long as she stuck to water and paced herself throughout the evening, she'd be fine.

Along with the water, she grabbed a bag of peanut M&M's and some potato chips and met up with Klootey at the register.

"Listen, don't go flashing those peanut M&M's in front of Bishop. Ever since his neutering, he's been very sensitive at the sight of any nuts and balls and so forth. Grapes. I even saw him tear up over a bag of baby carrots once."

"Got it. I'll be discreet."

The smile on his face vanished, and he leaned closer.

"So hey, I'm glad I got you in here alone," he said, glancing through the front windows of the gas station in the direction where his partner stood pumping gas. "Bishop's a great guy. My best friend. But he did two tours on a tank crew in Iraq, and his ears are all fucked up. You ever hear the main gun of a tank being fired? Thing's basically a cannon, so imagine standing right next to that thing when it goes off. You gotta speak up when you talk to him. And really enunciate, you know?"

Darger nodded.

"Yeah. Thanks for the heads up."

"Not a problem," Klootey said.

Back on the road, Bishop made good on his promise to stop for burgers. Darger and Bishop ordered their burgers "animal style," which came with pickles, grilled onions, extra sauce, and a bit of mustard fried with the patty. Klootey opted for the 3x3 — essentially a triple cheeseburger.

Five minutes later, they were parked a block away from Ivan Sablatsky's house. Plucking the radio from the mount on the dash, Klootey contacted the surveillance detail already in place.

"This is Bobcat, in position at the corner of Drake and Mount Olive."

The radio crackled and then a voice said, "Roger that, Bobcat. Cobra, you can take off now."

Down the street, a dark gray Ford Fusion pulled from the curb. As it passed by, Luck waved at them from the backseat.

Bishop raised an eyebrow at his partner.

"Bobcat?"

Shaping his fingers into claws, Klootey imitated the sound a growling cat would make. He grabbed for the paper bag of food and rifled around for his burger.

"You said you didn't care what our codename was."

"That was before I knew you were gonna pick something like Bobcat."

"You got a problem with bobcats in particular?"

"Just seems lame."

"This from a guy who's worried sick about eating burgers in his crossover, saying in earnest, and I quote, 'Tanya will have my ass.' End quote."

Bishop grumbled something, but Darger couldn't make out the words.

Klootey handed out the food, each of them receiving a paper-wrapped burger and cardboard sleeve of fries.

"Y'all are nasty with that 'animal style' nonsense," Klootey commented. "Mustard does not belong on a burger."

Ignoring him, Bishop angled so he could see Darger in the rearview mirror.

"So how come you aren't taking your own shifts?" Bishop asked, mouth full of half-chewed French fries. "You and Luck, I mean."

Darger took a bite of her burger. She'd had In-N-Out a few times before, and in the interim, she always convinced herself that maybe it wasn't as good as she remembered, not as good as the hype. But she was wrong every time.

She swallowed the food and took a drink to help wash it down.

"I probably shouldn't say anything, but we were explicitly asked to play tag-along."

"Why? Doesn't the FBI do surveillance?"

Darger suddenly remembered Klootey warning her about Bishop's hearing loss. She'd forgotten until now.

"We do," she said, speaking more loudly.

"So they can't be worried you're gonna fuck it up somehow."

Shaking her head, Darger picked up a fry, then thought better of it. It was easier to speak clearly if her mouth wasn't stuffed with food.

"I think it's more about who gets all the credit when we bring this guy down," she said, making sure to enunciate each word.

Bishop took a long pull from his drink.

"Who gives a fuck about credit?"

With a shrug, Darger said, "Not me."

"You're telling me we're doing round-the-clock surveillance, and we could have a whole extra team to take one of these shifts. But instead, the higher-ups want to saddle you and Luck with babysitters to make sure you don't try to steal all the glory?"

"Pretty much."

"Ree-diculous."

"I couldn't agree more," Darger said, tearing off a hunk of cheeseburger with her incisors.

"Can I ask you something, though?" Bishop said.

Darger chewed and swallowed.

"Sure." Her voice was loud and clear.

"Why are you yelling?"

A loud hissing sound emanated from Klootey's mouth. It was a moment before Darger realized he was laughing.

"Aw, man," Bishop said, shaking his head. "The hard-of-hearing joke again?"

The laughter shifted to coughing. Klootey must have

inadvertently inhaled some of his food in all the hilarity.

Bishop ate a fry and stared at his partner.

"You really are an idiot."

This nor the choking dampened Klootey's amusement. He continued half-coughing, half-chuckling for the next several minutes.

CHAPTER 25

They'd been parked outside the Sablatsky residence for three hours with nothing to report. The In-N-Out was long gone, the wrappers and cardboard cartons from the fries stuffed into the takeout bag. A faint aroma of fryer grease and onions permeated the car.

Darger took a sip of water. She didn't have to pee yet, so that was good.

The bright yellow of the bag of M&Ms caught her eye. She looked away, but she could hear the candy inside, begging to be eaten. She wasn't really hungry, but she was bored. And that was the real reason you brought ample snacks on a stakeout.

The plastic crinkled as she tore the bag open. She grabbed a handful and set the bag in one of the cup holders in the front console so everyone had easy access. Soon the car was filled with the sound of three mouths pulverizing chocolate, candy coating, and peanuts. The noise reminded her of footsteps on a gravel path.

Suddenly the radio on the dash squawked.

"We've got eyes," the voice said. "The subject has exited the residence."

The chewing in the CRV stopped. No one breathed.

"He's on foot, heading toward the street. He's carrying something," the voice continued.

Darger and the two policemen stared intently out through the windshield, waiting for him to come into view. A moment later, they got their first glimpse of Ivan Sablatsky in the flesh.

He was on the shorter side of average height, muscular, and he carried a plastic shopping bag tied at the top in one hand.

"I think we caught him taking out the trash, boys," the voice on the police radio announced.

Indeed, Sablatsky proceeded to the bin near the curb, flipped open the lid, and tossed the plastic bag inside. He closed the lid and headed back toward the house.

Darger continued to study him for as long as he was in sight. His brown hair was trimmed into a tight crew cut. Below that, a well-kept goatee. She knew from his driver's license that he was 26-years-old and had green eyes.

When Sablatsky disappeared from their view, Klootey swiveled in his seat to face her.

"What do you think?"

"About him being our guy?"

"Yeah," Klootey said, taking a few M&Ms and tossing them in his mouth. "From a profiling standpoint."

"The thing that stuck out most for me was that he seemed very neat. The crew cut. Fussy-looking facial hair. That takes some upkeep. And did you see his belt?"

"Looked like one of our duty belts."

"Yep. Classic law enforcement wannabe," Darger said.

"But why would law enforcement appeal to him? Or any of these guys?" Klootey asked. "You said before it's not uncommon. But I mean, they're criminals, right? Outlaws. Isn't wanting to be a cop like the opposite of that?

"Sort of. And maybe even that sense of irony is what appeals to them," Darger said, leaning back against the seat. "The idea that they could be in this respectable position in the community while also committing heinous crimes. Look at

Joseph DeAngelo, the guy accused of being the Golden State Killer. Thirteen murders, over fifty rapes, and at least a hundred burglaries, all while he's a police sergeant in charge of a task force focused on burglaries. It's like they're getting away with a little something extra."

Loosening the cap on her water, Darger drank before continuing.

"But the main attraction is the power that comes with being a cop. You get guns, fast cars, and best of all, authority. Cops are to be obeyed. And for someone that feels a chronic underlying sense of insecurity, that would be very appealing."

Klootey stared at her for some time, squinting slightly, like he was deciding just how much of this profiling malarkey to take seriously. Finally he shrugged and let his gaze slide back to the M&Ms. He snatched up a palm-full of candy and shook them in his fist so they rattled.

"Not to brag, but I've actually got a profiling system of my own. The pop-psychology version, I guess you could say."

"Oh yeah?"

Groaning, Bishop rubbed at his eyes.

"Here we go. Do I really have to hear this again?"

"Take your boy Luck, for example," Klootey said, ignoring the protests of his partner. "He drives a Lexus, right?"

Darger nodded.

"See, I think that's hilarious."

"Why is that?"

"A Lexus is just a Toyota that costs more. Made in the same factories and everything. From what I see, they don't even look much different. The Lexus might have gold accents instead of chrome, but the body shape is about the same. At least Cadillac has the decency to make huge boats instead of just putting a different logo on a fuckin' Malibu and charging more for it, you know?"

"Is that true?" Darger said, leaning forward to snatch a few M&Ms from the bag. "They're literally made in the same factories?"

"Oh yeah. Same for a bunch of brands. Domestically speaking, Lincolns are just Fords, and like I said, Cadillacs are Chevys. But Infinitis are Nissans. Acuras are Hondas."

"Huh. So do you think most of the people buying the luxury version know they're basically just buying an overpriced brand name?"

Klootey shook his head.

"Some of them must. But it's really only about the idea of luxury, anyway. People like Luck don't pay more because they think the product is better. They pay more because of what they want to believe about themselves. The story they want to tell themselves and everyone else. It's a status symbol above all, a way to feel better about yourself. This is a person who wants to feel important and needs other people to feel that way as well."

"Oh," Darger said. "I thought you were going to say he was overcompensating for… you know… what's the euphemism I'm looking for? Small sausage."

Klootey laughed.

"Hey, maybe some of that, too. Anyway, I could sense that about ol' Agent Luck before I even saw his ride. Just has that… fancy lad feel about him, I guess. The stiff posture. The slick haircut. I would've guessed BMW or something for him, maybe even a Mercedes, but… a Lexus? Come on, dude."

Darger smiled to herself, thinking about the crappy

minivan Luck drove when she'd first met him. He'd certainly upgraded his image in that regard.

"Well, now I'm curious what kind of car you drive."

"I don't," Klootey said.

"You don't… have a car?"

"Nope," he said, crossing his arms. "Southern California is made for an open-air experience. I ride a Harley."

"Interesting. So you bring an outsider's perspective to this whole thing."

Bishop scoffed, but Klootey seemed to like the idea.

"Exactly."

"OK, then," she said. "What about me? Any guesses about what kind of car I drive back home?"

Klootey's eyes narrowed to slits.

"Hm… Well, you seem like you'd value individuality quite a bit, so that'd almost make me think of something like a MINI Cooper. You can customize them pretty much however you want right on the website. Get one that's exactly to your taste in every way: color, tires, exterior accents. That's why you see MINIs with the union jack on them and crap like that. However…" He sucked his teeth, thinking. "Something about the MINI isn't quite right for you. A little too rich for your blood, I think. Lacks practicality. You'd go for something no-frills. Efficiency above all else."

There was another pause, which Darger suspected was mostly for drama.

"That makes my final answer a Toyota Prius."

Darger stopped chewing.

"Well, damn. You're right."

"Don't tell him that," Bishop moaned. "Now he's really

never gonna shut up about this."

"Hey, I have to give credit where it's due. That was some decent profiling."

"Aw, I don't pretend to be anything fancy. I just call 'em like I see 'em, Agent Darger."

The keywords of Klootey's speech echoed in Darger's head: Practical. Efficient. No frills. She couldn't help but feel a surge of pride. She wasn't one of the people trying to prove something to the world with her car. That had to be a good thing, right?

"So based on your explanation, I take it that you see the Prius as the superior choice to Luck's Lexus?"

Mouth full of M&Ms, Klootey said, "Oh. Fuck no."

Darger flinched. Her mouth popped open.

"A Prius is a soulless machine designed for yuppies and their kin," Klootey said. "Let's just say the things should come with a goddamn Apple bumper sticker pre-attached. And every time you start it up, it should just automatically whisk you through a Starbucks drive-thru."

He paused to chew and swallow.

"It's more like driving a computer than a car, anyway. You jam on the accelerator, and the thing whirs a little like a laptop fan kicking on or something. No soul at all. I mean, say what you will about the upper crust wannabe snobs like Luck who drive a Lexus — at least the thing is a real fuckin' car."

Darger started laughing then.

"No offense," Klootey said, popping another handful of candy into his maw.

Still chuckling, Darger shook her head.

"None taken."

CHAPTER 26

The surveillance on Sablatsky was done in eight-hour rotations. When the teams assigned to the graveyard shift arrived at 11 PM, Bishop put the CRV in gear and headed back to LAPD headquarters to drop Darger off.

Luck called as she was walking to her rental. She paused to dig the keys from her bag and answered the phone.

"Anything happen?" he asked.

"Oh yeah. You missed the exciting moment when Sablatsky took his garbage out."

"He barely moved while we were there, too. Doesn't seem to be a particularly active guy."

"If he's our arsonist, we'll catch him in the act sooner or later. As long as he doesn't figure out that we're watching," Darger said.

Klootey's pseudo-profiling came to her then, and she couldn't help but antagonize Luck a little.

"Did you know your car is just an overpriced Toyota?"

"What?"

"A Lexus is just a Toyota with gold trim instead of chrome."

"That's... not true," Luck said, though he didn't sound very sure.

"It is. They're made in the same factories and everything."

"Yeah, but... I mean, I've driven Toyotas before. It's an entirely different driving experience."

Darger scoffed.

173

"Driving experience?"

"Yeah, a Lexus is smoother. Quieter. And all of the control buttons are easier to press."

Laughing fully now, Darger pressed the key fob to unlock her door.

"You're joking, right? The buttons are easier to press?"

"Hey, some of us care about the little things, OK? The details."

"I guess," she said, snickering. "I'll talk to you about your 'little things' tomorrow."

On the drive to her hotel, it occurred to Darger that she hadn't eaten since that afternoon. She considered the bag of peanut M&Ms they'd polished off over the course of the evening and amended that thought: she hadn't eaten real food since the afternoon.

The red and yellow rotating sign for a Chinese restaurant caught her eye ahead. Her stomach gurgled in response, and she pulled into the parking lot. A few minutes later, she was back on the road with a bag of takeout.

The first thing she did upon entering her hotel room was kick off her boots. Then she walked down the hall in her stocking feet to grab a Coke from the vending machine. Back in her room, she hopped on the bed and dug into the chicken lo mein and spring rolls she'd picked up.

There was a late night talk show on the TV, celebrities having some canned conversation about their canned celebrity movies and canned celebrity lives. She wasn't particularly interested in watching it, but left it on for background noise. She leaned back against the pillows. It felt good to stretch out her legs after eight hours hunched in the backseat of a car. She sighed, realizing she might be looking forward to days or even weeks with more of the same. How long would they have to watch Sablatsky before he did something incriminating?

Darger's phone chimed out Tchaikovsky's "Dance of the Sugar Plum Fairies." Her hands were greasy from the spring rolls, so she used her pinky finger to nudge the screen closer.

It was Beck.

Wiping her fingers on a paper napkin, Darger answered the phone.

"Agent Darger, this is Georgina Beck. I'm sorry for calling so late."

"No need to apologize. What can I do for you?"

"Well, I was off duty today. We took the kids to Knotts Berry Farm, something we do every year around this time." Beck sighed. "I feel like an idiot telling you this, but I left my phone at home. So when my office called this morning to tell me you guys had a person of interest, I didn't get the message. Obviously. By the time we got home, and dealt with the whole bedtime routine for the kiddos, I didn't even check my phone until a few minutes ago. Jeez Louise, I sound like the biggest flake in the world."

Darger chuckled.

"It's fine. Really. The only thing you missed out on today was a lot of boring, uneventful surveillance."

"OK, but... I feel like you guys are working your tails off out there, and I just, you know, I want to contribute. All those people killed and wounded in the church fire... those are my people. They need justice, and well, it's my responsibility to get it for them."

Darger had an idea then. Chief Macklin might be opposed

to the FBI doing their own surveillance, but he could hardly stand in the way of Beck's department getting in on the action. A devious smile spread over her face. She could just hear Loshak's voice in her head, accusing her of stirring the pot. She couldn't help it, though. Sometimes the pot was just asking for it.

"What would you say to partnering up for a stakeout detail tomorrow?"

"Of course," Beck said. "What time?"

"The morning shift starts at 7 AM."

"I'll be there."

"Great. We can meet at my hotel."

CHAPTER 27

Night settles over the city in different shades — the degree of darkness dividing into sections by neighborhood. Downtown, the neon glows all night, bright and warm to the touch, but working one's way out toward the suburbs, the light pollution dims, softens, retreats. Weak streetlights try to fight off the shadows with mixed results. In some places, the light falls off entirely save for a sliver of moon and, of course, the stars — all those little pinpricks some trillions of miles away.

It's dark outside Betsy's apartment. Dark enough, anyway.

The waitress lives in Echo Park in one of those oversized Victorian houses dating back 100 years or so, now converted into four apartments by some slumlord who slapped tan vinyl siding on the place circa 1986 and has ever since left it to slowly rot in the California sun, the porch looking spongy and mossy and soft.

What catches Jim's eye is not the degrading porch, however, but the dumpster alongside the building. A mattress pokes out, its polyurethane foam the perfect fuel for his purposes — essentially petroleum in foam form. Each time his eyes crawl over that off-white rectangle protruding from the dumpster, his tongue flicks out to touch his lips.

He sits in his SUV for a long time, drumming his hands on the steering wheel, keeping up with the frenetic drumbeats of the fast songs playing softly on the stereo.

Waiting. Waiting for the last lights to go out in one of the upstairs apartments. For the last witness to wink off to

Sleepyland so he can get to it.

He shifts in his seat. Finds it increasingly difficult to sit still.

He pictures Betsy again. Drenched in gas. Slow blinking. That lighter creeping ever closer to her shimmering skin.

Hey, she made her choice. No turning back.

A giddiness comes over him. A restless on and off giggling that always seems to afflict him just before a fire, like the prospect of torching something or someone somehow turns him into a hyper child. ADHD.

His eyes outline the mattress again. God, it's almost perfect. The discarded slab of bedding reaches right up to touch the vinyl siding, and some part of him wonders if the piss-stained Sealy broke out into a sweat at the sight of him. Do these household objects he sacrifices to the gods harbor any fear of him, tremble when he comes near? He believes they should.

Traffic shouldn't be a problem. Not on a quiet little side street like this one. So long as no one comes by just as he's standing at the dumpster, it should be no problem at all.

Tonight it's paraffin that'll do the deed. A white plastic bottle of lamp oil sits on the passenger seat next to him. He paid cash for it at some dollar store an hour south of here. No cameras. No credit card records. Gotta start throwing off the scent, mixing things up. Patterns of behavior are what get most idiots caught. He must avoid them.

He only waits a few heartbeats after the last light goes out upstairs, though in that short slice of time, a sheen of sweat already slicks his skin. He tastes the salt of it the next time his tongue flicks out to touch his lips.

The giggles have fled him. Instead an almost religious level of stimulation quakes in the center of his person. A thrill so powerful that he feels like he needs to throw up.

He swallows a few times in a dry throat. Tries to shake that vomitous feeling now swelling in his middle. It always feels like this right before. An intense, oddly specific nausea, like spaghetti will come flinging out of his throat, tangled cords of it slithering past his teeth. Always spaghetti, whether he has eaten any recently or not.

No more waiting.

He opens the door. Arms and legs shaking from the adrenaline. Steps down into the night. Clutches the plastic bottle of paraffin to his chest. Closes the door ever so gently behind him.

The night clings to him. Heavy night air with a chill to its touch as though he can feel the darkness itself. Makes his skin crawl with goose bumps just beneath his shoulders.

He crosses the street. Veers toward the alley. Watches the dumpster grow larger. The camera in his head zooming in for the close-up.

He peels open the tab on top of the bottle. Squeezes. Tiny spurts of liquid paraffin jet out, douse strips of the mattress. The shine of it somehow discernible as oily under the yellow glow of the streetlight, that touch of efflorescence.

His shoulder blades rattle a little now as he arcs more and more ropes of paraffin onto the mattress. Hands jittery. Arms spasming.

But Jim doesn't get scared, he tells himself. Jim lives for these moments. That stretch of quiet focus right before all hell breaks loose? Jim fucking lives for that.

Headlights light up the intersection a half a block down, and Jim holds his breath. The growl of a car's engine swells in the dark, but the sports car zooms past, unknowing, uninterested. The lights gone faster than they appeared.

Jim blinks a few times. Close. Too close.

What if it'd turned down Betsy's street? Would that have saved her? Would Jim have backed down?

He mulls it a second. He thinks not. Jim would press on in the face of such adversity. For better or worse.

In any case, best to be quick now. Best to be done with it.

He leans into the dumpster, his top half lowered into the shadowed place. He squints. Sees just what he wants to see. Squirts a few more spritzes of paraffin on some broken down cardboard boxes at the bottom of the dumpster. Someone too lazy to put this in recycling? For shame.

Good news for Jim, though. Better to light it below the fold, so to speak. To give himself time to get away before the blaze really picks up.

His lighter snicks in his hand, little gritty wheel spinning against his thumb, and then the flame snaps to life.

He gasps a little at the sight of it. A reverent breath like he's witnessing something spiritual here, something mystical. A glowing, flickering thing he holds in his hand. So small yet so goddamn powerful. This little light of his could bring down buildings, turn cars to smoldering rubble, melt faces clean off of skulls.

And with him at the helm, it would do just that, again and again and again.

He tosses the rest of the bottle of fuel into the fire.

CHAPTER 28

His body trembles as he watches the fire from across the street. Squirming in the bucket seat of the SUV like some strung-out junkie about to get off after much too long. Maybe that isn't so far off from what he is.

Black smoke twirls up from below the mattress, the gyrating cloud breaching the open lid, expanding into the night like a living, thrashing thing. Thick coils of it partially block his view of the fire itself. Solid in some areas. Gauzy in others.

The flames rage higher and higher. Growing. Becoming. The tallest orange tendril is a nasty spiraling thing reaching out for the siding of the building. Closer. Closer.

He hears it breathing, sizzling, snapping at the foam. Melting it to a plastic puddle. The sound in some ways more intimate than the sight of the fire, more personal, more sensual.

And his arms fold in front of him as though to embrace himself, his hands clasping the opposite upper arms, massaging at the meat of himself. Skin so slick with sweat it almost feels like touching a fish now, something gutted and wrapped in brown paper at the supermarket.

Panting like a beast. All his skin tingling with an electric throb. Pins and needles prodding every follicle. Little pokes like the time he touched an electric fence as a kid.

It's too much. Overwhelming. Sensory overload. Even still, he only wants more. More more more. Smoke it. Snort it. Put it in his blood. Boil this destruction on a spoon and slam it into his veins with a syringe.

The twisting orange flame touches the siding now. Little licks at first. Lapping at it almost daintily like a snake's tongue flicking out of its mouth. Something tender about the contact. Gentle. Almost loving.

But soon the beige vinyl siding begins to bend and buckle and shrivel and blacken. He can see it go malleable, the textured vinyl going smooth, turning to goo. Softening like a milkshake. Liquefying.

And it weeps now. Melted vinyl seeping down the side of the building in slow motion. Viscous vinyl jelly a consistency somewhere between taffy and pudding.

"Yes," he says, breathing it more than speaking it. "Yes. Yes. Yes."

In the mirror, dilated pupils stare back at him. Gaping black pits where his irises should be. A glimpse into the void within. Whatever secrets might wriggle in there almost visible in this moment. The wild animal inside almost brought to the surface. Almost.

A big patch of vinyl falls into the dumpster, stretching two strings of melted goo off each side like strands of drool hanging from the corners of a St. Bernard's mouth.

Yes.

The fire brightens as it climbs to the top of the mattress and wraps itself fully around the foam thing. Embracing it. Engulfing it. The orange now veers toward white.

Bigger. Faster. Hotter. Meaner.

Fuck yes.

And it occurs to him that this fire is his. His doing. His being. This uncontrollable force he loosed upon the world. His power. His self projected outward onto the world.

This little light of mine.

His eyes water from staring into the brightness, but he dare not look away. Dare not miss so much as a second until he hears sirens.

Now the vinyl seems to fry in place. Bubbling. Blackening. Sticking to the plywood like cooked bits of scrambled egg sticking to the edge of the pan.

The wood begins to glow right along with the mattress. Blazing and brilliant and ready to go up any second now.

And he can see her in his imagination. Cowering. Whimpering. The fire soon closing around her like a bear trap. No hesitation. No mercy.

And his body shakes. Sweat pouring down his face. Electricity thrumming through every cell of his being.

But then the mattress shifts. Lowers. Sagging some in the middle. Sinking.

The fireball of foam slides deeper into the dumpster. Releases the wall from its touch. A plume of sparks rise from the point of impact, bursting out of the dumpster and floating up — the fire's last hurrah.

And the red coals where the plywood had started to ignite dim to black all at once. Still smoking. Still smoldering. But fading.

No.

The mattress sinks further. Most of it now encased in the metal walls of the dumpster.

The word sunk echoes in his head.

It feels like something has been torn from his chest. Some vital organ ripped clean. Still beating. A gaping vacancy where it's supposed to be.

A hole. A hole in his being.

The fire still rages in the dumpster, but it's contained now. Caged like a zoo animal. Neutered and toothless. No longer a threat. No longer the wild, savage thing it was just seconds ago.

His fingers fumble for the keys at the ignition. He starts the engine and shifts into drive in one motion. Moving on. Moving away. He wishes this was another homeless face he could forget, but no. This is more than that.

The emptiness creeps over him again. Some void opening in his belly. All those jittery stimulated feelings fleeing him, leaving him alone again.

No joy. No satisfaction.

He passes under streetlight after streetlight as he flees the scene. Those metal limbs reaching out above him to hold up their glowing bulbs to the heavens for no good reason. Feels like a dotted line hung up there, light and dark doing battle as always. Marking the time. Blinking. Counting down to nothing.

Again he sees it. The mattress sagging, sinking, falling into a fiery heap in the dumpster.

All his efforts thwarted just like that. The damsel escapes the villain with ease. She didn't even need a hero to intervene on her behalf.

He twists his hands on the steering wheel. Tries to push the pictures in his head down, away.

When the fire fails, he fails. When the fire is nothing, he is nothing.

He is no one. The worst thing you can be in L.A.

There exists no fate lonelier than being nobody.

CHAPTER 29

Pale yellow light seeped in through the curtains of Darger's hotel room. She'd woken early to make a donut and coffee run before Beck arrived, and now she set the food and drink down on the dresser and shoved the curtains aside. Might as well have a little light in the room while she waited for her ride.

She ate half a donut and checked her watch. A quarter to six. Beck should arrive any minute now.

Just as she reached for the other half of her donut, a digital chime spurted from her phone. It was a text from Captain Beck.

I'm here.

Darger hoisted the box of donuts and the cardboard beverage carrier and headed down to the lobby.

Beck waited at the curb in her Nissan. As Darger climbed into the passenger seat, she noticed the package of assorted muffins in the backseat. There were also bottles of orange juice and water.

She glanced at Beck, who was eyeballing the coffee and donuts. Their eyes met, and they both started to laugh.

"Well, we won't go hungry."

Fastening her seatbelt, Darger directed Beck to Sablatsky's house. It was another perfect California day, with clear skies and just a hint of a breeze. Darger turned Beck's radio to the channel the surveillance detail was using and announced their arrival.

"Unicorn is on the scene."

"Greetings, Unicorn. This is Mountain Lion. If you're all set here, we'll return to the den now."

"Roger that. Have a good one, Mountain Lion."

The tail lights of a black Jeep Cherokee came to life, and Beck slid into the parking spot behind it. The driver leaned over so his face was visible in the side mirror and gave them a nod before pulling into the street.

"Did I hear that right?" someone said over the radio. "Team Unicorn?"

Darger recognized Luck's voice. She squinted against the bright morning sun and spotted Luck's Lexus parked on the opposite side of the street.

"Considering we're the only all-female team on the detail, it seemed appropriate," she said. "Plus, unicorns symbolize wisdom."

"And which one of you is the wise one?" Luck teased.

Darger glared through the windshield, though she doubted Luck could make out her scowl at this distance.

"You know what a unicorn's horn symbolizes, don't you?" Darger asked.

"No."

"Stabbing idiots."

There was a burst of laughter over the radio, and then they went quiet. Darger pulled one of the cups of coffee from the drink carrier and lifted the lid.

Beck eyed it wistfully.

"God, that smells good."

"Well it's decaf, which I know is generally a sacrilege. But nothing really goes with donuts like coffee. The other two are hot water in case you'd prefer your herbal tea."

"Lord, no," Beck said, snatching up one of the coffees.

She sipped the steaming black brew and sighed.

"So close. And yet... there's something missing."

"Isn't that weird?" Darger said. "How you can just instantly tell it's decaf?"

Beck nodded.

"And it's not the taste, either. It's the texture, I think. Or maybe... am I crazy or does real coffee almost leave a little tingle on your tongue?"

Darger took a drink from her own cup.

"I'll let you know the next time I have some."

Frowning at the beverage in Darger's hand, Beck said, "I hope you're not drinking decaf on my account."

Darger's lips quirked into a smile.

"No, I have a strict No Caffeine policy during stakeouts. It's embarrassing to have to announce to the rest of the teams that you have to use the Little Girls' Room. Especially when you're the only woman on the detail."

"You need one of these," Beck said, patting her belly. "No one gives you any crap when you're pregnant."

The radio crackled, Luck's voice bursting through the static.

"How are you ladies doing over there?"

"We're fine," Darger answered.

"I just feel a little guilty, is all," he said. "Over here in my Lexus, we were just commenting on how comfortable the seats are. It's one of the many benefits of the brand, you know."

Beck frowned at her, looking perplexed.

"I was giving him shit about his Lexus being an overpriced Toyota," Darger explained. Into the radio, she said, "I'm happy for you, Luck. I know how delicate you are. Does the Lexus make you a glass of warm milk at bedtime, too?"

Chuckling, Beck helped herself to a donut.

"So what's up with you two?"

"Me and Luck?"

"Yeah."

"Nothing."

Beck arched one eyebrow.

"Nothing?"

"We dated. Briefly. And it was a long time ago."

Snapping her fingers, Beck said, "I knew there was something."

"How?"

"All that adorable banter? Dead giveaway."

Darger made a disgusted noise.

"What?" Beck asked.

"'Adorable banter.' Sounds like a phrase they'd use to pitch a really bad sitcom. I feel guilty subjecting other people to such a thing."

The police captain chuckled.

"It's not so bad," she insisted. "Anything to pass the time, right? Speaking of which, I've got a few podcasts we could listen to."

"Sure," Darger said. "If today turns out like yesterday, we're in for a very long, very boring day."

Tapping the screen of her phone, Beck loaded a podcast about conspiracy theories and the people who believe them. After that came a story about a police officer who had once been called to a car accident scene and found a chimpanzee driving the car.

Darger's attention waxed and waned. With her eyes glued

to Sablatsky's little yellow box of a house, she couldn't help but wonder what he was up to in there. Her mind concocted sinister scenarios, picturing him digitally stalking his next target via Google Maps or prepping one of his soda bottle gas cans. The next moment, she imagined him doing something mundane: sprawled out in an old chenille recliner watching ESPN news or feeding his pet goldfish (which was, as far as Darger knew, entirely imaginary).

It was easy to picture these guys up to nefarious things at all hours of the day, but the truth was, most of them lived pretty normal lives the 90% of the time they weren't committing heinous crimes. That's what made them so hard to spot. They hid in plain sight. Pretending to be normal folk, just like the rest.

They'd been on the detail for four hours when Beck blew out a long breath.

"I've been trying to fight the good fight, but at some point, it becomes a losing battle."

Darger had no idea what she was talking about, so she waited for Beck to explain further. The other woman threw her hands up.

"I have to pee."

"Oh," Darger said, laughing a little. "Me too."

"Yeah, but you could hold it if you had to. I'm jeopardizing the whole operation here with my weak bladder."

"They'll be fine. Sablatsky's probably in there trimming his toenails or something." Darger picked up the radio. "Hey, Toyota — oops… I mean, Timber Wolf. We need to make a quick pit stop if that's OK."

"Roger that, Unibrow. Timber Wolf will hold down the

fort."

Beck swung her neck around to make sure the way was clear before pulling into the street. As they passed the Lexus, Darger considered giving Luck the finger. Then she remembered Beck's comment about "adorable banter" and decided against it.

The marquee outside the gas station a few blocks from Sablatsky's place boasted 2-for-1 Nacho Cheese Filled Hot Dogs. Darger wondered — not for the first time — who bought gas station hot dogs. This new addition of cheese filling perplexed her even more.

She and Beck took turns using the facilities inside, and then headed back to the Altima. Darger twitched her shoulders and rolled her neck back and forth a few times before getting back in.

"I'll tell you what," she said, ducking into the passenger seat, "just being able to get out and stretch my legs for a few minutes? A dream. Not to mention being able to go to the bathroom. I'm good for another eight hours after that reset. I should team up with a pregnant woman for every stakeout detail."

"Or yourself," Beck said.

"Pardon?"

"Well, you could be your own pregnant lady."

Without intending to, Darger must have made a face, because Beck laughed.

"Sorry, that was supposed to be a joke, but I know some women are sensitive about that," she said. "I take it you're not big on the idea of kids?"

Shaking her head, Darger said, "Oh no. I love kids. I'd love to have kids, even. But the actual pregnancy part?" Darger made a noise. "It's so... weird."

Beck raised her eyebrows and looked down at her swollen midsection.

"Yeah, it is pretty dang weird, I guess. Kind of like having a little stowaway inside, helping itself to whatever it needs."

"Exactly!"

"But you get used to it," Beck insisted. "I had terrible morning sickness my first pregnancy. But the last two have been pretty smooth sailing. Knock on wood."

Back in place outside Sablatsky's house, Darger settled in for a few more hours of sitting. She fought the urge to doze off for a while, blinking and yawning every few seconds. She remembered suddenly that Beck had never reported back on what, if anything, she'd found on the owner of the old church.

Darger sat up straighter, stretching her shoulders a little.

"Did you ever get a chance to look at Howard Thorne's history?"

Beck gasped and smacker herself in the forehead.

"Georgina, you airhead!" she said, then sighed. "I meant to tell you first thing, and it just completely slipped my mind."

"Does that mean you found something?"

"Yes. I mean, no." Beck shook her head. "Jeez Louise, I'm even messing up the telling. We didn't find anything on Thorne. But we found something else."

"What is it?"

"Well, I had my guys go through the fires for the last five years, like you said."

Nodding, Darger waited for her to continue.

"We didn't find diddly. Nothing that matched our guy's

M.O., anyway." Beck held up a finger. "But then I went back a little further, and that's where things got interesting."

Darger was growing restless with Beck's protracted method of storytelling, but urged herself to be patient.

"Three summers in a row, there was a rash of small fires at different campgrounds in the county. The fire investigator at the time put them down as accidental. But in several of the fires, they found melted plastic bottles near the scene. And all of the fires had some kind of accelerant used."

"And they didn't figure arson?" Darger asked.

Shrugging, Beck said, "I talked to the guy. The arson investigator from back then. He said he figured it was idiots dousing their fires with lighter fluid or kerosene. People being stupid, not evil."

"How far back did you go?"

"This all took place ten, twelve years ago."

Darger pondered this, considered how to incorporate this new information with where they were in the investigation. She'd suspected before that the arsonist had been to the San Bernardino area before, that he hadn't chosen the church by accident. This could be the connection she'd been looking for.

"We need to find out if Sablatsky has ties to your area. Maybe he had family there or something."

"Exactly what I was thinking," Beck said.

They settled back into a pensive silence. Beck had unearthed something. That was good. But for the moment, it didn't change the fact that they were stuck in a holding pattern of watching and waiting.

At a quarter to three, Darger let out a long sigh. Their shift was almost done. Another day of nothing.

"I'm gonna get myself a pocketknife and a wooden stick," she said. "Every day we spend out here, I'll carve a notch into the wood."

"And in the meantime, you can teach yourself to whittle." Darger laughed.

"Maybe that's not a bad idea. My partner's always bugging me to get a hobby."

A few minutes later, a silver Honda arrived on the scene.

"Manta Ray, reporting for duty," a voice over the radio said.

"What do you say we let Luck's team leave first?" Darger suggested. "Considering they let us go for our mid-day pit stop?"

"Fine with me," Beck said.

"You go ahead, Timber Wolf," Darger said into the radio. "You guys take off."

They watched the silver car trade places with the Lexus on the opposite side of the street. As Luck drew alongside them, he slowed and rolled down his window.

"It's almost a shame for this shift to end, what with my Lexus being so dang comfortable."

Suddenly the radio squawked.

"He's on the move!"

"What?"

Darger couldn't see Sablatsky's house. Luck's stupid Lexus was blocking her view. She scooted forward in her seat just in time to see Sablatsky's SUV reverse rapidly from his driveway and speed away.

"There's a goddamn school bus over here. We're blocked in," the other car reported. "I repeat, this is Manta Ray, and we are blocked in."

"Oh shit," Darger said. "Let's go."

Beck put the car in gear, but Luck's vehicle was pinning them to the curb. And he wasn't moving. He was staring at his own radio, seeming to not quite understand what was going on.

"Luck!" Darger shouted through the window.

His head snapped up.

"Move!"

"Fuck. Sorry," he said, rolling forward so they had room to merge into the street.

Beck cranked the wheel and gunned it out of the parking spot.

CHAPTER 30

The SUV rips out of the driveway. Something savage in the way he turns the wheel. Jams the accelerator. His body all tense, veins on his arms rippling, pulse banging like a war drum on the side of his neck.

He slept late. Still half under even now. But this is his chance. He's watched this target for weeks, got a feel for the schedule, balancing his ease of access with the ebb and flow of the traffic, the best day of the week, etc. Right now measures out as his best window of opportunity, and he slept through half of it.

Reminding himself this fact makes his mouth clench involuntarily. Jaw jutting back and forth whilst fully clamped down, teeth gritting out little sounds — bone grinding against bone.

He can't lose focus like that. Can't let up. Can't lose his edge.

Unless he wants to be no one forever, that is. Irrelevant. Never was. Forgotten. Then he's doing it just fucking right.

He fishes for his sunglasses in the center console as he drives. Fingers scuttling like crab legs, clambering over loose change, Kleenex, some ancient hair scrunchies, a bag of menthol cough drops that he can smell faintly at all times in here. At last they find the shape they seek, smooth plastic curves.

He slides the sunglasses on. Watches reality dim a few notches. Better. He's loath to admit it, but he's never fully Jim until he has these things covering his eyes, bending that harsh reality out there to better suit what he wants.

He takes a hard left, tires squealing, barely makes it. Almost missed the damn intersection because of the stupid sunglasses.

Get a grip, fuckhead. You're being very un-Jim.

He takes a few deep breaths. Needs to focus. For real.

You get one shot at this. Make it count.

At the next stoplight, he reaches under the sunglasses to scrub the sleep from his eyes with his knuckles. Wills the drowsiness to flee his body. Harnesses some kind of hate like a cramp in the center of his torso — a knot of discomfort just beneath his sternum. Focusing on it, he can channel that energy elsewhere. A warmth. A tingle. He directs the feeling to his hands, concentrating on them. Then to his feet.

Closing his eyes he sees this energy as a ball of orange light spreading outward from the center of his being to touch the rest of him, to brighten every cell. Light it the hell up. Make the whole thing glow with life.

He opens his eyes just as the light turns green.

And he can feel it as the SUV picks up speed again, as he takes in the bustling street around him. The energy persists, that roiling warmth still occupying one part of his mind as he moves on.

Now he's focused. Now he's ready.

A few blocks down, he takes a right, and a little shimmer in the rearview catches his eye. Light reflects from a windshield that just traced his path around the corner. A dark sedan hovering a few car lengths back.

He scans his memory. Tries to remember how long the vehicle has been behind him, if he's ever seen it before today.

He's not sure.

It could be a tail. Could be. But it could also be paranoia, which Jim seems quite prone to. That might be the Achilles heel of old Jimbo now that he considers it — delusions of dread, his anxiety getting out of hand.

Better safe than sorry, no?

Yeah. Yep. He can't disagree with this particular voice. Paranoid or not, Jim is sure right about this one, the son of a bitch.

He scans the area. Ponders his options.

Pedestrians swamp this little shopping district. The mindless hoards carrying bags of fresh junk back to their cars, others setting off on missions to shop their hearts out.

Yes. A crowd. That will work.

He pulls over. Squeezes the SUV into a parking spot in front of a smoothie place. Kills the engine.

Waits. Holds still. Watches the mirror. Holds his breath.

The black sedan grows bigger and bigger in the rearview. Then it zooms past. Doesn't even hesitate.

He chuckles to himself. Shakes his head as he eyes Jim laughing along in the mirror. Just paranoia then. Good.

Still. Better to head in the rest of the way on foot. Just to be absolutely certain. The few minutes difference won't matter now.

He waits for a dead spot in the traffic and climbs out into the throng of shoppers. Head still swiveling to seek out that dark sedan and not finding it.

Maybe it doesn't matter either way. Five paces onto the sidewalk, the crowd swallows him up.

CHAPTER 31

Sablatsky's Mariner was not in sight as they sped down the road after him. Darger couldn't stop gritting her teeth, terrified that he was going to get away from them. If he managed to slip through surveillance and start another fire in that time, she was going to be furious with herself.

Beck slowed at the next intersection, and Darger spotted the silver-blue SUV heading east.

"There," she pointed and grabbed the radio from the dash. "We've got eyes. He's eastbound on Hawthorne Street."

Luck's voice came over the radio. "Copy. This is Timber Wolf. We're running parallel to you on Eastmont."

"Unicorn, this is Manta Ray," the other car said. "We are tailing you at a distance."

"Copy that," Darger said.

She glanced over at Beck, whose knuckles seemed wrapped around the steering wheel like claws.

"You good?"

Beck nodded.

"You think he's up to something?" the other woman asked. "He sure flew out of there like he has somewhere to be."

There was a part of Darger — likely fueled by adrenaline — that said this had to be it. They were about to catch him in the act and end this whole thing. Another part said it would be a while before they got that lucky.

"We'll see," she said.

As they kept pace with Sablatsky, Darger periodically

198

glanced at the speedometer. He drove aggressively, weaving in between cars to get ahead where he could, but he rarely went more than a few miles-per-hour over the speed limit. Still, the constant shifting of lanes made it more difficult to tail him from a discreet distance.

Darger continued to give updates over the radio as they drove through the streets of Los Angeles. They entered a residential area with stately Spanish Colonial homes lining both sides of the road. The white stucco and red roof tile went by in a blur.

After they'd been following Sablatsky for a few minutes, Beck let out a nervous laugh.

"Well, I hope he's not going far. I got quite the burst of adrenaline back there, and now I have to pee again."

Sablatsky kept weaving in and out of traffic, gaining a car-length here and there. They watched him switch lanes ahead, cutting in front of a white pick-up truck. The driver of the truck honked and threw his hands up angrily.

The traffic light at the intersection ahead flipped from green to yellow. The mass of cars slowed, anticipating the red light. Darger leaned back in her seat, relishing that they'd have a few seconds to breathe before the chase began again.

They came to a standstill as the light turned red. Sablatsky was ahead of them and one lane over. Darger could only really see a sliver of his face in the side mirror, but that didn't stop her from staring. Her eyes roamed the length of the vehicle, noting the Volunteer Fire Dept. sticker on his rear windshield.

There was a man standing in the grass median, selling roses out of a five-gallon bucket.

Darger could hear him saying, "A pretty flower for the

pretty lady in your life. Let your wife know how much you love her."

A sudden thought occurred to Darger. Something she'd forgotten in all of the frenzy.

"Did you happen to notice his car making a noise?"

"Sablatsky?"

"Yeah. Like a high-pitched chirping."

"No," Beck said. "Why?"

"It's nothing, really. Just that we have a witness and surveillance video of an SUV with a squeaky serpentine belt. We thought it might be him."

Beck's eyes wandered to the Mariner.

"Could have had it fixed."

"Yeah," Darger agreed. "Maybe."

Squinting up at the traffic signal, Beck said, "Well this might just be the longest light in history."

She had barely finished speaking when Sablatsky's vehicle veered into a break in the cross-traffic. With no warning, he'd taken a hard right despite the fact that he hadn't been in the turn lane.

"Damn it," Darger said, swiveling in her seat to peer at the cars surrounding them.

They were boxed in on all sides. There was no way they could follow until the light turned, and even then, they'd have to go to the next intersection before they'd be able to take a right.

She mashed the button on the radio.

"This is Unicorn. He just threw us at a traffic light. He's headed south on Highland Avenue."

"This is Manta Ray. We're in the same clot. Not moving."

"Copy. This is Timber Wolf. We'll try to head him off."

Ten or fifteen seconds passed, each one feeling like an eternity. When the light finally turned green, Beck wheeled into the far right lane as swiftly as she could and took the next right. Darger crossed her fingers that Sablatsky hadn't gotten too far.

Luck's voice came over the radio.

"OK, we spotted him. He's still going south on Highland, but we're stuck in traffic and not able to pursue."

"Fuck," Darger said. "We're going to lose him."

Beck slammed her open palm against the wheel.

"I should have been following closer."

"No. We were doing everything right." Darger shook her head. "The guy drives like a lunatic."

Beck turned right again and then made a quick left on Highland, stepping on the gas.

"Ahoy, Unicorn. This is Timber Wolf on your six."

In her side mirror, Darger spotted Luck's Lexus directly behind them. She waved before returning to scanning the cross streets for Sablatsky. A moment later, Beck was braking. The traffic ahead was moving at a crawl.

"Fucking traffic in this town," Darger said. "It never lets up."

She spotted a park with booths and tents set up in rows. Some sort of festival from the looks of it. People milled about on the sidewalks and crossed between the cars stuck in traffic, further slowing things down.

"Hopefully he got stuck in this mess, too," Beck said.

And then she spotted it. The silvery-blue Mercury SUV with the volunteer fireman decal. It was parked down a side street that ran along one side of the park. Better yet, Sablatsky stood only a few feet away, swiping his credit card at a parking meter.

"I see him." Darger said. "Stop here."

Beck brought the car to a stop, and Darger hopped out, signaling to Luck to pull over.

"Stay on his car," Darger said, turning back to Beck. "I'll try to track him on foot."

A horn blared from behind them.

"Move, bitch!" the driver shouted.

Darger was sorely tempted to move as slowly as possible just to spite the impatient woman, but she didn't want to lose Sablatsky again. Thankfully, he was still fiddling with the parking meter. She closed the car door and moved to the sidewalk where Luck and his Lexus were now stationed in a No Parking zone. He and the LAPD officers he'd teamed up with were climbing out.

"He's at 10 o'clock," Darger said. "Bright blue Dodgers t-shirt."

They formulated a quick plan. With the two cops positioned deeper within the park, Darger and Luck would fan out on either side of Sablatsky and follow at a short distance.

"Remember that he hasn't done anything yet. We're just watching," Luck reminded them. "Obviously, if we can catch him in the act, we'll take him down, but short of that we have nothing to arrest him on."

"Not even the shitty driving?" one of the men joked.

"If only," Luck said.

Just then, Sablatsky pocketed his wallet and hustled into the throng.

"Here we go," Darger said. "He's moving."

CHAPTER 32

Jim cuts across a landscaped yard in front of a real estate office — raised beds of tall exotic grass and a pair of magnolia trees manicured like fussy facial hair. His feet slip a little in the wood chips still moist from the sprinkler, and he kicks up little clusters of the wet mulch, but he doesn't slow.

He hustles. Focused. His body gone taut with anticipation. That glowing energy still pulsating inside.

The shortcut takes him to the next block where the foot traffic dies back considerably. This particular block won't really come to life until after dark. He knows this from watching, sitting off to the side in his SUV, letting the prey come to him. The lack of pedestrians is part of the plan.

He pulls the baseball cap down so it covers his brow. He knows from practicing in the mirror that this greatly changes his appearance, the angles of his cheekbones and jaw somehow appearing quite a bit more chiseled and angular with his big forehead covered up. He'd read quite a bit about manipulating these kinds of things in blog posts by various con men trying to sell losers the secret to getting girls. They all preach the same bullshit, too. Just act "cocky and funny," they say, and these girls will be falling all over each other to get to you.

Yeah? Not so much in his experience, but that's OK. Better to give them fire. All of them.

Tonight his target will go another direction, though, won't it? He snickers a little just thinking about it, a wicked chill reaching up to touch his shoulder blades, make him squirm a little.

The destination takes shape before him. A corner building. Brick facade on the front.

Now he picks up speed. Almost jogging. Sliding the little bottle out of the cargo pocket in his pants.

He stands in the shadow of the open doorway. Steps inside. A wood-paneled foyer comes to view as his eyes adjust, a flight of wooden steps leading up to the main floor of the bar. Chipped black paint covers both the wall and floors.

Yes.

This small passage serves as the bottleneck of this business operation, the one little chute where everyone must go in and out. It's a perfect target.

Despite the lack of foot traffic up and down the street, the bar itself sounds packed. Voices and music competing with each other inside, glasses clinking and thumping down on bars and tables. Happy hour on Tuesday afternoon always draws the regulars in a few hours early.

He licks his lips. Tastes the salt of his sweat once more.

He doesn't hesitate.

He dumps the gasoline over the steps. Slooshes it all out of the wide mouth bottle in one motion. The liquid almost slapping the wood more than splashing.

And no longer can he hear the voices nor the driving bass of the music through the door beyond. These sounds fade. Filter out of his perception. In their place, he hears only the thud of his own heart, the swishing patter of the blood roaring in his ears.

His hand shakes as he flicks the lighter. Trembling so badly it takes three tries to light. But the sight of the flickering flame itself seems to calm him. Soothe him. A balm applied directly to his troubled thoughts.

His arm steadies as he lowers the flame to the stairway, those strange waves of energy in his chest once again finding strength, finding reassurance now that the star of the show is alight center stage. The smell of gas is everywhere now, bright and acrid. He tastes it. Feels it in the wet of his eyes, on the roof of his mouth, in the back of his throat.

The fire leaps to life, all of the steps going up at once, and whooshing further after a second, some draft catching and exciting the blaze. He stumbles backward, off-balance, eyes watering to blur everything. The flames are quickly waist high and climbing, an indistinct brightness reaching for him, hungry for him, seemingly unaware that they are on the same side.

But he evades the orange coils, stands in the doorway, blinks the tears from his eyes, and right away he sees big patches of paint peel off the wall from the heat, the fire already having its way with the wood paneling there. Chewing into the building.

The wood veneer glows already, the orange of it swelling and waning and swelling again like the fire is breathing, living.

Catching. Growing. Becoming.

Yes.

He watches it for two ragged breaths, his whole body slick and throbbing and alive, tongue gliding back and forth over wet lips, arms once more embracing each other, kneading at the meat of himself.

And then he darts back the way he came.

CHAPTER 33

The crowd in the park was a blessing and a curse. The sea of people gave Darger plenty of cover — she doubted Sablatsky would ever notice he was being followed in this mess — but part of her attention was required to keep her from plowing into people. That meant taking her eyes off of Sablatsky every few seconds and running the risk of losing him amongst the horde, especially if he made a sudden change in direction.

She had to hope that between her and Luck, he wouldn't get away.

Sablatsky wove through the mob much the way he'd driven here. Shifting and zipping around anyone moving too slowly, an endless zig-zag pattern. Always trying to find the fastest way around an obstacle.

It spoke to his impulsiveness, this inability to wait even a moment, to slow down for a half-second. Anything to reach his destination as quickly as possible.

Was he planning to start a fire here, in the park? It didn't really make sense. With so many people around, he'd be easy to spot, for one. Not to mention the fact that it would be too easy for people to flee the fire, if he was looking for casualties.

So what then? He didn't appear to be interested in any of the tents. He hadn't even so much as glanced at any of the wares or food stands as far as she could tell.

Darger tried to peer ahead to determine where he might be headed, but all she saw were more people and trees.

He ducked around a booth selling an array of tie-dyed

merchandise, and she momentarily lost sight of him. She hurried along the other side of the booths, watching in the gaps for the blue shirt. He was there, still moving roughly in the same direction as before.

Her phone buzzed in her hand, and she glanced down at the screen.

He got away from me, Luck's text read.

I've got him, she wrote. Heading deeper into the park still.

She trailed alongside and slightly behind Sablatsky. She kept on him for another minute before she ran into an obstacle: a large, tightly-packed group of people were blocking the way ahead. A marimba band was set up in front of a fountain in the center of the park. Six or seven of the instruments spread across the pathway, and they'd drawn quite an audience.

At the far end, she watched Sablatsky slip through a narrow gap and disappear in the mass of bodies.

She jogged around the crowd and the band, where a dozen or so hands struck the wooden plates with their mallets in unison.

When she got through the swarm of people, she found herself at the far corner of the park. There were no booths here, so it was quieter, less packed with people. But Sablatsky was gone from view.

She moved roughly in the direction he'd been headed before, reaching a small parking lot that served this end of the park. Where was he?

Spinning slowly in a circle, her eyes searched desperately.

"Slippery motherfucker," she said.

She was about to text Luck, hoping someone still had Sablatsky on their radar when a flash of blue caught her eye. He was moving through an alleyway between a row of buildings beyond the park.

Darger couldn't help but think of the alleyway that ran behind Judy Galitis' house.

She made for the alley, texting Luck as she walked. She couldn't imagine her description of the place was much help. She'd gotten turned around in the park and wasn't really sure where she was in relation to where they'd started on foot.

She kept the phone out after sending the message to Luck. It was more for show than anything. There was nowhere to hide here, and she hoped the appearance of being glued to her phone would be less suspicious if she were spotted by Sablatsky.

At the mouth of the alley, she peered down the passage. It was empty, but further down she could see where this narrow lane intersected with another alley running perpendicular to it. He had to be around the corner of one side or the other.

As she approached the intersection, the hair on the back of her neck stood on end. If he were to torch one of these buildings, the packed park would be the perfect place to return to after the fact. He could melt back into the crowd in seconds, maybe even stick around to watch the aftermath, hidden in plain sight.

Her fingers itched for her gun, but no. Not now. Not unless she spotted Sablatsky in the act of starting a fire.

She forced herself to walk through the middle of the intersection as if she were just a pedestrian passing through. With her face still aimed down at her phone, she glanced in both directions.

No blue shirt. No nothing.

Shit.

She considered the possibilities. He was out of sight so quickly, he must have turned one way or the other. But which way?

She chose left first, hurrying down to the street entrance. Peering both ways at the barren sidewalk, she felt a jolt of panic run through her.

Wherever Sablatsky was, he could be starting a fire right now.

Turning on her heel, she hustled to the opposite end of the alley, eyes desperate to spot a flash of bright blue t-shirt. But this side was empty, too.

How?

She studied the line of businesses across the street, with more alleyways running between them. This section of town was like a rabbit warren of back alleys. He could be anywhere.

Not willing to give up, Darger crossed the street, hopping over the double yellow line. As she drew closer, she saw that the nearest alley was a dead end.

Movement danced in the periphery of her vision. A flutter of white from behind the glass of the storefront to her left. Beside the door, a red, white, and blue cylinder rotated, looking like a patriotic candy cane. The motion she'd seen was nothing more than a barber covering a customer with a smock.

Her only choice now was to check the other alleys. If Sablatsky didn't turn up then, she'd have no choice but to admit defeat.

As she moved past the front window of the barbershop, she glimpsed the face of the man sitting in the chair awaiting his haircut.

Sablatsky.

She almost stopped dead in her tracks at the sight of him but forced herself to continue walking. Face calm and impassive.

The fucker was just out for a wash and style. She couldn't believe it. Part of her wondered if he knew he was being watched. Had led them on a wild goose chase and then capped it off with a really mundane errand. But no. That was the adrenaline talking. It made her want to believe this had been a genuine fight-or-flight scenario. The more realistic version was the one where they'd all just busted their asses following a guy to his weekly trim.

Ducking into the next alleyway, she texted Luck and then called Beck.

"Jeez Louise, what's going on out there? I'm on pins and needles over here!"

"He's getting a haircut."

"Sorry... did you say... a haircut?"

Darger chuckled, letting out some of the tension she'd been holding in for the last half an hour or so.

"Yeah. Kind of an anticlimax, right?"

"I'll say."

"Radio Manta Ray and give them my position. They can sit on him until he finishes up here."

"Roger that. The second team from the afternoon detail is here with me now. They'll keep a watch on Sablatsky's car, and I can come get you."

"OK. See you in a few," Darger said and hung up.

The team known as Manta Ray showed up a few minutes later. Darger pointed out the barbershop and suggested they park in one of the alleyways with a clear view of the front of the place.

When Beck arrived, she looked a little shaken.

"Are you OK?" Darger asked. "You look pale."

Beck wiped the back of her hand over her forehead.

"I really thought I screwed that all up. I couldn't stop picturing him getting away from us and starting a fire."

"It's fine," Darger said. "We got eyes on him again in the end."

"Yeah, but if we didn't? If we'd lost him for good, and he'd ended up setting another fire? It would have been my fault."

The corners of Darger's mouth turned into a half-smile.

"What?"

"You sound like me." Darger shook her head. "Always blaming myself when something goes wrong in a case, like I'm somehow solely responsible for the outcome. Only now, when I hear someone else saying it, I realize how ridiculous it sounds."

Cocking her head to one side, Beck said, "I'm not sure if I should be offended by that or not."

"Look, this guy is fucked up in the head. Who knows why he does what he does? The thing is, he's going to set fires whether you're on the case or not, right? You matter not at all to his process."

Before Beck could respond, her phone rang. It was Luck.

"Where are you?" he said by way of greeting.

There was a note of panic in his voice. Darger frowned.

"In the car. With Beck."

"Turn your radio to Fire and Rescue's frequency."

There was a burst of static as Darger adjusted the radio.

"Structure fire. 100 Stark Avenue," a male voice said.

There was a mechanical beep and then a robotic female voice spoke.

"Station 41, Engine 14, Engine 2, Engine 4, Engine 6, Water 5, Water 3, Rescue 2, Battalion 4, Battalion 3, Car 220. Structure fire at 100 Stark Avenue. At 100 Stark Avenue. Cross of West Kane Street."

Darger stared at the scanner, not quite sure if she was hearing what she thought she was hearing.

Finally, Luck stated the obvious.

"Our guy set another one."

CHAPTER 34

Realizing her mouth was hanging open, Darger closed it. It didn't make sense. They'd only lost Sablatsky for a few minutes at most. And she'd just seen him, settling into the barber's chair as calm as day. Could he have possibly set the fire in the small window of time he'd been out of their sight?

"The fire is at a club across town. The Blue Handkerchief over in West Hollywood," Luck said.

"Wait," Darger said, still catching up. "That's like twenty minutes from here."

"Yeah."

She exchanged a glance with Beck, who looked just as dumbstruck.

"Sablatsky's not our guy," Darger said. "He can't be."

"It's looking that way." Luck sighed. "I'm headed over there now. Meet you there?"

"Yeah. We'll see you then."

It was rush hour by this time, and the roads were clogged with traffic. It took longer than Darger's estimated twenty minutes to arrive on the scene. When they did, the entire building was engulfed in flames.

The fire crews had cordoned off the street around the blaze. They found Luck positioned near one of the barricades, his gaze fixed on the inferno. Camacho stood nearby in a crowd of other task force members, conversing with his partner, Murphy.

"Was anyone inside?" Darger wanted to know.

Luck's face stiffened, and she instantly felt her gut clench.

"Apparently the bar does a 3-6 o'clock happy hour on weekdays, so they had a decent-sized crowd when the fire broke out. A lot of people got out, but we don't have a final count."

She wasn't sure if it was the smoke or the idea of people trapped inside the burning building, but her throat was suddenly very dry.

This was one of those times she hated being right. Klootey had asked whether the arsonist was a serial killer, and she'd told him it depended on whether he continued to target places that would ensure a body count. She was pretty sure she had her answer now.

"So how do we know for sure this is the same perpetrator?" Beck asked.

"One of the unis first on the scene found an almost empty soda bottle tossed on the ground nearby," Luck said. "He remembered from the task force meeting that plastic bottles had been recovered from the Galitis and church fires, so he picked it up."

"You said almost empty?"

"Yeah. He opened it and gave it a sniff. Said he figured it was 50/50 that it'd be Mountain Dew or urine, but he wanted to be sure. Turns out it was gasoline."

Crossing her arms, Darger frowned. Luck went on.

"Looks like he doused the stairs leading up to the bar. Lit them up and dumped the bottle after."

Luck shrugged.

"They'll test it for trace evidence, obviously, but it's looking more and more like you were right. He's leaving them on purpose. He wants us to know he's responsible for this."

He gestured at the burning building, and Darger's gaze couldn't help but follow, locking on the writhing flames.

Sometimes she really hated being right.

CHAPTER 35

Darger watched from the perimeter as a team of firefighters pointed two large canvas hoses toward the big front window of the bar. Streams of water jetted into the jagged opening where the glass had been, disappeared into the black.

She couldn't see anything through the little opening but churning smoke disturbed by the water's flow. Was the water helping? Was the fire dying down? Could they even tell at this point?

The roar of the hose seemed to drown everything out, so much so that Darger didn't feel like she was standing in a small crowd of onlookers, most of them fellow members of the task force. When she stared up at the burning building, she felt alone. Closed off from the outside world, save for the image of this building with the black smoke twirling out of its open places.

Just her and the fire. Nothing else was quite real in this moment.

Something brushed against her shoulder, startling her.

"Sorry," Beck said, projecting her voice over the din. "I'm heading out. Want me to drop you at your hotel?"

Darger envisioned herself pacing back and forth across the ugly carpet in her stocking feet, waiting for news updates on the fire from the TV. She couldn't fathom leaving the scene. Not when there were so many questions still unanswered. But she didn't have a 90-minute drive home or a family waiting for her.

"I'm going to stay. I can catch a ride with Luck later."

Nodding, Beck patted her arm. "You'll keep me updated?"

"Of course," Darger said. "Thanks for coming out today."

"Part of the job."

With a final wave, Beck ducked into the mob and out of sight.

Darger turned back to the smoldering building, focusing her eyes on the streams of water shooting from the hoses.

The white noise of the spray lulled her back into a daze. It almost seemed like a version of silence after a while. And the voice in her head returned, louder in the quiet. Urgent and forceful.

How many dead this time? Surely it can't be worse than the church.

Could it?

The flames had spread upward rapidly, touching the upper floors of the structure. Darger could see the flickering orange ribbons now and then, dancing somewhere beyond the upstairs windows, flitting in and out of view as though being coy about all of this, playing hard to get or some such nonsense.

Darger knew enough to know that what she was seeing wasn't good. It had spread too quickly. All that could be accomplished from here, in a best-case scenario, would be what the corporate types called "damage control."

A second team of firefighters now sprayed the place next door — a fitness studio with a hot pink leotard on its sign. The hose's powerful stream bashed right through the windows. A fist made of water. The steady spray darkened the concrete facade in haphazard strips that reminded her of graffiti.

Within minutes a third team joined the first two, readying

to douse the vegan brew pub next door on the other side. So maybe they'd stop it from spreading. She hoped so. That would be something, at least. Some kind of progress.

How many dead, though? How many burning inside even as we stand out here and watch?

More windows fell as the third hose loosed its stream, glass panes shattering one after the other. Darger realized that she could hear the breaking glass this time, if just barely — little high-pitched tinkling laid over the water's roar. It reminded her of cymbals crashing in a noisy song.

The sirens sang over all of it, wailing and warbling in the distance, more trucks and police on their way. More and more and more. Another spectacle to descend upon.

The sheer volume of water now being sprayed on this little chunk of brick and concrete became hard to fathom. It sounded immense, the outpouring, and she supposed it was. The water just kept shooting into the building. Impossible quantities. Approaching 1500 gallons per minute out of each of the hydrants, if she was remembering correctly.

Another group of firefighters seemed to appear from nowhere, three of them climbing up onto the truck closest to the building. They looked up at the top floors of the building and then back at each other a few times. Yelling and gesturing all the while, all of their movements exaggerated to a ridiculous degree like they were slapstick actors from the silent film era. Finally one of them moved to act.

He scampered into place toward the back of the truck, and now the tower ladder ascended, its huge boom arm unfolding, lifting the lone firefighter in the bucket up and toward the building. He pulled up just shy of a third-story window and stopped, jerking a few more times, final adjustments to position himself just where he wanted to be.

Then he too began spraying water into the building from a nozzle attached to the front of his bucket. It was hard to be sure from the ground, but it almost looked like this could be a more powerful stream than that of the hoses. Thicker and faster. It made the bucket quiver just a little, the firefighter gripping the bars on the sides for support.

Here, at last, Darger could see some sign of progress, too. Steam billowed from the opening where this fresh jet of water entered the building, the clouds of it giving way to tendrils and then dissipating into the sky as it rose up and away.

Still, that voice in her head wouldn't let up.

How many dead?

How many dead?

How many dead?

She clenched her jaw. Closed her eyes. Tried to silence that nagging internal monologue.

She listened to the spray, the endless sizzle singing a four-part harmony. And she breathed. Deep breaths. Counted to ten. And maybe the tiniest sliver of peace came to her, offered its paltry comfort or some muted version of such. A moment of stillness.

Yelling brought her back from her spell. Frantic sounds. Words she couldn't make out. Mostly it centered around a vowel sound — an elongated O. It almost sounded like they were booing.

She opened her eyes.

The men on the ground waved their arms and screamed at the man up in the basket. A couple of them jumped up and down, as though that might somehow help them be heard over the din. It almost looked like they were doing jumping jacks in full firemen gear.

If the fireman in the basket heard any of the chatter below, he showed no signs of it. His head and shoulders stayed trained on the gaping window where he sprayed his nozzle.

Darger felt a tug at her elbow. Looked.

Luck's fingers pulled at her sleeve. His eyes met hers.

"Roof," he said, eyebrows lifting as he enunciated as hard as he could. She could distinctly see that final F-sound forming as his bottom lip touched the tips of his front teeth.

She blinked. Twice.

Roof?

Oh. Roof.

Darger looked up just in time to see the roof of the building collapse.

CHAPTER 36

The roof buckled and crashed down onto the floor below it, sparks exploding from every opening in a great glittering gust. The biggest swirls of orange specks shot out of the top of the building, now peeled open to the sky as though a can opener had made its way around the perimeter of brick facade. The sparks danced on the wind, spiraling and bobbing and weaving, strange floating fireworks.

But rivulets of embers and flame poured out of the windows of the top floor as well, strange whooshing tentacles reaching out for fresh objects to touch, heat, consume. They seemed to move in unison, flowing and twisting together like some glowing flock of the tiniest birds.

Watching this brick and concrete structure pulled apart with such seeming ease, the words burst at the seams sprang to Darger's mind. It was hard to fully grasp, the destruction somehow awe-inspiring in its own disturbing way.

Shock and awe.

The fireman in the bucket squatted and hugged his arms around the bars, his little platform trembling like mad, the boom arm rattling all the way down to the truck. One of the guys on the ground had manned the controls, jerking the bucket away from the building just before the roof came down. That had kept him well out of the fire's reach, and so far there was no falling debris.

Darger could read relief in the body language of the men on the ground. The panicked arm-waving and jumping jack motions had fallen off into slumped shoulders, a few fist pumps, and smiles beaming out from behind the clear shields protecting their faces.

And even if the sun plunged into the horizon now, the sky darkening around them in shades of an orange and purple smog sunset going dim, there remained an incredible light shining through this time and place. A softness. A warmth. Some lightness seeming to occupy existence itself, a weightlessness, if only for this moment.

She still didn't know how many had died here, but the firefighter in the bucket was going to be OK. That was something.

For the first time in what felt like a long while, Darger tore her gaze away from the burning building above to examine the crowd around her.

It had grown rapidly — probably more than a hundred onlookers huddled along the sawhorse perimeter with more lingering further back. Some could be survivors or regulars at the bar — there'd be potential witnesses and people of interest in each group. That'd be an angle they could work, which meant they should probably start filming the crowd immediately and canvassing sooner than later.

More members of the task force had arrived by now, all of their faces solemn as they watched the blaze. Crazy how fire did that, she thought. Turned even the hardest law enforcement officers into spectators, numb and listless in the presence of the great burning spectacle, held them in rapture for a time.

They had to break that spell now and get back to work.

She noticed something else about the crowd, however — Agent Luck was no longer standing next to her.

Darger swiveled her head. Eyes scanning the crowd and beyond. Seeking Luck.

She looked for a suit amongst the hoodies and t-shirts and other casual garb most of the onlookers wore, then remembered that everyone on the surveillance detail had been in plainclothes. If she was remembering right, Luck had been wearing jeans and a polo shirt. Gray or navy blue, she thought. Not much help in either case.

The flashing lights on top of the first response vehicles wasn't helping either. It cast the whole scene with a disorienting strobe effect.

Finally, she spotted him. Luck had crossed the perimeter and now advanced on the truck with the tower ladder extending from its rear end. Two men in uniform stood near the back bumper of the massive vehicle, conversing with a group of firefighters in full gear. She recognized the L.A. Fire Chief but blanked on his name just now. The other uniformed man was Chief Macklin. He must have sensed Luck's approach, because he lifted an arm and waved him into the huddle.

Darger watched the parley from a distance. The men seemed to take turns ducking their heads near each other to better be heard. She couldn't help but think of a gaggle of geese as they craned their heads low one after the other. She chewed her lip a little as she wondered what they were talking about. They had to be discussing the body count, and that thought filled her with a mix of anticipation and dread. She resisted the urge to fidget, to bounce up and down on her feet. She'd know soon enough.

After a few seconds, Luck turned back. This was it. In moments, she'd get word about how bad this one had been, a definitive answer to that question that kept repeating in her head, pumping along like the sound of her heartbeat: How many dead?

Her throat got tight as Luck padded back over the asphalt toward her. She tried to read his facial expression. Did she see a grim line occupying his mouth, a mournful crease between his eyebrows, or was that just paranoia intruding into her perceptions? Fact or figments?

Luck sidled between two sawhorses and leaned close to her. Without even getting that near to the actual blaze, he already smelled more like smoke than he had — that acrid, industrial smoke smell that made the odor of cigarettes seem like freshly bloomed roses by comparison.

"Good news," he said, his lips finally quirking into a smile. "They're pretty sure everyone got out."

Darger blinked.

"Everyone?" she said.

Luck nodded.

"Someone smelled smoke pretty early on, stood up on the bar, and directed everyone to the fire exit toward the back of the bar. A very lucky thing. It's almost hard to believe looking at the wreckage now, but there were no casualties. Not even any injuries, as far as they know."

"Aside from the building itself, I guess," Darger said.

With that, they looked up at the structure, sparks glowing bright in the plumes of black smoke that seemed to twirl endlessly toward the heavens. Watching it now, it was hard not to think that the building would be a total loss.

Bad, but not so bad, she thought. The building was a casualty she could live with.

CHAPTER 37

All of the law enforcement officers on hand at the scene of the bar fire huddled around the two Chiefs. That lackadaisical quality that had settled over everyone as they watched the early stages of the fire seemed to have fled the faces of these men and women. Darger noted a fierceness having arisen to replace the listlessness — creased brows and clear eyes — and she felt good about that.

"Listen up, we got lucky tonight," Chief Macklin said, his voice hitting some note reminiscent of a football coach giving a rousing halftime speech. "We believe everyone in The Blue Handkerchief got out in time. That's significant for multiple reasons, obviously. But for right now, in terms of working this case, it means any potential witnesses lived to tell their tale. The way I see it, that means our unsub just made his first big mistake, a mistake we can make him pay for. So take a look at that crowd over there."

He extended his arm and swept it to the side, an oddly fanciful gesture, a little like one of the models on The Price is Right showing off a pair of Eddie Bauer edition jet skis.

"One of those onlookers might just hold the next big break in this case. It's a lot of interviews to process, and I know some of you are off duty just now, but we've got the right people here to make this happen. So let's get after it."

After Coach Macklin's pep talk had rallied the team, he asked Darger to give a few basic instructions for the impromptu canvassing session to come. Her words came out in a strange stream that she couldn't quite keep track of herself, her mouth somehow talking on autopilot, as though the message were channeled into her brain from elsewhere. She'd only ever experienced this in moments of intense focus, in moments when she was in the zone.

She knew why. Her instincts told her that something would shake loose tonight. Something important. And in her best moments, she often found that she wasn't thinking, not consciously. She let her gut guide her.

"The first step will be dividing the crowd into witnesses and onlookers. Let's pull anyone who was inside the bar over to this area here," she said, gesturing to an open space near one of the ambulances. "We'll also be interested in talking to anyone who was outside the bar around the time the fire started. It was broad daylight. Someone very likely saw something. A suspicious person. A car speeding away."

The heat coming off the building was starting to make her sweat, and Darger pushed up her sleeves as she spoke.

"When you question your witnesses, focus on the moments leading up to the fire. Where were they? Who were they with? What did they notice first? Adrenaline has a way of jumbling up our memories when we try to recall an intense event, so asking for a chronological narrative usually helps them to sort things out."

The fire was to Darger's back now, the orange light flickering against the faces of the task force personnel.

"We'll want to compile a master list of witnesses, including anyone who may have left the scene since the start of the fire. It's important that we speak to anyone who might have seen something. And on that note, we want to know if any of the witnesses noticed anyone or anything suspicious in the area not just today, but in the last few days or even weeks."

Darger was certain this particular arsonist was more organized than most. Already they had evidence that suggested he liked to case his targets for days or even weeks ahead of time. Just another in a long line of Hollywood location scouts combing through these streets for the perfect setting, she thought. And while the organized behavior made him more careful in some ways — and thus harder to catch — it also increased the possibility of someone having laid eyes on him somewhere along the way.

"We'll need someone to take video of the crowd, and that will include both the witness group and anyone that was just here to rubberneck."

Having filmed numerous crowds without it leading to anything, she didn't hold terribly high hopes that the killer would be here tonight, hiding amongst the crowd, but it was certainly a possibility. John Orr had often shown up to watch the fires he created, typically going so far as to volunteer his help in investigating them.

"We'll want a list of the surrounding businesses so we can get in touch with management. Not only are we interested to know if they've seen anything out of the ordinary, but if they have security cameras. Any footage we can get for this afternoon and the last few days will be key."

Before she'd fully caught up with the rush of canvassing tactics exiting her lips, she heard herself dismiss the crew, and then everyone began moving at once. Most of the officers knifed into the crowd, each pulling someone aside and asking him or her a few key questions. For the first time, Darger noticed that most of the crowd of spectators was made up of men, perhaps close to 90%.

She nudged Luck with her elbow.

"Is The Blue Handkerchief a gay bar?"

"Yeah. You couldn't tell by the name?"

"What about it?"

"The hanky code. It was a thing back in the 70s. You wore a different colored handkerchief depending on what you were… you know… into," he said, blushing at the implication.

Squinting, Darger said, "And how do you know about this?"

He shrugged, shifting his feet. She'd forgotten how easily he embarrassed and couldn't help but laugh.

Luck cleared his throat.

"You think that's significant, him targeting a gay bar? I mean, is he a homophobe or something?"

"Could be," Darger said. "I was thinking earlier that some people might consider a bar to be the opposite of a church. And maybe in some ways they are. But there are also similarities. People often have a regular bar they frequent the same way they have a chosen church. They're both community gathering places with built-in rules and rituals. Maybe he hates churches and bars because they represent all the ways he doesn't fit in."

Luck smiled and shook his head.

"What?"

"You just always have a way of spinning things that I don't see coming," Luck said. "I mean, it all makes sense. But the inside of your head must be a bizarre place."

"I'll take that as a compliment." Darger thrust her hands in her pockets. "Anyway, the fact that it's a gay bar may or may not be significant. He might be homophobic. He might be gay himself, and this is his way of lashing out at a group he wants to belong to but feels alienated from."

Her eyes wandered over to Murphy, who stood filming the crowd with a digital camcorder a little bigger than a can of Pepsi, panning across the mob slowly, trying to get clear shots of each and every face. Here and there she spotted members of the task force mingling among them, so many people chatting all at once after a long quiet stretch under the fire's spell. She realized that she was examining the body language of the bystanders, looking for signs of nerves, jitters, paranoia. Maybe part of her did think the killer was out there.

A chill crept up her spine at the thought, made the hair on the back her neck prick up.

Her eyes flicked from face to face, scrutinizing as though somehow, someway her intuition would just know him when she saw him. Another part of her tried to quantify this absurd fantasy by drilling down to the minutiae. Would he have a goatee? A cleft chin? A crooked nose like a boxer? Would he wear glasses? Have tattoos? Crow's feet around his eyes?

So many faces, and one of them could be his, but no matter how hard she focused her stare, there was no way for her to tell. If only she could peek inside each brain, peel away the skull like a candy shell to see what kind of filling lay hidden inside, all of the secrets exposed, plain to see with the naked eye.

She knew the truth, though. He probably looked ordinary. Plain. Just a man like anyone else. Indistinguishable.

Like a dad or a husband or a brother. Maybe he even was some or all of those things when he wasn't off setting fires.

Normal. He probably looked normal, whatever that even

meant.

She caught movement out of the corner of her eye and that reeled her back in from the abstract place her mind had wandered to.

Luck stirred, adjusting the collar of his shirt. Readying himself. Almost preening, she thought. She followed his gaze.

Two witnesses were being lead over to them by Bishop. For now the shadows swathed their features, rendering them as two silhouettes tailing behind the towering officer, but Darger knew she'd shine her light on them soon enough and see what was there to see.

Good. Time to get to work.

CHAPTER 38

Alejandro Zapata was a slim Latino man with blue hair and a single diamond stud in his ear. He'd been tending bar when the fire started, the first to smell the smoke, and the one responsible for immediately evacuating the place.

"At first I thought someone had lit up. Everyone knows it's illegal to smoke inside, but every once in a while we get someone trying to light a cigarette in the bar. I've even caught people trying to smoke pot in the restrooms a few times. But usually it's late at night. People drunk enough they aren't quite thinking straight. So I looked around, thinking I'd find some frat boy trying to be cute. They come in sometimes, thinking they're woke or something for being in a gay bar."

It was instantly clear to Darger that Alejandro was someone who liked to tell a story. He was quite theatrical, making faces, and acting out certain things with his hands.

"But you didn't find anyone smoking," Darger said, urging him along.

"Uh-uh. No, ma'am. And then I got another whiff and thought it didn't smell so much like cigarettes. It was… nasty. And not in a good way," he said, waving his hand in front of his face. "So I hopped over the bar and went over to the door that leads to the stairwell, and I could see the smoke seeping in through the cracks around the door. I tested the door handle to see if it was hot, and my hand was a little wet from juicing limes. I swear to you that the tips of my fingers sizzled when they touched that handle! I'm lucky I didn't burn my hand off."

Darger nodded.

"What happened next?"

"Well I knew then I had to get people out. So I marched right back inside, and I told Richie here," Alejandro indicated the other man Bishop had brought over, "I said, 'you go open the fire door in the back and make sure the ladder on the fire escape works, because we need to get these people out of here.'"

Richie, who barely looked old enough to be in a bar, nodded. Darger was momentarily distracted by the image on Richie's t-shirt, which depicted Mario and Luigi, though both were much more well-muscled and well-endowed than she remembered from the video games.

"I jumped up on the bar and told everyone that we needed to evacuate the bar. I made sure not to say 'fire' because I didn't want anyone to panic. I got everyone in an orderly line and directed them to the fire door. I used to be a flight attendant, so I have a teensy bit of experience with that kind of thing."

He then did a little mimicry of a steward directing passengers to where the emergency exits were located.

"And that's pretty much it. People keep saying I'm a hero, but the truth is, it was all instinct. I didn't really think about what I was doing at all."

There was a bandage on Alejandro's wrist. Darger pointed at the white cotton wrap.

"What happened there?"

He clicked his tongue.

"Just my luck. We got everyone down the fire escape safely, and I was the last one out. Then right at the bottom of the ladder, I scraped myself on this big rusty nail. The paramedics say I have to get a tetanus shot now." He shuddered. "I hate needles."

"Still pretty lucky, all things considered," Darger said, though Alejandro didn't look convinced.

"Any patrons in the bar lately that struck you as out of the ordinary? Or strange?" Luck asked.

One of Alejandro's eyebrows quirked upward, and a mischievous smile touched his mouth.

"Who among us isn't strange?" he said. "It's the ordinary ones you have to worry about."

"This might be someone that's only shown up recently. In the past few days or weeks. The kind of person that was more interested in studying the place than drinking. He might have even seemed a little nervous or keyed up," Darger said.

Alejandro shrugged.

"We have a small regular crowd, but the early happy hour brings in a lot of randos. Tourists. College kids. I can't say any of them stood out to me." He clicked his tongue again. "Those boys all look the same in their pre-distressed jeans and flannel shirts."

There was a distasteful look on Alejandro's face, as if the idea of a plaid button-down upset his stomach.

"Besides that, I have a pretty good sense for weirdos. I feel like I would have noticed the guy if he'd been hanging around."

Darger's gaze shifted to Richie.

"What about you?"

"Me?" His voice was soft and quiet, and he seemed startled that Darger was addressing him directly.

"Yeah. Did you notice anything odd before the fire? Or see anyone loitering outside when you came in today?"

Arms crossed, he shook his head.

"Well, thank you for talking with us," Luck said, handing them each a card with his name and phone number on it. "If you do think of anything else, even it seems like it might be small, please give me a call."

As the two men walked away, a cluster of reporters just beyond the police line clamored for Alejandro's attention.

"Mr. Zapata! Just a few more questions!"

"He'll be getting the big hero edit on the news tonight," Luck said, watching the cameramen swarm into position.

The sun was beginning to set now, and the lights mounted on the cameras were so bright Darger had to turn away.

"The irony is that the media are probably the only ones aside from the killer that are disappointed no one died."

Luck's eyebrows rose. He blinked once, slowly.

"But you're not a misanthrope…"

Darger couldn't hear Alejandro from here, but she didn't need to. She could follow his story from his hand gestures and facial expressions alone. Off to the side, Richie stood away from the glare of the cameras. He glanced back at her, as if sensing her gaze.

"Here's an idea," Luck said, luring her attention away from the media frenzy. "Since we're probably gonna be here a while, someone should make a coffee run."

"Good thinking."

His fingers disappeared into his pocket and came back with his keys. They dangled and clinked as he held them out to her.

"So by 'someone' you meant me. Is this because I'm a woman?"

"This is because I know you've been dying to get behind the wheel of my Lexus," he said. "All that Toyota talk was such obvious misdirection."

Darger choked out a disbelieving laugh.

"The way you've been giving me such a hard time about it? Totally transparent," he said. "You've got Lexus envy, and you've got it bad. Just be gentle with her."

She snatched the keys from his hand.

"No promises," she said, taking off before he could issue a command to drive five under the speed limit.

She crossed the street and side-stepped the police barricade, where passersby were still stopping to stare at the ongoing blaze. As soon as the fire was far enough behind her to be out of sight, she felt an instant shift in the air. It was cooler. Less smoky. She took in a deep breath and let it out.

The police had been redirecting traffic away from the fire, so the streets were dead. It was almost peaceful.

She passed between two buildings, footsteps echoing against the brick facades. And then she heard another sound behind her. The scuff of a shoe on concrete, she thought.

Turning back, she squinted into the last sliver of sunlight as it disappeared on the horizon. She'd expected to find Luck there — not trusting her to drive his precious car unsupervised after all — but there was no one. Goose bumps prickled on the skin of her arms.

She rounded a corner and spotted the Lexus farther down the block. She held the key fob closer to her face, trying to figure out which button would unlock the car.

And then she heard it again. A shuffle of feet. She was sure of it this time. And they were getting closer.

She spotted two dumpsters tucked alongside the building, and without a second thought, she darted into the space between them, huddling in the shadows there.

As the footsteps drew closer, she tried to tell herself she was being paranoid. But after the attack on Camacho, she knew the killer was watching the investigation. He must be.

And now the footsteps were hurrying, thinking they'd lost her.

Darger slid her hand to her holster and drew her weapon.

A figure stepped into sight. A man. She couldn't make out any defining features in the strange monochrome dimness of twilight. But it wasn't Luck, she could tell that much. He wasn't tall enough.

He stopped just beyond her hiding place, unaware of her presence. His head swiveled to the left and right. Searching for her.

Heart thumping, she aimed her weapon at the man's chest and drew to her full height.

"FBI," she said. "Hands in the air."

The man recoiled at her voice, but obeyed. His hands floated into position above his head.

"Why are you following me?"

Trembling, he swiveled to face her.

It was the kid in the ridiculous Mario and Luigi shirt. Richie.

"I need to talk to you. Alone."

CHAPTER 39

Darger lowered her gun to her side.

"You can put your arms down," she said, holstering her weapon.

They fell like limp noodles, and then Richie hugged himself, rubbing his thin biceps with his hands as if he felt a chill.

"If I had something to report, but I wanted to stay anonymous, could I do that?"

His eyes were stretched so wide she could see the whites. She feared that any sudden movement might cause him to flee, like a startled rabbit. Darger kept very still, barely allowing herself to breathe.

"Sure."

Chewing his lip, Richie's gaze swept the alley, then returned to meet hers. His finger flicked toward her chest.

"And you said FBI, right? You're not a cop?"

Glancing down at the badge she wore around her neck, she nodded.

"That's right."

"I saw something. Or someone, rather. It might be nothing, but…"

"But it's better to tell me what you saw than to leave it to chance," she said.

Richie swallowed, his throat clicking audibly.

"There was a guy in the bar a few days ago. I don't remember seeing him before, and he was… I don't know. You said that stuff about him casing the place, or whatever? This guy was like that. Eyes all over the place. Real uptight. I mean, we get our share of that, straight guys dragged in by their girlfriends or whatever, but this was different. The straight ones, they usually loosen up after a drink or two. But this guy, he didn't even touch his beer. Just stood with his back to the wall, watching everyone. He was so tense he looked like a rubber band stretched to breaking point."

"OK," Darger said. "Do you remember what night?"

She was thinking that if their guy paid for his drink with a credit card — a long shot, maybe — they might get a name.

Richie shook his head.

"That's fine," she said, concealing her disappointment. "What about a description?"

His head shaking went up a notch in intensity.

"It'd be anonymous," Darger said.

"No, it's not that." Richie pointed over her shoulder, back toward the fire scene. "It's the guy. He's here right now."

CHAPTER 40

She wanted to play it cool, but as they walked back toward the scene, Darger couldn't help but pepper Richie with questions.

"You said you spotted him in the crowd. But you didn't see him in the bar tonight?"

Lips pressed in a tight line, Richie shook his head.

They swung around the corner and crossed the street. The smoldering building came into view. Darger could already feel the warmth of the fire on her cheeks, even from this distance. She halted and turned to Richie.

"Can you see him from here?"

The kid's eyes bounced back and forth, scanning the crowd. Then they stopped, and he nodded.

"Can you point him out to me?" Darger said, then seeing Richie's hesitation added, "You don't have to physically point. Just describe where he's standing. What he's wearing."

"See the fire hydrant?"

Darger's eyes swiveled in their sockets, locked on the hydrant.

"Yes."

"And the tallish guy with the baseball shirt. Black sleeves. Holding a video camera."

The man in question was Officer Murphy. Darger immediately focused on the man Murphy was talking to.

"The guy with the bowtie and mustache?"

Richie's eyebrows came together in a frown.

"No. The guy in the baseball shirt. He's the one I saw in the bar."

Now Darger was the one frowning. That didn't make sense. Murphy was the one wearing the baseball shirt.

Officer Murphy.

And then the realization hit her full force.

Hadn't they been looking for someone in or adjacent to law enforcement this whole time? They assumed he'd have washed out or been fired because of his impulsiveness, but that wasn't always the case. Sometimes these guys were able to fly under the radar. John Orr certainly had.

She inhaled sharply, her eyes darting around until they found Luck.

"Hey," she waved at him and then crooked her finger.

He looked confused when he saw her, no doubt wondering why she wasn't off on her errand to fetch coffee, but he started toward them.

"No. Wait," Richie said. "You said this would be anonymous."

Darger saw the panic in his eyes, knew he was thinking that accusing a cop in the presence of his colleagues was a risky move. She held her palms up.

"It's OK. He's FBI, like me. We can trust him."

"No coffee?" Luck joked.

"Later," Darger said, swiveling to face Richie. "Tell him what you told me."

Richie shifted his weight from foot to foot as he recounted his story. Darger watched Luck's eyes go wide when Richie identified Officer Murphy as the man he'd seen acting suspiciously in the bar just a few nights ago.

After dismissing Richie, Luck and Darger huddled together,

discussing their next move.

"You think he's for real?"

"You tell me," Darger said. "Because he sounded convincing as hell. And he was scared. He knows what he's up against, fingering a cop for this. That's why he waited until he could get me alone."

"What about Camacho?"

"What about him?"

"The fire at his house. Why would Murphy target his partner?"

Darger shook her head.

"Because he knows him. Knows where he lives. Knows his house well enough to know where to keep in the shadows. Thought he could get away with it." She threw her hands up and let them fall against her hips. "Or maybe they're in cahoots."

A tiny hint of a smile played on Luck's lips.

"Cahoots?"

"Shut up. You know what I mean."

"Yeah. I do," he said, sobering instantly. "What the hell do we do next?"

Darger chewed her lip.

"Let's talk to Camacho first. If they were on duty when the fire was set, then Murphy has a pretty solid alibi. This ends right here, and we don't have to ruffle any feathers."

"OK." Luck nodded. "How do we approach him without making him suspicious, though? If we march over there and start asking pointed questions about their whereabouts when the fire broke out, he's gonna know something is up. He's a cop."

"Good point."

Despite the glow of the still-burning building, night descended around them. Darger could see the moon hanging over Luck's head.

"I've got it," he said, holding up a finger. "Coffee."

CHAPTER 41

As Darger handed out steaming cup after steaming cup to the men and women of the task force, she realized Luck had been right on both counts. She saw the expressions in the faces lift. And she was able to walk straight over to Camacho, hand him a cup, and strike up a conversation without seeming the least bit shady.

"Oh man. Thanks, Agent Darger," Camacho said. "I was running on fumes."

"Me too. Figured I wasn't the only one."

She took a sip of her own cup, wincing a little at the heat as it ran down her throat and into her stomach.

"Not how I expected the day to go," she said.

Camacho shook his head.

"Me neither. And you guys had just got off a full shift of surveillance duty, I heard?"

Darger nodded.

"Actually, I was surprised you guys weren't there. You and Murphy, I mean."

Camacho scratched the back of his neck.

"Nah. Me and Murph had the day off."

It was a struggle to keep her face impassive. She had so wanted Camacho to tell her they'd been on duty today. It would have made things so much easier. But now? Now she had to wade in deeper.

"Well, you missed out. Sablatsky led us on a bit of a chase. And in the end he was just getting his hair cut."

"Jesus." Camacho chuckled. "Pretty wild that we were sitting on the wrong guy this whole time, right?"

"Yeah."

She let the silence stretch out for a bit, planning her next move. She watched the embers on a piece of the fallen roof throb brighter and dimmer, brighter and dimmer. No pattern to it. A random flutter controlled by the flow of oxygen over the burning wood.

Darger swished her cup around so that the liquid inside swirled into a spiral. She needed to tread lightly for this next part.

"So that kinda sucks for you. I mean, this probably really fucked up your plans for your day off," she said.

"Eh, not really," Camacho said with a shrug. "I was just bumming around at home. Doing my best impression of a couch potato."

That ruled him out as an alibi for Murphy then. Her only hope now was that Murphy could prove he was miles away from this side of town when the fire broke out.

"I did miss Dr. Phil, though. Can't lie... I'm pretty upset about that," Camacho said, the corners of his eyes crinkling.

Darger forced herself to laugh at the joke, but it was hollow. She took the next opportunity to excuse herself to find Luck.

They met up on the fringe of the crowd, making certain they weren't within earshot of anyone else.

"You go first," Luck said.

"Camacho said he had the day off."

Luck nodded, confirming that Murphy had said the same.

"And he said he spent it at home. Watching TV."

"Alone?"

"Yeah."

Luck sighed loudly.

"That's a problem," he said.

"Why?"

"Because Murphy just told me he was with Camacho all day."

CHAPTER 42

Wind whips into the driver's side window. Cold air assailing the left half of his face. Flinging smoke from his cigarette into his eye, making the skin around that eyelid pucker and paunch with wrinkles.

It's getting late. The full dark of the night prevailing. But some parts of the city never sleep.

He drives there, to where the lights still burn bright, to where the creatures still wriggle and writhe and crawl out under the moonlight.

Better to drive out among them, he thinks. Better than being alone.

He's failed. Again. No life lost at the queer bar, according to the news reports. Unbelievable.

And it makes him feel small. Powerless. This is supposed to be his rise. His ascent. His ticket to the top.

Spectacles must build in momentum, in scale, in the extent of the damage they inflict, in the sense of awe they create. Not like this. He'd announced himself to the world with the church, the grand set piece that left so many dead, that grabbed headlines across the globe, and ever since he'd come up empty. Not only did he fail to top his opening act, he'd failed to even matter after it.

He flicks a cigarette out the window. Lights another.

The church feels like a long time ago now. Months instead of days. Like it happened in another life, in some other protagonist's story. Like he's merely a pretender to that legacy.

A nobody again.

He grits his teeth. Eyelids shuddering.

But no.

No use in dwelling on it. All of that is over. Better to force himself into the now. Into the present moment which infinitely unfolds.

It's always now. Always. So embrace it.

Introspection, like therapy, is for losers, he reminds himself. For pussies who want to sit on their hands a whole lifetime long, moaning about feelings and telling the sad sack stories of their inner children to any dope who will listen. For the weak. For the soft.

Fuck that.

The past is always over. The present is always here.

Now.

Right now.

So transform. Evolve. Morph. Become something new. It happens, right? Change happens.

The single-celled creatures evolved into more and more complex things. Impossible changes. Over and over.

Sometimes it takes a long time, that kind of evolution, but the change itself happens in a single second, he thinks. It has to.

One second: old.

The next second: new.

Permanent change. Dramatic. Like tectonic plates shifting. Never again to return to the way it was.

He inhales. Smoke spiraling down his throat. Entering the vacuum of his chest cavity. Roiling there for a few seconds before twirling back from whence it came, venting first through his nostrils and then through the open window. Into the night.

It feels good to breathe smoke in some small way he can't explain. A little death. Just a taste of it.

It's the little things like this that make human existence bearable. Smoking. Driving. Eating something tasty. Sex. Sating all those appetites as ancient as whenever that first amphibious creature slithered up onto the shore and somehow learned to breathe the air.

Did that happen in a single second, too? In some sense, it must have.

How many crawled up onto the sand and died? Thousands? Millions? Billions?

But one didn't. He lived. Thrived. Emerged. Made the great leap forward that would affect the course of all life on the planet going forward.

The first.

Did he will it to be that way? Force it by sheer focus of all of his energy?

Probably. Probably.

Some beings are wired differently, he knows. Intense, like him. Ripe for change. Born to make things happen.

The vivid ones. The sharp ones. They dream the impossible until they make it real, until they can touch it, until they live and breathe it.

And it suddenly occurs to him how he can right these wrongs, how he can get back on the attack, back on that climb to where he wants to be.

Again he flicks his cigarette butt toward the gutter, and again he lights another. All of this in one motion, like if his hands work quickly enough, he can never stop smoking. Never ever.

Night on Fire

The night is young. It'll be dark for hours still, he thinks. Time enough to make something happen before dawn.

No rest for the wicked.

CHAPTER 43

Darger tapped her boot against the dull tile floor, her stomach a bundle of nerves. The hallway outside the interview rooms at the station was lit by harsh fluorescent fixtures that reminded her of being at the dentist's office for some reason. This would be about as enjoyable as getting her teeth cleaned, she figured. The vending machine in the corner clicked on, filling the air with a low, steady hum.

"You ready for this?" Luck asked.

"Not really," Darger said. "But we've kept them waiting long enough. Let's do it."

Both Camacho and Murphy had been brought down to be interviewed, and efforts had been made to keep the men separate. It'd taken some time to convince Chief Macklin that Darger and Luck were his best choice for conducting the interrogation. The cynical part of Darger thought he was probably still worried about who'd get credit more than he was trying to protect his men. But finally he'd seen reason. He couldn't argue against the fact that Darger and Luck were infinitely more impartial than any of his own people, all of whom were Murphy's colleagues.

They pushed into the first room. Murphy sat hunched over the table, but he pushed himself upright immediately as they entered.

"Finally. I feel like I've been sitting in here forever. No one's told me what's happening."

He kept his voice light, bordering on jovial. And though he

smiled, it looked forced to Darger. A man trying his damnedest to appear innocently curious about why he'd been hauled down to the station with no explanation. Sat down in an interview room and left to stew for a while.

It smacked of guilt, especially for a cop. He should know better than anyone that they didn't pull this kind of maneuver without good reason.

"Sorry about that," Luck said. "We're just trying to figure some things out. Establish a timeline."

Murphy blinked.

"Timeline for what?"

Luck took a deep breath and leaned forward.

"There's a leak. On the task force." His voice was low, like he was sharing some big secret.

She saw Murphy relax then. A tenseness in his neck and shoulders that seemed to melt away.

It was a lie, of course. As cops, Murphy and Camacho would be instantly suspicious at being brought in for questioning. Darger and Luck needed a plausible explanation that pointed away from the notion of Murphy being the arsonist. They needed Murphy and Camacho to think they were being questioned about something else entirely. The idea of a leak on the task force had been Luck's idea.

With a hand on his chest, Murphy's eyes went wide.

"You don't think it's me, do you?"

"No, of course not," Luck said, shaking his head. "But we have to talk to everyone, you understand."

"Right. Of course."

Luck sat back, crossed one leg over his knee.

"The thing is, chances are it's something innocent. A guy

talking to his girlfriend. Maybe giving a little more information than necessary when he mentions the investigation."

"Sure. Right." Murphy swallowed. "So what do you need to know?"

"Take us through your day. What time did you get up?"

It was the same thing Darger had told the task force to do with the witnesses: get the statement in chronological order. Liars had a tendency to jump around in their story. To skip ahead to the dramatic bits. The parts they'd spent time embellishing. When you forced them to tell you what they ate for breakfast and when they took out the garbage, it was a chance to trip them up. To catch them in the web of lies they'd spun.

Murphy was starting out rough right from the gate.

"What time did I get up?" he repeated. "Geez, I guess it was... 9:30 maybe?"

"You don't set an alarm?"

"Usually I do."

"But not today?"

"Actually, I did have an alarm set, but I turned it off. Slept in."

Luck nodded, as if this made perfect sense. But it didn't. He was already contradicting himself. Over whether he'd set an alarm or not. He was hiding something.

"And what'd you do then? Shower? Breakfast?"

"Shower, yeah. Then breakfast."

"What'd you have?" Luck asked.

"Scrambled eggs," Murphy said, then scratched his head. "Sorry, what does this have to do with a leak on the task force?"

"Nothing really. But I haven't eaten in hours, and I'm

starving."

Murphy chuckled. Darger could sense him wanting to believe this was nothing serious. That this was a routine interview everyone was going through.

"After breakfast? What then?"

"I, uh… think I did a little puttering around the house. Loaded the dishwasher. Folded some laundry. Boring stuff. And then I went over to Camacho's place."

As he spoke, Darger noted that Murphy was suddenly gesturing a lot with his hands. It was something he hadn't done before that she could recall.

"Who called who?"

"Huh?"

"You and Camacho. Or I guess you could have just popped in without calling."

"Yeah, I mean, we'd talked about meeting up on our day off, so…"

"You hang out a lot outside of work?"

"I don't know. A normal amount? What's a lot, really?"

"Nah, it's just cool to be buddies with your partner, I bet. When I was on the force, most of the guys were older than me. We didn't have so much in common, you know?" Luck paused. "You remember what time you got to Camacho's?"

"Uh…" Murphy's throat constricted as he swallowed, thinking. "I'd guess it was around noon?"

"Noon. OK. And what'd you guys end up doing?"

Shrugging, Murphy said, "Just hanging out. Had a couple beers. Watched some football."

Luck froze.

"You sure about that?"

Murphy blinked. "Yeah. I mean, that's what we did."

When Luck didn't respond, Darger's gaze slid over to him. His lips were pressed into a tight line.

"Come on," Murphy said, trying to smile but not quite pulling it off. "What is this? How does what we watched on TV have anything to do with a leak."

"Maybe nothing," Luck said. "Let's take a little break. You want anything? Something to drink?"

Murphy shook his head.

"How much longer is this going to take?"

"Shouldn't be long. Just hold tight."

Darger followed Luck back into the hallway, and they put some distance between themselves and the interview rooms. They were supposed to be sound-proof as a rule, but Darger had been in many that weren't.

"He said they watched football," Luck said, "Only the thing is, there's no game on today."

Letting out a sigh, Darger said, "He's hiding something. And not just what he watched on TV."

"I know," Luck agreed. "This isn't looking good."

She could tell by the look on his face that he'd been holding out hope that there'd been some kind of mistake. Even though Luck was FBI now, part of him would always be a cop. No one in law enforcement wanted to believe one of their own was capable of crimes like this. The problem was that cops were only human.

"Let's go talk to his partner."

CHAPTER 44

Jim parks behind a Walgreens and exits the SUV to prowl Skid Row on foot.

He has a plan. More like the first stages of a plan, he supposes. The vaguest glimpse of a plan. He's not quite sure where Jim is going with this one, a thought that makes him chuckle a little.

But it's better to act. To press forward. Therapy is for fucking losers. Introspection is for lily-livered cucks. Forward. Attack. Keep attacking. Never apologize, inside or out.

It's dark now — the night thicker than usual, almost humid for once, something that almost makes the darkness feel blacker, heavier, impenetrable — but he leaves the sunglasses on nevertheless as he moves out of the Walgreens lot and onto the street. If he's honest with himself, this is no true choice of his: Jim simply wouldn't have it any other way.

The vagrants stir everywhere here. Flitting in and out of alleys. Milling on the street. Clustering on the sidewalk. Circling under the gauzy light of the street lamps like moths.

Their faces always look strange. Foreign in some way he can't pin down. Gaunt. Dirty. Lonely.

He can't help but think of rodents, watching them all scuttle about in the dark, some of them spooked by his presence and scattering, animal instinct telling them to keep their distance. Probably not a bad idea, that.

Behold the desolation.

Such is life in Skid Row — the homeless capital of the

United States.

A seemingly endless row of tents lines the sidewalk on one side of the street, the camping gear butting up against the thick steel bars of fences installed to keep the bums off private property. Tents and tarps and mobs of bums stretch on as far as he can see. It looks like a horrible concrete campground, or maybe people forming a line to get concert tickets for some awful boy band, people waiting for something special. But no. These people aren't waiting for anything in particular, he thinks. Maybe waiting for life to magically get better. Dare to fucking dream.

On the next block, he finds shopping carts loaded with trash bags — one soul standing guard over a small fleet of carts while the owners of the others presumably scavenge elsewhere. They must work it in shifts. Teamwork.

Inside the bags? Collections of worldly possessions. Trinkets, clothes, and shoes jut out of the tops of the carts. Perhaps small caches of food and drink hide below the top layer. All of it secured in black plastic. On wheels, of course, for the mobility.

None of this provides quite what he's looking for, so he keeps moving, avoiding eye contact. The eyes who watch him look more tired than anything. Listless.

What exactly does he hope to find? Good question, Jim. He couldn't define it except to say that he will know it when he sees it, when it feels right.

Skid Row seems a little disturbing at night, though he's not sure why. The homeless strike him as an overwhelmingly peaceful lot, especially compared to the gang members and random thugs that swarm in other neighborhoods. In so many ways, this place is safer than the rest of the city.

Still, the eerie feeling persists here after dark. Gives him that nervous self-conscious tingle. Like he's always being watched, and he supposes that for the most part he is, those sleepy eyes tracking him as he passes through.

There's something more to the feeling, though. Something strange.

He thinks maybe it's the sheer quantity of homeless here that feels off. Of the roughly 17,000 souls residing in Central City East, a solid 5,000 to 8,000 are homeless at any one time — the largest stable homeless population in the country. Of course, they only account for 20% or so of the 60,000 homeless in Los Angeles County. Still, something about this little slice of the city draws the biggest congregation of them. The lost ones flock here and set up shop, bedding down on concrete, scraping by indefinitely.

Why here? Maybe there's safety in numbers. Maybe even the homeless can find support and comfort by building a community. Something very human in that notion, he thinks. Something at odds with the society the mainstream world has built. A kind of warmth that stands in glaring contrast to the city itself.

He walks on. Watches the crowd around him thin. The endless rows of tents grow sporadic and then die out entirely. Even after moving out of the main thrust of the homeless living area, he feels like he's being watched. Strange faces tucked away somewhere, observing him from the shadows. He can almost hear them whispering amongst themselves.

He sees it then — a dark lump along the curb — and he knows he's found what he came here for.

The human form sprawls in the gutter, a man with gaunt features sleeping there on a sheet of tattered cardboard. He looks diseased or dead or perhaps both. Probably both. Cheekbones protrude from the face like two doorknobs, the skin there pulled so taut that he looks hollow, dried out, some empty husk that probably had hopes and dreams at some point, probably seemed human at one point.

"Hey," Jim says, making his voice loud and hard.

The figure stirs, alive after all. Maybe just diseased, then. Good for him. He says nothing as he props himself up on his elbows, the little stick arms barely enough to support the rest of him or so it appears.

Jim gets to the heart of the matter.

"You know where to score rock candy?"

"Hell yeah," the man says, his words a little mushy in a mostly toothless mouth.

He knows by the enthusiastic response that he's picked a winner. A companion for tonight's big task whose services can be procured for a mere $20 in crack rocks.

"Well, ain't it your lucky day? I'm buying for both of us if you handle the purchase for me. I can't be seen down in, uh, those places, if you know what I mean."

The stick man jerks up onto his feet, almost seems to levitate for a moment, suddenly animated after being so still just seconds ago.

"Yes, sir. I understand. Happy to help." This last part comes out "happy to hep."

Jim thinks it oddly brave for a man with such a pronounced lisp to make no attempt to avoid "s" sounds whatsoever. He holds out his hand to the stick man.

"I'm Jim, by the way."

"Carl. Nice to meet you."

Carl pumps Jim's hand a few times, his own palm cool and so dry to the touch it almost seems flaky or scaly or something. Like shaking a firm iguana.

"Excellent," Jim says, reminding himself to smile. "Nice to meet you, too, Carl. We'll head back to my ride."

Jim leads the way back through the slums to the SUV. The bounce in Carl's step seems almost comical.

Of course, Jim has no intention of smoking crack himself. He wouldn't mind getting out of his head for a bit, but he can't risk that level of losing control for now.

Still, having a partner in crime for the night should be useful. He's considered doing something like this before but never seriously pursued it — it always seemed just a little too risky. After the string of recent failures — the Mustang, Betsy's place, and the cocksucker bar all providing no satisfaction — he's ready to try anything. You know what they say about desperate times, Jim.

Crack makes the perfect bargaining tool round these parts, but Jim can't dare buy the stuff in person. Too risky. Someone could see, could recognize him. Trouble could circle its wagons around him, focus its wandering eye in his direction and give him a good hard stare, and that would be Bad News Bears, wouldn't it? That would spoil the fun for everyone.

But not to worry. Enter Carl. In truth, any number of bums bedding down on concrete tonight would be happy enough to perform the task of buying narcotics for him. They'd be downright thrilled. By and large, the homeless don't want to hurt anyone, don't want any trouble or conflict. They just want to get high and kill another slice of time as pleasantly as possible. Just like ol' Carl here.

CHAPTER 45

Before they could even close the interview room door, Camacho was on his feet.

"You guys wanna tell me what's going on? I mean, why am I in here?"

"We just have a few things we want to clear up. That's all," Darger said.

"About what?"

Camacho's tone was combative, which Darger thought was interesting. Where she sensed an underlying nervousness in Murphy, Camacho was all fierceness.

"There's a leak on the task force."

"A leak?"

"Someone's been passing information to the press. Information that could compromise the investigation. We're trying to find out who."

Eyes swiveling from Darger to Luck and then back to Darger again, she thought Camacho's face softened ever so slightly.

"Good. Then you can let me out of here now. Because I didn't leak shit."

"I'm glad to hear that. And I'm sure it's true. But we have to get statements from everyone."

The heavy muscles of his biceps flexed as he crossed his arms over his chest.

"Let's get this over with then."

Darger nodded her head once.

"I asked you earlier what you did today. You said you were home alone, watching TV."

"Yeah."

"What'd you watch?"

"Are you guys fucking serious? You brought me in here to ask what I was watching on TV?"

"Miguel, this is going to go a lot easier if you answer our questions," Darger said.

With a subtle shake of the head, Camacho sniffed with disgust.

"I watched some football."

She didn't blink. She kept a level gaze on Camacho, determined not to lose her cool. But inside, her mind was screaming, What the fuck?

"How is it that you were watching a football game on a Tuesday?"

"I have NFL Game Pass. They keep games on there for a year. I missed the last Raiders game because of work."

Now she turned to Luck, who could only offer her a shrug.

The unsettled feeling in Darger's gut intensified. One of the two men was lying, but where was the lie? They'd thought Murphy's story about watching football had been the clear fabrication, but now Camacho had given them a perfectly clear explanation for it. But he was still insisting he'd been alone all day. Why would one of them say they were together and the other deny it?

She could see only one choice remaining to her now. She had to lay it all out and hope something shook loose. No more games.

"Here's our problem, Miguel," Darger said. "We have a

witness from The Blue Handkerchief fire that picked Murphy out of the crowd as someone he'd seen in the bar recently. Someone he described as seeming nervous and out of place."

Camacho's eyes stretched wide.

"Murphy? You think Murphy set the fire? That's… insane!" he said.

His shock seemed genuine to Darger, though that wasn't worth much. Bad people fooled the ones closest to them all the time.

"There's no way," he insisted. "No fucking way. It's a mistake. I can prove it."

"How's that?"

"Murphy was with me when the fire started. It couldn't have been him."

"Come on, man," Luck said. "You expect us to believe that?"

Darger leaned forward.

"You just spent the last ten minutes telling us you were alone all day. So, what is it? You forgot you weren't alone after all?"

Darger saw fury in Camacho's eyes. And something else. Fear?

He sat back, crossing his thick arms again.

"Yeah," he said, his tone bitter. "I forgot. And I just remembered something else."

"What's that?"

"I want a lawyer."

CHAPTER 46

The glass pipe adheres to Carl's lips. The flame licks at the white rock in the rounded end of the pipe, a sphere like a miniature fish bowl there at the end of the tube. A little hunk of Chore Boy bronze wool filters the chamber from the shaft, keeps the rock from sucking up into the bum's mouth when he hits it.

Jim watches the whole process through the glass like he's peeking through a window. The flame dancing around the bowl, the smoke swirling off the rock and sucking up into the tube, little black marks smudging the glass from the fire's touch, the rocks shrinking as the heat devours them.

They sit in the front seat of the SUV, a few blocks from where the purchase was made. Jim can't help but lean away from the man in the passenger seat who has just finished smoking his $20 worth.

Carl writhes in his seat now, his body undergoing a series of tics and gestures that only a crackhead could produce. Knees pumping up and down in some jerky time signature. Shoulders rotating, shimmying, almost dancing. Head pointing up toward the ceiling.

Outside of himself or maybe pulled deeper inside. His brain on fire. His soul on fire.

Jim knows from his own experiences some years ago: smoking crack is very much like setting a fire inside. Lights everything in the brain the fuck up. The whole body, for that matter.

It pushes the edge of the limits of human experience. Pushes past stimulation. Past joy.

Crack pushes so far past joy that it ruins it forevermore. A glittering, throbbing, glistening world draped around the user. A glow so bright inside that it cannot be sustained. Cannot be forgotten. Can only be longed for again and again.

When you smoke this, you cross a line permanently. For the rest of your life, part of you will want only this. Ache for it. Itch for it. Pine for it. Nothing else can ever measure up.

You find a hole in your soul you never knew existed, and there's only one way to fill the fucker: with that potent smoke inhaled through a glass tube.

"You ain't gon' smoke yours?" Carl says, wide eyes locking on the foil in Jim's hand. His top lip quivers in fast motion as he stares.

"Not yet," Jim says. "Let's see where the night takes us first, Carl my boy. I suspect we've got an interesting journey in front of us. Yeah?"

Carl hesitates a moment, eyes flicking to Jim's sunglasses and then back to the foil. At last, he nods.

Jim tucks the foil into the left front pocket of his pants, not realizing until he does it that he's keeping it across his body from Carl. Probably smart. Crack can turn any man into a fiend, no matter how peaceful his disposition. Jim has watched crackheads crawl over the floor for hours, fingers raking along, scouring the carpet for anything remotely rock-like or white to toss into their pipe and smoke, hoping beyond hope for that .01% chance that they will randomly find some crack on the floor to smoke.

They merge with traffic on the 101, straddling the border

between Chinatown and Little Tokyo. Concrete walls encase the cars just here, as though this highway is sunken, partially buried beneath Los Angeles. Their view of the city reduces to just that image: gunmetal gray walls, drab and industrial, periodically peppered with graffiti.

Even fifteen minutes after clearing his pipe, Carl's chest still heaves as though he's just run the 400 meters. Hands drifting up to smear at the greasy skin of his face and forehead every few seconds.

Getting off the highway and onto Sunset Boulevard, they move through Angelino Heights toward Echo Park. A spa, a motel, and a large, modern-looking church occupy the sides of the road here, taking the place of the endless row of tents.

Jim realizes he's driving straight toward Betsy's apartment. Jumping the gun, he thinks. Shit. A fast food billboard gives him the idea to change routes for the time being. Buy some time. Let the night mature some. Besides, ol' Carl looks like he could use a bite to eat.

"You hungry, Carl?"

This time there's no hesitation. Carl nods with gusto, that excited look flashing in his eyes.

Jim chuckles.

"You know what I like about you, Carl? There's no wasting of words. You're the strong, silent type, right? I respect that."

The haggardness of Carl's appearance stands out again under the glow of fast food signs, the reds and yellows gleaming on those doorknob cheekbones. Acne scars give his face the texture of paper mache.

"Me?" Jim continues. "Guess I've always been a talker. Too much energy, you know? Keyed up. Can't sit still or shut up.

Always been that way. I was a hyperactive child and the whole deal. It's like my turbo booster got flipped on when I was a kid, and I never quite figured out how to turn it off. Even when I'm alone, my mind just keeps kicking out words. Monologuing away up in my dome, audience or no. It's like I'm always talking to myself inside, you know?"

"Right," Carl says, eyes again flicking to Jim's sunglasses and then away.

They fly through the drive-thru, commandeering a bag of burgers, fries, and a pair of Cokes. Part of Jim had expected Carl to get a milkshake for some reason. Food in hand, they park and begin to eat.

The silence stimulates at first, some strange energy swirling in the SUV, but it only takes a few minutes for the quiet to become comfortable. Funny how that works, Jim thinks, how a little quiet time can sort of seal a bond between two men, especially if there are burgers involved.

"You grow up around here?" Jim says.

Carl answers between bites of his second burger.

"No, sir. Grew up outside of Memphis. Moved out here when I was 19 or 20. Been just about that long again now, I guess."

Jim crunches the numbers in his head — that'd make Carl around 38 years old. He looked closer to 50 or 60.

"Only thing I really know about Memphis is that they have good barbecue. Watched some Food Network shit about it a few years ago. Or maybe Anthony Bourdain or something. Anyway, I hear it's rough out there."

Carl catches his tomato from falling out of his sandwich and pushes it back in place with his thumb. Then he nods.

"My brother, Stevie, got caught up in the drug game. Killed over some turf squabble when he was 17. I moved out here a couple months after that. It's like you get so tangled up in trouble in some place, so enmeshed in it, that the only way to disentangle yourself is to get as far away as you can. Physical distance. So I went all the way to the Pacific Ocean, you know? I'd need a boat to get farther."

"Why L.A.?"

Carl sips his Coke as he considers his answer.

"California seems like a land of opportunity, I guess. I mean, you got the movie stars out here and everything, but I didn't have grand dreams or nothing. Just wanted to find work and get by. Press the reset button on my life. Find a place. And at first, it all worked out. I got a job in construction. Made decent money. Shared a dumpy little house with some of my coworkers, you know, but it was great. Looking back, it was a great time."

"What happened?"

"A couple years in, I got to partying more. Just beer and pot, at first, maybe a little cocaine from time to time. But then I got into the harder stuff. And it's like after a while the drugs get pretty deep under your skin, I guess, start warping your thoughts and stuff. You start seeing that paycheck in terms of how much dope you could buy, how much fun you could have. Paying a big chunk of it for rent — basically to have a mattress to sleep on at night — stops making sense. It starts seeming like an unbelievable rip-off. So a couple of us working in this crew set up tents in Skid Row. This was, like, 2003 or 2004 or some shit. Of course, none of us kept our jobs more than two months after that, but…"

"So it's been over 15 years, you've been living on the street all that time?"

Carl shrugs.

"Guess so. But it's not all bad. Probably not how people think it is, looking in from the outside. You find ways to get by, ways to feed yourself — both your body and your addiction, I guess. People are kinder than you'd imagine. Generous. Especially the tourists on the weekends. You meet a lot of interesting people, homeless or otherwise. Like I'm out here riding with you right now, you know? Eating burgers. Never could have seen that coming when I woke up this morning. I guess a lot of the people I meet, it comes down to drugs, that's the common denominator that pulls us together like a magnet, but not always. I think a lot of people are just lonely. Just really lonely, and they go out and find anyone they can maybe connect with. Just a companion, you know. Someone to wander the earth with for a little bit. Life can be beautiful when you have someone to share the moments with. Same reason people get dogs, I think. Friendship is at its best when it's simple. You don't even have to say much. You can just be."

Jim feels his eyebrows push up past the top of his sunglasses, some strange feeling creeping over him as Carl talks, and then he gets a hold of himself. Feels that aggressive part of himself clench inside like a fist.

"I'll say this: I don't have much to worry about in this life, you know?" Carl says, throwing his hands up. "Nothing to lose. I think that's an underrated piece of business."

The homeless man at last falls quiet, the subtlest smile on his face, and then Jim chimes in.

"See, I just met you, and hearing you talk a little bit, I think you have potential, man. Potential for more than this. I ain't talking about joining the rat race and selling junk bonds or anything dumb like that, I'm just talking about doing something that matters to you. More than sleeping on cardboard and panhandling and all that. Feeding those basest appetites and nothing more. There has to be more to life than… than…"

He trails off. Realizes that what he was thinking is that there has to be more than life than setting fires, lashing out at the world over and over, seeing how much damage you can do, measuring your life and self by the destruction you dole out.

He swallows in a dry throat, something clicking deep in his neck. Jim does not approve of these types of thoughts. Loser thoughts. Jim needs to act now and put a stop to this.

Without thinking, he fishes the crack out of his pocket. Holds up the little foil in the palm of his hand, movements delicate as though he's handling some precious gem instead of street drugs.

"Well, I got a chance for you to do something tonight," he says, his voice changing, going flat again. "A little prank, yeah? Revenge. All you have to do is help me scare someone, and I'll not only give you this little bundle of joy, I'll throw in $50 for your trouble."

Carl is transfixed, gone mute, eyes locking on the foil again, head bobbing up and down in slow motion.

CHAPTER 47

As Darger and Luck exited the interview room, she got the faintest whiff of smoke. Her first thought was that there was a fire here, but then she grabbed a handful of her hair and sniffed. It was her. Her hair and probably her clothes, too. They'd sucked up the acrid smell of burning like a sponge.

"Well that didn't go how I expected," Luck said.

"No," Darger agreed.

She leaned against the wall, then let herself slide down until she was sitting on the floor. God, she was tired. She rubbed at the corner of her eyelid with a knuckle. And her eyes itched. Another parting gift from the fire.

Luck squatted down across from her, forearms resting on his knees.

"I mean, I wasn't totally shocked that Camacho tried to cover for Murphy. It's clear they're pretty tight, as far as partners go."

She considered Loshak. If he was accused of something, something she didn't believe he could possibly be guilty of, would she lie to help him? She supposed it would depend on what he was accused of and what kind of evidence they had against him.

"Loyalty only goes so far. Once I told him how deep Murphy is in this, I thought he'd waffle. Go back to his original story. I sure as hell didn't think he'd ask for a lawyer."

Scratching his jaw, Luck nodded.

"Makes him look guilty, doesn't it?" he said. "I mean, I

271

know it's his right. And maybe it's the right move. But if Camacho doesn't know anything, why would he ask for a lawyer?"

What she'd said before to Luck, about the two of them being in cahoots, she hadn't meant it. But now she wondered. Could the fires be the work of two men? Or could Camacho have known what his partner was up to and decided to shield him for some reason? Why? Would he really stick his neck out like that?

Luck straightened to his full height and crossed to the vending machine. He fed in a handful of dollar bills and came back with two Cokes. He handed one to Darger.

"Thanks," she said, twisting the lid off and taking a long swallow.

"How'd Murphy know to say they were watching football?"

"A good guess," Darger said with a shrug. "They're partners. They know each other."

Luck took a swig of his soda and wiped his mouth, looking unconvinced.

Darger replaced the lid on her bottle and set it on the ground beside her.

"OK, let's say I need an alibi for some reason, to cover my ass for something or other. So I tell people I was with you yesterday evening. And then they want to know what we did. I'd tell them we ate dinner and watched a movie with your daughter. If they asked what we watched, I'd say it was some kid's movie. I don't remember the name. Once you've seen one, you've seen them all. How far off am I?"

"Not far," Luck said. "But you don't count."

"What does that mean?"

"You've got profiler spidey sense."

With a groan, Darger stood up.

"Let's go see if Murphy can tell us what game they were watching."

☾

Murphy's knee, which had been bouncing up and down at a frenetic pace, froze as soon as Darger opened the door.

"Just one more quick question," she said. "What game was it?"

"What game?"

"The football game you watched at Camacho's house."

Murphy frowned.

"I don't remember," he said. "I don't watch a lot of football, to be honest. Is this really that important?"

Darger shot an I told you so look at Luck.

Then Murphy said, "Oh wait. It was the Vikings and the uh… Raiders."

She saw worry cloud Luck's face. Darger felt a mixture of frustration and confusion. None of this made any sense. It felt like they were moving in circles.

She slid a pad of paper over to Murphy.

"I need you to write down your whereabouts for today, and then I need the same thing for August 11th, August 20th, and September 4th."

He took the paper and pen, looking bewildered.

"August 11th and 20th and… hold on. Those are the dates of the other fires," he said, and then it hit him. "Wait. Wait, wait, wait. What's going on here? Why are you asking me about that?"

"When we asked the witnesses from The Blue Handkerchief if they'd seen anyone hanging around recently that seemed suspicious, one of them picked you out of the crowd. He said you were there last week."

His head shook from side to side, then he stopped and sat up a little straighter.

"But I was with Camacho when the fire started. I have an alibi!"

"The problem is Camacho says he was alone. He kept up with that story until I told him why we were asking, then he suddenly changed his story, said you were, in fact, together."

"Well, there you go! That settles it, doesn't it?"

"Not really. Because how do we know he isn't just lying to cover your ass? Or that you didn't set the fires together?"

"You can't actually believe that!"

"I don't know what to believe right now. All I know for sure is that both of you are lying about something," Darger said, her voice cold. "And here's another problem, Murphy. Your partner? He just lawyered up. And my guess is his counsel will advise him to cut a deal. Sell you down the river for a plea."

"He wouldn't do that," Murphy said.

"No?"

"No! Because he knows I didn't do this."

Darger shrugged.

"In that case, you'll both go down for it." She sighed and laid her hands on the table. "Look, Rodney. I want to believe you. I think this is probably all a misunderstanding. But I need you to tell me why a witness from today's fire could possibly ID you. And why Camacho would change his story like that."

"Fuck." Murphy's hands shook as he ran his hands through

his hair. "Just... give me a minute."

They waited. Darger wanted to look over at Luck, to see what he made of this, but she was afraid to take her eyes off of Murphy even for a second. They were finally getting somewhere.

"God he's going to hate me for this," Murphy said, his voice barely a whisper.

"Who?" Darger asked.

Murphy took a deep breath and looked her square in the eye.

"I've been to The Blue Handkerchief before," he said. "But I didn't start the fire."

"You can't expect us to believe you ended up there by accident. It's a gay bar."

"I know. I'm gay."

Neither Darger nor Luck spoke. She thought he was probably just as dumbstruck as she was.

It was Murphy who broke the silence.

"The witness said I was acting suspicious?"

"Yeah."

"That's because I was nervous as hell. In case you couldn't tell, I'm not exactly out."

Darger chewed on this.

"Why lie about being with Camacho, then? You just figured he'd cover for you?"

Murphy let out a mammoth sigh.

"It wasn't a lie. I stayed the night at Miguel's last night," he said, his tone pointed.

It was a moment before the full realization hit her.

"Oh."

And now it all made sense. Murphy had been telling the truth all along about being with Camacho. Camacho had been the one who was lying. Covering up the fact that he was sleeping with his partner.

"Everyone's going to know now, aren't they?" Murphy said, shaking his head. "Jesus, this isn't how I imagined coming out."

"No." Darger tapped the pad of paper. "It doesn't have to be. Give us those alibis, for the other fires. We're going to need them to clear all of this up."

"What about Miguel?"

"We have to get him to corroborate it."

Murphy slumped in his chair.

"He's never going to forgive me."

CHAPTER 48

Camacho's lawyer was in the interview room when they entered this time. He got to his feet and stood so that he blocked the way into the room.

"I'm curious, Agents. Are you planning on rounding up and interrogating every able-bodied man in Los Angeles?"

"Excuse me?"

"My client tells me that just today you've suspected three different people of being the arsonist. It sounds to me like you're playing eenie-meanie-miney-moe, blindly accusing any innocent person that crosses your path, and hoping something sticks. It's nothing short of harassment, and let me tell you, the DA is not going to—"

Darger pushed past the windbag lawyer with his shiny shoes and shinier hair and focused on Camacho.

"Miguel, Murphy said he was with you earlier today."

"Yeah, and I told you he's telling the truth."

"Mr. Camacho, I would advise you not to say anything," the lawyer said.

Darger ignored him.

"He also said you were together last night."

There was a long pause. Camacho's jaw clenched and unclenched. His eyes fell to the tabletop.

"He told you?"

"Yes," Darger said. "It's true?"

Camacho nodded, still not making eye contact.

"Why hide it?" Luck asked. "It's not like we're in some

backwoods place. And it's nothing to be ashamed of."

Camacho's head snapped up, eyes burning.

"Ashamed? Fuck you, Luck! I'm not ashamed of anything. Just because I'm not out there waving a fucking rainbow flag doesn't mean I'm ashamed of who I am. It's my fucking choice. My fucking life. Who are you to tell me how to be?" He jabbed a thick finger at his own chest. "I control my identity. Not you. Not anyone."

Luck held up his hands defensively.

"Fair enough, man. I didn't mean anything by it."

Camacho made a disgusted sound.

"Does this mean I can go?"

"We're still confirming Murphy's alibis for the other fires. But yes. You can go."

He was on his feet and halfway out the door before Darger could think to say something.

"I'm sorry, Miguel," she said, knowing a mere apology was woefully inadequate.

Before disappearing through the doorway, he scoffed and said, "Murphy's the one you should be apologizing to."

And apologize they did, once they saw the security footage of Murphy at the department firing range on the day of the church fire. Unless he was able to be in two places at once, he was not their arsonist.

After releasing Murphy and reporting to Chief Macklin, they took the elevator down to the parking level.

"So," Luck said, letting the silence hang there for a moment. "That was rough."

"Yep. That sucked."

Darger propped herself up in the corner of the elevator,

letting her head loll back against the wall.

"We should have asked for alibis for all of the fires before we did anything else," she said. "We could have saved everyone the headache."

Frowning, Luck shook his head.

"No. We did this right. If we'd asked about the other fires, he would have spooked. Probably would have lawyered up like Camacho. We were wrong in the end, but we made all the right moves."

The elevator dinged, and the doors swished open. They filed out, footsteps echoing across the vast concrete chamber of the parking garage. Darger spotted Murphy and Camacho at the far end despite the dim lighting. The two men looked in their direction, and Darger held her breath, thinking they might be in for some sort of confrontation. But Camacho only turned away, and then Murphy followed suit. So it'd be the cold shoulder instead.

Once inside Luck's vehicle, Darger settled into the passenger seat.

"OK," she said. "I'll admit it. This seat is pretty comfortable."

He smiled.

"That's it? You're not going to gloat?"

"I'm too tired to gloat."

She sighed.

"I hear that."

As they drove, Darger thought back to the first interview she'd ever conducted with Luck. It was her first case with the BAU, and she was in Ohio hunting a man who'd killed and dismembered four women. When they spoke with the fourth victim's mother, she'd been more concerned with a piece of jewelry her daughter had been wearing at the time of her death than about making funeral arrangements. Luck had invited her out for a drink afterward, perhaps sensing and sharing Darger's raw emotional state after the encounter.

She wanted him to do that now. Wanted to go somewhere loud and dark, where they could hide in the corner and take the edge off with a drink or two. Most of all, she desperately did not want to be alone, regardless of the hour.

They rolled through the streets of L.A., the dark silhouettes of palm trees outlined against the streetlights. Why not just ask Luck herself? She was a grown-ass woman, after all. But what stopped her was that he had a family waiting for him at home. She didn't want to keep him from his daughter. Not when that was where he probably wanted to be.

When they reached her hotel, Luck pulled alongside the lobby doors and put the car in park. Her eyes traveled up the side of the building, imagining her stark little room. She really couldn't stand the idea of going up there just now. As tired as she was, she had a feeling she wouldn't be able to sleep. The idea of lying on the rock hard mattress, numbing her mind with vapid TV made her want to scream.

Fuck it. They were going to go get a drink, damn it. And she'd do the asking.

Her lips parted. She was about to speak when Luck suddenly threw his head back and swore.

"What is it?"

"I was supposed to pick up cleats for Jill," he said. "She's starting soccer next week, and I keep forgetting to get the damn cleats."

Darger couldn't help but take this as a sign from the universe that a drink with Luck was not in the cards for her tonight.

"Ah well… there are 24-hour places for such things," Darger said. "You still have time."

Luck glanced at the digital clock on the dashboard and nodded.

"That's true. Somewhere will still have cleats."

Darger unbuckled her seatbelt and started to slide out of the car.

"Thanks for the ride," she said.

"Hey," Luck said, stopped her. "Were you about to say something a minute ago? It looked like you had something on your mind."

"Nothing important," Darger said and closed the car door.

CHAPTER 49

Carl wades all the way into the bush — a gnarly dried out thing, mostly dead, surrounding an abandoned church — and starts flinging gas around from an old bottle of Ruby Red Squirt. He backs out of the brush slowly, thoroughly coating the shrub from front to back as he moves. Jim has to admire his initiative in being so thorough.

Crack truly is the mother of ingenuity.

The gasoline glistens on the twisted branches, the wetness seeming to imply life in the jerky movements of the bush as Carl pushes his way back through it, the knotty places looking more and more like knuckles flexing and grasping and trying to grip. Jim feels the slightest ripple of goose bumps just where his neck meets his spine.

"There," the homeless man says, now standing outside the foliage but still detaching prickly stuff from his shirt and pants, the plant reluctant to let him go. "That good enough?"

"Oh, I reckon that'll work."

Jim stalks close to the dying plant and kneels, close enough now to see the gas drizzling down everywhere, beads pattering at the dry dirt below. The stench of the gas hits then, makes his head a little light, an electric tingle tremoring in his skull, but subtly so. Mild. Almost reminds him of the nicotine buzz he got the first time he smoked a cigarette behind the tennis courts in 7th grade.

He flicks his lighter. Holds it close to the wet bush.

Let there be light.

The blaze flares. Fire reaching up into the night. Lifting the darkness. Attacking it.

So bright it makes Jim's eyes water. Everything smeared and blurry. But the raw energy is still there to be felt even in that first fraction of a second. Undeniable.

He stumbles back from the rush of heat, a violent gust of air that seems hell-bent on pushing him down.

And then they're off. Scurrying away. Two rodents partially hunched as they flee across the grass toward the street. Jim watches their crooked shadows running alongside, and the word scoundrels pops into his head.

Giddiness overcomes both men as they climb into the SUV and speed away from the scene. Some thrill of victory mixing with something else. The giggles erupt, infectious as always, though in the panic and rushing about, Jim can't recall who started laughing first. Could it have been Carl? Is that possible?

"That was great," Carl says. "Didn't think it would be so fun, I guess."

"Yep. Told you, didn't I?"

"So that's it? That'll scare your, uh, whoever, then, I take it?"

Jim's laugh comes out in an uneven cackle. He sounds a little unhinged even in his own ears.

"Oh, lord no," he says, giving Carl the sunglasses stare down. "That was just the opening act, my friend. The real deal is just up here."

Carl's brow wrinkles. He tilts his head to the side. Is he trying to puzzle this out, or is he angry that he's still a step away from his beloved crack rock?

"So the bush back there," he says, his voice softer now.

283

"That was like a decoy?"

Now it's Jim's turn to nod and smile.

"You're sending all the firemen and cops down that way to handle the burning bush, so they won't get back this way fast enough to do anything about… well, whatever you've got up next."

"See? I told you, you have potential. You cracked that shit like Sherlock Holmes."

"Yeah. Guess I did."

Carl falls quiet after that, a thoughtful expression occupying his face, neither suspicious nor not suspicious, from what Jim can tell.

Carl. A mystery wrapped in a riddle.

They drive in silence for a couple blocks, and then Jim takes a right.

"It's just up here," he says, his voice hushed as though someone might hear.

Betsy's apartment building takes shape before them. The image zooming in, growing larger and larger on their windshield screen.

But something is wrong.

The dumpster still sits there on the alley side of the big Victorian house, and that blackness still pocks the wall above it. The melted siding now holds still, crispy blackened folds of it, no longer the molten, malleable stuff it was when Jim last laid eyes on it.

Police tape cordons off this little area. A rectangular perimeter of yellow encasing the dumpster, flapping a little in the breeze.

The rest of the building looks mostly the same as last time.

All dark on the ground floor, the old fogeys who live there in bed for hours now, most likely. A few lights on upstairs, but nothing crazy.

It's the police cruiser in the driveway that takes Jim's breath away, renders him mute. They should all be en route to the burning bush by now. Putting the window down, he can even hear the sirens warbling in the distance.

And then he sees it. The downfall of tonight's festivities. No fun for anyone.

An officer stands near Betsy's window, jotting something in a little notepad. They're here. Now. Working this goddamn case at this hour? Probably asking her to talk about anyone she had a conflict with.

Pain. Rage. The same core emotion somehow coming out in two different ways. He felt both of them now like a pair of blades jammed into his gut.

He says nothing. Just grits his teeth and drives on. Leaves it behind, for now and for always.

For just a second, he gets those dual flashes again. Naked Betsy pressing against him flashing straight to her gas-drenched hair going up in flames at his lighter's touch.

It's never to be now. Never ever ever.

"There a problem?" the homeless man says, interrupting Jim's internal monologue.

"So much for the strong, silent type, eh, Carl?" Jim says. His voice sounds sharp, more angry than he intended.

"Sorry," Carl says. "Just… you seemed upset. And you're speeding. Seems like something changed."

"Well, something did change, Sherlock. We're off for tonight, I'm afraid. I'll take you back now. Drop you off."

"Damn. I don't know. I was kinda lookin' forward to it, I guess."

"Weren't we all?"

Again a quiet comes to them, intent on riding along with them. But even in his frustration, he finds this silence to lack that awkwardness he might experience with another. Carl is all right.

Jim pulls the foil from his left pocket. Tosses it to Carl who looks like a little kid getting a new toy.

Carl doesn't go to smoke it right away, though. He holds the packet in his open hand, and his eyes seek out the sunglasses, trying for the third time to look through the dark lenses and see who lives behind them.

"So you're him, huh?" Carl says.

Jim holds his breath for a few heartbeats. There was something in the tone of the man's voice to be read, but he's not sure how to take it. A threat? Mere intrigue?

"What?" Jim says after the silence grows too long to bear.

Carl turns away. Looks out the window.

"Nothing," he says. "Forget it."

Jim wants to. He wants to forget it, but he doesn't think he can.

CHAPTER 50

The first thing Darger did upon entering her hotel room was to strip off her smoke-drenched clothes and take a shower. She dressed in fresh clothes and milled around for a few minutes before the leftover frustration from the day built to a peak. First the failure with Sablatsky and then again with Murphy and Camacho. It seemed like they were running down dead end after dead end.

She tried to remember the relief she'd felt after learning no one had died at The Blue Handkerchief, but that had faded now. What remained wasn't nearly enough to erase the guilt she felt over accusing two members of the task force, being wrong, and then outing them in the process. It was the cherry on top of a shit sundae of a day.

She grabbed her bag and room key and headed downstairs. There was a restaurant down the street with a neon sign outside that said "Open Late." She found an empty stool at the bar and ordered a drink. Scotch. Neat.

Darger downed the first drink and set the glass back on the bar for another.

"That kind of night?" the bartender asked.

She was young, with long black hair that was buzzed on the sides. Her smile was accented by a double lip piercing that Darger had heard someone refer to as "snake bites" at some point.

"Pretty much."

The girl nodded and refilled her drink. Darger took it

slower this time. Now that the warmth and numbness from the first drink had spread a little, she'd just maintain for a while.

"Want anything from the kitchen?" the bartender asked, sliding a menu across the bar.

Something about standing in all that smoke earlier had zapped her appetite, but it'd been hours since she'd eaten.

"I'll take an order of fries," Darger said, handing the menu back.

Her thoughts turned naturally to Luck. She wondered if he'd made it to the store to get the cleats for his daughter. She'd made the right call, she decided. He should be with his kid.

Her phone buzzed then, and Darger couldn't help but hope it was Luck. He'd psychically picked up on the fact that she was in this bar and was heading over to join her.

But no. It was a text from Beck, thanking her for updating her on the outcome of the bar fire.

Darger slid her phone back into her pocket and sighed. She pictured Beck's happy little family of four, with number five on the way. Maple syrup disasters not-withstanding, Darger envied her. Because Darger? Darger had no one. Which was how she found herself here in this moment, drinking alone.

The bartender plopped a basket of fries down in front of Darger, shattering her thoughts.

"Ketchup?"

"Yes, please," Darger said, taking the proffered bottle.

She'd been headed down an awfully mopey train of thought and was glad for the interruption. Self-pity wasn't a good look.

Besides, she had more important things to think about.

She dunked a fry into a swirl of Heinz and considered the case. They'd ruled out Sablatsky, Camacho, and Murphy. So that only left a few million people in the greater Los Angeles metropolitan area.

And then it hit her: they'd landed on Sablatsky because of the fire outside of Camacho's house. And then Murphy because he'd been inside The Blue Handkerchief.

They'd assumed after the Camacho fire that the arsonist was targeting the task force. Now she was certain of it. Not only that, but it seemed they had become his sole focus.

Her next thought sent goose bumps scuttling up her arms.

Who would be next?

She couldn't resist the urge to glance around the bar, but it was mostly couples and small groups. She was one of only a few lone patrons, a thought that had her reaching for her glass again.

(

It was a good thing Darger had walked to the bar. By the time closing time came around, she was definitely tipsy, though not completely shitfaced. That would be irresponsible. This thought made her chuckle to herself, which left her wondering if she was possibly a little closer to shitfaced than she'd originally considered.

It took her three swipes of her room card before she got the timing right and opened the door before the green light turned back to red. Why'd they have to make hotel room doors some kind of rocket science, anyway? It was a Marriott, not Fort Knox.

Trying to remove her boots as she walked to the bed, she stumbled and fell against the side of the mattress, thudding to the floor.

She simultaneously wanted to laugh and cry. She settled for thumping her fist into the carpet and grunting.

She imagined the people in the room below hearing the sounds and envisioning some manner of wild sex. But no, it was just a depressed, drunken FBI agent having a temper tantrum.

Darger peeled her boots off the rest of the way and crawled onto the bed, not bothering to even get under the covers.

At some point, while she waited for the room to stop spinning, she fell into a dreamless sleep.

CHAPTER 51

Carl huddles in the dumpster. Shivering. Too scared to move, Jim thinks. Probably rightfully so. The gun in Jim's hand would be enough to scare anyone, wouldn't it?

Jim had come to this decision on the ride back to Skid Row. The way he saw it, Carl left him no choice. He'd painted himself — perhaps both of them — into a corner.

Now Jim stands on the hood of his car to peer down on his partner for the night. He'd chosen a tall dumpster. Eight feet high or so. Smooth steel walls to contend with. If Carl wants out, he'll have to work at it. Jim doubts any full-time crackhead could manage a single pull-up.

The gasoline drizzles down on the homeless man now. Dumping out of the bottle in little spurts with each shake he gives it. Muffled wet sounds rising from where the dribbles slap into the fabric of Carl's clothes.

And it looks like the bum is crying, but it's hard to be sure. Hard to tell the difference between what might be tears and the beads of gas streaking down his face, especially tucked down in the shade of the dumpster's chamber.

A wad of muscles clench in Jim's gut as he fishes in his pocket for the lighter. And he keeps waiting for Carl to say something. To beg. To plead. To pray.

But the man says nothing. Not so much as a single word. He just slumps there in the metal tomb, blinking, eyes fixed on the middle distance, piercing empty space.

Maybe he's ready to die. Good to go. Maybe he's made

peace with it. He's not quite all the way here, anyway, is he? Sleeping on concrete. Living from fix to fix. It's not much of a life. So let it go.

Mixed emotions churning in his gut or not, Jim can't help but feel the thrill creep over him as his fingers find the lighter and pluck it free of his pants. A tingle in his chest, an electric chill in his hands. This is the fun part, right? It's a cold feeling that comes along with this thought, and yet he finds himself verging toward laughter. Lips shimmying with the threat of the giggles just like earlier tonight.

He's never done it like this. Lit someone up face to face. At close range.

He's terribly excited to experience the sheer aesthetics of it — to see how it will work, how it will look, what sounds this man will make with the fire adhered to his skin by a sheening layer of gasoline. This will be his most jaw-dropping special effects sequence yet.

Sweat seems to arrive on Jim's skin everywhere at once. A thin layer of moisture slicks his body. Prepares him.

And he breathes through his teeth now, ragged breaths, his lips parted involuntarily, tip of his tongue running back and forth along the sharp edge of his incisors.

God, it's sick to be so titillated by something like this. He knows this. Acknowledges it. But it changes nothing.

He leans his upper body toward Carl. Flicks the lighter. Loops his arm down into the dumpster. Presses the flame toward the damp hair.

Brightness shoots through the night. An overwhelming glow enveloping everything. Pure white, or so it seems in the dark.

Night on Fire

Jim's upper body rocks back, avoids the rush of the flame. His eyes water, and everything blurs, smearing and smudging, all the shapes bleeding together into a flailing mindless glow.

The fire hisses. Right there. Its heat a wall in front of him. Writhing. Reaching. Taking.

Carl screams, silent no more. He screams like a child. Shrill. Shredded. Small and powerless and very scared.

Goose bumps plump on Jim's arms, down his back, rippling across his chest. He pants for breath now like a dog. Moaning a little. Sweat weeping down his forehead, stinging in the corners of his eyes.

And he stumbles back a step, the sound too much. The sound somehow worse than the sight of it, somehow worse than the burning pork smell.

Blinking a few times, he sees the man thrashing in there, torso thumping against the metal walls, the dark of his limbs visible through the flames, whipping and flopping. He looks like one of the bunnies panicking in the wildfires, running deeper into the flames.

Mindless with fear. Lost. No escape.

Now wings flap behind Carl, beating and burning, frantic like the screams pouring out of him, trying to lift him from this fiery grave before it's too late — or maybe it's the tears rushing to Jim's eyes that make him see it that way.

He doesn't know. He never will.

He wants to rush off the hood of the SUV. Race away from here and never look back. But his feet stay planted in place. Paralyzed.

He watches the burning. Can't take his eyes away. Blood beats in his head. In his skull. In his brain. Rushing heat inside and out. A violent throb he can only associate with an erection.

And for just a second, he considers slumping forward. Leaning over the edge. Letting himself fall into the dumpster, into the flames. Letting the fire embrace him with its special touch. Consume him. If he wants it, it's right here in front of him. A short drop. A single second away.

Death.

Carl's scream cuts out all at once. Jim thinks the man dead for a split second, but no. He squirms still. Lives on though his voice is gone. Kicking and flailing. Limbs somehow thinner than before. Spindly. He looks like a black beetle trapped on its back, succumbing to a child's magnifying glass.

And even after the figure stops moving some twenty-odd seconds later, the fire hisses out its endless exhale. Some great release of energy. Some revelation to behold.

And he is scared of it now. Scared of its power.

No longer Jim. This moment reduces him. Leaning over the dumpster. Watching the corpse continue to burn. It reduces him to Klootey. To T.J. Klootey, a nobody cop. A fucking loser with no friends. With nothing but fantasies of being someone else.

Even stripped down like this, he can't look away. He can only watch his creation.

Destruction. The sublime.

This primordial heat. Something as primal as blood and skin and sex.

The fire takes everything in the dumpster, reduces it to a shapeless glow, a melting of all forms within, every contour surrendered to the flames.

CHAPTER 52

The thumping sound coming from the next room over was uncalled for. She'd intentionally turned her usual phone alarm off, figuring she owed it to herself to sleep in. And now it sounded like the jackholes next door were doing parkour on the shared wall.

"Violet?"

The voice was muffled and came in a break between thumping episodes.

Now that was something she hadn't expected. How did the jackholes know her name?

Several bleary-eyed seconds passed with her staring at the wall before she realized it wasn't noise from the next room that had woken her. It was someone knocking at her door.

And the voice belonged to Luck.

She scrambled out of bed, smoothing her hair and attempting to clear her throat before answering, not wanting to appear like a groggy cave troll.

She opened the door, squinting against the brightly lit hallway.

"Hey. Sorry to just show up like this, but I tried calling, and you didn't answer."

"It's fine," she said, ushering him inside, and closing the door behind him. "What's up?"

"Chief Macklin called me. They found a body."

"At The Blue Handkerchief?" Darger asked, unable to keep the dread from creeping into her voice.

She should have known it was too good to be true. The fact that no one had died in yesterday's fire had been the one bright point in an otherwise dreary, unproductive day. But after seeing the fire at the bar firsthand, it had been almost shocking to learn there had been no loss of life.

"No," Luck said. "This is a separate scene, over in the Fashion District."

Darger found herself struggling to catch up.

"There was another fire last night?" She brushed a strand of hair from her face. "How did we not hear about this?"

"Not a fire, so to speak. Well, that's not true either," he said and then sighed. "Sorry, I haven't had any coffee yet, and I don't think I'm making sense. This wasn't a structure fire. It looks like… well, it looks like he doused someone with gas and set them on fire in a dumpster."

The ability to speak left her for a moment. She felt the air sucked from her lungs.

"I'm about to head over there now," Luck continued. "I can wait for you, or you can meet me over there."

She was already moving to her suitcase.

"Give me five minutes."

CHAPTER 53

After the fire, Klootey can't sleep. Restless energy pulses behind his eyes. Beats in his blood. Works his jaw back and forth over and over.

He drives. Speeds. Goes ripping into the night. Deeper and faster. Like if he builds up enough sheer velocity, he can flee this plane, flee this life. Drive off that sheared edge of the city into nothing, into the void. Leave it all behind.

Trying to touch the darkness.

Is that what it is? Is that what he's doing when he goes out like he does? Spreading destruction everywhere he goes. Setting the night on fire.

Flashes of the dumpster blaze in his skull. The orange leaping. Lurching and spitting.

Carl turning. Changing. Body going wispy, going frail at the fire's touch. Black as charcoal.

Fire on his skin. In his hair. Melting his clothes. Adhering the fabric to his body.

Fire dancing. Fire thrashing. Fire flailing and glowing and blistering and breaking down the meat of him.

That oily fire stuck right on him, the gasoline binding it to his flesh, holding it to him. Morphing the shape of his face, sort of smearing the skin down the skull in slow motion.

He shudders remembering it, remembering Carl's scream. Jesus.

The hair on his arms stands up, skin pulling taut with a chill. He swallows in a dry throat.

And a big breath sucks into him. A wet gasp so big it makes his vision flutter, eyes watering. Some religious feeling coming over him, holding him in its sacred grip.

Awe. He trembles with it, body immediately glistening with sweat. The perspiration weeping down out of reverence, out of wonder, out of astonishment.

It's time, he realizes all at once. It's time.

He sits forward in his seat. Blinks the water from his eyes. Not upset anymore. Not wallowing anymore. He knew this day would come, knew that he would feel it when it was right, that it would pick him more than he would pick it, that it would happen to him as much as anything.

He's paid something, paid some due with the dumpster fire. Suffered something for his art, for his passion, for his life's work.

And with the price paid at last, he can be done. He can finish this now.

He veers left down a twisting street. Heads out toward the hills again. Out toward the spot he's picked for this. The shed that will become the point of origin.

He puts the window down. Lets the cool night air rush in to tousle his hair. It chills the left side of his face, makes the muscles around his eyelids spasm.

And his mind is blank. Vacant. At peace, finally.

Here. Two little gashes break up the foliage, barely visible — tire tracks leading out to the sacred ground.

He parks the SUV along the side of the road. Kills the engine. Sits a second in the quiet, in the dark, just breathing and sweating. Some restless tension eventually pushing him forward, pushing him out of the car, into the night. He'll take the last little way to the shed on foot.

His body feels strange now. Electric. The normal tingles he gets before a fire intermingling with some awkward wad of nerves clenched in his belly. Is he nervous? He must be. He must be. And maybe that's to be expected.

He's imagined this moment for years. Waited most of a lifetime for this. Patiently. Waiting for the moment to come to him like a sleepy spider lingering along the edge of its web. The moment arrives without warning, jarring, almost feeling surreal.

Something animal kicks in. Something savage that takes him whole. It prickles over his skin, every little follicle and pore alive with it, slicked and crawling with it. Fierce with it. Makes him grit his teeth.

And now what will happen will happen. For now and for always. It will ever be.

If all goes well, many will die in the coming days. Burned. Melted. Crisped and disintegrated. Horrific deaths like Carl screaming in the dumpster but everywhere, everyone. The whole city consumed by flames, surrendered to the fire.

He will give the city what it deserves. He will give them fire.

The dark closes around him as soon as he's under the trees, the air thicker here, though still dry. He feels his way along the dirt path, knowing the shed is ahead somewhere but not able to see it for the moment. His feet pick their way, sort of sliding forward over stones and dirt, plunging down the left tire track, and he can feel the scraggly stuff just next to him on both sides brushing against his pantlegs, tangles of brush and shrubs about knee-high, filling in the place between the tire tracks like overgrown stubble.

He feels outside of himself. Apart. Watching the climax of the movie. The hero taking those inevitable steps that will set the finale in motion. Crossing a line. Irreversible.

And the whole thing will be decided from here, the path already certain, all the momentum pushing it where it wants to go, where it must go, the whole thing spinning on its course as if directing itself, in some way out of anyone's hands now.

L.A. should brace itself for a special effects sequence like none before it. A stunning technical achievement. Oscar-worthy, if there were any justice in this town, in this world.

He tries to picture the woods going up. Wonders if the wind will do its piece today. It feels right, he thinks. The air warm and dry and moving along, wrinkling his shirt against his front.

And he smiles as he pictures the flames, because he knows now. It is inevitable. Always was.

He paid his price. Offered up his dumpster sacrifice. And now the fire will smile back at him, pay him back many times over. It will rage and hate and kill, express the mess of feelings in his head for him. The ultimate artistic statement.

As he opens the shed door, he pictures all the king's horses and all the king's men coming for him soon, coming for his fire. All those fire trucks and police cars, lights twirling, sirens screaming. Camacho and Bishop and everyone. A fleet of news choppers flying overhead to get those raging fire shots they love to show so fucking much. Even the feds in their shiny Lexuses would be after him, after his work. Here in just a few hours, it'd be a total and complete shitstorm.

He'd be the biggest star in Hollywood, the talk of the town. A star, at last. Little laughs puff out of his nostrils at the thought.

Want to try to stop this? Well, come and fucking get it.

CHAPTER 54

The year Darger graduated from high school, her stepfather had decided to deep fry the Thanksgiving turkey.

"But I always make the turkey," her mother had argued. "Don't you like my turkey?"

"Of course, honey. But deep frying is supposed to yield a very juicy bird."

"And my stuffing. You can't stuff the turkey if you fry it, can you?"

"Well no, but you can make it on the side. There's always more dressing than fits in the bird, anyway."

Despite her mother's doubts, they went ahead with the deep frying. Her stepfather bought several gallons of peanut oil and a giant turkey-sized pot for the frying. He set up in the garage on Thanksgiving morning, brought the oil up to temperature, and slowly lowered in the turkey. Nearly an hour later, when he pulled the turkey out of the oil, it was solid black. Charred to a crisp. Her mother never let her stepfather forget this incident, and he never again suggested deep frying the Thanksgiving turkey.

Darger thought of the burned turkey now as she looked down into the dumpster. Because that's what the body looked like to her. A charred piece of meat.

"We're sure the person was alive when they were set on fire?" she asked.

They hadn't determined a sex yet. It was that bad.

Luck pointed to some outlines in the soot and charred areas

inside the dumpster.

"The fire investigator said you can tell by the burn patterns here and here that he was moving around while he burned. Probably trying to climb out."

"Jesus," Darger said, her stomach feeling sour.

"The medical examiner will be able to confirm it once the autopsy is done, of course. If there's smoke in the lungs, then we'll be sure."

She'd been to scenes with burned bodies, but in those cases, the person had already been dead before they were burned. The idea of someone being set on fire while alive was just… unimaginable.

Luck helped her climb down from the scaffolding the LAPD crime scene techs had erected outside of the dumpster. Two assistants from the medical examiner's office waited nearby to assist with moving the body. They'd brought along a hydraulic lift, the kind hospitals used to move patients who lacked full mobility.

"How do you think he got them in there? The victim, I mean," Darger asked, her gaze focused on the coroner's assistant who was now climbing over the edge of the dumpster. There was a loud metallic thud as the man let himself drop to the bottom.

"Good question," Luck said. "I would say he had them incapacitated and threw them in, but it's too tall for even that."

"If he has a pickup truck, he could have put the victim in the bed and backed up to the dumpster," Darger mused, gauging the height of the metal container. "I bet he could have thrown them in that way. Or he had a weapon and forced them in."

Luck shook his head.

"Can you imagine? Being forced to climb into that thing? And then this psycho starts pouring gas over you?"

Darger left the question unanswered. She watched one of the techs bagging the soda bottle the killer had left behind. Again. Wanting to claim this dark deed as his own.

To set a living, breathing person on fire, to watch them die so horribly and violently in front of you… that was quite a progression from setting a house fire. If he hadn't technically been a serial killer when this all started, he surely was now. No doubt about that.

Chief Macklin stood a few yards away, phone pressed to his ear. Judging by the drawn expression on his face, whatever the person on the other end of the line was saying wasn't good. He ended the call and beckoned the two agents.

"That was Chief Rubio with L.A. Fire. They've got a brush fire out in one of the canyons north of here."

Darger's already dark mood went a shade blacker. She closed her eyes and asked the inevitable question.

"Do they think it was set intentionally?"

"They traced the point of origin to a shed on an abandoned property. Not far from there, on the side of the road, they recovered a plastic bottle with gasoline residue."

"Sure seems like he's going on a tear," Luck said, gesturing to the soot-smeared dumpster. "First this, now a brush fire?"

Darger rubbed her temple.

"It's probably because everyone got out of The Blue Handkerchief alive. The fire isn't enough anymore for him. He wants blood and death now."

Eyes fixed on the body being hoisted from the dumpster via

the hydraulic lift, the three of them spent a few seconds digesting that. What lengths would he go to now to ensure a body count? Darger wondered.

She turned away from the scene to face Chief Macklin.

"How bad is the brush fire?"

"They've got it under control for now. They're lucky, really. It's been a pretty still day. With something like this, the wind is what really wreaks havoc." He wiped a hand across his brow. "I've scheduled another meeting for 1600 hours so we can present the latest details to the task force. The M.E. has promised to expedite the autopsy. I'm hopeful we'll have an official cause of death and possibly an ID by then. And I'd like the task force to hear from you as well, Agent Darger."

With a single nod of her head, she said, "I'll be ready."

((

Hours passed as they watched the scene being processed. The techs bustled about in their protective booties and gloves, bagging the evidence from in and around the dumpster.

"I hate this part," Darger said, shifting her weight from one foot to the other. "It feels like I'm just standing here, doing nothing."

From behind his aviator sunglasses, Luck looked over at her.

"That's because you are doing nothing."

"Yeah well, I don't like waiting." She shook her head. "I mean, I get that this is how it has to work. The techs have to move carefully and methodically. And I'd rather they be slow than sloppy. But I wish I could wave a magic wand and have the scene fully processed. All the evidence bagged, logged, and ready to be analyzed."

She felt Luck's eyes on her.

"I'm whining, I know." She nudged a pebble with her toe. "I'll shut up now."

"What about your other two wishes?"

"What?"

"You wished for a magic wand that would process crime scenes in an instant. Pretty sure you get two more."

Darger laughed.

"OK. Well, while I'm at it, I'd like a second wand that gets all our evidence through the lab at the blink of an eye."

"Double-fisting the magic wands. A bold move." Luck nodded, looking impressed. "And your third wish?"

She answered without hesitation.

"A pet unicorn," she said. "Duh."

CHAPTER 55

Darger spent the early afternoon helping canvas for witnesses with Luck. Unfortunately, the fire had taken place late at night, and this wasn't an area known for its nightlife.

Which is why he'd chosen it, Darger thought bitterly.

The dumpster in question belonged to a floral supply warehouse, which closed at 4:30 PM. All of the employees were gone by five, hours before the fire had taken place.

The business next door to the floral supply was a designer jeans outlet store. Across the street, two wholesale fabric suppliers and a tailor. All of them closed by 6 PM. None of the workers they talked to had seen anything, because they simply hadn't been there when there was anything to see.

To make matters worse, all of the businesses on the block had security cameras, but they were mainly located inside the buildings, with the exception of a single camera focused on the front entrance. The dumpster and the alley leading to it were well out of sight of any of the cameras.

The tailor had a TV on in his shop, and Darger couldn't help but notice the local news snippet about the brush fire. Back outside, she searched for updates on her phone. She found a live L.A. newscast online and played the video.

"Reports from earlier today were all good news. The fire crews made excellent progress and believed they had the blaze firmly under control. Unfortunately, that all changed over the past two hours. Channel 2 News is getting word now that strong winds have moved into the area, feeding the fire and threatening that progress."

A bird's eye view of the fire showed a steep green hillside ablaze. The camera panned right, showing rows of houses clustered along a nearby ridge. A helicopter swung into view, dumping a load of water on one end of the flaming ravine.

"As of this moment, there have been no injuries reported, nor have any homes been lost. However, the Los Angeles County Fire Department has issued a tentative warning to residents of the Whitney Canyon area that they should be ready to evacuate their homes at a moment's notice, should things take a turn for the worse."

"That's not good," Luck said.

"No. Definitely not."

By the time they'd finished canvassing the neighboring businesses, a large truck had arrived to pick up the dumpster. Darger spotted Captain Beck amongst a group of LAPD officers clustered not far from the dumpster-loading activity.

Seeing Beck reminded Darger of what the Captain had told her on the surveillance detail, about finding a string of old fires in the San Bernardino valley that fit the pattern. God, was that only yesterday? It felt like days had passed since then.

Darger made a mental note to address this at the task force meeting. The task force had been looking for more fires that fit the pattern, but they'd only been looking at the past five years. Beck had uncovered something by expanding the net, and they should do the same for all the localities. Because if he was setting fires as far back as eleven years ago, he hadn't stopped in the interim. Darger was certain of it.

Waiting for a break in traffic, Darger and Luck crossed the street to join the group near the loading truck.

"I can't believe they're taking the whole kit and caboodle to the crime lab," Beck said.

"Seems like overkill to me," one of the unis said. "I figure he torched the guy and got the hell out of here. How much trace evidence could he leave behind?"

The mechanical winch on the back of the truck roared to life, whining as it cranked the chain that pulled the dumpster inch by inch onto the truck bed.

Luck crossed his arms.

"With a case this massive, I'm guessing the LAPD wants no stone left unturned."

The breeze ran its fingers through Darger's hair, blowing a strand across her mouth. She reached up and plucked it away, turning toward Beck.

"I didn't expect to see you until the task force meeting."

Beck hooked her thumbs into her gun belt.

"Well, I figured I ought to come down a little early and check out the new scene," she said, eyes on the dumpster. "I have to admit, when you texted me last night to let me know there were no casualties in the bar fire, I'd thought we'd gotten off easy."

"Me too," Darger said. "You heard about the brush fire in Whitney Canyon?"

"Caught some of it on the news on the ride over. Is it our guy?"

"From the sound of it, yes."

Beck shook her head.

"Shoot. I was worried we'd end up with something like this eventually. This time of year, you can't ignite a spark without worrying it'll turn into a beast of a wildfire. I guess it was only a matter of time."

The dumpster landed on the back of the truck with a clang. The driver of the truck moved around the sides now, affixing a tarp over the top. The crime scene techs began breaking down their tent and packing up their kits.

Luck glanced at the watch on his wrist.

"We've got some time before the meeting. You guys want to grab some food?"

Darger realized she hadn't eaten anything since the Egg McMuffin she scarfed on the drive to the scene this morning. Her stomach rumbled at the thought of food.

"I'm in," Beck said.

"Me too."

And then every phone in the vicinity seemed to go off at once. A cacophony of digital chimes and chirps. A burst of activity from the police radios added to the din.

Before Darger could get her phone out of her pocket, Luck was reading the text he'd received.

"Task force meeting canceled. All personnel should report immediately to Whitney Medical Center to assist with emergency evacuation efforts."

CHAPTER 56

The Lexus rocketed down the winding canyon road — a tiny speck ripping along that gash of asphalt mankind had carved into the hills. Engine roaring. Speed climbing. Floor and dashboard vibrating along with the rising RPMs.

Rocky slopes stretched up on both sides at sharp angles. Steep and tufted here and there with chaparral. The scrub almost seemed to flicker like a strobe light as they tore past, branches flashing into view one second and gone the next. There and gone, and there and gone. Behind them in a blink. Forgotten.

As they zoomed deeper into the valley, the trees thickened along the sides of the road as though they were watching a time-lapse video of a woods forming, a dense forest taking shape where once there had been nothing. Thicker and thicker like green stubble filling in on the hillsides before swelling into a haggard beard.

Darger stared out into the gnarled oaks, peeking into the gaps to steal a glimpse, but she spotted no signs of the fire yet. No glow. No flicker. As the Lexus crested a small rise, she thought she could see smoke twirling up from the place where the road met the horizon, black tendrils undulating there, climbing into the sky, but it was hard to be certain in the waning light.

She gripped the handle on the passenger door, her stomach lurching along with the car's movements — that strange weightless feeling in the center of her torso making her gut a touch nauseous. The road seemed to be growing rougher the further they got from the city. Pocked and weathered and crooked. They rocked up and down dips. Zipped around bends. Tilted as they took long banked curves that seemed to turn the world half sideways.

Luck hunched over the wheel, eyebrows furrowed in concentration. The cords in his neck stood out, flexing and adjusting every time he swallowed. He'd barely said a word since they'd gotten the call about evacuating the hospital.

Darger couldn't help but think of Klootey's earlier comments about the Lexus. If Luck were truly fussy or prissy about his car, there existed no signs of it now. They hit higher and higher speeds, undaunted by the twisting curves, completely unfazed by the rough patches in the road. The obstacles only seemed to make Luck jam on the accelerator harder, some jolt of frustration expressed through the ball of his foot.

For this moment, at least, he was a man possessed with one task — getting to the hospital no matter the cost.

Darger swallowed. Tried not to picture the fire even as she scanned their surroundings for it. She didn't know why. It felt like it'd be bad luck to picture it, a jinx of some kind. Images of orange flicked into her skull, but the flashes were so tiny she couldn't make much of them.

A wooden bridge took shape ahead of them now, an antique-looking thing, its angular sides rising up from the road like some flourish of detail in a Bob Ross painting. It looked like it should lead directly to a barn in 1890.

They moved onto the bridge, and the road under the Lexus changed all at once — the hum of the asphalt shifting to a lower pitch as they drove directly over beams of wood as thick as railroad ties. Darger could hear the tread of the tires abrading the different texture of road here, almost like the buzzing of electric shears. The vibration of it shook them in their seats.

And for a moment, the woods around them parted. Out on the bridge, a strange openness surrounded the Lexus, an endless abyss of sky held back only by the wooden frame of the bridge.

They rumbled over the bridge, jostling like crazy. Darger gripped the handhold on the door even tighter, knuckles quivering, and then the smooth ride came back as the normal road resumed beneath them. The sudden lack of vibration shocked at first, felt wrong.

Darger took a deep breath, realizing only afterward that she'd held it as they crossed the bridge. As she inhaled, she smelled it for the first time: smoke.

She looked at Luck, found him still locked in the same hunched position, eyebrows as creased as ever. Focused. Driven. Whatever happened from here, it felt good to have him at her side.

Again she gazed into the hills, trying to see something — anything — in the openings and finding nothing out of the ordinary. They had to be getting close if she could smell smoke.

The Lexus whined as they climbed another steep rise. Darger's stomach sank as the car went up and up and up, the changing pressure somehow too much for her digestive system. It felt like something solid inside was weighing her down.

When the car finally reached the top of the ridge, she saw it. The fire.

Flames raged on both sides of the road ahead — hateful

orange overtaking this stretch of land. Ravaging brush. Devouring pine and oak and sycamore indiscriminately. Climbing the branches of even the tallest trees, some 100 feet or so off the ground.

Twirling. Flickering. Insane.

The fire would consume all that it touched here. Right away that was plain to see.

Luck grunted in the driver's seat, and the sound brought Darger back to herself, back to the car. She turned to face him, expecting him to do the same, make some kind of eye contact with her, but he didn't. His shoulders remained squared toward the road, eyes locked on the burning landscape up ahead.

The smoke enveloped them then, as dense as a thick fog. It darkened the sky, blotting out the last vestiges of daylight remaining in the day.

Darger had an urge to reach for Luck. To grasp his arm or take his hand in hers. It seemed embarrassing, like something a little kid would do.

The walls of orange grew closer, brighter, taller. The Lexus once again seemed to pick up speed, racing toward the place where the dark on the sides of the road gave way to the flare of burning.

She had to force herself to breathe, kept finding that she was instinctively holding her breath every time she stared into the flames, chest frozen, eyelids fluttering. She concentrated.

Breathe in. Breathe out.

Breathe in. Breathe out.

It seemed so wrong. This much fire. This much loss. And to drive straight into it? Madness. But there was no other way. No choice.

At last, they crossed the threshold, the Lexus racing into the fire, into the gleam.

Immediately, Darger could feel the heat surrounding the car, something suffocating about it even with the asphalt keeping it at arm's length for now. The fire made noise, too — an endless rumbling hiss, as though the fire let out one continuous breath.

And up close, the destruction was laid bare now. The fire erased bushes. Gnawed and toppled branches. Turned bark to hunks of shimmering ember.

It was everywhere. Lurching and flailing. Crackling and spitting.

And spreading endlessly.

It was too much, too powerful, Darger thought. People were going to die. They couldn't get them all out in time, could they?

She watched a branch fall out in the woods, sparks exploding everywhere as it disappeared into the flames engulfing the forest floor. The little glowing specks swirled up and spread on the wind, lifted by the hot air rising from the inferno.

She sensed some shift in Luck's posture out of the corner of her eye, his shoulders hunching further in a way that reminded her of a possum. She followed his gaze to the road ahead.

Police lights spiraled there. The red and blue shine almost drowned out by the scarlet and yellow glow fluttering over everything. After a second, she could hear the sirens, too — a many-voiced warbling, crying out. They sounded tinny and small from back here.

They'd caught up with the rest of the pack, and now they

followed the twisting road in single file. She watched the line of them rise over a little hill and then fall away to nothing on the other side, noting an ambulance and at least one city bus among the procession.

Darger felt her resolve strengthen the tiniest bit at seeing the fleet of vehicles. At being a part of the cavalcade. They were part of something bigger now, her and Luck.

She cast off her bashfulness, reached out and entwined her fingers with Luck's.

She expected him to balk. To at least raise an eyebrow. But he only squeezed her hand, as if holding hands with her was the most natural thing in the world.

A moment later, he turned to look at her. When he spoke, his voice was quiet and low, a little raspy.

"Almost there."

CHAPTER 57

Klootey's hands vibrate along with the steering wheel. The rough patches where time and the elements had worn away this rural road seem to wreak havoc on the cruiser. The tires judder over the chewed up stuff and jolt at the potholes, that latter always seeming to stand the vehicle upright, like the car keeps stubbing its toe.

Unperturbed by the choppy ride, he writhes in the driver's seat. Snakelike movements twisting his torso. That electricity throbs through his body again. Pins and needles. He feels it surge in his blood, in his bones, in his teeth.

He rockets out toward the hospital along with so many other law enforcement and fire department vehicles. A whole fleet of them springing into motion. Too late, he hopes. A doomed mission.

Tonight is the night. The night he has waited for his whole life long.

The grand finale unfolds upon them. Blooming. Becoming.

The forest fire he set into motion some hours ago rages fierce. Releases its fury upon an unsuspecting public.

The wind chose to aid him, chose to become his ally. The Santa Anas blow just so, just right, flowing northwest to southwest, the heat picking up as the gusts curl back toward the Pacific. It feeds the flames. Nurses them. Looses them like something wild, something meant to run free, something that could never be tamed. Never.

And so the flames creep over the hills and down the valleys,

317

crawling ever closer to the hospital. Even now, the fire's fingers begin to close around it, the fiery grip growing tighter by the second.

He snorts as he crosses the wooden bridge. Tires rocking over the planks in a series of thumps.

The giddiness swells until he can't contain the giggles. They come spilling out. Intense laughter. Insane. High-pitched little chirps like some noise a squirrel would make.

And he can't stop. Can't stop the laughing that cascades from his mouth, drizzling little specks of drool now and again.

Thank Christ Bishop had the day off. If his partner had been here, it would have really killed the mood. Not to mention that Klootey isn't entirely sure he would have been able to keep a straight face through this whole thing. It's just too much.

Tears are rushing down his cheeks now. An ache forms in his abdomen, something like a cramp in the cluster of muscles where the laughter seems to spring from.

He looks out at the woods through tear-filled eyes. Cheeks sharp with the pain of a held smile, all clenched up to bare his teeth.

The laughter grows so intense it becomes unpleasant. Reminds him of being a little kid, being tickled so long and hard he began to worry the laughs would never stop, he'd be stuck that way, hurting and laughing and scared. Powerless to control himself at all.

When he crests that fateful hill, reaches the edge of the fire, sees the blaze consuming the woods with his own two eyes, he laughs even harder.

CHAPTER 58

The hospital took shape, a dark form nestled into the crook of a valley, with steep ridges surrounding it. A dead-end location, that was for sure.

The lights in the parking lot shone brighter than those on the building, somehow making its bulk murky and ominous — something muscular waiting for them in the shadows.

It was clear to Darger that the building had been situated to take advantage of the scenery of the surrounding hillside. She imagined the rooms on the back of the hospital had spectacular views, but she wasn't sure just now that it had been worth it.

The woods there were already burning — another slope of writhing orange stretching up to form a strange backdrop to the scene. The trees seemed to thrash with the blaze, ripping swells of fire that moved without pattern, without mercy.

The fire encroached on the building from all sides, closing around it like a trap. The vast sea of asphalt out front helped keep it at bay for now, held it at a distance from this side, but from what they'd been told, the back would offer little such protection. That was where the problems would arise, where the building would eventually succumb to the inferno.

The patter of the blood beating in Darger's ears grew stronger, louder. Here was yet another sight to take her breath away. She fought it right away this time, concentrated to keep breathing.

Everything here was tinted red, she realized. A flickering red light reflecting from every surface, glittering over all the windshields in the parking lot, dancing over the building's facade, scarlet ripples that shimmered and twisted, bright and hot and threatening.

Drawing closer, she could see movement in the parking lot now. The people scurrying out of the building like rodents. Lines of them streamed into buses and vans parked out front. Another mob clustered on the sidewalk in front of the building, waiting to be directed to a vehicle. Everyone looked twitchy, antsy, nervous, scared — their body language screamed it with such force that she could read it from a great distance.

Two uniformed officers directed traffic in the lot, one swinging glowing sticks like an air traffic controller, another doing the same job with bare hands. They mostly seemed to be keeping the way clear for the buses and other cargo vehicles full of people to get out, halting the incoming swell of law enforcement to make it happen.

The Lexus slowed as they entered this line of waiting vehicles, and Darger watched packed buses go by one after the other, heading for safety, getting out. They still had a ways to go to clear the hospital, judging by that twitchy mob out front, but they were making steady progress.

Finally they reached the front of the line. So close to the action. A bare hand held them just shy of the gates as a couple of vans squeezed out, and then the glowing batons waved them through to the lot.

They zipped up toward the front of the building, the Lexus growling a little as Luck jammed on the accelerator. They parked as close as they could, the brakes squealing and all of reality seeming to jerk to a halt as Luck went from full speed to parked a little too quickly, the car crooked as hell in the spot.

Before Darger could comment on the rough landing, he was out of the car, jogging toward the crowd at the front of the building.

There was a line of nurses and other hospital staff pushing wheelchairs. A few were even maneuvering gurneys across the parking lot. Darger hadn't even stopped to consider that some of the patients wouldn't be mobile.

Another group of uniformed officers directed the foot traffic here, waving groups into the buses and vans and keeping the others as calm as they could. Luck raced up to a mustached cop in the middle of the fray, Darger following a few paces behind him.

"Is everyone out?" Luck said.

The officer squinted at him a second, and then seemed to either recognize him or realize who he must be.

"Yeah, we think so."

Luck scoffed.

"You think so?"

The officer grimaced, lips curling down hard at the corners and nose wrinkling like he'd just taken a big swig of skunky beer. His mustache twitched twice. He went back to waving another load of people into a police truck as he answered.

"It got chaotic, OK? We ran out of gurneys. The nurses were having to load the patients into vehicles before going back inside for more, and we're out here loading people up as fast as the buses arrive. It made it impossible to keep count. But the group that just came out, they say this is everyone."

The muscles along Luck's jawline twitched with irritation. He looked at Darger.

"What do you think?"

"I think we go in and make sure."

The mustached officer grabbed Luck's sleeve as they pushed past him.

"Look, buddy, they're saying we've got minutes until the fire breaches the back of the building. No one's going to wait around for you just because you got a hard-on to play hero. You got that?"

Luck pulled out of his grip.

"Yeah, I got it."

As they approached the front doors of the hospital, Darger could see the fire occupying the hill behind it, the flames creeping closer and closer. It felt like they were walking into Hell.

CHAPTER 59

Darger pushed through two sets of front doors to enter the hospital, Luck trailing just behind her.

The lobby smelled like menthol cough drops, the air in here cooler than outside, quieter — lacking both the sizzle of the fire and the smoke smell. The only sound was the muted buzz of the fluorescent bulbs above. The quiet made Darger's skin crawl.

It looked strange with nobody behind the front desk — no bustle of nurses answering phones and checking charts, no sign of life at all aside from the potted palms manning every corner with their fronds outstretched, and even those may have been artificial.

They seemed to take in the lobby slowly, walking the first few paces as they sized it up. Once they had the lay of the land, their walking picked up to a jog.

Hallways sprawled out from the desk, three branches.

"Should we split up?" Darger said.

Luck squinted as he answered.

"Yeah, but let's take this first piece together. Get a feel for the building."

Darger nodded. He must have felt the same niggling doubts about being here, about going off on his own in this expansive building.

They hustled down the hall, Darger taking the left and Luck the right, checking each doorway for anyone left behind. The clatter of their footsteps echoed everywhere in the quiet, in the emptiness, his and her steps falling in and out of time. Something about it gave Darger a chill she couldn't quite shake.

She peered into room after room, spotting empty beds in each of them. Most of them sported mussed sheets, wadded up blankets. Some beds had half-eaten trays of food suspended over them — Jell-O cups and what looked like congealing beef stroganoff. All evidence of the rapid escape the patients made not so long ago.

And it occurred to Darger that she was experiencing that strange sensation that only occurred in the most dramatic moments in life — the camera in her brain was on now, recording this moment. Saving every image, every thought, every feeling to be parsed, picked over, analyzed in detail at a later time and date. However all of this turned out, she would play these memories back over and over again. The point-of-view shot of her running down the hall, heart pounding, breath heaving in and out. The movies would open in her head at random, come to her when she least expected it, infect her dreams from here on out.

She swallowed. Felt and heard a click in her throat, dry flesh shifting there inside her neck. It almost seemed to be cracking, though she knew that couldn't be true.

When they reached the end of the hallway, they returned to the lobby and split up.

"I'll take right, you take left," Luck said.

Darger nodded.

"Let's do it."

They parted ways then, and she got the faintest jolt of adrenaline as she veered down the empty hospital wing, a tingle roiling over her scalp. Now the sound of the footsteps changed, parting, Luck's trailing off and Darger's lighter footfalls echoing on their own.

She pattered on, considering a zigzag to check both sides of the hall and quickly decided to stick to one. She could check the opposite side on the way back.

The tile floor shifted by underfoot, square frames of beige terrazzo flecked with black sliding by, one by one, reminding her of an old TV with a vertical hold problem.

The hospital seemed larger now that she was alone. More desolate, its sense of eeriness enhanced. It ultimately was small by hospital standards, just one floor, perhaps a hundred beds at the most, but it didn't seem small just now. Not at all.

Something crashed ahead and Darger jumped, freezing on the spot. A nurse appeared, tugging a gurney through a doorway.

Spotting Darger, she said, "Oh, thank God. I thought I was the only one left."

Regaining her ability to move, Darger took a step forward. "Do you need help?"

"No, I've got this. I'm pretty sure there's just one more after this. Down the hall. Second to last on the left."

And that was it. The woman disappeared around a corner before Darger even realized what she'd meant.

There was another patient still waiting to be evacuated.

Darger hurried down the hallway, coming to a halt in front of the second to last door. A sign on the door read Authorized Personnel Only. It appeared to be a stock room and when Darger tried the door handle, it was locked.

Well, that couldn't be right.

She backed away from the door, looking both ways,

checking her count of the doors. This was undeniably the second to last door on the left. The nurse had even gestured to this side of the hall.

She checked the last door and found the room empty.

Moving across the corridor, Darger peered into the last and second to last rooms on this side. Empty.

Fuck.

She ping-ponged back to the other side, thrusting her head into the third door, expecting more of the same. More empty beds and mussed sheets.

But then she saw it. Bulges plumping the blankets in one of the beds. The undeniable shape of legs outlined in layers of fabric.

She stopped. Gaped. Bobbed back onto her heels as though she'd slammed the brakes. She held her breath a second as she processed the image laid out before her.

The legs had a withered look. Frail. Skinny as sticks. She couldn't see the face from this angle, but she knew it must be a kid or an elderly person just based on the scrawniness of the limbs, likely heavily medicated to have somehow missed on all the commotion.

She glanced about for a gurney or a wheelchair. Saw neither. Then she remembered the policeman out front saying they'd run out of gurneys.

She could wait for the nurse to return, but there wasn't time. And that was assuming the nurse was planning on returning at all.

She stepped into the room, the frame of the doorway slowly relenting to reveal the patient little by little — first the chest, then shoulders, then face.

It was an old woman, eyes closed, chest rising and falling. She had gray hair bordering on white in closely cropped curls, and something in the tangle of wrinkles near her eyes and lips spoke of someone who smiled a lot — even now she seemed to wear the subtlest grin, the corners of her lips turned up just a bit. Her eyelids moved, that thin skin shifting as the eyeballs beneath flicked back and forth. She must have been dreaming.

Darger approached slowly, not sure why exactly, some reverence taking hold of her. When she reached the bed, she put a hand on the lone exposed arm, some halfhearted attempt to wake the woman that had no effect. Her skin felt warm and soft.

Darger took another breath, moved her hands to the woman's shoulders and gave her a good shake.

"Ma'am. Can you hear me? The building is being evacuated."

Still no response.

She shuffled quickly back to the door.

"Luck," she yelled out. "I've got one!"

She heard his footsteps stop in the distance, hold quiet for a second, and then resume, this time growing louder as they moved back toward her.

Back at the old woman's bedside, Darger peeled back the blankets to reveal the rest of the stick body swathed only in the thin hospital gown, light blue. Then she unhooked the IV from the back of the woman's hand, the pump shrieking angrily.

Luck clattered into the room behind Darger. Stopped. His wild eyes flicked from the woman in the bed to meet Darger's.

"What have we got?"

"She's out. Medicated, I think. We'll have to carry her."

Luck nodded, resolve seeming to replace whatever shock had been in his eyes a second ago. He bent over, collecting the woman in his arms like a sleeping child.

Her eyelids stirred again. Opened for a split second. Some expressionless look occupying them for a moment, a couple of nonsense syllables murmuring from her lips. And then she was out again, her limp arms dangling like noodles.

Out from under the blanket now, the floppy body somehow reminded Darger of a baby bird, frail and featherless.

"You got her?" Darger asked. "I can help carry."

"She barely weighs anything. Just help me with the doors when we come to them."

Darger nodded and led the way, turning back to watch Luck finagle himself and his burden sideways through the doorway. In the open expanse of the hallway, they picked up speed.

Darger realized her heart was pounding again, hitting that out of control gallop like it had in the car, but this time it wasn't a bad thing. They were fucking doing it.

She surged forward, feet thudding against the tile floor. Glancing back, she realized Luck was falling behind. She slowed her pace to let him catch up.

"You see anyone else?" he asked.

"I passed a nurse. She said she was pretty sure this was the last patient."

Luck let out an angry huff.

"Pretty sure?" he said in the same tone he'd used to the policeman out front. "Just like they think they got everyone out? Jesus Christ. This whole operation is a shitshow."

The hallway opened up into the lobby, seeming to arrive

much faster on the way back. Darger picked up speed again, reaching the door ahead of Luck and pushing it aside for him. Through the first set of doors, Luck braced his shoulder blades to back his way out of the second set, moving carefully to ensure he didn't bash the frail head into any steel bits.

Just as they eased over the threshold, the woman spoke.

"I'll have the pudding," she said, her eyes still closed. "But not the tapioca. The tapioca looks like boogers."

CHAPTER 60

As soon as they were past the outer door, the fire's hiss returned. Breathing. Crackling. Sizzling. Everywhere.

Luck's toe caught on a seam in the sidewalk, causing him to lose his footing and stumble a little. Darger reached out to steady him, but he righted himself and got moving again.

Sensory overload hit then — so many noises and movements compared to inside. The heat. The smoke. The fire's glow thrashing in the distance. The police lights twirled, and the crowd chattered. Cars and people moved everywhere. Elbows, tires, shoulders, facial twitches. One of the buses let out a sibilant swoosh. And wavering over all of it, that evil red flicker.

Darger blinked a few times to try to take it all in and make some sense of it, overwhelmed as though she couldn't hold it all inside at once without something bursting.

Right away she noticed a change in the crowd. It had thinned to almost nothing while they were inside. Perhaps a dozen or so civilians still milled on the front walk, waiting to be taken away. That was good.

Many of the police vehicles were moving now as well. Falling back. Retreating. A policeman nearby shut a van door, and then tapped on the hood to signal that another load was clear to move out. The van jerked to life, careening off toward the mouth of the parking lot, brake lights flaring once before it tore out onto the road.

Luck and Darger shuffled toward the remnants of the

crowd. They moved to the last few policemen still directing the foot traffic.

"Got one here," Luck said, making his voice hard to be heard above the din. "She's unconscious. Mostly, anyway. In and out a little."

Uniformed officers swooped in, surrounded them, helped load the floppy bird lady into a van, plucking her from Luck's hands. Darger watched as a female officer secured the woman in the backseat of the van, snaking the seatbelt over her shoulder and down past her hip. And then it was done. She was loaded. The van door was sliding shut, the vehicle veering away.

The policeman who they'd spoken to earlier came near, gesturing a hand at that last smattering of people, and then at the last bus idling in the looped drive.

"This is it. We got the order to clear out," he said. "We load these folks up, and we're gone."

Darger knew what Luck was going to say before he spoke.

"There were two patients and a nurse still inside when you told us the place had been cleared," Luck said, his tone harsh. "We need to make sure no one else gets left behind."

The cop ignored Luck's anger. His tone was level and calm.

"Look, buddy, I ain't been inside. I only do what they tell me. And right now, they're telling me we're done here." He shrugged. "I suggest you come along with us. We've got word that the fire's getting out of hand up the road. Might not be a clear way out much longer."

Luck was already shaking his head. And he was right, she knew. There could still be someone inside. She'd only checked half the rooms before she found the bird lady. Maybe less than half. And Luck surely hadn't searched all the rooms on his side before she'd called out to him for help.

Luck dipped his head to the side and their eyes met.

"One more sweep?" Darger said.

Luck gave a firm nod.

They turned back to the large front doors, and in they went again.

CHAPTER 61

Back inside, Darger and Luck didn't need to talk. They veered in opposite directions just past the lobby.

It'd take several minutes to clear the rest of the hospital, even if they both sprinted all the way through. Darger tried to prep herself to stay patient, stay vigilant. Assertive. Decisive. Do the job, and then get out. No more. No less.

Luck's footfalls trailed away, seeming lighter and faster than before, and once they'd faded out, she was on her own again, back in the quiet of the empty hospital. A little chill crept up her spine.

More doorways flitted past. The beds inside coming up empty, empty, empty. That was good. In her heart, she suspected the place had been cleared — but she had to be sure, had to see it with her own two eyes before she could move on.

Still, Darger didn't feel nearly the same dread she'd felt on the first pass. Damn near everyone was already out, and after this, they'd be certain. This notion lifted the caul of anxiety from her head, cleared her thoughts, strengthened her resolve.

She felt so good in fact, that she picked up her jog into something approaching a sprint seemingly without suffering consequences for it. It felt like she could run forever. Weightless. Free. Endorphins, she figured. She throttled her speed down a touch. Better to stay patient.

At the end of the hall, she turned to double back, feet squeaking a little on the tile floor as she changed directions. Now she worked the opposite side of the hall.

More empty beds. The feeling only grew that this place was empty, that they'd done it.

She called out.

"Anyone there?"

Her voice echoed down the hall, the copies of her words fluttering in the space a while and then going quieter, seeming to fly away from her.

No response. Only the quiet.

Then she heard Luck call out as well in the distance.

"Hello?"

Nothing.

And the sound of her footsteps faded then. Her consciousness sucked up into her head so she heard only the beat of her heart, steady and firm like a kick drum plodding through a break in a song.

Another left took her along the route she'd run the first time through, moved her toward the back of the building at top speed.

The back corridor was wider than the rest, almost cavernous. Some of the lights were off back here as well, and the space seemed eerie in the half light.

Darger called out a few times. Had to be sure.

"Hello? Is anyone here?"

The echoes seemed louder in this hallway. Denser. Flying away on heavier wings.

She tried again, louder this time.

"Anyone here?"

Her voice broke up a little this time, a rasp coming out with the yell.

No response. The echoes faded to slushy whispers. When

they faded to quiet, the hair on the back of her neck stood up.

Darger slowed. Something wasn't right here. She could feel it, could sense it, even if she couldn't see it yet.

Then it came to her. Movement at the end of the hall. She couldn't make it out in the shadows, but something stirred there. Something dark and quick.

She crept closer. Still not sure what she was seeing. She almost wanted to draw her weapon, but that would be silly. Wouldn't it?

After a few more steps, she knew what it was. She smelled it before she saw it.

The charcoal stench hit her. Smoke.

The black twirling along the back wall at last came clear to her.

The hospital was on fire.

CHAPTER 62

They hesitated just outside the door. Darger stopping first and Luck joining her. They stood. Stared. Took in the vision of the parking lot as it looked now.

Empty. The lot sat empty. A few cars still waited, penned in their little yellow lines, scattered here and there, abandoned by their owners, left to fend with the flames on their own. But no life stirred here. The crowd had been loaded up, the cops and paramedics and firemen all having retreated, the whole lot of them racing for safety even now.

The sky had grown darker as well. Blacker. But it wasn't dusk giving way to full night. Not yet. It was too early for that. It was the smoke that was causing this artificial twilight. The clouds of black stretched over the sky like layers of ebon gauze, filling the heavens with its murk. At this rate, she wouldn't be able to tell when night did fall. The smoke would blot out the moon and suffocate the stars.

Nothing moved save for the fire all around. The orange glow still thrashed, flailed, shook trees, devoured plant life, created heat distortion that made everything shimmer, a blur roiling in all directions. The fire's endless exhale once more provided the only sound — the sizzle that stretched its white noise out to eternity.

The heat had swelled from warm to hot to stifling. Darger could feel her body going damp just standing there, doing nothing more than breathing and looking.

She took off first. Ran through the empty lot, Luck close

behind her, and she couldn't help but feel a strange exhilaration come over her. Her feet clapped against the asphalt, the heat reaching out to adhere her shirt to the small of her back via a thin film of sweat, then wetting her hair to her scalp seconds later. Something extraordinary was happening here. Awful, yes, but extraordinary nevertheless. In this moment, the lot seemed the only thing that was real, concrete, material. The rest of the world, the rest of the universe, was merely an idea.

Her mind still recorded everything — every image, every thought, every clipped exchange of conversation, every feeling inside and out. Stowed them all away to be examined later.

They broke into the open expanse of the lot, the place beyond the looped drive, and for just a second Darger thought the Lexus was gone. Vanished somehow. Emptiness occupying the place it had been.

But then she saw the rear end of it sticking out from behind an SUV. She changed her trajectory to close on it. Just a few steps more.

Weaving around a pair of small Ford sedans, they veered at last toward Luck's Lexus. Drawing up on it. In what felt like one swift movement, she opened her door, slid into the seat, and sealed herself inside. Luck already had the key in the ignition. Neither one needed to tell the other to hurry.

He put the car in gear and ripped out of the parking spot. A sharp turn pulled Darger into the door, the tires screeching a little, but then they leveled out.

In the side mirror, Darger watched the black smoke curl up from the rear of the building now. Wispy but turning thicker before her eyes. It'd go up fast, she thought. Thank God they'd gotten everyone out.

Their speed only climbed as they swung out of the lot and onto the road. Luck lifted himself off the seat a little to jam the accelerator even harder, put his body weight into it. Time to see how fast this gussied-up Toyota could go.

They drove into the open place in the flames. The thin sliver of road amidst the walls of orange, everything smeared and indistinct as though the air itself had been greased somehow, glass smudged with something cloudy that moved and glittered a little.

She couldn't even smell the smoke anymore. It had wormed its way into her mouth and nose, settled into her skin and hair and clothes as if it were a part of her now.

The trees flicking by looked like stop motion animation — a child's flip book going too fast. Bleary. Pulsing. Almost indistinct. Just flashes of something solid yet among the flames. Long, tall shapes. Cylinders of dark crawling with fire.

Darger gripped the handhold on the door until her fingers hurt. Knuckles quivering. She gritted her teeth and stared into the flames.

Wild feelings clawed at her insides. Primal fear that reached all the way to her core. This was wrong. Madness.

The night was on fire, and they were driving into it.

A downed branch seemed to materialize from nowhere in the smoke just ahead, blocking their lane. Darger braced herself for impact, and then her stomach flopped and squished as Luck swerved.

She caught a passing glimpse as the car zigged and zagged around the obstacle. It was a massive limb, still glowing orange like an ember at the bottom of a campfire, its color brightening and darkening with the shifting winds.

A creeping nausea settled into Darger's gut. This was going to be a hell ride, she thought, wiping a line of sweat from her upper lip.

The Lexus again picked up speed when they straightened out, started shaking — the floor, the dash, the seats, all rattling, vibrating — the movement growing more intense along with their acceleration. The seat convulsed beneath Darger, the ride growing rough, the whole car shuddering like it was about to come apart.

And then the car seemed to top out at last, reaching the edge of its limits and smoothing out, the final plateau, the rattling and shaking no longer strengthening, dying back, the car itself going no faster.

Darger thanked the universe that the asphalt couldn't burn, because it would if it could. The fire ran right up to the edges of the road now, threatening them, grass and bushes all aglow, flaming tree branches hanging up above.

She gazed into it, no longer able to differentiate the bits of foliage, lost in the orange and the haze. The woods seemed to be one burning mass, a writhing creature surrendered to the flame.

The night itself burned. Decayed. Offered itself up for sacrifice.

Luck gasped next to her, a little hiss escaping his lips.

Before she could turn to look at him, the whole world shifted, jerked at her, rocked her forward in her seat, momentum tugging, tugging.

The squeal of the tires told her that Luck had slammed on the brakes. Inertia kicked in, thrusting them forward.

The Lexus fought against the forward momentum,

fishtailing like mad, laying thick strips of rubber down on the asphalt from the sound of it.

Darger braced both hands on the dash to keep her upper body from jerking forward any further.

Out of the corner of her eye, she could see Luck fighting to keep control of the car. Elbows out wide to get a little extra torque as though he were strangling the steering wheel, his whole body jerking one way and then the other.

At last the car angled into a diagonal skid and held steady there, skidding, slowing. Finally coming to rest. Everything around them seemed utterly motionless after all that thrashing about.

Finally, in the stillness, Darger turned to look at Luck, finding his mouth agape, lip quivering. He blinked a couple times.

"No," he muttered under his breath. One tiny syllable. Nothing more.

She followed his gaze to the road ahead. Gasped herself when she saw it.

The fire overwhelmed the wooden structure before her, saturated it, engulfed it entirely.

The words entered her head as if from some outside source, shattered the shocked silence there:

The bridge is on fire.

CHAPTER 63

Klootey waits in the parking garage until he spots other members of the task force returning from the evacuation. He's the first one back, naturally, but he doesn't want it to look that way. So he waits.

When he sees them filing in like bees returning to the hive, he climbs out of his squad car and merges with the group as if he's been with them all along. Follows the buzzing swarm into headquarters and takes a seat in the conference room.

A woman he vaguely recognizes from another district moves into the chair directly behind him. She's got a phone pressed to her ear and is loudly arguing with one of the van drivers about whether or not he's supposed to shuttle his evacuees to White Memorial or Keck Medical Center.

"No," she says in a grating voice, "you're Van 3. I have it right here. You're on the list for White Memorial."

Klootey's leg pumps under the table. Calf pistoning away in fast motion. He needs to appear calm, needs to appear normal or however close to that he can achieve. A certain amount of nerves here would seem natural enough, he knows, and that's good. But unbridled glee? Maniacal laughter? Jumping up on the fucking table to do a touchdown dance? Well, his esteemed colleagues might notice something like that.

He keeps his eyes on the shining tabletop, the reflection of the fluorescent lights there. Better to avoid eye contact, avoid conversation. He didn't want to trip up, lapse into some weird behavior someone might notice. No chances. To fuck this up after coming so far would be tragic. Truly tragic.

Better to retreat into his mind. Pull his focus away from this room, these people. Stay safe in his shell.

So he pictures the fire. Remembers pieces of it. That slope of burning woods stretching up from the back of the hospital flares once more in his imagination. Burning bright and hot. The heat he could feel coming off that even 100 or 150 yards away was incredible. Palpable. It touched his cheeks, his top lip, the backs of his hands. Much more than he anticipated.

He knows fire. Lives for it. But a fire this big is beyond his experience. Overwhelming. He struggles to wrap his head around the realities, the logistics, the sheer size and force of the thing.

Even now it grows. His creation grows. Swallows acre after acre. Pursues a path of annihilation. Takes no prisoners. Knows only total destruction. Means to spend itself destroying as much as it can. Here and now.

He pictures the trapped people. Scared. Crying. Helpless as newborn kittens.

He pictures the flames taking a bus. Orange fury wrapping around the hulk of steel. Devouring it.

The tires blow out one after the other, back then front, the popping tubes as loud as shotgun blasts, and then the bus sinks a few inches to the ground, shorter now.

The white paint on the sides blackens. Char marks crawling up toward the roof. Blistering the enamel. Little bubbles bulging everywhere.

The passengers all dark shapes behind the windows. Panicking silhouettes. Banging on the glass. Screaming. Their open mouths the one detail he can make out.

A hand on his shoulder brings him back to the conference room. Klootey flinches a little. Startled.

"Sorry, Teej. Didn't mean to spook you like that," Bishop says.

Klootey plasters a big, stupid grin on his face and shakes his head.

"Nah, it's just I'm still a little jacked on adrenaline, you know?"

"I bet, man. Sounds like I missed out on all the excitement." Bishop glances around the room. "So what was it like?"

It takes a moment for Klootey to find the right words. To do it justice.

"Absolute fucking chaos."

Bishop nods, and Klootey practically has to bite a chunk out of his cheek to keep from laughing. Even his own damn partner has no idea. Not a fucking clue.

Isn't it grand that no one cares? That you're invisible? Isn't it a fucking delight to walk around in a world that cannot see who you really are?

The giggles crawl up his throat again, but he stops them there. Clears his throat a couple times, which somehow squelches the laughter just shy of his tongue.

Someone flips on a flat screen TV mounted on the wall at the front of the room. Big yellow letters glow against a black background at the bottom of the screen: Forest Fire. And the news shows aerial shots of the blazing forest. Dramatic camera work. Sweeping visuals that give a sense of the scale.

It looks like an expensive shot from a disaster movie. The camera rolling on and on, hill after hill, dip after dip. Everything on fire for as far as you can see.

A few houses burn among the trees. Rich fucks saying goodbye to their fortresses up in the hills. Watching their dreams melt.

And he wonders if the liquid remains of these mansions will ultimately drain down that grate at the center of Los Angeles. All the scum flows through there, one way or another. Always a matter of time.

Bishop turns away from the TV, swiveling back to face him. "You seen Camacho and Murphy?"

Not taking his eyes from the screen, Klootey waves a hand in the air. "Yeah, they're around here somewhere."

Bishop says something about heading out to find them, raps his knuckles against the tabletop as a farewell gesture, but Klootey hardly notices.

The newscaster yammers away on the TV, but he can't focus on her words. He just watches her teeth while she talks. Big white teeth. Big fish lips flapping up and down over those big ol' choppers.

And he wishes for the feed to cut back to his fire. His legacy. Aches to see it. To stare into the flames for as long as he can, let that trance take hold of him and carry him away. His desire for those images of the burning woods is so intense it borders on sexual.

He realizes that he is breathing too loud. Hot breath heaving in and out of his mouth. And he coughs to cover it. Fist clenched in front of his lips, shaking just a little. Phlegmy sounding hacks emitting from him.

Someone slides him a plastic cup of water. And he takes it and drinks. Croaks out a thanks. Hand massaging at his throat.

The news cuts back to the fire. Same loop of shots as before, but he's glad for it nevertheless. The camera gets so high up and shoots straight down, a true bird's eye shot. He wonders if it's from a drone.

Then another uniformed body elbows through the door. The Chief. He plants himself right in front of the TV, raises a hand to get everyone's attention.

The room goes quiet. Klootey tries to see around the Chief to watch his fire.

"Listen up, all. We just got word a moment ago. Everyone got out," he says.

The small crowd gathered in the room erupts into jubilant noise, but the Chief holds up his hand again, looking to finish his statement.

"It was a nick of time type of deal, OK? The wooden bridge went up, but all the buses, vans, and cruisers are accounted for. The hospital is clear. We did it, people. Rose to the occasion. You saved a bunch of lives tonight, OK? So give yourselves a round of applause."

The crowd is louder on the second upheaval. Raucous.

Klootey's arms go numb, the blood draining from his face so quickly he thinks he might pass out or vomit or both, but he manages to slowly clap along with the rest of the room. Wincing inside.

Police from various divisions stand and shake hands, pat each other on the back. There's a little whooping and the like. Someone offers up cigars, and a big group bustles out to the parking lot to indulge.

Klootey feels like he is going to fall out of his chair. Just slide down under the table and die there in a pile.

It's impossible. Impossible that they would all get out. He

doesn't understand.

"You feeling OK?"

It's the podunk policewoman. Captain Beck. She stands near the doorway, hands tucked in the sides of her gun belt, a funny look on her face.

"Oh yeah. All good here. I just… I think the reality of all of this is catching up to me or something."

She slips into the seat next to him, eyes still locked on him.

"It's a lot to process. That's for sure," she says, scooting her chair back further to make room for her protruding middle.

"Just glad everyone got out," he says.

He can't believe he doesn't projectile vomit before the words get out of his mouth, foam and flecks of food rocketing up from his gullet, spreading over the big conference room table in a puddle the exact shade of Cheez-Its.

For the first time, it occurs to him that he should kill himself. Get out now. Exit stage right. Be done.

He wonders how he'll do it. Gun? Rope?

No. The fire should take him. That seems right. Feels right. That big forest fire should get one major victim to its name, shouldn't it?

He pictures driving out into the apocalyptic scene. The earth on fire as far as the eye can see. All the plant life, all the land glowing and smothered in it, shriveling and twisting within the inferno. Everything sizzling and popping.

And the flames will jump for him when he arrives. Elongated tendrils of orange leaping for his car, wrapping him up, writhing over his body like snakes.

Yes, that feels like a Hollywood ending, he thinks. Appropriately dramatic. Appropriately morbid. It fits.

Then one of the detectives on the task force, Brill, rushes to the door, feet thudding over the floor. He sticks his head in, a frantic look about him, lips and eyes twitching in repeating patterns that seem to have their own strange rhythm to them. Once again the room falls silent.

"Heads up. We just got word that someone's trapped in the fire after all. It's a single car from what we're being told," he says, licking his lips before he finishes. "It's not confirmed yet, but they think it's the two federal agents. Luck and Darger."

CHAPTER 64

Darger's breath caught in her throat, fear seeming to afflict her eyes so she couldn't stop blinking them for a few seconds, tears bulging at the corners.

Trapped. They were trapped here. Walled in by fire on all sides.

No place to go. No way out.

The Lexus rolled to a stop about a hundred feet shy of the flaming bridge, and Luck and Darger just sat there. Motionless. Both of them staring. Watching the orange flicker where the way out should be. Their chests and shoulders kept rising and falling, but nothing else moved inside the car.

"What do we do?" Luck said eventually.

Darger hesitated, unsure. But when she spoke, her voice sounded calm in her ears. Strangely tranquil. Totally disconnected from how she felt inside.

"We go back to the hospital parking lot. That's a big chunk of asphalt that the fire can't touch. Eventually they can send someone in to get us."

Luck muttered a response, seeming to talk more to himself than to her, she thought.

"Right. Right that makes sense."

The Lexus wheeled around, swerving near the fiery edge of the road, eventually pointing itself the opposite direction.

Luck's shoulders heaved once. Some breath to reassure himself. And then he stomped on the gas, and the Lexus lurched forward once more.

Night on Fire

They rocketed back the way they'd come. Tearing over the asphalt again, that dotted yellow line in the middle of the road going faster and faster, ticking off their progress.

It felt better to be moving again, Darger thought. Momentum. Action. Right now, doing anything was better than doing nothing. Stasis was death, even up against a fire raging out of control.

Luck said nothing. He sat utterly still in the driver's seat save for the spasms of his breathing, his chest fluttering a little on every inhale, little quakes of the ribcage somehow reminiscent of a baby that can't quite stop crying.

Darger thought he may be on the verge of panic, which she could understand. She thought about saying something, using some counseling technique to help him calm himself, center himself, at least get that breathing under control. But some instinct told her to hold off for now. Let this play out a little more. Find the right time to reassert a sense of calm. For now, she'd let him process this, give him time to absorb the shock.

The heat encroached now as they advanced deeper into the blaze. The kind of hot that wrapped itself around her throat, her forehead, building steadily in her core. Darger could feel it flushing her face, cheeks red and splotchy and fevered.

She watched beads of sweat form on Luck's forehead. Little budded jewels seeped out of the pores there, gathering and then slowly draining down toward his brow.

She was just as soaked, her body already leaking out its last defense against the fire. That thought scared her more than anything else. The loss of moisture, of hydration, rapidly underway even now. It was only going to get hotter from here, wasn't it? The worst was yet to come.

Movement in the woods caught her eye. The fire heaved all at once. Lurching. Careening. Big chunks of it leaping for them.

Her words hissed out of her, a strange whisper that sounded foreign in her ears.

"What the fuck?"

Luck snapped out of his daze. Glanced at her and then out the window. Gasped.

He jerked the steering wheel.

The Lexus swerved, tires screaming beneath them. Shrill and harsh.

A cluster of burning trees crashed to the road beside them, one by one, some domino effect taking down three together, flaming limbs all tangled.

The lumber hit with a force that shook the ground, an incredible thump that Darger felt in her sternum, in her teeth.

Sparks exploded everywhere into the sky. A glowing cloud of them fluttered away like swarming insects, beating back the dark for this one moment with the sheer volume of glittering orange specks.

Embers cracked away and thudded to the ground as the great hulking trees shuddered and came apart. The Lexus fishtailed a little as Luck steered it off the rocky shoulder and back under control.

And then Darger watched the fallen trees in the rearview mirror. Burning shambles growing smaller and smaller as they zoomed away. A strange flickering object in the strip of darkness. Harder and harder to make out.

Darger kept watching even after it was gone. Speechless. Panting for breath.

She and Luck made eye contact. Faces blank. Lips parted.

No words passed between them, and yet much was communicated.

They both sheened with sweat from head to toe now. Glistening. Slicked like fish.

A strange lightness entered Darger's head. The interior of her skull went hazy, like the heat and smoke were leaking inside. Smearing. Blurring. Obscuring. Like steam fogging a mirror.

And a little distance grew between her and the outside world. A gap of quiet, of peace. Her mind pulled away as though it might be able to protect her from this fucked reality. Like it could keep her safe and sound in the shell of her cranium, blot out the horror and trauma of what was happening by retracting from it like a tortoise.

No. That was shock, and she needed to fight it. Keep her wits. Survive.

She breathed. Sucked in a great lungful of air, the wind dry and hot in her throat. She held the breath for a few seconds, ribcage swollen for this moment, and then she let it out slowly. Counted to ten as she did.

That cleared the fog some. Brought her back to the Lexus. Brought the fire's hiss back. Brought the fevered feeling back to her cheeks, her throat, her forehead.

She licked her lips.

A crack outside drew both of their eyes ahead and to the right. The sound resonated. A deep splintering of wood.

More ripping movement writhed in the fire there. Towers of flame leaning impossibly. Teetering. Slowly at first and then gravity took hold and tore the cluster of branches and trunks down. Another tangle of four trees came crashing down to the road ahead of them.

Thump. Thump. Thump. Thump.

Luck slammed on the brakes. Jerked the wheel. Veered out into the left lane. Tried to edge around the tops of the trees.

But this time there was no opening. No way around. No place left to go.

They stopped a few feet short of the burning mess of plant life. Stared at the blocked path before them. Watched the mess of sparks catch on the hot wind going up and up.

Neither of them spoke. They just watched the night on fire, the world burning for as far as they could see.

CHAPTER 65

Klootey focuses on his breathing. Forearms resting on the lip of the conference table. Eyes staring hard at nothing.

Luck and Darger. Trapped. Helpless. The fire closing in on them now.

Jesus fucking goddamn Christ. It's perfect. There's your Hollywood ending, Jimbo. Fear not.

He reaches for the pitcher of water in the center of the table. Pours himself a cup. Drinks. Needs to look normal. Not show this room full of L.A.'s finest that he's bordering on jizzing himself.

He scans over the faces in this room, making sure to look none in the eyes. Concern draws between the cheeks and noses. Puffs those folds of skin beneath the eyes. They look like lost puppies in here. Bunch of fucksticks.

He thinks back on that vision of driving into the fire. Sacrificing himself to the flame. Orange death surrounding his body. Cooking him like a hot dog on a grill.

Fuck that noise, Jim. I'll go ahead and do you one better. I'll offer you Luck and Darger in my stead. Let the fire take them. Raise the stakes or whatever you want to call it.

He pictures Luck's Lexus going up quick. Smoldering for a few seconds, smoke billowing off it in sheets, and then the fancified Toyota blowing. Coming apart when the gas tank succumbs to the fire. Blown to bits.

He takes another sip of water to stifle the laugh moving for his lips.

These will make his most significant kills to date. Darger is practically a celebrity for God's sake. The hotshot profiler, swooping around the country to catch the worst of the worst. Not this time, thank you very much. Jim has other plans for you, I'm afraid.

She would have been the most likely to figure him out, too. Smarter than most. Sees humanity a little clearer, maybe. Almost like Jim in a certain sense.

With her out of the picture, he will get away with all of it, especially if he's smart about it. Shit, if he paces himself, he can carry on for decades. Pop out every six months or so, release the inner Jimbo to burn another church or movie theater or preschool.

His tongue flicks out to lick his lips.

He likes this idea of the future. Likes it very much.

Yes, indeedy.

Trap all the people inside like grasshoppers in a jar and light 'em up.

CHAPTER 66

Darger stared at the flaming hulk of the downed tree blocking the road. They were boxed in. Surrounded on three sides by fire.

Beside her, Luck shuddered in the driver's seat.

"It's OK," she said, sensing his panic. "We'll go the rest of the way on foot. We can do this."

She unhooked her seatbelt and reached for her door handle before realizing that Luck hadn't moved. He still sat with both hands locked on the steering wheel, arms and torso quivering out of time from each other. Jaw clattering as though he were frigid instead of burning up.

"Luck. We have to go. It's not safe to stay here."

His eyebrows flicked up a second, but otherwise he showed no sign of hearing her words. It finally dawned on her that he was in shock.

She slapped him.

"Luck," she said. "You need to take a deep breath, OK? Just focus on your breath, let it bring you back to the now. Take one big breath and count to ten."

His eyes looked glassy. Dead doll eyes that swiveled the opposite way and then back at her. They held there on hers but maintained that vacant look. At last, his head bobbed once.

He sucked in a big breath. Held it. Blew it out in slow motion, a little whistle accompanying the wind on the way out. That seemed to sharpen the look in his eyes, at least a little. He did it again. Better still.

"You good?" she asked.

His head bobbed again, more decisively this time.

There was a water bottle in the center console of the Lexus. Darger plucked it from the cup holder and shook it. There were a few swallows left. She grabbed Luck's jacket from the backseat and doused it with some of the water.

She sensed Luck's eyes on her.

"To filter out the smoke," she explained, handing him the dampened piece of clothing.

"Does that really work?"

"No idea," she said. "But it's gotta be better than nothing."

She did the same with her own jacket and looked over at him.

"Are you ready?"

He nodded.

"Say it."

"I'm ready," he said. "We can do this."

They climbed out of the Lexus into the burning night. The air dry, dryer than what seemed possible, somehow reminiscent of toasty paper fresh out of a copy machine.

Everything turned up as soon as she stepped through the door — the noise, the brightness, the heat — all of them intensifying. Overwhelming.

She didn't hesitate. Her feet carried her to the fallen trees, pausing for only a moment to pick out the clearest path, hopping and skipping her way through, feet finding just the right marks as though she were using a stone path to cross a stream.

The fire was right there, surrounding her from the shins down, strange orange shapes licking at her ankles, forked tongues touching her but somehow not quite able to leave their marks.

But she cleared it. She hurdled the tangle of burning deadfall and kept going, pressing deeper into the dark, peering behind her shoulder to make sure Luck made it all right. When she confirmed that he was right behind her, she continued on.

They ran down the middle of the road, the sound of their footsteps somehow dull against the rumble and hiss of the fire. Moving away from the cluster of fallen trees, away from the trapped Lexus.

We just need to get to the hospital parking lot. That's all. That's it. It was the only thought worth having just now, Darger knew. The only thing that was real in this situation.

The fire roared, angrier than before. A raging force. Chemical fury.

The world around them blurred with heat distortion. The air itself dancing the hateful dance of the fire. Shimmering with sadistic glee. Bending all the lines. Warping reality.

Darger pulled farther ahead of Luck. Lifting her knees. Landing on the middle of her foot. Keeping her feet beneath her, under her hips. All these things she half-remembered about running form came from some long-forgotten high school gym class, her brain regurgitating the tips now, coughing them up in bits and pieces, fragments of memory somehow jarred loose by the crisis.

Her new mantra played over and over in her head, slowly breaking down to simpler and simpler grammatical constructions. We need to get to the hospital parking lot, turned to Need to get to the hospital, which turned to, Get to the hospital, and finally just Hospital.

The trees cracked everywhere around them. Deep, thick cracks from the heat, like snapping bones but bigger and meaner and louder.

She held her wadded-up jacket to her mouth. The makeshift respirator seemed to be working so far. She didn't know how long that would last. Didn't even want to think about it.

Just go.

Perhaps a half-mile into the run, deliriousness began clawing at Darger's brain like a beetle in her skull. That dizziness twirling in her mind again. A throbbing nothingness that made her queasy. It gave her thoughts a feverish hysteria, sent them racing down nonsense paths that lost track of the real and the imagined.

The shimmer seemed to intensify around her. Everything warped and smeared and swimmy along the edges. The smoke stung her eyes, and the steady flow of tears only made it all the worse, refracting light into orange halos around everything.

She felt insane. Doomed. Running through a fucking nightmare. Through the gates of Hell.

To where? For what?

She tried to focus on her task, the singular word pumping in her head in time with her heartbeat. Hospital. Hospital. Hospital.

But the fire was right there. All around them. A thrashing thing that seemed alive. Only wanting to get closer, closer, closer. Fire only knew how to destroy, seemed to want it more than anything.

The heat swelled in her cheeks until they stung with it. The fire was brighter now. Blinding in its intensity. She had to squint to see at all. Eyes slitted. Just able to make out that pair of glowing yellow lines in the middle of the road.

She tried to look ahead, to see the hospital somewhere in the distance. But she could make out only fire and darkness. Form and void with no detail to be discerned. For all she knew they were still miles from the building, may never even get close.

She couldn't let that thought in, though. Could only keep going. Keep that word pulsing in her head, the carrot just out of reach.

Hospital. Hospital.

And then the Lexus exploded behind them.

There was a concussive boom like thunder. It seemed to travel along the ground, flinging her forward like a stiff push. She felt the rumble of the blast in the arches of her feet, in the meat of her ankles and calves — a miniature earthquake that sent a quiver into her bones.

They both stopped. Turned to look at the blaze rising where the car had been, shoulders squared to it, hands cupped around their brows to try to make out details in the endless bright. Finally Darger saw the contours of the twisted metal — what was moments ago Luck's prized Lexus.

The debris rained down for a bit. Audible sprinkles of luxury automobile pelting the ground, now closer to a fine powder than the body of a car.

He swiveled back the other way, ran on toward the hospital, his face blank from what she could see.

Darger followed his lead, relieved to be in motion again. She stayed close to Luck for now, keeping pace alongside him. Watching him in a series of little glances, trying to read his reaction.

She half-expected him to bemoan the loss as they carried on, to make some sarcastic little jab about Lexuses and Toyotas, at the very least. She thought for sure the adorable banter would chime in here, lighten the moment if just faintly.

But Casey Luck said nothing at all.

CHAPTER 67

Darger fought for breath now as she ran. Lips wheezing where they adhered to the wadded up jacket. The air seemed thinner, as if the fire burned out the oxygen and turned it to tufts of black smoke. She didn't know if that was real or not, but it felt that way.

The road looked shiny and wet. Perhaps the asphalt going soft from the heat, partially melting beneath their feet.

"How much farther?" she said between pants, removing the fabric from her maw long enough to be heard.

Luck squinted. Pulled his jacket away from his lips. He seemed to be struggling for breath even worse than she was.

"It's around one more bend and down a hill."

Darger thought about that a second.

"So how much farther?"

"Maybe half a mile. Probably less."

Luck swiped a hand at his brow before he went on, sweat leaking down from everywhere he touched. Rivulets running free like little rivers. He looked soaked now from head to toe, hair all mashed to his head, clothes sopping, hanging heavy with the moisture as though he'd just climbed out of a pool after having been thrown in.

Darger looked down and noted that the same was true of her clothes as well, that sogginess making the shirt bag funny. Rumpled and slack.

"I've been thinking," Luck said. "About what we'll do."

He took a couple breaths from his wet jacket before he went

on.

"When we get there, I mean. We should head for the center of the lot and then lay low."

Another breath from the jacket. His voice sounded hoarse now, thin and raspy, and he lifted it to be heard above the fire's roar, almost yelling.

"We'll try not to breathe smoke, mostly. I'm hoping that a chopper will be able to swoop in and get us sooner than later."

This time he took a longer breath, eyelids fluttering as he did.

"Obviously the parking lot gives them ample room to land, but the concern is the smoke. Visibility. Also maybe heat. It affects the air, could mess with the propellers if it's hot enough. We might have to wait a while before it's safe for them to make a landing. I'm not sure."

He locked eyes with her then, and she thought he looked more like himself finally. Tired. Scared. But he looked like Luck.

"I think that's our best hope, anyway," he said, wrapping up his speech.

He shrugged this time as he took a breath, which she took to mean he wasn't sure about any of this.

Darger nodded along with all that he said and kept nodding even after. It felt good to look forward, to see a picture painted in her imagination, a picture of the future, a picture of a way this might work out. It was the first time she'd dared to think about how they might survive in much detail, and it seemed more promising than she'd anticipated. Not the worst odds after all, maybe.

Now Darger saw the bend Luck was talking about, the fire

seeming to curve oddly around the little slice of land, that void and flaming form twisting in a way that it hadn't until now. Strange but reassuring in this moment.

Almost there.

She picked up her knees a little higher again, inspired. And she pulled a few paces in front of Luck, her endorphin rush finding a second wind, flooding her veins with faith, belief, conviction, hope. The chemicals in her brain convinced her once again that she might be able to run forever if she needed to. Probably could, in fact.

The tree cracked just next to her. Shattered. Burst. A two-syllabled split as loud as a shotgun blast.

And she saw the tumbling tree trunk out of the corner of her eye, a hulking sequoia-looking motherfucker, another disturbance in the flames. Tipping. Listing. Falling right at them.

She powered forward, opening up into a full sprint. Knees lifting higher and higher. Jacket no longer at her mouth as she pumped her arms. Not sure where she got the energy for this burst but thankful for it.

The massive tree bashed into a row of smaller trees as it sank, the whole mess of them dropping. Headed straight at her place in the road.

But Darger zipped right past all of them, weaving a little to miss a few scraggly branches. She felt weightless in this moment. Unstoppable.

The impact once more seemed to shake the earth itself, threatened to bash a hole in the asphalt.

Sparks exploded everywhere around her. Blinded her for the moment. Hands lifted to protect her eyes and hair from the tiny embers flitting around.

She stopped then. Waiting to hear the footsteps catching up behind her. Waiting. Waiting until the goose bumps rippled over her soggy flesh, streaks of cold creeping up her spine to grab her by the scruff of the neck.

When she looked back, she saw that Luck was down, a dark lump slouched among the fallen trees.

CHAPTER 68

"My heart can't take this," Beck says, her voice all soft.

It takes Klootey a second to realize she's talking to him, big eyes blinking in his direction.

"I can't stop thinking about Darger and Luck stranded in that." She gestures to the news footage of the fire on the TV.

"Yeah, yeah. Me, too," he says.

He hopes that's the end of the conversation, but she goes on.

"I just keep picturing them out there. Trapped. The fire raging toward them."

He almost laughs again. Mops the back of his hand over his lip to avoid it.

"Oh, same here. I been picturing nothing else, believe me."

She squints at him. Then shakes her head. A little shudder grabbing her by the shoulders and shaking.

Damn it. He needs to get her off the scent, off the topic. He's too tense to talk about this. Maybe if he reassures her.

"I mean, I think they'll make it," Klootey says. "Somehow, some way. If anyone is smart enough to get out of a situation like that, it'd be Agent Darger, you know?"

"Yeah, maybe."

It occurs to him only after this exchange that he is covering up, redirecting her. Feels threatened by her. Like maybe she can see him a little bit. Those little glimpses of Jim people sometimes get in his other life, his real life.

Could that be what he's seeing in the squint of her eyes? In

365

the way she looks at him with her head angled a little bit, an expression that reminds him of a suspicious dog?

Could be paranoia, though. She's pretty green as a cop. Pretty naive. Some backward bitch from way out in the boonies. Probably washes her clothes in a stream, runs it up and down a washing board or some nonsense.

"So you're from out there in Yucaipa, right?"

"Yessir. I don't blame you if you're only vaguely familiar with it. Most people on the task force hadn't been there before the church fire. Some hadn't even heard of it."

"Nah. I know it well. Used to go camping out in Wildwood Canyon State Park every summer when I was a teenager. I went through a survivalist phase, big time. Sleeping out in the roughage. Catching and cooking random shit like Bear Grylls or something. Kind of nuts, right? I guess there are worse hobbies a young kid can have."

Beck nods. A little smile taking the place on her lips where the frown had been. Good.

"That's for sure."

Talking about her hometown seems to trigger her hospitality, polite conversation now. Perfect. Keep her mind off Darger and Luck for a bit.

"What do folks do for fun out in Yucaipa? I remember thinking the fishing would be good, back when I used to hang there."

"Oh yeah. We've got all kinds of wildlife and outdoorsy interests to partake in. Fishing. Hiking. Hunting."

Just in the middle of her spiel, Klootey's phone rings. He checks the display. Holds up a finger.

"Sorry, it's my ma. Probably saw the fire on the news and

got spooked."

"Take it."

He answers the phone. As always, his mom's voice is so loud in his ear that he has to hold it away from his head and turn the volume down.

By the time he catches up with what she's saying, she's mid-rant.

"Gas it up. That's all I ask. If you want to borrow my vehicle, it's the least you can do, T.J. It's common courtesy."

"What are you ranting about this time, Ma? You realize I was just in a harrowing situation? We're talking life-threatening."

"Oh. Well, it must have been the life-threatening situation that prevented you from putting gas in the car last night."

"It's just a major forest fire. That's all. No big whoop. Turn on the TV. Any channel. You'll see what I'm talking about."

"I'm watching Wheel right now. No fire I can see."

He looks up to see Beck making a funny face at him again, her lips pursed. He can't decide if she's amused or disgusted. Even with the volume down, his ma's voice is still loud. No doubt Beck can hear every word of this conversation.

He winds his finger next to his head and points at the phone, then moves the phone away from his mouth and makes some cuckoo clock noises, which Beck huffs out a laugh at.

"I don't suppose you'll be around for family dinner on Sunday. That'd be typical," his Ma says, launching into a new line of verbal assault.

Beck steps away then. He watches her exit through the glass door and disappear around the corner as he fends off his mom, whose rant continues on, changing subjects every minute or so as though she's working from a list.

A few topics later, he sees the podunk cop on the phone in the hallway, pacing back and forth. Maybe his call reminded her to call her own mother.

Anyway, he is glad to be rid of her. One less thing to worry about.

CHAPTER 69

The flames licked up from the fallen mess of tree branches as Darger rushed to get to Luck. The heat swelled, pressing in on her from all sides. She waded into the fire, eyes squinted to slits, taking choppy steps, arms out wide to keep her balance, feet finding gaps in the orange and weaving, weaving.

Air whooshed up endlessly from the conflagration. That endless exhale breathing on her now, hot breath that smelled like smoke and ash. So close. It occupied the air around her, the time, the space, the night around her.

Her mind remained clear, though, finding that intense focus she sometimes experienced in the most stressful moments.

One thought mattered for the time being. A singular idea. She needed to get Luck out of here. Free of the fire. After that, she could worry about everything else.

She was close now. A few more steps and she could reach him, touch him, pull him out.

She found him crumpled in the fetal position among the burning debris, the odor of burnt hair hanging everywhere. It was an acrid stench that clung to Darger's nostrils, seemed to attach itself to the flesh in her sinuses, never to leave her. Part of her wondered if it was hers or his or both.

Luck moved not at all from what she could see. A motionless lump. Face down on the asphalt. Utterly still. A dark place among the wreckage. The one thing not on fire.

He was unconscious. Maybe worse.

She stooped over him and felt along the clammy shoulders, searching for a place to grab him securely. Her hands snaked under his armpits, scooping and lifting. His jacket looked like a dark puddle in the flickering light. She grabbed it and draped it over her shoulder. He may need that later. She hoped he'd need it, anyway.

She dragged his dead weight along. He was heavy and slippery, and she had to stop every few steps to regain her grip on him. He still lay face down so she couldn't see the extent of the damage, maybe didn't want to see.

She just needed to pull him clear of the fire. That was all she could think about. The rest of the night, the rest of her life, would happen after that. It could be worried over when it arrived.

She muscled him over a couple of small branches, moving quickly to try to keep the both of them out of the flames for more than fleeting encounters. It was during the heave that got him over the second branch that she saw it.

Luck's ankle was broken. Badly.

White bone jutted out from the bottom of the calf. Glittering in the fire's glow. The foot tilted at the wrong angle. Floppy like an uncontrolled puppet. A compound fracture. Possibly a dislocated ankle too.

The injury was wrong. Deeply wrong. She almost puked at the sight of it.

Blood sheened on the leg, the ankle, the edge of the bone, the sides of his shoe. With the limb tucked partially in shadow, it was too dark to see how bad the bleeding was, but she didn't think it was too bad. At least that was a positive.

She kept moving, powering through.

If the ankle was the worst of it, he'd be OK. He would be OK. And if he wasn't...

She could worry about it when she pulled him clear of the fire. She could think again, breathe again, feel like a human being again, when she pulled him clear of the fire.

She repeated this affirmation to herself. Tried to focus on it like a prayer. Transmit the sentiment to a better place. Make it real somehow.

The dragging sped up as they cleared the last of the roughage. Luck started slipping through her fingers again, so she looped an arm under him to get through the last of it, her gait going to an uneven stagger for those last four steps. She strained, struggled still to hold onto the heavy, sweat-slicked body. Pushed herself to the finish line.

And then she was out. Clear. Free.

She lowered Luck's body to the asphalt, moving slowly, delicately, with care. Her mind recording every detail.

She saw the blood on the back of his head just as she pulled her hands away. With the fire of the fallen trees no longer backlighting the agent's features and swathing him in shadow, she could see the red soaking the hair where the neck and back of the skull met.

So the ankle wasn't the only injury he'd suffered. He must have gotten walloped pretty good all over. Battered by the branches. Agent Luck was laid low.

But how low?

And then she was coughing. Gagging on her hands and knees next to him. The smoke invaded her lungs, her throat, her eyes, worse than before. Dry hacking sounds sputtered from her throat, tears spilling down her cheeks. Some part of her knew that she could feel it now, could suffer now, because they were clear of the fire. The outside world could get in once more, could assail her.

She fought it. Tried to stop whatever was wracking the muscles along her ribcage, squeezing cough after cough out of her. It took time and effort to slow it down, time she didn't have.

She swiped tears from her eyes, and the coughing stopped at last, dying back to muffled little croaks that spilled out of her spontaneously, hoarse sounding barks. She took small, shallow breaths, afraid to breathe too deeply lest it start all over again.

Her focus shifted back to Luck. Time to see how bad it was.

She turned him over in slow motion. Nestled his shoulder blades to the blacktop. Cupping the bloody cranium as she lowered him.

He looked dead. A lifeless kind of still. Face as blank and slack as could be. Skin waxy and glistening and strange. Wet. Like a mannequin that'd been spritzed with a spray bottle a few times for no good reason.

She needed to be sure. Needed to. Now or never.

She held her breath as she checked. Almost didn't want to know, even if she had to.

Her fingers snaked along the clammy neck. Finding the proper place. Feeling for a pulse.

Nothing.

She held the two fingers there for a long moment — the tips of the index and middle fingers motionless just in front of the curved muscle of Casey Luck's neck, the flesh a little cool to the touch.

And no thoughts occurred to her as she sat there, the fire

swirling in the forest all around her. A vast black sea of nothingness entering her skull instead. The void. The abyss. Endless. Nameless. The big nothing that stretched out to span eternity, to swallow all life in time. Waiting only to take us all.

And then she felt it.

A pulse. Thready. Weak.

But it was there.

CHAPTER 70

Luck's eyelids fluttered. Closed again. For a second Darger thought he was back under, out again for the time being, but then he opened them once more, and his gaze locked on hers.

She could see the moment when the pain of his ankle hit, a wince wrinkling his features, a wet hiss escaping his lips. His hand squeezed hers. Hard. The other hand clutched at his shirt, ringing sweat out of it.

"Your ankle is broken," she said, removing her jacket respirator to speak. "But we still need to move. You can lean on me. I'll be your crutch."

She gestured to the road, hand flinging the way the hospital lay.

Luck stared that direction, eyes seemingly clear enough but hard to read. After a moment's hesitation, he nodded.

Darger helped him up, and he draped one of his arms over her shoulders so he could hop along on his good leg. She hesitated another second, wanting to get a better read on him before they moved out.

"You remember what happened?" Darger said. Again she watched his eyes for signs of his state of mind. "You got your bell rung pretty good."

"I remember the hospital, the car exploding," Luck said. "Burning trees falling. It's all kind of jumbled up, I guess."

"That's OK. That's most of it, anyway. Let's move."

The heat was overwhelming, the smoke thicker than ever. But they hobbled forward, finally approaching that bend in the road after staring at it for so long.

Luck did his best, but it was a slog, and their progress was reduced to a slow shuffle. Darger was happy to be going at all with the way his ankle looked. Tattered meat with goddamn bone sticking out of it, the dislocated foot flopping around enough to turn her stomach if she made the mistake of looking at it.

She focused on the surrounding forest instead. It had been transformed, the leaves and brush eaten up by the fire. What was left had a sparse look. Stark. Columns of orange with skeletal lines of black where the tree trunks remained. The tinder may have burned up, but the inferno still had fuel enough to keep going for a long time.

"That's it," Luck said, prying Darger's attention away from the trees.

They'd reached the end of the curve in the road, the hospital now visible in the distance at last. The building squatted at the bottom of the hill, the expanse of parking lot lying at its feet. It was a long way off yet, but it was there. Real.

Luck fumbled with his jacket as he went to press it back to his mouth, almost lost it. He caught it, though. Pinned it to his chest and regained his grip.

And Darger's confidence began to grow for the first time during this ordeal. Her eyes fixed on the parking lot ahead. Their destination was in sight, as impossible as that notion seemed until just now. They could do this.

Survival is the only thing now. The only thing.

They moved to the hill, starting down the final descent. The incline made it tough for Luck to hop along, gravity constantly trying to pull him into a downward stumble. His progress came in big uneven jolts forward.

Maybe she was crazy, but Darger thought the smoke seemed to be clearing as they took those first steps down the hill.

Fresh air? Maybe it made sense. Hot air rises. Smoke rises. Maybe it would drift up and away. Leave them air to breathe in the valley where the hospital lay. Maybe.

The words echoed in her head again.

Survival is the only thing.

They kept fighting the slope, working their way down the hill in fits and starts. Based on how they'd handled it so far, the hill would take them another five minutes or so, Darger thought. Then they'd be done and whatever would happen from there would happen.

For now, she only had to get through the next five minutes. She could do that. She could do anything for five minutes.

She felt lighter than she had all night. Alive. Filled with passion, inspiration, hope.

Survival is the only thing. And it might be within our reach.

A strange sound shook her out of the abstract — a wet cluck emitted from Luck's lips.

And suddenly he was pulling, pulling, jerking away from her. Falling. Spilling down to the strip of dirt and gravel that divided the asphalt from the wall of flame. A little mew came out of him as he hit the ground — the pain of the broken ankle prying a cry out of him, Darger thought.

Luck picked himself up, held himself steady on hands and knees.

"Are you OK?" she asked, reaching for him to help him stand again.

His only answer was to vomit into the dirt of the shoulder, head lolling along with the heaves.

Darger closed her eyes. Breathed deep, the faint damp from her jacket trying and failing to fight off the smoke invading her mouth, her throat, her lungs.

She'd been afraid of this, ever since she'd seen the bloody spot on the back of his head.

Luck had a concussion.

CHAPTER 71

Thankfully, Luck's vomiting spell was over quickly. Darger leaned down, offered her shoulder to him. He climbed her torso the best he could, getting up onto his knees, looping himself around her collar bone, and then the two of them stood together. He spoke as she helped him back to his feet.

"I'm sorry, Jill," Luck said.

Darger didn't know what to make of that. Was he mistakenly calling her Jill — his daughter's name — or was he apologizing to the actual Jill even if she weren't here to hear it? She licked her lips.

"Sorry for what?" she said.

"I didn't know... I mean, it caught me off guard is all. Came out of nowhere and just..."

He shook his head. Re-gathered his thoughts. Tried again.

"I'm just sorry I threw up, Jill. Left a mess to clean up. That's all."

She thought about correcting him, let the words form on the tip of her tongue, and then she thought better of it. What would it help? He didn't know what the hell was going on, did he? What would pressing him accomplish?

"Let's not worry about that right now," she said after a second. "You're doing fine. We're almost there now."

He stared a hole into her then, blinking. She wasn't sure how much of what she said was getting through.

He seemed more confused than he had been before, the disorientation settling over him all at once, as though his concussion hadn't fully taken hold until he sealed its existence with a spray of vomit, completed some bodily ritual. She knew that wasn't true, of course, but it seemed like it.

Had he been this loopy since he woke, and she couldn't tell until now? It must be so, but she could hardly believe it.

He babbled on a little as they shuffled down the hill in slow motion. Fragmented thoughts spilling out of him. Sometimes lucid, focused on the hospital ahead, getting out of the fire. Other times he lapsed into various levels of confusion, hallucinations, a couple times talking as though they were back in Detroit or Ohio instead of LA.

"Holy shit," he said after a stretch of silence, startling her. His shoulders twitched a little, and Darger realized he was flinching back from the fire.

"What?" she said.

He pointed at the woods around them, engulfed in flames. Slurred out his response as though drunk.

"Fire. It's on fire."

By the time he said it, she could hear that the resolve was already draining from his voice, some part of him realizing that the fire wasn't a new occurrence after all, that he'd known about it all the while, and his scrambled brain had forgotten somehow. Momentarily. Swiss cheese holes in his short term memory. It was like he was stitching together the pieces of a dream, finding it a constant struggle to hold all of reality together in his head.

He let his soggy jacket flop to his side, and Darger redirected him to hold it up to his mouth, physically lifting the hand holding the wadded fabric and pressing it toward his face before something triggered in his addled mind and he remembered what to do.

"Forgot. Sorry, mom," he said.

Yikes. Jill was better than mom, Darger thought, if only a little.

They trudged on, picking up speed as the land leveled some toward the bottom of the hill. Luck still stumbled every few steps, but the recovery didn't take as long on the flatter surface.

The lot seemed to grow before them, looked more like a body of water than something solid — a spreading pool of asphalt, a puddle growing wider and deeper. Closer. Closer.

Orange jumped and flickered in the windows of the hospital. The lobby was a gleaming brightness shining through the front glass. Burning bright.

Smoke twirled off the top of the building. Plumes of black coils rising without end, up and up and up. And Darger could see where the fire's tantrums had taken out chunks of the roof, the flames licking up from the freshly opened wounds, raging tendrils reaching for the sky.

The final step on the road almost caught her off guard. She looked down from the building in the distance just in time to see their feet cross onto the shinier blacktop of the lot. It felt softer, just a little more give under her boots, but it was solid ground. Real. They'd made it.

For the first time, they were able to move away from the fire, feeling the faintest touch cooler as they hobbled out toward the center of the lot. Whatever chance they had of making it through this, their best hope was right here, on this black smear of land coated with a layer of bitumen and stone.

Darger let out a big breath, and the exhalation seemed to carry physical weight off of her person. Lighten her load.

They'd made it. A tingle spread over her body, the disbelief making all the tiny hairs perk up across her arms and along the back of her scalp.

They moved to a decorative bed of mulch in the center of the lot and huddled there — an oval-shaped landscaping flourish encased by curb, a ring of red woodchips encircling a lone maple tree. This one would be OK, she thought. If any of the trees might make it, this little guy would. He had a whole parking lot between him and the rest of the fire, after all.

After she made sure that Luck got to the ground safely, she leaned her back up against the little tree. Felt the strain release in the muscles of her back, in her neck, along her abs.

She closed her eyes and focused on the feeling of relief spreading through her body. Took a few deep breaths out of her wadded jacket. It felt incredible to sit. She'd forgotten how good that could feel, the simple act of sitting when you needed the rest. She'd taken it for granted for so long.

It was still hot. Infinitesimally cooler than the road, maybe. Faintly detectable. It wasn't quite the level of difference that she'd hoped for. Still, the fire was a good couple hundred feet from them now. That had to be good for something, didn't it?

Her gaze landed on the scattering of cars still in the lot. Maybe one of them had something they could use, if only a bit of water to drink. Her mouth was so dry she was having trouble swallowing. But the idea of standing up again, of having to do anything more strenuous than blinking, made her want to cry. She'd do it, though. In a minute. For now, she'd gather what strength she had left.

She drifted. Let her mind go still and blank, relax for this tiny fraction of time. She had to enjoy this little victory, even if she could only muster a sliver of enjoyment at that.

Then her eyelids fluttered open. She couldn't forget about Luck, though. She had to keep an eye on the concussed bastard.

Glancing over at him, she watched his chin bob down toward his chest, eyelids drooping closed. Another concussion symptom, she knew. He was passing out.

Years ago, it was thought dangerous to let a freshly concussed person sleep. Coma was a feared result. These days, they knew that wasn't true.

Still, she wanted to keep him talking. Better to keep him conscious in case they needed to move out again.

"You alright over there, Agent Luck?"

His eyes snapped opened — too wide for a second. A few blinks and a head shake seemed to clear them, bring fresh life to them. He nodded once, gave her a thumbs up.

"Yeah. Yeah. All good here, Darger."

"Want to sit up? Put your back on the other side of the tree there?"

"Uh, yeah, sure."

He slid over, moving gingerly due to the ankle, which Darger still couldn't bring herself to look at.

"Good," she said. "I know you're tired, but let's try to stay alert for now. Just in case, right?"

Because who knew what the wind and flame might bring next?

CHAPTER 72

Updates flood into the conference room now, seeming to come in little waves. Endless streams of people pour in and out of the room.

A suited and coiffed higher-up who Klootey doesn't recognize currently dominates the room. He stands at the lectern in a suit that costs a little more than what Klootey makes in a month — probably Gucci or Brooks Brothers or some fucking thing — chattering away on his phone. He's getting updates from some personal contact in some federal agency or other — maybe the NSA? — about satellite imagery of the land surrounding the hospital, a bird's eye view of the fire via some hunk of metal orbiting the planet, maybe a hundred and forty-four miles or so straight up.

The smoke blocks most of the view, but the team is going through the archived footage. Looking for any signs of Luck or Darger. They should know soon, and this suited slack dick will tell them all about it as soon as they do.

Klootey clutches a sweaty can of Mountain Dew in his paw. He's already guzzled down two of the things and several glasses of water before that, but he can't stop himself. Needs something to fill the time, something to fill the void, something to do.

The suit holds up his index finger, and everyone in the room goes silent all at once.

"Got something. They think they've spotted the Lexus. Looks like it didn't make it. Tangled among some downed trees and burned. Exploded even. A total loss."

After a stretch of quiet, a woman's voice speaks up from the back of the room. It might be Beck.

"Do they think… Were Darger and Luck still in the vehicle?"

"They're working to confirm that now."

Klootey takes a big pull on his Mountain Dew can, accidentally making a loud slurping noise, lips smacking on the can in the hushed room. Heads snap his way. A lot of dirty looks taking aim at him and his beverage.

"Sorry," he says, almost under his breath.

Mr. Fancy Suit's finger stabs the sky again.

"Wait. We've got footage of Darger and Luck fleeing the vehicle on foot. Moving down the road. Back toward the hospital."

Everyone falls quiet as the suit listens to the talk on the other end of the line, nodding his head along with the rhythm of the words in his ear.

"We've got eyes on them now. They're in the parking lot outside the hospital. The male subject, Casey Luck, looks to have suffered injuries. But they're alive."

CHAPTER 73

Darger and Luck still huddled near the tree when the wind changed. She could see the currents adjust, the ripples in the air morphing, shifting gears, changing directions. The smoke once spiraling away from them now closed on their location, veered toward them as if seeking them out.

The black clouds grew thicker and thicker in the air around them until she couldn't see the liquid movement of them anymore. Only the black sheen of it, the shadow of it as opaque as a steel wall.

The night grew darker as the smoke descended and blackened around them. No more stars. No more fire hemming them in on all sides. The raging, writhing orange replaced by a velvet curtain of blackness.

The smoke stung her eyes even if she couldn't really see it anymore. She felt a couple of tears drain down from the corners, streaks running down her cheeks. There should be more, she thought, but she was running dry now. The heat was cooking the fluid out of her little by little.

Her mouth was so dry, her tongue kept getting stuck to the roof of her mouth, felt like some weird sponge in her face. She tried to swallow, tried to get the saliva flowing, but she only started to cough again, a dry rasp that shook her ribcage.

"We better get low," Luck said, his voice coming out of the darkness to her left.

She wasn't sure it mattered now, couldn't imagine the smoke was any less dense at ground level, but it couldn't hurt.

She reached for him, found his shoulders. Kept him steady as he rolled over onto his belly, trying to make sure that the bone protruding from his ankle didn't jab into the ground and jolt fresh pain up the limb.

And then she scooted onto her stomach as well, her chest and arms poked by the pointy bits of the mulch. She pressed her face down into the jacket. Breathed what fresh air she could. The fabric was mildly damp at best now. She wasn't even quite sure it was wet enough to truly be considered damp.

"We're going to be OK, yeah?" Luck said.

His face was closer to hers now. His voice near her ear.

"Yeah," she said. "I hope so."

"Nah. I wasn't asking. I'm telling you, Violet. We're going to be OK."

She wasn't so sure about that, but she didn't say anything. Even if a helicopter pilot could brave the conditions, if the chopper could handle the heat technically and fly in here for them, there was no way anyone could see them or much of anything now. Nothing but smoke.

She pictured the bird's eye view of it. The smoke rolling over the land, over the parking lot, over the hospital. Endless black clouds. Impenetrable dark that blotted everything out, making what seemed like the whole world an indistinguishable black mass. A writhing, darkling nothingness that snaked over and over itself in strange rivulets.

Smoke inhalation would most likely kill them now. She knew that. Understood it, even if it was hard to make much meaning of it here in the dark, face jammed down in a jacket tucked into some wood chips.

Luck's hand found hers again. Gripped it. His palm was

warm and dry and strong.

And she wondered what any of this had meant. Any of it. What was the use? The purpose? Why did all the people keep going? Keep fighting? Keep holding out hope for as long as they did? What for?

She shoved her face deeper into the jacket, burrowing her head down into the mulch, and the world seemed to drift away. To grow quiet.

Her thoughts turned to the man who had started all of this. He was getting what he wanted, wasn't he? More destruction. More death. She wondered if they'd catch him after all of this. And as she fought to keep that last spark of hope from being extinguished, she wondered if it even mattered.

CHAPTER 74

The Chief paces the floor of the conference room, no less than thirteen distinct lines creasing his forehead. He hisses into the phone more than he talks into it, the little smartphone wedged against his ear, quivering along with the hand holding it there, inching back and forth as his nervous twitches adjust it endlessly.

Klootey can't help but stop thinking about anything else to listen to him, piece together this conversation based on the one side he can hear. He notices that Beck is doing the same, eyes tracing Macklin's path to one side of the room and then the other, pupils swinging back and forth like pendulums.

"I know that. You think I don't know that?"

He listens for a few seconds. Goes on.

"Well, check again. Look, I'm asking you to check again."

Klootey knows he's asking after the helicopter, whether it will be able to make it into the hospital parking lot to retrieve Luck and Darger. It had been looking good, but the wind changed directions. Smoked everything up. Now, they aren't so sure.

The Chief stops in his tracks. The whole room has gone quiet now. Watching him. Waiting to hear the news.

"No. We can't... Are you serious? Hours? That's not acceptable."

Klootey looks over at Beck, sees tears beading along the bottoms of her eyelids, clear sparkles ready to spill down her face. Once again, he has to stifle a laugh, biting at the inside of his cheeks.

"Fine," the Chief says. He rips the phone away from his ear and ends the call, jaw muscles rippling.

Then he seems to gather himself as he realizes the whole room is watching and waiting. He closes his eyes. Takes a deep breath and lets it out slowly. The deep creases on his forehead relax, now mere hairline folds.

"The smoke is going to be a problem," he says, addressing the hushed room. "They said... I mean, if it doesn't clear up..."

The tension in the room thickens like Cream of Mushroom soup.

Klootey is giddy inside. Ecstatic. He has to stop himself from tumbling across the room in a gymnastics routine full of handsprings and cartwheels and culminating in a series of pelvic thrusts. Has to cup a hand over his smile and cough a little to conceal the truth.

The Chief goes on, his voice sober as fuck. He's just as oblivious as Bishop and Beck and all the rest, and that makes Klootey want to laugh even more.

"They think it could be hours before they can get a chopper in there to attempt the extraction. They just don't know."

CHAPTER 75

The wind moaned as it ripped past. Endless gusts of air
brushing over her, prying at her shirt, her hair. Wind. This was
what brought the never-ending smoke to them. Smothered
them. Even after all they'd braved, all the energy they'd
expended, the sacrifices they'd made to get to this parking lot, it
would kill them in time. Nothing more than a strong breeze
would kill them.

Darger kept her head down, face shoved into her wadded
up jacket as deeply as it'd go. Eyes closed, each shallow breath
tasting and smelling of wood chips and smoke.

Her throat burned, and her head swam. She felt on the
verge of passing out, and despite the fuzziness in her head that
made her thoughts sluggish and nonsensical, knew that would
be bad. She had to fight. She took a deep breath and then
another, fighting the urge to start coughing again.

Luck's hand still gripped hers. She gave it a squeeze, and
after a second of hesitation, he squeezed back, just barely. She
could feel the strength leaving his fingers. He was still there for
now, though. That was something.

With every breath, she wondered how many she had left.
Twenty more breaths? Less? All of life was a countdown,
though, wasn't it? The number of heartbeats. The ticks on the
clock. Always winding down to our end, one way or another.

How long had they been lying here like this now? Ten
minutes? An hour? It felt like an eternity.

When she couldn't stand it any longer, Darger lifted her

head to look. She expected to see nothing but the writhing darkness. She braced herself for it, for the endless clouds of smoke that meant to suffocate them.

Instead she found patches of translucence perforating that thick wall of smoke. Bars of light that broke through the murk, lighting up the twisting coils of black and gray.

And through the gaps, she could see glimmers of the fire again. Coals of withered trees gleamed orange and angry in the night. The forest as it had been was gone. Only bones were left now.

Darger shoved her face back into her makeshift respirator. Breathed. Tried not to think about the ache in her throat where the heat and smoke had abraded the flesh.

Instead, she pictured those beams shining through the smoke again. Glimmers of hope that played in her head over and over.

A low-pitched whir entered her consciousness. It was so subtle and quiet at first that she wasn't even sure if it was really there or if her pulse had suddenly taken on a strange beat. But after a moment, she recognized the sound.

A helicopter.

It whoomphed closer, the sound growing bigger, louder, crisper. Propellers slicing the night air.

God, let it be real. Don't let it just be my imagination. Please.

She squeezed her eyelids closed hard. Would have cried if there were any tears left to spend.

She wondered if Luck could hear the chopper. He must, right? She gave his fingers a little squish. Waited.

His hand stayed slack. No response.

Then she felt a stirring of the air. A change in the wind that disturbed the wood chips around her, made them tremble and throb. Unlike the winds that had ripped past for the last while, coasting over them from northeast to southwest, the pressure now came straight down at them. It beat into the ground, snuffled at her shirt which had gone so dry as to feel stiff and overstarched at some point.

The chopper sound suddenly swelled in volume. Louder and louder.

She peeled her head up to take another look. Blinked smoke out of her eyes.

The helicopter sliced a hole in the murk and descended into it, seeming to appear there out of nowhere. It hovered just above the ground some 100 or so yards from them, between their tree and the hospital.

The circular motions of the propellers assailed the black cloud above. Twisted it up like a tornado. And the smoke seemed to dissipate over the lot.

Darger didn't think now. She stood and waved her arms over her head. Jumped up and down.

There was no response from the shapes in the helicopter. The two silhouettes in the cockpit seemed oblivious. Unmoving.

One of them poked his head out the side door, cupped a hand over his brow. He scanned from left to right. Looking. Searching. Not seeing her.

Darger jumped higher, waved her arms harder. She tried to scream but something more like a croak came out, dry and raspy and small.

The man lowered the hand from his brow, and Darger was

certain then that he was going to climb back in the chopper and move on. Leave them there. Surely they had other survivors to look for.

Instead, he lifted the hand again. His head bobbed as he turned and said something to the other man in the helicopter. It was a beat before she realized he was pointing at her.

Then he waved at her. A big, happy wave that reminded her of something a little kid would do.

The helicopter descended the last twenty feet or so and landed. The man jumped down from the cabin door and started running for her. The vortex of air from the spinning propellers fluttered against his bright yellow shirt, wrinkling and pressing the fabric flat to his chest and belly.

Darger stooped to Luck's side, part of her unsurprised that he hadn't moved even with all the commotion. She reached out a hand for him, grasped his upper arm.

His skin was strangely cool to the touch, and when she shook him, he did not wake.

CHAPTER 76

It's a bad omen. Darger surviving? It puts a kind of fear in Klootey, in Jim.

He goes to take another slug of Mountain Dew and finds the can empty. Hollow. Sucks on the little glowing green liquid in the lip of the can. He feels the zing of the acidity touch his lips, but it's not even enough to really taste it.

The bustle turns jubilant around the conference room once again. Someone put on some horrific dubstep music and now a couple of the younger officers dance in one corner of the room, making fools of themselves and giggling about it. Giddy like children. Another fleet is already headed down to the outdoor break area to celebrate by breathing smoke. The irony.

Word is, the choppers have both Darger and Luck in sight. Any moment now they'll be loaded and lifted. Maybe it's happening right this second, Klootey thinks, trying not to picture the heroic rescue. Barring some kind of Stevie Ray Vaughn type chopper crash, they'll get out.

And he can't sit here any longer. Cannot. Needs to get out of the conference room. Away from these people.

Probably better to lay low for this next little bit anyhow. Let things play out. If he leaves right now, he can still get the jump on hiding out, if that becomes necessary.

That's what he'll do. Stay one step ahead. He'll feel out what they know at this point and react accordingly. He knows there's no logical reason to believe that Darger has figured him out, but he fears it with such intensity that he can't sit still, can't stay

394

here a second longer.

He pushes through the glass doors. Moves out into the corridor. The camera in his head pans down the hall, not dwelling on any of the faces as he rushes past, keeping them in that soft focus that seems less threatening, less real.

He'll take the back stairs. Stepping into an elevator right now would feel like entering a cage. There's less foot traffic that way, too. His bike sits in a parking garage a few buildings down from here, and he can cut along the backs of the buildings this way. Stay off the street.

He fishes his keys out of his pocket before he's even outside. Clutches them in his hand as though simply touching them puts him closer to where he wants to be. A talisman he can focus his desire on, sharpening the edge of it in his mind.

A steel door angles out of the way, and he's outside. One step closer. Almost there.

He's half-startled by the small crowd on the other side of the door. But it's only the smokers. A bunch of uniformed officers, most of them from the task force, mill around the pair of big ashtrays. The ceramic cylinders look like birdbaths full of sand. Cigarette butts pock this little beach, though. All their heads submerged, the filter ends sticking up at various angles.

Some of the officers still suck on the big stogies handed out earlier, probably having saved and relit them. Others opt for traditional cigarettes. A few vape instead, blowing out huge dense clouds of the stuff.

Klootey recognizes some of the faces. Gives a little wave. Better to play it cool. Just a dude heading home for some much needed shut-eye. No one worth noticing. Nothing to see.

The crowd seems pretty occupied in any case, a loud

conversation bandying back and forth among the ring of smokers. They talk over each other to the point that Klootey can't pick out any strands clearly.

He almost doesn't hear the sound of the door opening and shutting again behind him. The noise certainly doesn't register or mean anything until her voice comes just after it.

"Freeze."

Right away the little mob of smokers falls quiet. Total silence fills the space behind him. Makes that cold surge of adrenaline course through his hands.

But Jim detects a note of fear in the voice. A shakiness. Doubt. He ignores it, takes a step.

"Officer Klootey," she repeats. "I said, 'Freeze.'"

When he hears her pull the bolt of her gun back, he stops. What the hell?

"Hands up."

Whispers erupt from the crowd. Klootey picks out one sentence among the murmuring.

"What's going on here?"

Captain Beck stands just behind Klootey now. So close he feels her breath on the back of his neck. She plucks his gun from his holster. Tells him to put his hands behind his back.

By the time she tightens the cuffs around his second wrist, he can't feel his arms, his legs. Can't feel anything at all.

CHAPTER 77

A knock came from outside of Darger's hospital room, and then the door opened. Georgina Beck poked her head inside.

"Are you awake?"

Darger gave a thumbs up. Her throat was so fucked she still couldn't talk, even after several hours of oxygen and IV fluids. The oxygen mask would have made conversation awkward anyway, so she supposed it didn't matter.

She swiped her phone from the bedside table and typed out a message. She pressed a button and the bionic voice of her phone spoke for her.

"You did it. You saved the day."

Beck settled into the chair next to Darger's bed.

"Oh heck. It was your profile that did it."

"The profile is just words on paper. Applying it is the hard part, and you're the one who did that," Darger said.

Beck didn't look convinced.

"At the very least, you deserve credit for an assist," she said.

Darger's thumbs danced over the screen, typing out a new message. Beck was the first visitor the nurses had allowed into her room, and though she'd gotten bits and pieces of what had transpired since she and Luck had been stranded, she was starved for more information.

"How long did you suspect it was Klootey? And when did you know for sure?"

"That's what I'm trying to say," Beck said, throwing her hands in the air. "I didn't know anything for sure until I called my station and had them run a records check on vehicles registered to Klootey's mother."

Darger raised an eyebrow, indicating that Beck had jumped too far into her story, and she wasn't following.

"OK. So the first thing was that he mentioned having been to Yucaipa before. Said he used to be into all this outdoorsy stuff when he was younger, went on camping trips in Wildwood State Park. That's where one of the old fires was, the ones I told you about that were put down as accidental but fit the arsonist's M.O. when I dug a little deeper."

"How'd you end up talking to him in the first place?"

Beck frowned, her head rocking back a little on her neck.

"Well, I guess I hadn't thought about it before, but he was acting funny. Real jittery-like. I mean, we were all keyed up, so I don't know why he stuck out, but he did. I thought he seemed upset, so I asked if he was doing alright."

Raising an eyebrow, Darger gave her a knowing look.

"What?"

"Your gut knew something was off, even if you didn't yet."

A disbelieving scoff told Darger what Beck thought of that.

"Now you're making it out like I'm some kind of psychic or something."

"No. I'm just saying you sensed it, however faintly."

Beck folded her hands over her protruding belly and pursed her lips.

"Everyone's acting like I'm some kind of Sherlock, but it was just dumb luck."

Darger's fingers moved furiously over the screen.

"You had to put all the pieces together. You've done jigsaw puzzles with your kids, I bet. You don't assemble it with luck.

You use your perception, your intuition. So yeah, you are some kind of Sherlock."

Beck's face flushed, a pinkness showing on her cheeks, but Darger kept typing.

"So is that when you started digging?" Darger asked. "After he mentioned being in Yucaipa way back when?"

"Heck no! It didn't even cause so much as a single hair to stand on end. I thought nothing of it."

"Until?"

"Until he got a call from his mother. She was giving him a bunch of guff about not gassing up the car. Sounded like she was talking to a kid more than a grown man, which struck me funny. I didn't know why, at first. I mean, beyond the fact that at some point you need to cut the apron strings, you know? And then I remembered that in your profile, you said he might still live with a parent."

Beck took a breath, adjusting her pregnant bulk in the chair.

"Obviously, I couldn't just ask him something like that. It's awfully personal. Besides that, my first instinct was to tell myself I was being paranoid. But my mind started going backward from there. I thought about him driving her car and wondered, what if that's what he uses when he's starting fires? Something unfamiliar to anyone that knows him. Something that wouldn't come up if you were searching vehicles owned by firemen and law enforcement."

Darger nodded.

"So that's when I looked up his mother's vehicle registration. Found a dark brown Buick Enclave. My heart was already pounding a little when my deputy told me that, but there was something else. We got a big traffic safety grant a few years back. The county put in a handful of traffic cams at our busiest intersections. Guess whose license plate got logged for running a red light in Yucaipa on the 4th of September?"

"The day of the church fire?"

"Yes, ma'am. That's when I got the willies, like a big ol' spider had just crept up my spine."

"So you went to Chief Macklin then?"

Beck shook her head.

"No, because after that I was afraid to let Klootey out of my sight. He'd been squirrelly the whole time, even more so once it became clear they were attempting a rescue mission. When he heard they were sending in a chopper, I could see on his face that he was thinking about running."

"He must have thought I'd figured him out. Or would soon," Darger typed. She sighed which caused her to wince in pain. "But I'm not so sure I would have."

"Of course you would. I only figured it out because of you. Because of your profile."

Darger shrugged noncommittally.

"What happened after you cuffed him?"

"He froze at first. I think it took him a minute to realize what was happening. And then he started to make a real fuss. I got pretty nervous, being surrounded by a bunch of his buddies, you know? That's when I said we'd better call for their Chief."

Darger said nothing, waiting for Beck to continue her story.

"He didn't much like what I had to say. Not until I showed him the traffic cam shot of Klootey in the Buick. Once he saw that, he got on the horn and got a warrant to search both the mother's vehicle and Klootey's bike. The Harley was clean, since there's not much you can stash on a bike, I guess, but the Buick had a little pyro kit in it. A five-gallon can of gasoline, some empty plastic bottles, matches, a ripped up t-shirt, and some scissors. All pretty innocent on their own, but together…"

"He'll still try to claim it's all just some junk his mom left in there," Darger said.

"Oh I'm sure he will. But by then, they'll have searched everything. His house, his locker down at the station, his phone, his internet search history. He's not nearly as bright as he thinks he is. I bet he left bits of evidence all over the damn place. We'll find them."

EPILOGUE

By the time she was discharged four days later, Darger had regained the ability to speak without turning into a gagging, coughing mess.

Her first destination was her hotel room for a change of clothes that didn't reek of smoke. The outfit she'd been wearing in the fire went straight in the trash.

Her second stop was the county jail. Beck had sounded shocked when Darger told her where she was headed.

"Your first taste of freedom after what you went through, and you want to go sit in a hard chair in a starkly lit room with Thomas James Klootey? Go to the beach and get an ice cream cone or something. Geez."

But Darger knew what she needed and that was to sit down with Klootey face to face. To look at the man who had fooled her and so many others and see him for what he really was.

Her voice was still raspy, and it hurt like hell to talk, but it would be worth it. She wanted to be the one to hammer the final nail into the coffin. For her, but also for Luck.

She signed in at the jail, stowing her weapon and valuables in a locker. When she entered the private visitation room, Klootey was already there, along with a wiry-haired man in a brown suit she figured for his lawyer.

He didn't even wait until she had the door closed before he started in on his objections.

"I don't know who arranged this little sit-down, but they didn't clear it with me. If they had, I could have saved everyone a lot of time, because my client isn't talking to you."

"Well that's not really up to you, is it?" Darger asked, taking a chair across the table from the two men. Beck had been right, too. The chair sucked.

The lawyer blinked at her from behind a pair of glasses. "Excuse me?"

"You can advise your client not to talk. That's all good and fine. But Klootey's the one who ultimately decides whether he'll talk to me or not." Darger let her gaze shift to the ruddy-cheeked man in the chair beside the attorney. "What do you think, T.J.? Do you want to hide behind your lawyer, or do you want to talk?"

Klootey's eyes narrowed to slits. She hoped the suggestion that he was hiding would goad him into opening his big stupid mouth. She didn't have to wait long.

"Sure, I'll talk to you, Agent Darger," he said, spreading his hands wide. "Because I have nothing to hide."

"I strongly advise against this," the lawyer protested, but Klootey waved him away.

"It's all a frame job anyway."

Darger raised an eyebrow.

"You were framed? By who?"

Klootey shrugged.

"Could be you for all I know," he said. "Every piece of evidence you've got is shady as hell. Not to mention circumstantial."

"Maybe at first, but not now."

She waited a beat before she gave him more.

"We've got prints."

"Fingerprints?" Klootey asked, then scoffed. "Bullshit. It's nearly impossible to get prints from a fire scene. Nearly all of the deposits left are destroyed by the fire. Anything that might remain is usually further destroyed by water when the fire crews show up."

Darger smiled. Even now, he couldn't resist trying to prove how fucking smart he was.

"See, if I were sitting where you are, that wouldn't be my argument. My argument would be that whatever prints you found can't be mine, because I wasn't there."

"I'm just presenting scientific facts, Agent. Nothing more, nothing less," he said in an overly patient manner. "But if it makes you feel better, the prints ain't mine, because I wasn't there."

She almost laughed then. He thought he was clever. So clever.

"Oh, I forgot to mention that part... the prints aren't from one of the fires. And they're not yours."

She watched him try to blink away his confusion.

"You're talkin' nonsense," he said.

Darger pulled the photograph of Carl Tanner from the manila folder and slid it over to Klootey. She watched his face for a reaction, saw what she thought was fear in his eyes before he quickly covered it.

"Who's this?"

"You don't recognize him?"

He sniffed and wiped at his nose.

"I've never seen this guy before in my life."

"Well then, allow me to introduce you," Darger said. "This is Carl Tanner. We pulled his prints from the Buick. Ran them through AFIS and got lucky. Ol' Carl here served a bit of time for burglary and drug possession."

Klootey's Adam's apple bobbed up and down as he swallowed.

"He also matches the demographics of our John Doe from the dumpster fire. And boy, did we just hit the jackpot there. See, Carl has a sister. And she made sure that Carl here got in to see a dentist every few years, because one time he had an abscess that almost killed him. She didn't want that to happen again."

Klootey stared her down, suddenly seeming to lose his gift of the gab.

"It's funny. I'll bet you thought you picked someone no one would miss. You assumed that some homeless guy you picked up on Skid Row wouldn't have a family. Wouldn't have anyone that cared that he was gone. But you were wrong."

She could see the muscles along his jaw moving now, clenching and unclenching.

"And you were stupid," she said, leaning back in her chair. "You were so sure you'd get away with it that you didn't bother wiping down mommy's car."

Nostrils flaring, Klootey finally spoke.

"I'm done," he said, turning to his lawyer. "I want this bitch out of here."

Darger only smiled. She plucked the photograph of Carl Tanner from the table and returned it to the folder.

"Oh that's fine. I was pretty much done," she said, getting to her feet. "Really, I just wanted to come down and be the first to wish you the best of luck on your one-way trip to Chino."

Klootey's eyes watered now, tears of rage.

"Fuck you."

Darger was already at the door. She stopped, pretending to wince.

"Oof. I'd work on my manners, if I were you. It's gonna be hard enough making friends in prison, being a cop and all."

And then she was out of the room, walking down the hall.

☾

Darger returned to the hospital after her talk with Klootey, taking the stairs to the ICU. She was out of breath by the time she reached the nurse's station, and her lungs felt like they were on fire. The doctors had warned her it would take time to recover from the smoke inhalation, but she hadn't expected to get her ass kicked by a single flight of stairs.

She recognized the charge nurse on duty behind the desk. Her name was Jackie, and she'd been Darger's nurse the night she was brought in.

"I thought they kicked you out this morning," Jackie said, smiling.

"They did. But I wanted to bring by a little token of my appreciation," Darger said, dropping a box of donuts onto the desk.

Jackie groaned at the sight of them.

"Get those out of here," she said. "I'm supposed to be starting that damn keto diet today."

Darger flipped the lid of the box open.

"Start tomorrow."

"Fuck it," Jackie said, grabbing a donut. "If I cave before I've barely started, I'll never make it."

Darger chose a cinnamon sugar donut and took a bite.

"Any updates?"

"He's still stable," Jackie said. "If you want more information than that, you can get it from his family. They're in there now."

Darger nodded, popping the last of her donut into her mouth and dusting the sugar from her fingers.

All of the rooms in the ICU had glass walls with curtains for privacy. The curtains on Luck's room were open, and she could see Luck's former in-laws and his daughter seated inside. She paused at the doorway and knocked.

Claudia, his ex-mother-in-law, stood and came to the door.

"Hello again, Agent Darger."

No matter how many times she'd asked Claudia to call her Violet, the woman refused.

"How is he?"

"Mostly the same. They did another bronchoscopy this morning, though, and the doctor was pleased with the results, so we're counting today as a good day."

"Well, I'm just here for a quick visit, if that's OK."

"Of course." Claudia glanced at her husband and granddaughter.

Jill sat on her grandfather's lap, a book in her hands.

"We were just talking about going down to the cafeteria. Jill spotted an ice cream machine yesterday."

"Please don't leave on my account," Darger said, but it was too late. At the mention of ice cream, Jill had leaped to her feet and was already tugging her grandfather toward the door.

"Come on, Grandpa. Do-it-yourself sundaes, remember?"

Claudia smiled.

"No, it's good that you're here, actually. I feel better leaving when I know there's someone else to sit with him." On her way out the door, she patted Darger's shoulder. "Talk to him, if you can. They say it helps."

When they'd left, it seemed to Darger that all of the sounds in the room were amplified. The whoosh of the ventilator. The steady beep of the heart rate monitor. A series of clicks and whirs from a piece of equipment she couldn't identify.

Luck's face was puffy and red, and stepping closer, she could see where patches of his hair had been singed by the fire. The blistered spots on his nose and cheeks were starting to heal, at least.

She took his hand in hers and stared down at her friend, wondering why she'd been able to walk away from the fire when he hadn't.

Sometimes when they caught the bad guy, it felt like they'd righted something. Like some wrong in the universe had been put right. Order restored.

Other times, she found it difficult to reconcile the fact that such disorder should be allowed at all. That a monster like Klootey could sow such destruction with so few repercussions. The man had killed twenty-eight people and wounded countless others, and yet he walked, talked, laughed, lied, ate, and breathed while Luck was here in this room, clinging to life by a thread, unable to do any of those things.

Darger's eyes filled with tears at the injustice of it. She sniffled and wiped her eyes, trying to compose herself.

"I saw him today," she said out loud. "Klootey, I mean. Beck was right. He thinks he's quite a bit more clever than he is. And he loves to talk. I'm hoping he'll talk himself right into a life sentence."

She sighed.

"Of course, his lawyer will probably try to keep him off the stand, but I don't think Klootey will be able to abide that. The attention he'd get from testifying will be too tempting for him. He'll see it as his chance to tell his version of the story. The version where he's the hero." She swallowed. "No, I don't think he'll be able to resist."

Darger's gaze landed on the fresh cast on Luck's ankle, which had already been thoroughly decorated by his daughter. She spotted an orange cat, some clouds, and a unicorn.

"Your daughter is quite the artist," she said. "When it's time for the cast to come off, I think you should save it."

She squeezed his hand then. If anything should stir him, she figured it would be talk of Jill. But nothing happened. It was expected, but no less disappointing.

"I fly back to Quantico tonight," she said, her voice hoarse from more than just the talking. "So I guess this is goodbye. For now."

Still holding his hand in hers, she leaned forward to kiss his forehead.

She was about to let go, was about to turn away and leave, but something kept her there for another few seconds.

And then she swore she felt something. The slightest twitch of the fingers she held entwined with hers.

"Luck?"

She squeezed his hand again, waited, waited.

His fingers didn't move this time, but when she glanced at Casey Luck's face, his eyes were open.

COME PARTY WITH US

We're loners. Rebels. But much to our surprise, the most kickass part of writing has been connecting with our readers. From time to time, we send out newsletters with giveaways, special offers, and juicy details on new releases.

Sign up for our mailing list at:
http://ltvargus.com/mailing-list

SPREAD THE WORD

Thank you for reading! We'd be very grateful if you could take a few minutes to review it on Amazon.com.

How grateful? Eternally. Even when we are old and dead and have turned into ghosts, we will be thinking fondly of you and your kind words. The most powerful way to bring our books to the attention of other people is through the honest reviews from readers like you.

ABOUT THE AUTHORS

Tim McBain writes because life is short, and he wants to make something awesome before he dies. Additionally, he likes to move it, move it.

You can connect with Tim via email at tim@timmcbain.com.

L.T. Vargus grew up in Hell, Michigan, which is a lot smaller, quieter, and less fiery than one might imagine. When not click-clacking away at the keyboard, she can be found sewing, fantasizing about food, and rotting her brain in front of the TV.

If you want to wax poetic about pizza or cats, you can contact L.T. (the L is for Lex) at ltvargus9@gmail.com or on Twitter @ltvargus.

LTVargus.com

CPSIA information can be obtained
at www.ICGtesting.com
Printed in the USA
LVHW101728300322
714782LV00011B/381/J

9 781954 203075